NO LONGER PROPERTY OF
SEATTLE PUBLIC LIBRARY

THE
SIN
COLLECTOR

THE

SIN

COLLECTOR

DARIA DESOMBRE

TRANSLATED BY SHELLEY FAIRWEATHER-VEGA

amazoncrossing

This is a work of fiction. Names, characters, organizations, places, events, and incidents are either products of the author's imagination or are used fictitiously. Any resemblance to actual persons, living or dead, or actual events is purely coincidental.

Text copyright © 2015 Daria Desombre
Translation copyright © 2017 Shelley Fairweather-Vega
All rights reserved.

No part of this book may be reproduced, or stored in a retrieval system, or transmitted in any form or by any means, electronic, mechanical, photocopying, recording, or otherwise, without express written permission of the publisher.

Previously published as *Prizrak Nebesnogo Ierusalima / Призрак Небесного Иерусалима* by Eksmo Publishing House in Russia in 2014. Translated from Russian by Shelley Fairweather-Vega. First published in English by AmazonCrossing in 2017.

Published by AmazonCrossing, Seattle

www.apub.com

Amazon, the Amazon logo, and AmazonCrossing are trademarks of Amazon.com, Inc., or its affiliates.

ISBN-13: 9781542047203
ISBN-10: 154204720X

Cover design by M.S. Corley

Printed in the United States of America

"Are you not seekers of the City of God? You, who have lost your native city, and now labor in the name of the City Itself?"

Ivan Shmelev

"He who fights with monsters should look to it that he himself does not become a monster in the process."

Friedrich Nietzsche

PROLOGUE

So cold, such a cold! Vera, also known as the Washpile, stood in the middle of Red Square. Though she was a veteran bum, this cold was too much even for her. She had never liked public squares, but especially hated this one. She felt small and alone, exposed. She told herself it was just the lurking cops making her nervous, but some sort of animal instinct insisted that danger was hiding up above. When you stand in the middle of Red Square, on the raised fortress wall around Lobnoye Mesto, right where everyone says they used to have public executions, you may as well be offering yourself up to the heavens.

Vera looked around and scolded herself. What had she limped up here for? It was too early for foreigners, who would sometimes give her a hundred rubles. Not even any GUM department store clerks around yet. There were a few students heading home from their night out, but nothing good ever came from those types.

And it was cold, so, so cold! The wind was blowing, too. Vera got so profoundly lonely on these gloomy mornings that she felt like getting loaded right then and there. But she had no money and no way to get any.

And then, suddenly, it seemed like the good God above was waggling a finger at her and saying something, something like, *O Vera, servant of God! You are but dust, of course, and ashes, but that's all right—here's a little something, from me to you!*

Daria Desombre

There, near the fence that surrounded St. Basil's Cathedral, there was a big, gorgeous, white plastic bag with the GUM logo on it. Vera practically shivered with excitement. Inside that bag was God's gift for her. She was sure of it! She turned toward the cathedral, crossed herself in gratitude, and hurried to claim her prize. The bag held something wrapped in white paper, which was stained with brown splotches. Vera pulled off her torn gloves and unwrapped the bundle to reveal something long, pasty white, and covered in sparse black hair. It ended in fingers clamped tightly together, gripping some sort of small picture. A painting. It showed a dark, strange-looking tree set off by an ultramarine sky. And a cow with human eyes looking straight into Vera's soul.

A few seconds passed while she considered the sight. Then Vera screamed one long note like an opera singer.

As she fell flat on her face on the ancient, mighty cobblestones of Red Square, she just managed—before she succumbed to the abyss—to see two police officers running in her direction.

MASHA

Masha woke up a couple of minutes before her alarm went off and lay there, staring fixedly at the wall across the room. Her father's favorite Turkish carpet hung on that wall, one part shining bright red in a patch of sunlight, the rest a dull, shadowy carmine with black ornaments touched with blue.

Hanging over the carpet was a shelf holding the books from Masha's childhood that she refused to give away. She sometimes read fifty pages at a time without her mother knowing, pulling out a tattered volume at random and letting it fall open. Sometimes it was Sir Arthur Conan Doyle, sometimes Jane Austen or a Brontë sister. She loved perusing the pages she knew almost by heart. Other people liked to look through old photo albums, smiling nostalgically at the pictures from their childhood. But for Masha, photo albums were a chore. Pictures from before she turned twelve were no fun because her father was in them. In pictures from after, the problem was that he wasn't.

From the other side of the wall came sounds of rustling sheets and labored breathing, and Masha, as always, shrunk away. Her mother usually spoke in precise, clinical terms, but she had once given in to mawkishness and called this particular activity "deliverance from solitude." As far as Masha could tell—why did these walls have to be so thin?—her mother underwent the process of being delivered from solitude a couple of times per week. And every time it happened, Masha felt less like an honor-roll student, less like a bright-but-not-quite-beautiful young woman, and more like a queasy little girl left behind on the platform, watching the train pull away.

It was a very unpleasant feeling, and a humiliating one. It would be stupid to blame Belov, the stranger who washed in their bathroom and brewed his own special coffee in their kitchen, for—well, for what? For taking her father's place? Or just for not being her papa? Yes, that was it. He was the UnPapa. The UnPapa sensed Masha's antagonism and, capable psychologist that he was, took Masha's side when things were rough with her mother, let her have plenty of space, and gave her silly presents. This alarm clock, for example, which played snippets of Glenn Miller swing tunes.

Just now the alarm clock sprang to life, and Masha vengefully let it play to the end. By the time the thing quieted down, the rustling in the next room had, too. Masha giggled and stretched. Glenn Miller was a little like Belov. He was great, sure, but nobody could stand swing music every morning. Masha picked her watch up off the nightstand, and gave her daily nod to the photograph hanging on the wall. It was a portrait of a man with a long, thin face and an ironic squint, whose hint of a receding hairline made his forehead look even higher.

"Morning, Papa," said Masha. "Why'd you have to go and get murdered?"

ANDREY

Andrey opened his eyes and nearly screamed bloody murder, but then he realized this enormous, shaggy, stinking face was not a beast out of his worst nightmares. It was only the result of yesterday's very unmacho bout of pity and temporary insanity.

As usual, he'd come home around eleven from police headquarters at Petrovka, tired as a dog, and stopped to buy some bread at the twenty-four-hour shop near his house. An actual dog was sitting outside the shop, scratching himself in a frenzy. While Andrey sipped his well-earned bottle of Baltika, he and the dog had a chat. Basically, Andrey talked about his own doggone life: his terrible but manly loneliness, how fed up he was with "ladies" (he didn't have to watch himself with the dog—we all know what they call the females of that species), how he worked himself ragged and lived on junk food. He also bragged a little about his culinary feat of the previous evening. He had fried ten frozen meat patties, and tonight he would warm them up in the microwave.

That had turned out to be a strategic error. The stray was no idiot. Sure, he had listened with sympathy and respect to Andrey's sad tales of bachelor life, but when it came to meat—well. The dog's eyes gleamed even more pitifully, and his tail beat on the cracked asphalt. Since Andrey was feeling generous after the Baltika, he invited the dog home. He thought he'd toss a patty onto the porch. Men had to stick together, after all.

But the mutt had different plans. He followed Andrey into the makeshift kitchen and sat there staring with eyes bigger and sadder than any orphan's until Andrey had fed him not one, but five of the patties. He didn't even chew them like a civilized dog—just gulped each one down whole, and noisily.

"You're supposed to chew your food," Andrey admonished him, his mother's voice ringing in his ears. "You won't digest anything that way!"

But to no avail. Andrey had to practically swallow his share whole, too, just to keep some of it away from the scrawny, clever beast.

"And you're a terrible actor. You're playing dumb, but I don't buy it," Andrey told him as he sipped some tea. "Who was that shameless blonde in the old Hollywood movies? Marilyn Monroe."

This shaggier Marilyn must have known there wasn't any meat left, and Lipton was clearly outside his expertise. The pitiful sheen in his eyes was gone now, and he stretched out on the floor next to the saggy old couch.

"Don't even think about sleeping here."

Andrey went to drag the dog out by the scruff of his neck. But Marilyn wiggled out of his grip, and that look returned, a suffering that permeated the whole damn room. Andrey gave in, spat on the floor, and told the dog he was overacting. He shut the door to the bedroom behind him.

By morning, though, clever Marilyn had evidently figured out how to pry the door open and come right up to the bed. Andrey swore again and walked out to the wash basin hanging outside. He took the towel down from the hook without thinking, then immediately hung it back up again. The towel was such a dingy shade of gray that there was no way he was going to use it. Andrey told himself very seriously that he was really going to have to do some laundry, and then he switched on the electric teapot and sat down on the porch. While the water started to boil, he took yesterday's teacup and spooned instant coffee into it, along with a couple of cubes of sugar. He sliced some bread. Then he locked eyes with the dog again. Those eyes seemed unimpressed.

"You can get the hell out if you don't like it, Marilyn Monroe," Andrey snapped at him. His mood that morning was rotten enough, and then he remembered that the night before, all wrapped up in his conversation with the dog, he had forgotten to buy the cheese he wanted for breakfast.

His cell phone rang, and Andrey swore quietly. The day was about to go from bad to worse.

MASHA

"Dean Ursolovich isn't here!" the disgruntled secretary told Masha. "You should have called first."

"But the schedule says . . ."

Annoyed, Masha trudged back downstairs, cursing herself for coming across town for nothing. Ursolovich never followed the schedule, except when it came to his lectures. Students were clearly not a priority. Masha had been proud, at first, that he'd agreed to take her on as an advisee, but as the weeks and months flew by, the seditious thought crept into her mind that maybe a less famous instructor, someone less busy writing textbooks and articles and flying off to conferences at Princeton, would have been a better fit. After all, she wasn't writing her thesis for him, or for the grade, or for—

Masha suddenly froze. Through the open door to the university cafeteria, past the bored food-service workers, she spotted Ursolovich's hunched back at a table by the window.

"I'm sorry to interrupt," she said, striding up to his table. "I tried your office."

Ursolovich turned to her, a chunk of sandwich distending one cheek. "Ave a cuppa chee," he mumbled to her, then turned his back again.

Masha obediently bought herself some tea and a roll and then returned, thinking gloomily that Ursolovich would surely punish her for interrupting his repast, just like he had done to another of his advisees. The poor guy had stumbled from his office pale and trembling, dropping loose pages covered in red ink, and practically run off down the hall.

"I can't eat when someone is sitting there just watching me," Ursolovich told her when she settled down in the chair next to him.

He dug through his worn-out briefcase and pulled out the painfully familiar folder. Then he wiped his fingers haphazardly on a paper napkin and began paging through her thesis. Masha gripped her teacup hard; her fingers had gone white. The margins of her manuscript were unsullied with comments.

"This is good work, Karavay," he finally said, raising his nearsighted, nearly lashless eyes. "With a little work, you could stretch it out into a doctoral dissertation. But you're not planning to go into academia, are you?"

Masha shook her head.

"Well, here's what I would tell you." Ursolovich leaned back in his chair. "The topic is really very . . . nontrivial. Rather particular, I'd say."

Ursolovich's attentive eyes were fixed on Masha's face, and she suddenly felt ill at ease.

"You know more about this, er, research topic than I do. More than anyone in this entire institution, to be honest. This sort of knowledge"—he slapped a hand down on the folder—"is not something that can be acquired in a whole year of training. Not even two. Maybe if you devoted yourself to it for five years, at a minimum. Which means this thesis has been in your head ever since you started the program. So tell me, young lady, what makes this subject so attractive for a girl of twenty-three?"

Masha felt the heat rush to her cheeks.

Ursolovich suddenly leaned over the table and asked her, quietly, "So you didn't believe them?"

Now Masha really met Ursolovich's gaze for the first time, and in a flash, he remembered the color of Fyodor's eyes. They had been just like hers, a light, light green, a rare color, very cold. The resemblance really was astonishing: she had the same sharply defined cheekbones, the strong, handsomely drawn mouth. And her gaze, too—definitely a Karavay family trademark. It was as if she were looking right through him as the gears turned in her brain.

"Listen." He dropped his voice to a whisper, even though there was nobody around. "No matter who it was, please, let this go! Don't waste your life trying to understand. And remember, no matter what, Fyodor is not coming back."

Masha shuddered, but Ursolovich looked away, closed the folder, and continued in a new tone. "I have a few other questions and suggestions about your work, mostly in terms of structure. There's a page stapled to the bibliography. All right, you can go."

Masha nodded, muttered something inaudible that might have been thanks, stuffed the folder into her bag, and nearly ran for the exit.

"Where's your internship?" Ursolovich's voice chased after her.

Masha froze, her spine stiff.

"At Petrovka," she called back, her voice even.

Ursolovich snorted and turned away. *It's hopeless,* he thought. *She'll never let it go. Just like her father!* Who would believe that behind that innocent gaze, that smooth forehead, those locks of straw-colored hair tucked studiously behind one pink ear, there was such a strange beast lurking, like something out of a Goya painting?

Masha strode away from the cafeteria, eyes forward, chin jutted out, trying with all her might not to let any excess moisture—that was her father's phrase—leak from her eyes. But that moisture was looming, compelled by helplessness and childlike anger. How could she have unmasked herself so stupidly? What was she thinking, revealing a secret she hadn't entrusted to her friends, her diary, or even her mother? Why, why, why hadn't she decided to write her paper on some other topic, something more innocent? A topic like . . . But here Masha faltered, because for her, there was only one topic.

She must have been working on it for five years, at least, Ursolovich had said. Five? Try ten. Masha's thesis had taken shape in her head when she was twelve years old, the age little girls put away their dollies for good. And what do they start playing with instead?

ANDREY

If someone had told Andrey he was suffering from the typical complexes of a guy from outside the big city—and not just a case of provincialism, but of *poor-person* provincialism—he would have laughed in that person's face. Considering yourself a provincial in Moscow was ridiculous. Ninety percent of the city's residents came from somewhere else. And the ten percent who insisted on their ancient and venerable Moscow roots? Look closely and you'll always find an auntie in Saransk and a grandpa in the Urals. Andrey considered Moscow his own because he knew it like the fingers on his hand. That knowledge was extremely valuable.

For the first few months of his life in the capital, Andrey had spent the weekends cabbing around the city in his old Ford, trying to make a little extra cash while getting to know the place. Andrey had never really known what to do with his free time. He didn't read much, he hated TV, and he definitely hadn't been raised to frequent the philharmonic. Andrey was a practical kind of guy, so he got into the habit of using breaks in his work schedule to fix things up at the dacha he was renting. He chopped firewood for the stove or did laundry. But that kind of thing wasn't much fun, either, so he was always glad when they piled on work at the office.

Andrey vaguely understood that he was one of the lucky few in the world who found real satisfaction in the job he got paid for at the end of the month. This satisfaction was just as strong as, say, the pleasure his father had gotten from his weekend drinking bouts, or that his mother seemed to get out of gossiping on the phone for hours. So for Andrey, the commute to work at Petrovka was a secret source of joy.

And then there was the fun of driving. Just a second ago he had cut off a sporty BMW with a snotty-nosed kid at the wheel. What was she going to do with all that horsepower, anyway? Andrey had a good reason for having a souped-up engine, not to mention the pleasure he got from seeing the shock on people's faces when his cheap-looking car left them in the dust.

"So your daddy bought you a car and a license, but not a brain?" He laughed. "Come on, you can do better than that!" he scolded the anonymous father, who looked, in his imagination, like the Monopoly Man.

Andrey turned skillfully into his usual parking spot. The phone squawked in his pocket, and the low voice of Andrey's boss, Colonel Anyutin, barked an order: "Report to my office in five minutes!" Andrey scowled.

Five minutes later, he pushed open Anyutin's office door—only to behold, of all things, a girl. He'd never seen her before, but she was just the type of brat he loved cutting off.

"Ms. Maria Karavay," the Colonel announced. "Soon-to-be graduate of the law school at Moscow State."

Well, sure, Andrey thought, his irritation growing. It wouldn't be some technical school in Nowheresville.

The girl stood up and extended a narrow hand. Andrey ignored it and just nodded once.

"Andrey Yakovlev."

"Andrey is one of our top detectives," said Anyutin, the compliment dripping with honey.

Would you like a little lemon with that, Mr. Chief? Andrey asked his boss—silently, of course. Anyutin normally spoke in the sort of choppy prose you'd expect from a soldier, and usually for the purpose of making heads roll.

"I'm entrusting you to Captain Yakovlev. You'll be working together," Anyutin continued in a melody like a nightingale's song. "He should be able to teach you a good deal."

Teach her? Who is she? wondered Andrey.

Then Anyutin turned to him.

"Ms. Karavay is working on her honors thesis—"

So that's what her daddy bought her, Andrey concluded.

"On a very interesting topic," Anyutin continued. "Serial murders passed off as accidents. She'll be a wonderful assistant to you!"

Andrey forced himself to look at the girl again. She was writing a paper on serial killers? Kid must be sick in the head.

This last thought must have been written all over Andrey's face, because Anyutin politely asked the girl to step outside a moment. As soon as the door closed behind her, Anyutin spun around to face Andrey. The fatherly expression was gone.

MASHA

Masha leaned against the wall outside Anyutin's office. It wasn't hard to imagine what was going on inside. Anyutin was spelling out for the disagreeable dude in cheap Turkish jeans that she was payback for some unofficial deal (as if the guy hadn't already figured that out) and that he would have to let the payback pretend to help him.

Worst of all, she really was part of a deal, a pawn in someone else's game. But without that deal she would never have gotten this internship at Petrovka, and she simply had to be here. After having her forced on him like this, Masha thought gloomily, the guy with the jeans was sure to hate her and gossip with all the other male detectives about her, and Masha would be the dumb kid nobody would deign to trust with anything important. Everyone would look at her with that knowing chill in their eyes, and wait impatiently until she finally relieved them of the burden of her presence.

She wondered if she really should have taken a court internship like everyone else, making copies and coffee. That dark train of thought was interrupted by the door swinging open. Yakovlev flew out, his expression even surlier than she'd expected.

"Follow me," he snapped, then led her down several long corridors to the door of a different office. She took in a windowsill sporting a long-dead cactus, a couple of desks piled with overstuffed folders, and about ten people who paid Masha no attention whatsoever.

Masha felt a glimmer of hope. Having outside parties around made it remotely possible that the detective's anger would dissipate a bit and that Masha would have a chance to join the team, who, she desperately hoped, would treat her a little better than this clod.

The captain, meanwhile, shoved some files to one side and pointed to the newly cleared patch of tabletop.

"This is your workplace," he told her drily, putting invisible quotation marks around "work" to make it clear that working was the last thing he expected her to do.

People who got to Petrovka due to their connections were only supposed to sit there and wear out the seat of their pants.

ANDREY

What a pile of crap, Andrey thought as he snuck an occasional glance at his unwelcome neighbor. Sergey sure had picked the wrong time to be out sick. If he were here, they would have dumped this little brat on somebody else.

They say there's such a thing as love at first sight. Andrey didn't think he had ever experienced such a phenomenon. But what he felt now was the exact opposite. There she was, this Maria—Karavay, was it? Even her last name sounded idiotic! Sitting at the desk like she had every right to be there. She was tall, which happened to be in style right now (Andrey didn't like tall girls on principle—the operating principle, in this case, being his own height). Her hair was straight, her eyes some light color that was hard to define, her nose annoyingly proportionate to her face. He was never going to be able to get any work done with her sitting there irritating him. Everything about her pissed him off! Her face, bare of makeup; her hands, nails cut short, no rings; her black T-shirt, black jeans, and moccasins. She sat there looking at him, and waited. *What for?* he wondered.

"You'll have to forgive me," the girl said. Her voice was soft and serpentine. "I know I must seem like a burden." Andrey felt himself blush, and his Adam's apple jumped. "But . . . do you think you could give me some sort of assignment?"

What is this, kindergarten? Baby needs an assignment? Fine, Andrey thought, and gave her a smile he thought must be laden with meaning.

"You're not a burden, Intern Karavay. As for an assignment . . . it should be something to complement your academic research, right?" And he grinned even wider, crocodile-style. "Why don't we have you collect information, let's say a statistical report, on all the homicides passed off as accidents over the past two years?"

The girl frowned. "Is that something you really need?"

Andrey sighed and gave her another false smile.

"In the work we do, Intern Karavay, anything at all might come in handy. We can get drunk on water."

That moment, the telephone rang. It was urgent. The police had found a body downtown. Fished it out of the Moskva River, pretty much directly in front of the Kremlin walls.

"On my way!" Andrey pushed his chair back noisily and grabbed his denim jacket.

The girl looked at him, eyes shining with hope. Obviously, she was already imagining how she might get out of her assignment. *Moscow State honor student, my ass.* Andrey smirked and pretended not to notice.

He had to park some distance away from the cordoned-off scene and push through the crowd of gawkers. An ambulance was already there to cart away the corpse. They were just waiting for him. Andrey took a look at the body and immediately noted that the victim, a middle-aged man, must have worked out a lot. A prison tattoo on one muscular arm caught his eye: a ring with a snake design.

"He did time," a young forensic expert confirmed.

Andrey took a couple of pictures on his phone, for his own use, of the man's arms and the frozen grimace on his face. Then he gave a nod to the men standing off to one side, smoking. While the corpse was being loaded into the vehicle, the man's head suddenly lolled over, and Andrey caught sight of a number shaved into the hair at the back of his neck: *14.*

"Wait!" Andrey hurried over and took another picture. That's when he noticed two kids, maybe fourteen years old; the girl nestled her face into the boy's shoulder, and the boy stood there uneasily, his own face white as a sheet.

Witnesses. Unlucky bastards. Andrey sighed. Here they were in the blush of first love, a romantic rendezvous, and out of nowhere, a dead man in the water. What sweet memories they would have.

Then he remembered his own first love and frowned. He would have preferred a dead guy. Andrey walked up to the young couple.

"You found him?"

The boy nodded.

"See anything?"

"No."

Which was to be expected. Andrey gave him what he hoped was an encouraging smile, like some sort of young Commissaire Maigret; took down their phone numbers; and sent them on their way. He watched the boy wrap his arm very sweetly around the girl's waist. Andrey snorted and walked back to the forensic experts.

"So, find anything?" he asked, even though his gut was already telling him there was nothing there to be found. If the murderer had left any trace, the Moskva River would have washed it away.

That body had been polished smooth as a pebble in the sea.

MASHA

It didn't take Masha too long to pull all the archived files for the last two years of murder cases. Nobody in the office paid any attention, but they weren't overtly hostile, either, like that detective in denim. What had she done to make him hate her so much? Good thing she'd been quick-witted enough not to ask him to take her along to the crime scene. He had made it perfectly clear: no field trips for her, just some statistical report nobody cared about.

How had she ever imagined she'd be in the thick of things? Maybe not chasing down a suspect, pistol in hand, but at least standing among the famous Petrovka detectives and their perfectly trained German shepherds, making brilliant deductions. They would exchange awed glances. *How young she is,* they'd say, *and yet soooo smart!* Masha understood, of course, that all her knowledge was just theoretical, but didn't they want to make use of Maria Karavay, valedictorian? Masha sighed, not realizing how much she looked like her father as she jutted her chin out proudly. To hell with him! Twice as stormily stubborn as before, she dove into the coroners' reports and crime-scene photos.

Until she suddenly ran up against something very strange. Here was a report on a murder along the Bersenevskaya waterfront. The file said three people had been killed in the basement of an old electric station, now a tram depot. Two men, one woman. Masha peered closely at the photographs, and after a stealthy look around—naturally, everyone was still ignoring her—she pulled a magnifying glass out of the cup on Andrey's desk. Yes, just as she'd thought. There were numbers on the victims' T-shirts. Damn these black-and-white photos. What were they written with, blood? The shirts were all covered with it, and blood was pouring out of the victims' mouths. Masha averted her gaze for a second. Maybe it wasn't such a bad thing the pictures weren't in color. She moved on to the interrogation reports. The chief witness, the man who found the bodies, was a security guard, an I. N. Ignatiyev.

Masha jotted down the name in her notebook and turned back to the pictures, magnifying more details, one after the other: the tied-up legs, the big, loud earrings on the woman, the chairs arranged in a semicircle, and those T-shirts . . . they were enormous, unsightly, one size fits all. They obviously did not come from the victims' own closets. No. The murderer must have brought them—the big white shirts were the perfect canvas for those Arabic numerals, written in blood: *1, 2, 3.*

ANDREY

Everyone should have a friend who examines corpses. Andrey chuckled to himself. Probably some people would disagree.

People on this particular career path fell into one of two categories. The first type were the mimics. Somebody who hung out with dead bodies all day could start to resemble their clients. Pale and gloomy, basically. The second type just got more hearty and healthy, optimists with a very specific sense of humor. The only thing they all had in common was a propensity for strong drink—and in this, Andrey could deftly provide company to either type. Business dictated that they could often be found together: Andrey; the coroner; and corpses, corpses and more corpses.

Pasha belonged to the second category. He had three kids and a very practical wife with her own travel business. She covertly supported the family and openly adored her husband, a guy who cheerfully spent his time digging around in dead people's guts.

Andrey had stopped by the morgue to pick Pasha's brain, but the coroner was on his way out; his middle kid had a middle school concert, and these horrific amateur performances—"You'll understand when you have kids, man"—could not be missed.

Before leaving, though, Pasha did tell him that the cause of death was asphyxiation under water. That was the first thing. Also, the corpse had been frozen. It could be that the guy had not in fact died just a few days ago, as the condition of the soft tissues might indicate. That was the second thing.

"Wait!" Andrey grabbed Pasha by his sleeve. "What do you mean, frozen? It's summer!"

"Let go!" Pasha twisted out of Andrey's grip. Running out the door, he answered in a sing-song falsetto. "Tomorrow, tomorrow, and not today, as all the lazy men say!"

And he left Andrey alone in the morgue, rubbing with annoyance at the bridge of his nose.

MASHA

Masha perused files until eleven o'clock that night, until it was completely dark outside and the office was empty. She was tired. Tired of the reports, tired of all the terrible photographs, and tired of this undefinable sense of awkwardness, or confusion, or whatever it was. She had the impression there was something else in the files having to do with numbers. But what? It felt as if there were a shadow lurking behind her back. If she just looked behind her, she'd see something, understand it. Something very important. But the shadow kept slipping away, her eyes were exhausted, and the impression was fading. It didn't make any sense to keep sitting there.

Masha made photocopies of some of the documents and put them in her bag. She glanced at Andrey's desk. *Where did he go?* she wondered. It certainly seemed he wouldn't be back tonight.

As she passed through the security gate, she caught sight of an exceedingly familiar man cloaked in an old raincoat.

"Nick-Nick!" Masha called.

Nick-Nick turned and beamed at her, baring his poorly made dentures.

For the first time, it occurred to Masha that Nick-Nick was getting older. He didn't look so much like a classmate of her father's anymore, and she thought sadly, *Papa would have changed over the years, too.* After all, Nick-Nick had always been in better shape than her father was, doing martial arts, playing tennis, even talking Masha's father into skiing with him once in a while. So, if Nick-Nick was on the decline, what would her father look like now? *What does that matter?* Masha scolded herself. He'd be however he would be. And whatever that was, it would have made her life so happy and so, well, different, that she couldn't even imagine it.

Masha hurried over and gave her father's friend an enthusiastic kiss on the cheek. Nick-Nick's bushy eyebrows shot upward.

"Oh-ho!" He backed away from her a little. "Have you forgotten where you are, missy? It's Nikolay Nikolayevich here. And no kisses, please! What if somebody sees?"

Masha glanced around. Sure enough, right outside the building her new boss was getting out of his car. Very careful not to look in their direction, he walked briskly into the building.

"Oh no!" whined Masha. "You're right!"

"Did we blow your cover?" Nick-Nick said in a conspiratorial whisper.

"It's not funny." Masha sighed. "Of course, he already knew someone pulled strings to get me in here. He just didn't know who. Until now."

"Not a nice guy?"

"He's terrible," Masha said.

"Don't worry. He'll take another look and realize you're so much more than pulled strings."

"I guess," said Masha, sighing again.

Nick-Nick smiled, then very innocently asked the question that Masha suspected was always on his mind. "And how's your mom?"

ANDREY

Perfect! snarled Andrey. Obviously, somebody at the top had pushed Anyutin to take the girl on, but Katyshev himself! Herr Prosecutor! An unblemished reputation, the best of the best, the people's avenger. Somebody Andrey wouldn't even be brave enough to ask for a light. And here he and the little honor student were bosom buddies. They might as well be family, the way she kissed him on the cheek.

Andrey was so pissed he opted to storm up the stairs instead of taking the elevator.

Only once he reached his office and sat down at his own desk did he start to recover a little. He turned on the electric kettle, opened a window, found a cigarette, and took a drag. While he smoked, he stirred up some instant coffee and dove into the computer. He went to the missing persons database and typed in his search criteria. Last six months, male. Faces flashed on the screen. Lots of people go missing in six months in Moscow.

But wait. Andrey grabbed for his cell phone and scrolled to see the photos, but he already knew. The drowned man they'd found today shared a not-very-pleasant face with one Mr. I. A. Yelnik, born 1970, missing since February. "Well!" whispered Andrey as the hot coffee burned his throat. His fingers trembled with excitement as he felt the case begin to gain ground.

The first tiny step, even just an inch, was the most important. Andrey thought of a new case like a boulder at the top of a hill. He pushed at it steadily, gradually, until it finally began to budge. Now the next step. *Who are you, Yelnik, old pal?* The database of past offenders did not let him down. Andrey's computer screen filled with text and pictures, views from the front and the side, in which Yelnik was clearly much younger than he had been this morning on the banks of the Moskva. Andrey rubbed his nose again, happily this time.

Old Yelnik was a murderer.

MASHA

As she drove, Masha tried to shake the nasty feeling that plagued her. It made her furious that Yakovlev had already connected her with Katyshev on her very first day, when she hadn't even had time to show him what she was capable of. Masha was sure her association with the wise old prosecutor would do nothing to improve her reputation with the denim-clad Yakovlev. On the other hand, she thought, braking smoothly near the gates of the old electric station, maybe she didn't have to prove anything to anyone.

It was late, and the tram station was empty. Nobody was there but a lone security guard, a big burly guy paging through a magazine. When he saw Masha looking he put the magazine down. *SuperAuto,* she read.

"Who you here for?" This one obviously wasn't the type for good manners.

"I need to speak with Ignatiyev," said Masha in a perfectly professional tone. So it was a rude surprise when the guy gave her a sassy grin.

"You a reporter?"

Masha nodded warily.

"Not much use coming around now. It's been two years since Ignatiyev got fired! Couldn't keep up." The guard looked pleased with the fate his colleague had suffered, then revealed why. "Five hundred rubles gets you inside. And I can tell the story as well as he could."

"Just a second." Masha rummaged around in her purse and pulled out a wad of cash. She figured she could eat apples for lunch the rest of the week.

The guard ushered her in and led her down long, narrow corridors. They finally emerged at a staircase, at the end of which loomed an iron door.

"They put this in after the murders," he explained, unlocking the door with a key he kept on a bulky chain he fished out of his pocket. The guard hit a switch, and the basement glowed with the type of blue halogen light you would expect in an office.

The basement was empty, and it looked just like the basement of any other government building. Masha asked herself why on earth she had come here, and spent her lunch money, too. But the guard was warming up now to his side job as a teller of sad tales, and he pointed out the place in the center of the room where the three chairs had been. Everything in his story matched the description in the files Masha had read. She had a copy in her bag right now.

"And so," the guard was saying dramatically, "all the victims had their tongues cut. But not in the same way, you know? For one it was just the tip. The woman's was half cut out, and the other guy's was sliced off at the root. The cops said that they might have been able to untie each other, and save themselves, if they had been able to talk. It was some sort of fancy knot, like a sailor's knot. But obviously those three weren't talking. There was a whole ocean of blood in here."

"What about the numbers?" asked Masha. "The numbers on their shirts."

"Nah." The guard shrugged. "I don't remember any numbers."

Masha went to bed early in the morning. Her head hurt, and a blurry negative of the scene in the basement, with the three victims, swam before her eyes. She could see their chins, dripping with blood, and the single rope that tied them all together, hands behind their backs.

Half-asleep, she heard her mother come in quietly. Masha guessed, from what she heard, that she was hanging up the sweater Masha had tossed on the ground. Then there was another rustling noise. That must be her mother picking up the photograph off the floor, the one from the file Masha had put together for the next day. She was annoyed. There was no way Natasha would be happy about a picture of three dead people.

Masha knew her mother was worried about her. She wished her daughter would do something else, follow in her own footsteps rather than Papa's, study medicine rather than law. The legal field, family experience had shown, contained more blood, more death, and less hope for a healthy recovery. Masha's father had thought that Moscow's best high school for math and physics, where Masha had started to go after she won a couple of city-wide math contests, would help his daughter learn to think logically. But in the end, her brain had become home to both the orderly logic of mathematical thinking and the chaos of a still-unsolved murder. The murder of the person who, for Masha, had been the measure of all things until she turned twelve. The person who was the only solid ground she knew, the reassurance that this whole miraculous world around her was not also just an endless putrid swamp. But then, suddenly, that ground sank beneath her feet like some sort of Atlantis, and nothing could replace it.

Masha's mother had never managed to step into that role for her young daughter. She might as well have been Papa's daughter, too, even though she was only a year younger. In her youth, Natasha had begun a residency under the famous Dr. Ryabtsev, who had expected great things from her—until Fyodor asked Natasha to have a baby. When Natasha reported her pregnancy to Ryabtsev, he shrugged and told her she'd need to find a new job, since pregnant women and young mothers couldn't do science. Their minds, he said, were elsewhere by definition.

She tried to convince the professor that wasn't true, that she was different, but Ryabtsev had only smirked, patted her on the shoulder, and told her, absentmindedly, to take good care of herself.

Natasha had rushed home in tears and unleashed her hysteria on her husband. What would become of her now? Was she going to be one of those old hens who only ever talked about diapers? No, it was unthinkable, impossible, she wouldn't do it! It wasn't too late to go to the clinic and—

Fyodor slapped her then, the only time ever. Then he hugged her and promised, in a soothing whisper, that she'd still be the most amazing woman scientist since Marie Curie, and that Ryabtsev was an idiot, bringing women as beautiful as Natasha into his lab and expecting them not to have families! And they would have an amazing daughter, he said, just as gorgeous as her mama . . .

"It's a boy," she had corrected him, sniffling. "We're having a boy."

Both parents turned out to be wrong. Masha was a girl, and she did not inherit her mother's good looks. Actually, she hardly took after her mother at all. But Fyodor Karavay didn't care. As soon as he came home from work every day, he rushed to the cradle, and stood enchanted with little Masha in his arms, just smiling happily as his wife scolded him, "Did you even wash your hands before you picked up the baby?"

Natasha complained to her friends, too. "He goes right to the baby! No thought for hygiene!"

But they just told her how lucky she was to have such a doting husband and such a sweet little bundle of a baby.

Masha knew from early on, however, that her birth had made her mother unhappy. Natasha's figure suffered: the tiny waist expanded, her breasts hung lower after nursing, her stomach grew folds. Natasha resented the fact that her backside had grown as wide as a truck driver's, and she hated that her feet grew a whole size and she had to give away her impressive collection of shoes. She looked in the mirror and didn't recognize herself, and she cried often. Giving birth coincided, in her, with the first symptoms of getting older, making it doubly hard. Nothing helped dispel her persistent melancholy—not her husband's reassurances or presents, not even their date nights when they left little Masha with her grandparents. Natasha sank deeper into depression.

Masha's father was the one to stop by the supermarket after work and cook dinner for the family. He read Masha bedtime stories, and then, after midnight, sat down to get back to work. Papa's head never hurt, unlike Mama's. He never brushed Masha aside when she started asking the thousands of questions that children ask. Natasha, on the other hand, would rant and rave, right in front of her daughter, about how having a child had wrecked her career. Fyodor would whisk Masha off to her room, but Masha still heard her mother's resentment, and also sensed that this wasn't the whole truth. Deep inside, Masha suspected that Mama had gotten that residency with Ryabtsev due to her youth and beauty, not because she was really a gifted scientist. But she needed to play on her husband's sense of guilt constantly, as sure as his beard grew every night. It was Fyodor's fault that she was no longer beautiful and would never get her doctorate.

It was around this time that Nick-Nick started turning up regularly at their apartment. His friendship with Papa had cooled for a long while, all because of their choice of profession. One was a prosecutor, the other a defense attorney. Even ten years later, the two friends were prone to long arguments in the kitchen. Katyshev, outraged, would go on about how everything was rotten, how the whole legal system was hopelessly out of date, how every investigative agency was corrupt but all the bad guys still needed to be proven guilty. To which her father would respond calmly that, here in Russia, they'd never had any problem finding somebody to put in jail. The more interesting question, he thought, was whether or not there would be anyone to defend them.

Then Mama would stride into the kitchen, sit down on Papa's lap, wrap her arms around his neck flirtatiously, and ask them to talk about something else, anything but work. And Katyshev would obediently settle down and change the subject.

It was only when she was much older that Masha realized that Nick-Nick had always been in love with her mother, and probably still was.

He came to see them frequently, even when her father wouldn't be home. He played with Masha (having no children of his own), and he tried to help Mama in the kitchen. She would always laugh at him, but she never chased him out. Masha wondered, sometimes, whether Papa had known. She thought he must have. They were playing an ancient game, with rules even the village idiot could understand. And whatever else he was, Fyodor Karavay was no idiot. But Mama came back to life in the glow of Nick-Nick's unspoken adoration. She started wearing her pretty dresses again, putting on makeup, and smiling. She even became a better mother. She cooked, she hauled Masha to gymnastics and ceramics classes (though Masha didn't excel at either), she took her to museums and historical palaces. Natasha was an extremely well-educated woman, and she began talking to Masha, teaching her all kinds of interesting things. But Masha still missed her papa, and in what would turn out to be the last years of his life, Papa was always working, and finding less and less time to spend with her.

When he did find an hour or two, though, that time was for them alone. He and Masha wandered the boulevards of Moscow and went fishing, swimming, and skating. He knew that sometimes, when they were out, Nick-Nick would visit Mama. But he trusted them both, and even felt sorry for them. Sorry for Nick-Nick because he had chosen the wrong career and the wrong wife, and had no children, which meant he didn't have the kind of happiness Fyodor did. As for Natasha . . . Well, why shouldn't she flirt a little? He thought he could trust them, and he was right.

After Papa died, Masha was terrified, and she secretly, fervently wished that Nick-Nick would marry her mother. The darkness around her was so thick that she craved the sight of a familiar face. But oddly enough, Nick-Nick's visits became increasingly rare, and finally dwindled to nothing.

There was something else, too. It seemed to Masha that Fyodor Karavay's last cases had dug deep, not just into personal injustice, but societal injustice, injustice mixed up with the more villainous aspects of human existence. She knew it was slowly wearing him down, although they never discussed it. But a couple of times Masha walked into the apartment and caught her father loitering in the dark hallway, staring into the brightly lit kitchen, where Mama, sitting across from Nick-Nick, tilted her head and giggled, as carefree as a little girl. In her father's face, Masha saw exhaustion rather than love. Having a charming, girlish wife was all well and good, up to a point. After that, a man wants a wife who is his peer, someone he can really talk to after the bedtime stories have been read and the door to the child's bedroom has been shut tight.

But there was no way to transform a charming pixie into a sober confidant. And in the end, Fyodor himself had shaped a world around Natasha in which she could remain his beloved little pet and never grow up. So it was his own fault. If her father had lived, maybe Masha would have grown into the role of intellectual partner, leaving Natasha free to live out her life as the spoiled little girl.

But Papa had died, their paradise had disappeared, and Mama did her best to make the leap out of the persona she had grown so used to. Because even if they were like sisters, Natasha was, nevertheless, supposed to be the responsible one.

Masha woke up a few short hours later to the optimistic swing tune blaring from her alarm clock. She listened for a second, just in case there were any suspicious sounds coming from the other side of the wall, and then jumped out of bed and headed for the shower, taking her work clothes with her. She didn't like walking around in a bathrobe in front of her stepfather, and so twenty minutes later she emerged from the bathroom in her usual uniform: black pants, a clean black T-shirt, and a dark-blue, high-necked sweater. Her hair was pulled back into a smooth ponytail.

"I've always hated that notebook," Masha heard her mother say from the kitchen, and she froze in her tracks. "No child should have murder on her mind, constantly, from the age of twelve! Crimes! Serial killers! I don't want that to be her career, her life!"

"Natashenka," came Belov's voice, calm and composed as ever. "I'm afraid there's nothing you can do about that. Masha has made her choice, and—"

"I know, I know, I'm the one who let her go to law school! I thought that she'd find something else to be interested in, something other than psychopaths! I thought she could have her own law office, maybe. But instead she's still obsessing about dead bodies—in Petrovka now, no less! I'm going to call Katyshev and tell him to find her a different internship."

"Look at it from another point of view," Masha's stepfather said. "She's doing something she's crazy about, and there's a good chance she'll be very successful."

"But I don't want—"

Masha pushed through the kitchen door. "Good morning!"

"Good morning." Only one of them returned her greeting, choking a little on his coffee. Natasha just nodded, standing there with her back to her daughter. When she did turn around, Masha saw that her eyes were red.

Embarrassed, Masha spoke up cheerfully. "What's for breakfast?"

Her mother handed her a plate of pancakes and, probably also wanting to change the subject, asked, "All black again?"

Masha's wardrobe was one of their most frequent topics of breakfast conversation. It came up as regularly as the weather. She had her usual retorts ready. When her mother asked whether any other colors existed in nature, Masha said they did, but you had to work hard to match them up. Black eliminated all the problems of good taste and wasted time. Black made her look too serious and washed her out? Sure, but she had this post-adolescent syndrome, see, and she wore black because it matched her mood. And on and on. In her head, Masha's responses were different. *No, Mama, these aren't mourning clothes, more than ten years later! No, Mama, this isn't a symptom of depression. No, I'm not trying to push people away.*

Her stepfather wisely maintained neutrality through these debates.

Once today's was finished, Mama sighed and offered Masha the car keys.

"That's okay," said Masha, giving her mother a kiss on the cheek. "I'll take the metro today. It's faster."

On her way out, Masha caught a glimpse of her mother straightening her stepfather's tie in a very maternal gesture, and she smiled sadly. There were so many ways a man could change a woman, inside and out. It occurred to Masha that her mother could have become a pixie again, with Nick-Nick. But she hadn't wanted to play that game with anyone except Papa.

Masha was lucky. She got a seat on the train, so she pulled her notebook out and started to sketch. Seeing things drawn out always helped her think more clearly.

So. Three of them. Masha methodically drew the semicircle of chairs and the three figures, two male, one female.

The young man next to her shot Masha a curious glance. He seemed to be the rare artistic type who found beauty in Masha's profile, Masha's thin fingers, Masha's bare lips.

1. Special knots, wrote Masha next to her picture.

2. Numbers.

3. Why were their tongues cut differently?

The artistic type, reading over her shoulder and probably hoping to find some interesting way to start a conversation, recoiled at that last sentence.

Masha smirked at the man (nothing to see here!), calmly slipped the notebook back into her bag, and headed for the door.

She'd already been at her desk for at least an hour when Captain Yakovlev walked in. She couldn't help but notice, with a twinge of pity, that he was dressed the same as yesterday. The same jeans, the same ripped denim jacket. And unless her revulsion at his personality was making her imagine things, he smelled faintly of dog. He said hello to the room without meeting anyone's eye, especially not Masha's. *Better that way,* Masha thought. She had been worried he'd have something snarky to say about her encounter with Nick-Nick the night before. But Yakovlev just shrugged off his jacket and tossed it over the back of his chair as he reached for the phone.

"Shagin? Hi. It's Andrey Yakovlev. Listen, I have a question for your underworld expert. Which of the lowlifes out there have started shaving the backs of their necks in fancy ways? You know, fancy, like, creative, shaving out numbers, for instance."

Masha suddenly focused on his voice. *Numbers?*

"Oh yeah? Well, it's a new trend. Okay. Write it down for your book on criminal folklore. Guy I saw had a fourteen. Seven plus seven? Double the symbol for good luck? Huh, never would have thought of that. Thanks. Talk to you later." Yakovlev hung up the phone, meeting Masha's eye without meaning to.

Numerology! Masha's heart sped up. The symbolism in numbers! She shuffled through the files on her desk again. One, two, and three were the first victims, at the Bersenevskaya waterfront. There had been a number four on the arm of the drunk they had found dead a year ago at Kutafya Tower. Then a six, on the dismembered arm on Red Square almost six months ago. Now there was a fourteen. Could they all be victims of the same perpetrator? Or was Masha's mania for maniacs driving her insane? She looked over at Yakovlev again and decided to take a risk.

"Excuse me?"

The captain unhappily lifted his eyes from his papers.

"Do you happen to have the coroner's report from yesterday's death on the riverbank?"

Yakovlev lifted his eyebrows, obviously annoyed at Intern Karavay meddling in his case.

"I mean," Masha hurried to add, blushing, "was there anything strange about it?"

Now his eyebrows reached a nearly unnatural height. "What do you mean by *strange*?" he asked coldly.

Masha shrugged her shoulders, feeling helpless, and tried to think. Yakovlev took the opportunity to turn back to the papers he was studying.

What a jerk. Masha was furious. *Fine,* she told herself, arranging her own eyebrows in a way that would make her mother say she scowled just like her father. *Fine. Screw him, and the numbers, too. Let's try a different angle.* There was the weird way the tongues were cut. And there was that other case, a bizarre one, with the drunk who had come to Kutafya to die with his throat all swollen. There was the severed arm and hand with the Chagall painting. *What else?* Masha went on reading old files, finding more and more strange things. How could she have forgotten? There was the terrible case all the papers had covered, not long after the severed arm, about the wife of the governor from Tyumen Province. She was one of the ten richest women on the planet, wealthier than the Italian boss of the Benetton Group and J. K. Rowling. They found her body, hacked into four pieces then neatly wrapped in old newspapers, at a gift shop at the Kolomenskoye estate.

Masha felt sick. The governor's wife had not been well liked—too many people depended on her business dealings. Everyone had to bribe her, grovel at her feet, and do their best to cater to the whims of this all-powerful woman. And Liudmila Turina had ruled with an iron fist. Her businesses grew, and money flowed into her Swiss bank accounts. The papers loved to describe her mansion outside London, wondering when she'd show some shame. But she never did, and anyone who dared to scold her for it was punished. Liudmila squeezed them dry.

Who could have done such a thing to a governor's wife, someone who was always surrounded by bodyguards? And who could have done it and not gotten caught? *That's the real question,* Masha thought. Would they let her take a look at the full case file, or at least the initial evidence they had collected? There had been a time when Petrovka's best resources had been directed at solving that murder, but Turina's widower had fled, one fine day, to the foggy shores of England, and after that, things had quieted down.

Masha sketched out a table (every line perfectly straight, though she hadn't used a ruler). In it, she wrote, *Liudmila Turina.* She entered the date of death, and the place: Kolomenskoye.

Then she dove back into her files. Yesterday she had spotted something else strange, but let it go, because she hadn't known yet what she was looking for. Half an hour later Masha stopped cold. There it was! Architect and builder Bagrat Gebelai had died in an exquisite apartment on Lenivka Street from severe enervation and physical exhaustion. The contrast between the words *exquisite* and *enervation* jumped out at her. And Masha thought she'd heard the name Gebelai in the news, too. Masha filled in the next line in her table: *Bagrat Gebelai, eight months ago, Lenivka.* She leaned back in her chair. Most of the strange cases were connected by one thing: the places where the bodies were found. Aside from Liudmila Turina at Kolomenskoye, on the outskirts of Moscow, all the rest had shown up right in the city center.

The detective sitting next to her announced that it was time for a smoke break, and Masha asked if she could use his computer. He told her to go ahead, then walked out, the rest of the office trailing after him.

First Masha pulled up a detailed map of Moscow. She fed some A3 paper into the printer in the hallway and printed out a full-color map of downtown. Down the hall she caught a glimpse of Captain Yakovlev, cigarette in hand, listening with an ironic gleam in his eye to the detective whose computer she was borrowing.

She went back to the computer and risked searching for a few numbers and the word *numerology*. Google didn't let her down. The number one, Masha read, was a symbol of glory and power, action and ambition. Someone born on the first day of the month was supposed to pursue those things, never wavering from his course, but never trying to make a big jump too early, either. Then there was two, which symbolized balance in a person's mood and actions, a personality that was gentle and tactful. Four meant an even-natured, hardworking disposition. Six predicted success in business, as long as the person could win the trust of those around him, attracting not just customers, but followers.

Masha closed the browser window and sat down again in her own seat, irritated. So the man who had the tip of his tongue cut off was ambitious, and the woman labeled *2* was supposed to maintain balance, despite the blood rushing from her mouth. Not to mention the alcoholic whose number indicated his hardworking personality. She had no idea how numbers had predicted destiny for the owner of the arm found on Red Square; nevertheless, Masha was sure the numerology idea was too simplistic to be useful. She didn't even know whether the numbers meant something, or if it was only her imagination.

"Captain Yakovlev!" Masha stood up and set a sheet of paper down before her supervisor, who'd just returned.

He gave a start at being addressed so directly, but his face stayed impassive as he picked up the paper.

"What's this?"

"These are deaths I picked out that seemed strange to me."

"Strange again?"

"Yes. Again."

"You know, I asked you to look at murders passed off as accidents."

Masha said nothing.

Andrey sighed. "I'm listening, Intern Karavay."

"You don't actually care what I work on," Masha said quietly. "Right? But without anything to work on, I'm still going to be here. You can't get rid of me."

"That sure seems to be the case." He smirked. "Fine. Go ahead and investigate your strange things."

Masha nodded quickly and almost ran out of the room.

"Why are you so pissy with her?" she heard someone ask as the door closed behind her.

Masha didn't wait around to hear the answer.

ANDREY

When Pasha finally called, Andrey raced off to the morgue. Something was needling at him. He knew his intern didn't deserve this treatment. She had been working hard all day. A couple of times Andrey had noticed the intense focus on that odd, striking face of hers. An honor student! He had to admit she knew something about navigating case files. He wasn't sure what sort of strange stuff she had dug up, but if it helped her with her thesis, then fine, why not? Why shouldn't she run around asking questions? Some people would tell her to fuck off, but some might tell her what she needed to know. It wouldn't hurt her to learn a little about working with people, too, instead of just paper.

In this pedagogical mood, Andrey walked into Pasha's office and shook his enormous hand, before accepting the latex gloves his friend held out for him.

"Crazy stuff," Pasha began, pointing to the dead man's open stomach.

Andrey winced and looked inside. A big, empty cavity.

"All his internal organs had been removed," Pasha said, nodding. "Somebody gutted the guy like a big fat chicken. All I found inside him was this." Pasha handed Andrey a plastic bag.

"Money?" he asked.

"Right. Soviet kopecks, to be precise. Pennies."

"How many?"

"Fourteen."

"Huh." Bewildered, Andrey sat down.

Pasha went on. "And on the back of his head—"

"I know. I saw the number."

"But that's not all. Look!" He lifted up one of the blue hands for Andrey to see. "I found ice under his fingernails. But it's not from a freezer. There are microparticles in there that indicate the ice occurred naturally."

"What does that mean?"

"Well, it's the middle of July, and the last time there was ice on the river was February, maybe March at the latest. His lungs are gone, but I can tell you for sure the guy was drowned. Dropped through some hole in the ice."

"Okay. And the body froze?"

"Yes, and I stand by that. Plus, he was only thrown back in the river again a couple of days ago."

"That's crazy." Andrey rubbed his forehead.

"I know," Pasha said, his voice tired.

"So, this is what we have." Andrey made himself look again at the man's contorted face. "The guy is dying because somebody chucked him through a hole in the ice, then he tries to claw his way out of there—"

"He gave it a good shot, too. He's covered in scrapes and scratches. Look." Pasha turned the corpse's head so Andrey could get a better view.

"Right. So the guy puts up a good fight, but he croaks. Then the murderer goes and reels him in, and puts his catch on ice for six months before tossing it back. Was he trying to cover up the time of death, maybe?"

"Well, if the killer's not a complete idiot, he knew we'd detect the frozen tissues. On the other hand, he might have killed him, say, three winters ago. If it was frozen well, the body could still be in this sort of shape."

"No, Pasha." Andrey looked again at the victim's wide-open eyes. "That's not possible; Yelnik disappeared last winter."

"That's the guy's name?" Pasha pushed the corpse back into the refrigerated compartment.

"Yep. Matched him to his mugshot yesterday. The tattoo helped. So if the murderer wasn't going to be able to trick us in terms of time frame, then why make such a big *tzimmes*, as an old woman I know used to say?"

"The place?" asked Pasha, pulling off his gloves.

KATYA

First she rang the doorbell. Not much chance that Natasha would be home, but it was best to be sure. Then Katya used her key to unlock the door, took a deep breath, and crossed the threshold, smiling at the familiar smells. While she was taking off her boots, she thought she heard someone in the kitchen.

"Natasha?" she called. But there was nobody there. Only a clock ticking, and the washing machine spinning in the bathroom.

Katya paused before the mirror just inside the door. She liked to look at herself in this mirror, as if she were the lady of the house. It felt totally natural. The soft golden light from the chandelier had the same magical effect she remembered from childhood. She was a princess again, not some poor shepherd girl, and everyone else could get out of her damn way. Katya tiptoed farther into the apartment. There was a new blanket on the sofa in the living room. Soft. Probably cashmere.

A new bottle of lotion sat on the shelf in the bathroom. Must be Natasha's. Masha never cared about things like that. Katya mentally put the lotion aside for later.

In Masha's room, everything seemed frozen in time. The summer sun beat through the window.

"So stuffy in here," Katya said out loud, and she opened the window to air things out.

She spent a bit longer in Natasha's room, standing in front of her closet. She took note of the chocolate-brown strappy heels and the businesslike pinstripe suit with its surprising leopard-print lining. Katya took a deep sniff. Natasha had switched perfumes again. Masha's mother could never stay loyal to just one. She was always experimenting. Katya liked that. She played a game with Natasha's perfumes, trying to decide which one would be best for her, and concluded they would all work nicely.

She moved on into the kitchen and peeked inside the fridge. But that always ruined her fun. There was no way, here, to pretend this was her own place, because the real-life lady of the house might notice if half a wheel of cheese disappeared (Katya adored this Dutch cheese, and it was crazy expensive), or a bunch of grapes went missing. So Katya devoured the contents of that enormous refrigerator with her eyes only, like a poor idiot visiting from the provinces might look at a fancy still life at the Hermitage.

Katya desperately wanted to take a bath, but it was too risky. It would be too hard to explain if they caught her lounging in a tub full of bubbles and aromatic oils. A shower, maybe. Katya had her alibi ready. "Oh, Natasha, I fell in a puddle, I got caught under a downspout, a Mercedes flew by and splashed me!" Katya knew Natasha would allow it. They'd even have some tea afterward, and Natasha would grill her about Masha's many admirers. She always wanted to hear about that. Sometimes, when there were clues that Masha had her eye on someone (bold but amateurish attempts at makeup, for example), Natasha even sent Katya out to spy for her.

And Katya performed well. One time she found out that the "someone" was in Masha's class, and his name was Petya, a respectable son of wealthy parents. He drove a Porsche, and when Katya caught sight of that Porsche, she practically jumped out of her skin. But silly Masha said she wasn't impressed—with all the huge SUVs on the road, you couldn't see a thing from a little sports car. It was never clear what

Petya saw in Masha. Katya would have said there wasn't much to see. Her thick hair, she supposed, or her eyes, maybe. She had even said something about them to Masha once. Masha had laughed and shocked Katya by quoting something in French about how people compliment a woman's eyes when the woman herself isn't very pretty. And she was smart, sure, but for guys that was more of a drawback. So what had Petya fallen for? Must have been her last name: Karavay. Real elegant, and pretty famous in some circles. The dead lawyer and all.

Katya remembered how much everyone fussed over Masha after he died, even Katya's own mother, as if she didn't have anyone better to pity. Oh, the poor child, losing her father so young! What a tragedy!

Katya had spoken up then. "What about me? Don't you ever feel sorry for me?" she objected. "My father deserted me before I was even born!"

Her mother said she did feel sorry for her, really. She patted Katya's head and told her not to be jealous, that it wasn't nice. But Katya was jealous. She thought she must have been born with that feeling inside of her, the feeling she felt when she looked out their first-floor window at the girl in the colorful jacket, riding high on her father's shoulders as he laughed, when she heard the old women praising him from their benches. *What a good father that Fyodor Karavay is,* they used to say. *And a big shot, too!* And she felt it when she saw Fyodor with Natasha, who looked so young and who dressed in the sort of clothes Katya's own mother had never even dreamed of owning, and every time she saw his picture in the paper with an article about some high-profile trial. Katya desperately wanted to be friends with Masha, but she also wanted to claw her eyes out. It was a strange, worrying, terrible feeling, one that Katya's mother correctly identified only ten years later.

The year that both girls turned thirteen, Katya's mother, Rita, was offered an enormous amount of money for their one-bedroom apartment downtown. They could use it to buy one twice as big in a less trendy neighborhood. Her mother was happy. The buyer made all the arrangements for them, even helped them move, and Rita was so grateful, knowing she never could have handled it on her own. She gushed to Katya about how they'd have their own bedrooms now, not to mention an extra room, an actual living room ("And maybe, Katya, it could be a nursery someday!").

"It won't be," Katya had snapped. She was determined to marry a rich guy.

Katya was glad about moving, though. She could finally get away from Masha's ugly face. Only months later Katya realized she was dying of loneliness in their dull new neighborhood. Life without Masha was boring. It was as if some sort of engine had been removed from her mind, one that had given emotional tone and tension to Katya's life. And Katya was no idiot. She knew she couldn't talk with her new neighbors the way she had with Masha. All these girls talked about was boys, makeup, and clothes—the three subjects she and Masha had never, ever discussed.

At first, she got a kick out of looking through their dog-eared issues of *Vogue*. Then she felt lonely again, remembering the guys from Masha's special math and physics school who used to come over. She didn't always understand the things they talked about, but those boys were a whole lot more interesting than the ones her new neighbors were always drooling over. Katya dreamed of eventually marrying one of those math-and-physics boys—provided, of course, that he made a lot of money, and didn't work as just a boring old researcher somewhere like her mother.

So Katya decided to get back in touch with Masha, despite the ten metro stops between them. She knew, deep down, that her jealousy was pointing the way like a compass, that Masha would continue rising up into the cream of society, and that Katya needed to hitch a ride.

And so, a year after moving away, Katya had dialed the Karavays' number, as nervous as she'd ever been. Masha was surprised to hear from her—but pleasantly surprised, thank God. She invited Katya to come visit.

When Katya had emerged from the metro station at Bolshaya Polyanka and breathed in the gasoline-infused air, she'd felt as if she had finally come home. That feeling only got stronger in Masha's apartment, so strong she didn't know what to do with herself. This was the apartment of her dreams, the apartment where she had spent half her childhood, the place she thought of as her real home. She sat down across from Masha at the kitchen table and felt the tears welling up in her throat.

"What's wrong?" Masha asked.

"I missed you," Katya said, and she wasn't lying at all.

Katya had wanted to impress her old friend. Getting ready for that visit, she had put on her makeup very carefully. But now, looking at Masha's bare face and embarrassed by her own tears (after all, Masha hadn't missed Katya enough to cry!), Katya realized the truth: she had lost again. Simply because Masha existed on a completely different level.

An awkward silence settled over the table. Masha and Katya drank their tea quickly, pretending not to notice the obvious: they had nothing to talk about. Katya was devastated. Friendship with Masha was her only excuse for being in this apartment.

"Know what?" Katya finally blurted out, desperate to break the silence. "There's a guy with a Harley who likes me!"

"A Harley?" Masha asked, confused.

"You know, a motorcycle, the really cool kind? He's already been in jail for stealing, can you believe it? He told me I don't look any older than sixteen. So I said, 'Well, I am sixteen!' And he said, 'Don't tempt me, baby girl!'" Katya jabbered on, her eyes growing bigger and bigger as she continued the story, holding Masha's gaze the whole time.

After the guy with the Harley, Katya talked about Sveta, who lived in her new apartment building and whose mother beat her up for wearing eye shadow and lipstick, even though she was already fifteen, can you believe it? Then there was the "Great Silk Road" that ran in front of their building, always filled with the people who sold things at the cheap marketplace next door. And a soldier who had come back from Chechnya sick in the head, who sat in the bushes until his mom came out and told him everyone was gone, the ambush was over, and it was safe to come inside for dinner.

Katya was turning out to have a real gift for storytelling. She played the part of the terrified vet peering out from behind the bushes, then the self-satisfied dude on the Harley, then Sveta's mother, cursing her out so loud everyone could hear. Masha laughed till she cried, wiping the tears from her eyes, and when Natasha came home from work, Masha told her mom she had to sit down and listen, too. Katya gave an encore performance of the best parts of her story, perfecting them as she went, and now she felt awesome, triumphant. She had won! It was working!

It went on like that for years. Katya sort of became Masha's personal court jester. With other people, Masha held very intellectual conversations. With Katya, she relaxed, and sometimes she would even gossip. That didn't bother Katya. Neither did the sideways looks Masha's school friends gave her: *Who are you? Where do* you *study?* They could see right away Katya wasn't one of them. But Katya knew that herself, and she didn't mind, just went right on playing the fool. Masha always introduced Katya as her oldest friend. *Oldest friend.* It was like an honorary title. Anyway, she'd be one of them, someday. Maybe even be better than them. There was no rush, she had time—that's what Katya thought.

Until Innokenty. Yes. Until Katya noticed Innokenty.

MASHA

"Okay, you, too. Talk to you soon," Masha said, and tucked the phone back in her purse.

"Your old neighbor friend?" Innokenty lifted his glass of white wine. "You should have had some of this. It's very light, and it complements the asparagus well."

"You're such a snob!" Masha said happily, stabbing at the asparagus with her fork. "By the way, she's still in love with you."

"Huh." Innokenty frowned. "And she's still jealous of you."

Masha snorted and shrugged.

"I wish I had something to be jealous of! You should see how my new boss ignores me. Yesterday he saw me with Nick-Nick. He thinks I'm just an annoying rich girl with no brain."

"But you do have a brain." Kenty smiled.

Masha sighed. "No, not these days, I don't. I'm just going around in circles. Around what, exactly, I don't know. I'm looking into these strange deaths."

"Aren't there always plenty of those?"

"No. These are strange deaths in strange places." Masha pulled the map of Moscow out of her bag. "Look."

Innokenty laid the map out next to his plate and glanced over it while finishing his asparagus.

Masha watched hopefully, afraid to say anything. She hadn't told Innokenty anything about the murders, so this map, marked with a cross at each crime scene, was his introduction to her puzzle. But they were used to trusting each other's mental abilities, and while logic reigned supreme in Masha's head, erudition guided Innokenty's.

Finally, Masha couldn't wait. "Well?"

"This is silly." Innokenty pushed the map away. "Nothing's coming to mind."

Masha obediently took the map back. "I have a little time before I have to get back to work."

"Let's have some dessert! That'll make you feel better." Innokenty winked at Masha and insisted on ordering the biggest slice of cake in the display case, a monster covered in fruit and whipped cream.

"I've just made a deal for a fantastic icon," he told her while they both dug in. "One made for the Old Believers, seventeenth century. I already have a buyer for it, too. I'll be able to take a month of vacation, and, if you want—"

"Yelnik is one of them!" Masha interrupted him, nearly stabbing Innokenty with her cake-laden fork.

"Umm, what?" he asked.

Masha took out the map again, and Innokenty pulled a heavy gold pen from the breast pocket of his cherry-colored velvet jacket. Masha scribbled some quick circles on her napkin to get the ink flowing, then added a new little cross on the map next to Red Square.

"Huh." Innokenty picked up the map again and looked over the points that Masha had marked. "Can I hold onto this for a couple of days? If I think of something, I'll call you."

"Take it. I can make another copy." Masha smiled happily.

She loved it when Innokenty took her up on a riddle. It felt like they were kids again, conspiring together. Of course, Kenty was all grown up now, a prominent antiquarian, as he called himself. He owned a private gallery downtown, and judging by his designer shoes and the platinum cuff links on his bespoke shirts, monogrammed *A. I.* for *Innokenty Arzhenikov*, Kenty's little shop was bringing in some money. Yes, her old friend had become quite a dandy, and since Masha had never moved beyond her simple black wardrobe, people often wondered at the odd pair. And they were both so different from everyone else, such introverts. Masha knew he deserved all the credit for their relationship lasting all these years.

"What does that map remind me of?" Innokenty murmured as he directed the last bite of cake into his mouth. "No, it's hopeless. I'm never going to remember with my stomach this full."

ANDREY

Where Andrey ate lunch, they were not serving asparagus with a nice Chablis. Nobody was wearing cuff links. Where Andrey ate lunch, it was smoky and stuffy, but the customers didn't take off their coats to eat. They dined at plastic tables on sandwiches of suspicious origin. They drank beer.

Andrey was sitting across from Arkhip. Arkhip's real name was Arkhipov, and he was Andrey's informant. Arkhip thought Andrey was an okay guy, so he held up his side of their arrangement in good faith. For his part, Andrey never threatened to lock Arkhip up, but despite the valuable information he shared, he'd never developed warm feelings for the man. He was kind of grossed out, honestly, by Arkhip's acne-covered face, narrow as a knife blade. And Arkhip had a way of moving that face closer and closer as he told you things in confidence, his breath smelling of yesterday's dinner.

"Yelnik went straight a long time ago," Arkhip whispered as he took another gulp of cheap, foamy beer. "After the last trial, nobody had any jobs for him. He went and lived out in the country. He wouldn't see anyone he used to know. He was, like, stay away from me, let me keep my nose clean in my old age. As if! Turka said some army men used to go see him."

"What army men?" Andrey asked, chewing on his stale sandwich.

"How would I know? Important guys, I hear, even though they always came dressed like civilians and drove crappy cars."

"Then how did your guy Turka know they were soldiers?" Andrey asked suspiciously.

"Whaddya think?" Arkhip sputtered. "Their posture, first off. And the way they walked, like they were in a parade, and faces like bricks. Looked at you like they were expecting a full report. Definitely no lower than a colonel."

Andrey thought for a minute, took another sip from a mug of warm swill the café called coffee, and frowned.

"Listen. Last time Yelnik was in, who did he do time with?"

"I can find out."

"Do it. Send me a text."

"Okay." Arkhip wiped his mouth. "I'm off."

Andrey just nodded.

So, Yelnik had gone straight. And then someone killed him. What was the logic in that? Punishment for getting out of the game? Some old score that had to be settled? And what did these military types have to do with any of it? He remembered the grimace on the dead man's face. The hollow body. The worthless, rusty coins. Some sort of mysticism? Andrey decided it was time to pay a visit to Yelnik's place in the country. He headed for the counter to pay for his lunch and Arkhip's.

In the hallway, Andrey ran into his intern—literally—as he charged around the corner with his characteristic fury. They bounced off each other like tennis balls, and the girl fell down hard, gasping. Andrey was scared at first that she was hurt, but then he saw the papers scattered all around her, copies of photographs.

He awkwardly sat down next to her and began gathering them up, quickly at first, then more slowly. The numbers on the murder victims at Bersenevskaya waterfront looked black in the photocopies, but Andrey vividly remembered how they had been written in blood. A close-up of a biceps tattooed with a *4*. His own memory served up the image of the fourteen on Yelnik's neck. Andrey got up off his haunches the same time the girl did. She was as red as a lobster.

"So you're doing some investigating, then?"

The intern nodded nervously.

"Very good," said Andrey, surprising himself, and suddenly realized that Intern Karavay's eyes were exactly level with his. Those expressive eyes—light green, with dark, almost wet-looking lashes—were embarrassed on the one hand, but on the other defiant. Her pursed, pale lips bent into a smile when he said those words.

"I'll do my best," Karavay said, and she walked away around the corner.

Man, she's tall! thought Andrey, without resenting that quality for once.

He needed to get some things together and head to Tochinovka, the village where Yelnik the hitman had attempted to retire.

MASHA

Masha sat on a narrow bench near the district police station and pretended to listen attentively to the young patrolman Dima Safronov. Dima was glad to be sitting here with this piece of ass from Petrovka, smoking expensive cigarettes, wondering if he should ask her to the movies. After that, naturally, he'd need to get her drunk . . . But something told him this chick wasn't much for dive bars.

He was telling her about Kolyan. But there wasn't much to tell. Guy was a complete and total alcoholic, but there were plenty of those around. Harmless. Not the criminal type. Must have been brought up right, because he didn't just piss wherever he felt like it. Kolyan had mostly stuck to the neighborhood, so how had he ended up at Kutafya Tower? Did he go there to die someplace beautiful? The cops are thick on the ground there, too. It was a nice enough place to finish off a bottle, but Kolyan had an apartment for that sort of thing. Why travel so far? Later, when that uptight coroner got ahold of him, he found out it wasn't Kolyan's heart that had killed him. He'd suffocated to death. The coroner thought a liquid dripped continuously into his throat had made his throat swell up.

"What kind of liquid?" Masha interrupted. She was still replaying in her head the slapstick scene of her running into Yakovlev in the hall. What an idiot she was.

"Vodka, what else? I read the report. You do it drop by drop, it's some kind of medieval torture. I think they tortured people in China that way."

"Not just in China," Masha said, frowning as she felt the shadow just behind her back.

Seeing her eyes go all weird—distant and sad—Dima decided he definitely wasn't asking the chick from Petrovka out. But he had more to tell her.

"And in his apartment," he said, "they didn't find a single fingerprint! Not in the kitchen, not in the hallway, not in the bedroom. On the one hand, any asshole could see that it's murder. On the other hand, why murder a harmless drunk? Maybe he saw something he shouldn't have?"

"Maybe," Masha said. That was a perfectly reasonable motive that could explain everything away, and Masha hated it.

Dima tossed his cigarette on the ground and stood up. Masha followed suit, and shook his hand in a very official manner.

"Thank you for your time," she said.

"You're welcome," answered Dima, embarrassed by all these good manners. "Call me if you have more questions."

"I will." Masha carefully withdrew her hand from his, just a little later than she would have liked. She had already crossed the street when she turned back and caught Dima watching her go.

"The tattoo on his arm!" Masha called. "The number four. Had you seen that before?"

"No. Kolyan didn't have a tattoo!" Dima shouted back. "He went around most of the time in just an undershirt, so I would've seen it."

A satisfied smile spread across Masha's face. She waved good-bye and hurried on.

ANDREY

Tochinovka turned out to be the kind of village you might see in a documentary about the dying Russian countryside. More than half the houses were boarded up, and the ones that were still inhabited seemed to be light-years away from the glamorous capital instead of sixty miles. While the gilded young people of Moscow tweeted on their smartphones at university lectures and learned the correct way to eat imported oysters, while they injected Botox into their jaws so they wouldn't grind their bleached teeth at night from the stress of modern life—here there was a stinking outhouse behind each little shack, like something out of the Middle Ages, and the villagers hauled water from a distant well and warmed it up over propane. The distance between those two realities could be measured in centuries. The people spoke the same language, but they didn't understand each other. Nobody in Tochinovka knew anything about oysters, Botox, or Snapchat. The only person here who had seen the world and all the paradoxes of the twenty-first century had been Yelnik. He was like a double agent. And he'd been murdered.

Andrey sat and smoked, pondering, without any particular bitterness, a remarkable quality all Russians seemed to share: complete disdain for an ordinary, decent existence. Disregard by the people in power for everyone else, for four generations now, at least. The abject humility of these people, who'd been the workhorses of socialism, who'd wired the whole country for electricity, but didn't think to ask for hot water or a sewage system. As if it were just the way of things, that of course you have to trudge through the snow when nature calls in winter, wipe your ass with torn-up newspaper, and rinse your hands with water from some rusty old bucket.

What on earth had Yelnik been hoping to find here? He had been set up well enough. He could at least have afforded a heated bathroom after he got out of prison.

The door to Yelnik's run-down house was locked, so Andrey, checking for a key in the usual places, peeled back the mat and felt around the heavy window shutters. Nothing. The property wasn't big, but it was well cared for. There were some vegetable beds, a small potato patch, even a greenhouse. That door was unlocked, and Andrey went inside. In contrast to the healthy garden, the greenhouse was badly neglected, which made sense since the gardener had disappeared over the winter. The air was hot and heavy, but it didn't smell of the usual cucumbers and tomatoes. No, it smelled of death and decay. Andrey shuddered. There was a dead bird lying on the floor, its thin bones glowing white through matted black feathers. *Must have flown in during the winter and, when no one opened the door again, it couldn't get out,* Andrey thought. So Yelnik's killer had a bird's blood on his hands, too.

"What makes people different from birds?" Andrey mused aloud as he stood, undecided, before the porch, playing with the coins in his pocket. "People know how to open doors."

He pressed a coin from his pocket firmly into the palm of his hand. He had a paper clip in there, too, precisely for occasions such as this. Andrey looked around stealthily. Not a soul.

"You understand, right, Yelnik? It's because I was raised on the streets, it's because of my poor family, it's all the bad examples in my life," Andrey muttered as he straightened out the paper clip. "Idle minds and so on!"

Andrey went to his car and opened the trunk, humming contentedly as he pulled out a narrow wrench. There was a gentle bounce in his step when he walked back to the front door of the house. He glanced around one more time. Still quiet. Andrey inserted the wrench in the lower part of the keyhole, then slid the paper clip into the upper part, tip pointed up. He turned the paper clip slowly, counting the contacts: *one, two . . . five.* There was a tiny click with every turn. Andrey looked dreamily at the summer sky, dotted with cheerful white clouds. He gave the door a gentle push and it swung open without so much as a creak.

"Anyone home?"

But all the house offered up in response was complete silence and impenetrable darkness.

He felt for a light switch. With a soft click, an enormous chandelier lit up, completely out of step with the rundown village.

Andrey whistled. Nothing inside this place matched Tochinovka. The chandelier, all bright-orange Murano glass, hung high above him, and it took a moment for Andrey to realize there was no second floor. His eyes took in a surprisingly large space, bounded only by wooden beams painted a dark chocolate hue.

The room was square, with a noble-looking oak parquet floor near the entryway and a sprawling Turkish rug farther in. Arranged on the rug were a white leather sofa, a pair of futuristic-looking armchairs, and a narrow coffee table. Deeper inside, the light flashed off a kitchen outfitted in chrome, the kind you see in glossy magazines. Heavy velvet curtains covered the windows.

Andrey made himself look outside. Sure enough, Tochinovka was still out there, poor and gray. *Surreal,* he thought, shaking his head as he explored. First a bedroom, white and minimalist, with a massive closet full of expensive clothing—Italian jeans and English suits. Then a guest bedroom in the same style. Plus a big bathroom, with an elegant shower made of a porous beige stone, and a modern flush toilet. Andrey turned the shower tap mistrustfully. The water responded immediately—hot with amazingly high pressure. Yelnik had enjoyed all the blessings of civilization, not in some ritzy suburb, but right here in run-down

Tochinovka. Was he trying to hide among the drunk old men and half-blind old women? If the former killer wasn't killing anymore, he must have been making money—and judging from this house, more than a little of it—some other way. Not by growing potatoes, that was for sure.

Back in the living room, Andrey looked at the fireplace with envy. It was sleek, modern, and set a couple of feet off the floor. Yelnik the hitman had taste. Maybe he'd hired a designer, a good one. How would he have described the job? *Make me a palace inside a wretched little shack?* But why? And if there were a designer and Andrey could find him, would he have any idea where his nutso client's money came from?

Andrey walked outside, sat on the porch, and lit a cigarette. He was completely confused. Getting ready to come here, he had been nearly convinced that Yelnik, tied up as he was in the murder business, had been caught on the wrong side of some old deal. But this house stank of new money, new trends, if you could put it like that.

The phone in his jacket pocket chirped. A text. *Yelnik's cellmate was Zitman. Goes by the Doctor.* Trusty Arkhip! The Doctor, covert soldiers, new business, murder by drowning, half a year in a freezer, and a body without its guts, finally tossed back in the Moskva River—

"Hello!"

Andrey jerked his head up.

A short man with Down syndrome, maybe twenty years old, stood in front of him. The man grinned shyly, his small eyes trusting and kind.

"Hi," said Andrey.

"Are you the new owner?" The man had started sidling over to the porch.

"No," Andrey answered honestly, shifting over to make room.

"I'm Andreyka," his new friend said. "Got a smoke?"

"Sure, buddy. That's my name, too." Andrey handed him his pack of cigarettes.

Andreyka took a few and tucked them behind one ear. They sat there smoking quietly for a couple of minutes.

"Igor's not coming back," Andreyka said suddenly, in a funny, high voice like an old woman. "No, not coming back!"

"Why do you say that?" Andrey asked, unnerved by this verbal contortionism.

"He went away! His friend came for him. He's a nice man. In a blue car."

"Oh yeah?" Andrey felt his body tense, as if getting ready to pounce. "What kind of car?"

"A blue one." Andreyka looked at Andrey like he must be stupid. "He said, 'Go on, Andreyka, I don't need your help anymore.' 'Cause I shoveled his snow in the winter. He said, 'My friend is here, he's an important man, I owe him my life. It's time to pay my debts.'"

"What did that man look like?"

"A man. You know. Important."

"What about his eyes, or his hair? Do you remember?"

"Dark. And he had a black coat. And a blue car."

Andrey could tell that was all he was going to get. He knocked at a few little houses, but none of the old women had seen a dark-eyed stranger, and they didn't remember any blue cars. Andrey circled the house and garden again, this time under the friendly blinking gaze of the other Andrey. Then he headed home, planning to send a few forensic techs out to search Yelnik's place. But he strongly suspected he'd already found out all they could about the man in the car, Yelnik's mysterious savior.

They wouldn't find anything more interesting, or more substantive, than that.

INNOKENTY

Innokenty sat looking idly at Masha's map and the series of crosses she had marked. Thank God Masha was tactful enough not to tell him all the details, over lunch, of what had happened at each of those places. As it was, his appetite hadn't suffered, but his curiosity—the most treacherous of sins, and the driving force of any historian—had definitely been aroused. Innokenty remembered seeing a map with crosses like these once before. Given the sort of things he worked on, the map must have been an old one. Sixteenth or seventeenth century, probably.

He dutifully reached for an atlas. Where was it? Ah, there it was. Innokenty looked thoughtfully at the book's cover. For him, old maps, just like old sepia photos—and the Dutch masters, really—held an extraordinary charm. The tiny horses racing far off in the background in a Bruegel, a slice of a street scene in a De Hooch, the costumes and facial expressions of a merchant family on a late-nineteenth-century postcard, and the Streletsky Settlement gardens here on the page he turned to first—they all had a particular quality in common, which was that their greatness was in the details.

And these details were powerful enough to make them real. If you followed those details, like Ariadne's string, through the dark labyrinth of time, they might lead you to a different reality. Wasn't that, in the end, why Innokenty had become a historian? Because it was a way of dipping into other worlds? Of distancing himself from this one, the world where fate had dropped him? He couldn't resist running his eyes over the commentary accompanying Herberstein's map of Moscow one more time. Full of small mistakes, it reflected an outsider's view. Innokenty smiled ironically. Who were modern Muscovites, if not outsiders observing the sixteenth-century city? They didn't even know that Moscow, which now ranked somewhere between Delhi and Seoul worldwide, used to be the fourth biggest city in Europe, after Constantinople, Paris, and Lisbon.

And where was that Constantinople? Kenty wondered abstractedly. Where was that Lisbon, all weighed down by New World gold? Where was old Paris, robbed by revolutions? In the Middle Ages, it took a man on horseback three full hours to ride all the way around the walled fortress here—the same amount of time his modern-day descendent spends in traffic every day.

Innokenty licked his lips over the text he already knew almost by heart. *Cathedrals in the city are sometimes constructed of brick, though most are wooden, and all the houses are made of wood. None are permitted to build from stone or rock save certain members of the nobility, and the most successful merchants may build vaults on their property, small and narrow, where they secret away their most valuable possessions in times of fire. The English and the Dutch, and the Hanseatic merchants, primarily store their wares here, selling fabrics, silks, and perfumes . . .*

He smiled again when he read the next sentence. *The local merchants are quite adept and inclined to make deals, and while they are extremely untrustworthy, they are markedly more pleasant and civilized than other residents of this land.*

MASHA

Masha sat in the hallway outside the prosecutor's office and waited obediently. Anna Yevgenyevna, a formidable woman who had been the lead investigator on the Bagrat Gebelai case, was giving someone a thorough hiding over the phone. Finally she let Masha into her office, and offered her a narrow chair upholstered in fake leather on the other side of her massive desk.

The desk was neat and clean, something that could not be said of Anna Yevgenyevna: her black sweater, stretched over her massive bosom, was littered with what must have been cat hair; her own hair, hastily swept back into a bun, was badly dyed and coming loose; and the manicure on the almond-shaped nails of her unexpectedly elegant fingers was flaking.

"So. Gebelai?" she said, tapping her nails on the surface of her desk. Then she shoved back, rolled her chair over to a cabinet, and skillfully pulled out the file she needed before scooting back to the desk. She opened the file, glanced at the papers there, and then turned her gaze back to Masha. "And why are you so interested, Miss Intern?"

Masha decided to tell her half the truth: she was writing a thesis on strange deaths passed off as accidents—

"Right," Anna Yevgenyevna grunted, then reached for a cigarette and took a drag. "It was a strange death, I'll give you that. Gebelai was an architect, a builder. He drew up the plans for some new metro stations, the kind with canopies. One day two years ago, it was pouring rain at rush hour, and people were huddled under one of those canopies to stay dry, a huge crowd, and the canopy collapsed. Hundreds of people died." The detective sighed and tapped the ash off her cigarette, half into an ashtray, half onto her sweater. "It was a terrible thing. Women, children. You probably remember."

Masha nodded silently.

"Gebelai and his subcontractors were found liable. The metro stations were falling over due to structural errors in the plans. They used the wrong materials, they calculated the loads wrong. But then there was a presidential pardon and Gebelai got out of jail. So. A couple of months later they found him dead in an apartment on Lenivka, all covered in dirt, black under his nails, too, naked, skin and bones . . . The doctors said his heart gave out due to some sort of major physical exertion. But what kind of extreme exertion makes any sense? The man was a decorated architect; he used to win medals. They found one of them pinned right to his skin, in fact."

Anna Yevgenyevna handed Masha two photos. One view, a little from above, was of an apartment that was striking for its ostentatious luxury. The other was a picture of Bagrat Gebelai himself, curled up in fetal position on the floor, a medal stuck into the dark thatch of hair on his chest.

"What is that?" asked Masha.

"That's an Akhdzapsh medal, third degree," the senior investigator answered wearily. "They give it to citizens of the Republic of Abkhazia for service to science, culture, and art. Our hero got his a few years before the station collapsed."

"But this wasn't his only award, was it?"

"No, he had plenty. Medals for honorable service in this and that, Honored Architect of the Russian Federation, Distinguished Artist, and so on. He built a bunch of churches in new neighborhoods, for one thing. So far those are still standing, thank God."

Masha lifted the photograph to get a closer look. The medal was shaped like a circle, with rays radiating out from it. Masha asked if she could make copies of several of the photographs from the file, and Anna Yevgenyevna graciously agreed.

Masha smiled and stood up. "Thank you very much for your time."

"Of course, of course, go write that paper, grind it out, let me know if you think of any questions." The detective stood up noisily at her desk and walked off farther into her office. She switched on an electric tea kettle as Masha left.

On her way out, Masha thought unhappily that the well-meaning investigator hadn't actually shed much light on the case. Just that medal. There hadn't been anything about it in the case file. Masha imagined the sharp tip of the pin poking through the blue-tinged skin. Her stomach turned.

I should be exercising more, Masha decided, shaking her head to chase away the horrifying image. *I'll make Mama happy and go to the gym.*

Natasha had bought her a gym membership six months ago, in an attempt to get her to stand up a little straighter, get some muscle tone, and forget about serial killers once and for all. She was willing to give it a shot. After that story of architectural negligence in the metro, though, she was done with public transportation for the day. She'd go home to get the car first.

Masha hated working out, and she trudged into the ritzy health club on Novoslobodsky like other people dragged themselves into the dentist's office. She'd been going nowhere on a treadmill, to a soundtrack of cloying pop music, for at least half an hour, when suddenly her rhythm faltered. Masha stumbled, then jabbed at the red button. Stop! The medal! There was something about that damn medal! Masha grabbed her towel and ran to the locker room. Still panting, she opened her locker, took out the file full of documents, and plopped down on the wooden bench.

A bead of sweat dropped onto the picture in her hands of the medal, close up, on Gebelai's hairy chest. Masha swallowed hard and lifted her head. Other young women were going about their business all around her, some in swimsuits, some in track suits, some wrapped in towels, rosy-cheeked and relaxed after their showers. Masha, sitting there with a murder file on her lap and staring fixedly straight ahead, was an unusual sight for these gym rats, and probably a disturbing one.

"The medal," Masha whispered. She counted the rays on it. "One, two, three, four, five. Five." She repeated the last number quietly, while around her women passed each other lotion, curled their eyelashes, fussed with hair dryers. *No, it doesn't make sense!* Masha thought, but she couldn't stop now. She shuffled through the file and found the business card with Anna Yevgenyevna's number.

"Yes?" came the low voice of the lady detective.

"Hello. It's me again, Masha Karavay."

"Ah, the intern. Hi there." The woman's tired voice slipped down another full octave. Masha could hear her working on another cigarette. "Did you come up with some questions, then?"

"Yes," said Masha, embarrassed. "You know, I was looking at these photos, and it seems to me that there used to be more little rays on that medal. It's probably not important," she rushed to add, suddenly ashamed to have bothered the detective.

"Good work, Miss Intern." Masha felt, rather than heard, Yevgenyevna blowing out smoke happily. "Being meticulous like that is crucial in this cruddy profession of ours. There should have been eight of them."

"But there were five," said Masha. "Could they have broken off, just like that?"

"Just like that!" snorted the detective. "Nothing happens just like that. They were sawn off, honey, and that's all there is to it. But why? What for? No idea. And I wracked my brains over that for a long time."

"Thank you," Masha said slowly. She said good-bye and hung up.

"Five," she repeated to herself, worrying that she might be going crazy. Did everything actually fit into this bloody puzzle, or was her subconscious just serving up pieces that matched the pattern? A pattern that began with the numbers one, two, and three on the shirts of the unfortunate people at the Bersenevskaya waterfront and then led to a distinguished architect in a luxury apartment on Lenivka Street? Masha jumped when the phone rang again. It was Innokenty.

"Masha!" he said. "I think I have something for you, but I'm not sure. There's somebody I want you to meet. Today, if possible." And he gave her an address.

It was getting dark by the time Masha picked up Innokenty at the park outside the hospital. The security guards made her wait at the front gate while they called the front desk. Then they drove slowly down a narrow road lined with old maple trees. The noise of the city gradually died away, and when Innokenty gallantly helped Masha out of the car, she heard birds singing their evening song, and it felt like they'd left the city altogether. They climbed the gently sloping stairs to a Palladian-style front porch with its semicircle of white columns, and Innokenty pushed open the heavy door, polished smooth by thousands of visitors' hands. Masha read the sign: "Pavlov Psychiatric Clinic."

Inside they came first to a much more modern-looking door of thick glass. The woman at the desk saw them and nodded, and the door buzzed open.

"Good evening," said Innokenty. "We're here to see Professor Gluzman."

Masha had assumed Gluzman was one of the doctors here, but the nurse's gentle smile and the way she said the professor was feeling well and could receive them today made her wonder.

"What does that mean, *feeling well*?" Masha whispered as they followed a carpeted corridor deep into the hospital.

"Ilya Gluzman was my favorite professor in college," Kenty replied, giving Masha's suddenly clammy hand a squeeze. "I must have told you about him. He's an expert in Russian medieval history. Don't let the hospital scare you. Dr. Gluzman is in good shape right now. He's writing books, and he just got back from an international lecture tour."

Masha still felt uneasy. No sound came from behind the doors along both sides of the hall. All she could hear was soft, almost inaudible, classical music, apparently meant to calm the nerves. *Whose nerves?* she wondered. Was the music for the guests, the patients, or the staff? Meanwhile, the nurse had stopped before one of the identical doors and knocked quietly. The door opened and another nurse appeared, so similar to the first that they might have been twins. She had the same warm smile and pleasant face.

"So it is Inno-centi himself!" came a rumbling voice from inside the room. The nurse nodded and stepped aside. The sixty-year-old man who greeted them had a gentle face covered with fashionable graying stubble, and a similar bristle covered his egg-shaped head. He was dressed more like an Oxford don than a mental patient, in a dark-green jacket with leather elbow patches, a wool turtleneck sweater, and corduroy trousers. He rolled his motorized wheelchair closer and shook Innokenty's hand. Then he grinned slyly at Masha.

"Ilya Gluzman, at your service." He lifted Masha's hand to his lips, not so much to kiss it as to express his gentlemanly intentions.

"Masha," she introduced herself, a little taken aback.

"Innokenty, thank you for bringing such a beauty to visit a lonely old man!" Dr. Gluzman looked at her like a curious bird, tilting his head to one side. "If only I could still fall in love at my age!"

Then he rolled back into the room and gestured to the nurse to put the teapot on a low table. The table was already set with a ceramic bowl of chocolates and a crystal dish overflowing with an artistic mess of dark, nearly black cherries and small, pungent strawberries. After her long workday and visit to the gym, Masha felt her mouth water.

"Please have a seat, mademoiselle!" Their host nudged a teacup in her direction and half filled it with strong amber-colored tea, then added hot water to top it off. Gluzman slid an almost-transparent slice of lemon onto a tiny dish for her, then graciously offered the silver sugar bowl. "Young ladies don't take sugar these days, do they?"

"You fool!" a creaky old voice suddenly rang out just behind Masha.

Masha jumped in surprise and turned around. Behind her hung an enormous cage, and inside it, an enormous parrot.

"You fool!" the parrot repeated.

"No need to tell me, I know!" Gluzman retorted cheerfully.

Masha laughed. The tension that had accumulated in her body during their long walk to the room was falling away now. Though Gluzman was eccentric, he didn't show any signs of insanity, as far as she could tell. His dark eyes seemed to take everything in hungrily, and his large mouth was twisted into a wry smile.

"My parrot very much resembles me, don't you think, my dear? Two silly old good-for-nothings!"

Masha smiled and took a sip from her delicate ceramic cup. The tea was excellent.

"I don't believe in the green teas and red teas they have these days, with their flowers and buds and petals and little pieces of straw, smelling like anything at all other than tea. I don't need my tea to be diaphoretic or calmative or anything else. My nerves, honestly, require a stronger medicine." Gluzman's fluttering hand performed its ritual over Innokenty's cup next, and then he sat back in his chair, clearly pleased with himself. "Well then, my young friends! What brings you to my humble abode?"

Innokenty bent down and pulled Masha's map from his briefcase.

"Dr. Gluzman," he said, "we need a consultation. Or, actually, a confirmation of my theory."

Gluzman took a pair of glasses with round, thick lenses from his breast pocket and perched them atop his fleshy nose. The expression on his face remained unchanged, but he tilted his head first to one side, then to the other as he looked the page over carefully.

"I believe there's a certain pattern to the points marked on the map, Professor. Do you see it?" Innokenty looked nervous, ready to spring up from his chair.

"It might just be a coincidence, but—" Gluzman turned to Masha, removed his glasses, and smiled. The old man's teeth were blindingly white. "Inno-centi must have seen just what I see here. He's a wonderful boy, mademoiselle. Don't you let him get away."

"I won't," Masha said, smiling. "I've been holding on to him since we were eight years old."

Gluzman nodded and turned to the blushing Kenty.

"Never be afraid of your own conclusions, young man! You must trust that whisper inside you! It is formed of knowledge, first and foremost, and of deep intuition. It comes with experience."

"Heavenly Jerusalem," Kenty said quietly.

"Heavenly Jerusalem," repeated Gluzman. "Precisely."

Masha looked impatiently from one man to the other.

"Masha, dear, judging from the discouraged look in your lovely eyes, you must be unfamiliar with the concept?" Gluzman chuckled and rolled his wheelchair over to the bookshelf that lined one wall of the room. "Here you are, for a start," he said, pulling out a leather-bound volume. "The Holy Scriptures. Have you read them?"

Masha felt her cheeks going red.

"Surely you have," said Gluzman, not waiting for her to respond. "But who remembers books like these? Only old dotards like me. Now, let me just find the place . . ." He thumbed through the pages. "Here we are. Listen. From the Book of Revelation: 'And I, John, saw the holy city, new Jerusalem, coming down from God out of heaven, prepared as a bride adorned for her husband.'" Gluzman removed his glasses again, and looked up at Masha. "You see, Mashenka, my dear—may I call you Mashenka?—in the religious tradition, the city of Jerusalem was considered the navel of the earth, because it was meant to be a prototype of the Heavenly City. And that Heavenly Jerusalem, in turn, is the kingdom of the saints in heaven." Gluzman smiled. "If you believe John, it is a city of uncommon beauty, built of materials that shine and reflect the light. Gates made of pearls, walls made of precious stones—jasper, sapphire, chalcedony, topaz, chrysolite, amethyst—and streets made of gold. And this description was not just something the storyteller dreamed up, his own fantasy. No!"

Gluzman looked to Innokenty, and his former student took up the tale.

"In those times, gemstones represented sources of sacred energy. They are eternal, and like eternity, they are perfect, unlike the mortal world of humans, plants, and animals."

Masha felt lost, which did not escape Gluzman's attention.

"It's rather a lot, isn't it? Here is the important thing. Symbolism aside, written descriptions of the City of Heaven are so precise, so suggestive, that they have allowed human beings, time and time again, to create their own models of that city, in essence transporting it from the heavens down to this earthly realm. Every description is architecturally detailed, and every detail carries symbolic value. For instance, all the descriptions agree that Heavenly Jerusalem is laid out as a square. Its walls face the four cardinal directions, and each wall has three gates, conveying the image of the Creator in all directions."

Masha cast a helpless glance at Innokenty, who winked back.

"Close your eyes and imagine this city, Masha!" Gluzman went on, reading from the Bible now in a singsong voice. "'Twelve gates, and at the gates twelve angels—'"

Masha had been following his description, her head tilted in concentration, but she stumbled at the angels.

"Dr. Gluzman, I really don't understand what all this has to do with—"

"Patience, my child. I know haste is the burden of the novice, and you are both still so young. Try to resist your urge to absorb knowledge on the run. Now, where were we? Oh yes. In the Middle Ages, the Gospels were often interpreted as instructions for action. Medieval architects had two models to work from: Heavenly Jerusalem and the earthly Jerusalem. The real Jerusalem influenced the cities people built to evoke the celestial one. Think of the Golden Gate in Kiev, or in Vladimir here in Russia. Those were intended to copy the Golden Gate in Jerusalem, and later in Constantinople."

Masha nodded uncertainly.

"Mainly capital cities tried to imitate the earthly Jerusalem," Innokenty added. "But plenty of smaller Russian cities were designed based on the descriptions of Heavenly Jerusalem. Kiev, as Dr. Gluzman said, but also Pskov, Kashin, Kaluga, and, of course, Moscow."

"Interesting," Masha ventured. "I always thought medieval architecture was completely chaotic. Narrow streets leading nowhere, improvised rebuilding every time a city burned down again . . ."

"That is a common theory, but absolutely unfounded," Gluzman answered heatedly. "As is this idea of the Dark Ages in general. Nonsense! It was a difficult but wonderful epoch, one which gave the world genius works of architecture, art, and literature. What have people ever made that is more wonderful than the spires of Gothic cathedrals, reaching for heaven? Or more noble than the Church of the Intercession on the Nerl? You might argue that by the eighteenth and nineteenth centuries, Moscow had fewer poor, fewer orphans, fewer cripples. Less filth, and not nearly as many brothels and saloons per capita. But the idea, the supreme religious idea that governed and inspired life in those earlier times, even for the lowliest pauper—that idea was gone."

Gluzman rolled back to the bookshelves and took down two more tattered volumes.

"It's only now, in the twenty-first century with all its blessings, that man has started building things any which way. But in those days, not a single stone was placed without a reason. It took years and years to build a church—three, five generations sometimes. Nothing like these Gebelai projects."

Masha gave a start at the murdered architect's name.

"Just think, Masha! People, their children, grandchildren, great-grandchildren, were born, got married, grew old, and died alongside a cathedral that grew higher and higher. Such a project could never be undertaken without a profound foundational idea around which life could take shape like flesh on a bone."

Innokenty and Masha exchanged looks. The improvised lecture was impressive. Innokenty was clearly enjoying himself.

"Now let's take a look at Moscow." Gluzman took on a calmer tone, and with the practiced gesture of an experienced speaker, adjusted the glasses on his bulbous nose. "You see, Mashenka, people often speak of Moscow as the Third Rome. But that idea is more secular or political—imperial, if you will. The idea of Moscow as a second Jerusalem is much older, and it has deep roots in Russian Orthodoxy. Moscow, as you no doubt learned in school, is the heir to Byzantium. On May 29, 1453, the Ottomans sacked Byzantine Constantinople, renamed it Istanbul, and made it the capital of their empire. With Constantinople gone, the political and spiritual leaders here shifted their focus to building a New Jerusalem where Moscow stood.

"With all our little daily worries, we cannot begin to imagine the power this idea of transforming Moscow into the City of Heaven wielded, in a young nation with no television, no radio, scarcely any literacy. Every single person, from the great tsars to the lowliest serfs, worked to make this city into the New Jerusalem. Just imagine if today the bums on the street and the oligarchs in their mansions joined forces.

Our medieval forebears believed that if Moscow were to become the New Jerusalem, all the Christians residing here would be first in line to enter heaven itself. That's why they started hauling in holy relics from all over the world. The more sacred items Moscow could collect, the more sacred the city would be!"

Gluzman moved the sugar bowl carefully to one side to make more room for an aging tome. He leafed through the yellow pages until he found the one he needed.

"This is the famous map from Sigismund von Herberstein's *Rerum Moscoviticarum Commentarii*. His contemporaries called him the Columbus of Russia. Herberstein visited Moscow in 1517 and 1526, and his map dates to 1549. Here is another map, from the Blaeu atlas, dated 1613."

Innokenty and Masha bent over the map.

"Look. Old Moscow is arranged in a circle, symbolizing eternity— the eternal Kingdom of Heaven, more precisely. Now compare that to the Book of Revelation: 'The City of Heavenly Jerusalem is new . . . and had a wall great and high, and had twelve gates . . . On the east three gates, on the north three gates, on the south three gates, and on the west three gates.' Moscow's old defensive walls, the Skorodom, perfectly match this description. An even earlier iteration of the city had the same arrangement of gates, three facing in each of the four directions." Gluzman looked up at Masha. "So what does this mean, mademoiselle? It means that Moscow was twice encircled by the twelve-gated walls of the City of Heaven, first in stone, then in wood. Now, moving on.

"'And the city lieth foursquare, and the length is as large as the breadth.' The length of the Skorodom fortress, north to south, was just under three miles, and almost the same east to west. You will agree, I think, that this cannot be a coincidence. And the height of the walls? In Heavenly Jerusalem, they are 'a hundred and forty and four cubits, according to the measure of a man, that is, of the angel.' If we assume a cubit is more or less one and a half feet, and multiply that by one hundred forty, we have two hundred ten feet—too high for a medieval wall. But the Spasskaya Tower was intended to be exactly one hundred forty-four cubits tall!

"Next, the color. Heavenly Jerusalem was decorated with green jasper, symbolizing the eternal lives of the saints, blue sapphires for the sky, and gold for righteousness. Moscow's cupolas could be only those three colors."

Now Innokenty joined in. "And in the seventeenth century, all the churches were covered in specific patterns, not just the carved stone and colored tiles we still have today, but also engravings of flowers and plants. You can see evidence of those in fragments remaining from the tile walls of the Cathedral of the Dormition on Goncharnaya, in places where they've stripped off the layers of plaster that got added on later. And—"

"Kenty," said Masha, quiet but determined. "Can you get to the point?"

"Mashenka!" said Gluzman, grinning victoriously. "The marks you made on your map? There is an explanation for every one of them. A very specific explanation."

ANDREY

Andrey sat holding the beeping receiver of his office phone in one hand and staring into space. The prisoner known as the Doctor, one Oleg Zitman, had apparently moved to Israel after being released early for good behavior. How had he managed to pull that off? Andrey had always thought jail time was supposed to make it difficult to get residency somewhere else.

The other tidbit he'd picked up was even more curious. The good doctor had made his fortune traveling around Russia, and sometimes Moldova, Ukraine, and other former Soviet backwaters too, buying human organs on the black market. Poverty and desperation drove people to sell whatever parts they had that came in pairs. Kidneys were most in demand. Here, former collective-farm workers, abandoned by the system, found hope again in fifteen- or twenty-thousand-dollar payouts. They fixed their homes or bought a cow, and while all around the world physicians and lawyers carefully debated whether or not to legalize the sale of donated human organs, Dr. Zitman grew very rich. But the world community finally rejected the idea, and the good doctor was caught and convicted, much to the dismay of many Moldovan peasants—who now had both their kidneys, but no prospects for making money.

Then Zitman did time with Yelnik, and naturally he would have told him how he ended up in jail. What would Yelnik have thought?

Perhaps what Andrey was thinking now: selling organs was nice work if you could get it. But Yelnik was no doctor. The only reason he'd ever held a knife was to murder somebody. Had Zitman and Yelnik joined forces? One could have done the killing, and the other could have collected the organs.

Andrey needed to find out the last time Zitman had visited Russia, and also, if possible, when he'd last contacted Yelnik.

He called around to every big security agency in and around Moscow. Printouts began coming through the fax machine thirty minutes later.

First Andrey skimmed a list of phone calls, looking for Israel's country code. Nothing. That would have been too easy. Besides, the numbers didn't mean anything by themselves. Yelnik could have used any number of phones and names. But just then, the Israeli embassy returned Andrey's call. No, they told him, Mr. Zitman had not crossed the Russian border since receiving his Israeli citizenship.

The tantalizing door that had opened in Andrey's mind slammed shut. Organs need to be transported quickly and carefully. Yelnik never could have handled them without the doctor. Still, Yelnik's own gutted belly was too strong a connection to ignore. Andrey nudged the door open again with one foot. Could Yelnik have worked with a different corrupt doctor, if not Zitman?

He squinted again at the densely printed faxes. *When you don't know what you're looking for, just try to spot anything unusual.* Another country, a distant province, calls that lasted too long or came too frequently.

Andrey searched and searched, and finally he found something. Several calls, a month apart, lasting ten seconds each. Andrey underlined them in red. He turned back to the computer. Bingo! The number belonged to a government office, one at the Ministry of Defense. Andrey sat back in his chair. So there was Yelnik, an unidentified doctor, and the mysterious military men. Andrey grimaced. It was all starting to come into terrible focus.

Night had fallen over Moscow. He was exhausted and starving, and he still had to stop and pick up some food for that shameless dog. Maybe some of those nasty brown pellets the commercials said were a guaranteed hit with hungry canine pests.

As he closed the office door behind him, Andrey looked one more time at Karavay's desk, and the thought crossed his mind—without the bile he'd previously associated with her—that his intern had probably been asleep for hours already.

MASHA

But Masha was only just getting in bed.

She and Innokenty had driven back from the hospital in silence. Masha needed to let Dr. Gluzman's lecture stew for a while. It was crazy, fantastical, impossible. But the impossible and fantastical fit so well into the pattern Masha had already spotted in the murders. It was logical, in an insane way. Masha's studies of serial killers had taught her that insane yet logical justifications were their forte. She stared out at the Garden Ring Road flying by her window. She needed to get into the killer's head. *Who are you, Mr. Heavenly Jerusalem?*

Expensive cars rushed by. Ah, Moscow. It was a city that never slept. Restaurants flashed by, too, and the lights from exclusive strip clubs. The last trolleybus of the night lumbered past, looking like a plant-eating dinosaur next to the Jaguars with their predatory grins. The bus was full of people with a very different look from that of the driver of the Porsche convertible waiting next to them at the stoplight. Masha frowned at his smug face.

"I bet our guy couldn't afford a Porsche," said Innokenty, seeming to read her mind. "He's probably a bus rider. On the other hand, if they haven't caught him yet, he must be well educated."

Masha shivered, remembering the architect with that medal pinned into his skin. *Cruel, too,* she thought. *He must imagine the shining wealth of New Jerusalem all around him. He hears the choirs of angels, so he can't*

hear the cries of his victims. He is as cold as the jasper and emeralds in the
walls.

Innokenty parked the car Masha shared with her mother in the
garage and walked her to her door.

"Good night, Mashenka," he said gently, looking at her with a sort
of tender sadness.

Masha smiled, and gave him a kiss on the cheek and a quick hug.
She really didn't want to sleep alone tonight. But the idea of sleeping
with Innokenty was ridiculous.

Masha crept into her apartment and took off her coat without turning
on the entryway light. She didn't want to bother her mother and stepfather. She could hear their calm, measured breathing from the back
bedroom, and Masha felt a sense of relief, for the first time, that there
was a man in the house. She tucked herself into bed and curled up
tight in a ball. She warmed her feet one at a time in her hands, trying
to banish terrible images from her head. Her dreams, when they finally
came, were incredibly beautiful.

Masha dreamed of medieval Moscow, a church at every crossroads.
The walls of the churches were decorated with herbs and vines, flowers and
birds, and Masha tilted her head back and stared up at a cupola shining in
the sun. She walked over a wooden roadway, casting her gaze hungrily in
all directions. Flowers were blooming everywhere; she heard roosters crow-
ing, cattle mooing, and birds singing; and the air smelled of freshly cut
grass. Any direction she turned, Masha could see the brick-red battlements
of the Kremlin, stretching in a toothy row above the lush-green banks of
the Moskva. In her dream, Masha effortlessly traveled from Borovitsky
Hill, where the Kremlin stood, to the lowlands on the far side of the river,
and then southwest to Shvivaya Hill. Everything she saw was fresh as when
the world began, when human beings had not yet been created—yet there

were already gardens and cathedrals with countless floating cupolas. And everything seemed very logical and correct. All streets converged at the Kremlin's gates; the towers of the concentric old walls—Kitay-gorod, Bely Gorod, and the Skorodom—grew taller and more numerous the closer they were to the Kremlin itself; and when Masha suddenly found herself sitting in the Ivan the Great Bell Tower, a breathtaking view spread out below her of ancient monasteries dancing in ancient circles.

Masha awoke with a feeling of delight she had not experienced since childhood—like the feeling when you open your eyes and know there are presents under the tree and you are wrapped warmly in your family's unconditional love. In the shower, the feeling began to fade a little. She thought, sheepishly, that the dream-Russia was the false image zealous nationalists clung to. They acted in the name of the blue sky, golden cupolas, ruddy-cheeked children, and maidens in traditional dress. But, she realized, one thing about her dream did make sense: everything had been beautiful and good and simple as far as the eye could see *because* there were no people there.

When she climbed out of the shower, a new question occurred to her: How did Moscow look in the murderer's mind? Could it really be so mawkish, so dripping with honey? *No,* Masha thought with confidence. Her killer knew everything there was to know about people. He did not forgive them; he killed them.

Masha made her way to the kitchen table. Her stepfather gave her a wink over his cup of coffee, but her mother kept her back to Masha, making an awful racket at the stove. Masha smiled. This was Natasha's way of proclaiming that, like any decent mother, she would like to have a little insight into her daughter's personal life. When Masha came home after midnight, what could her mother assume other than some romantic rendezvous? *Oh Mama,* thought Masha, pouring herself a cup of Belov's always-excellent coffee. *If you only knew!*

She could easily have cleared up the misunderstanding and informed them that there had been no romance last night. But then she would have to make a similar statement the next day, and the day after that. And Masha hated talking about herself. Her mother blamed it on the annoying sense of secrecy she had inherited from her father.

"You look great, Mama!" Masha said as she stood up and gave her mother a kiss on the side of the head, noticing her skillful new dye job.

"Really?" Natasha turned and grinned happily.

"Just what I've been telling you!" Masha heard her stepfather crow as she skipped out the door.

ANDREY

Andrey pondered the mysteries of the universe in the same place the vast majority of humankind did: sitting on the crapper. He thought about Yelnik's bathroom, the toilet with a tank and the marble floor, hidden away in that godforsaken village. Yet here under Andrey's feet were nothing but warped wooden boards. His outhouse was practically medieval. *Even the average villager has a septic tank these days,* Andrey scolded himself. And what did he have? Soviet-style sanitation, with newsprint tacked to the wall.

What a pile of crap, literally. And that newsprint . . . When he got inside again, there it was, the ubiquitous *MK*. On days when Andrey took the train home, he sometimes bought a copy. *MK* was the kind of newspaper that didn't tax your brain. Here, for example, were the latest shocking crime chronicles. Something itched at his memory, buried, like a dusty coin that had rolled under the couch. He had read something, not in a case file or a novel . . . something about a soldier's mother who had her son's body shipped home to her, and found it to be surprisingly light, because the body was missing its heart, kidneys, and liver. The official story was that the soldier had committed suicide. *The coins!* Fourteen of them in Yelnik's empty belly.

Andrey ran back to the house, where Marilyn Monroe was waiting for him with such a demanding expression on his face that you never would have guessed that after the kibble last night, he had also weaseled out of Andrey half a dozen sausages Andrey had bought for himself.

"You call yourself a dog?" Andrey asked as he pulled on his jeans and boots and chugged some lukewarm coffee. "No, Marilyn. You're a pig. I'm kicking you out of here so you can go die on the street, got it?"

But Andrey wasn't even fooling himself, he thought as he hurried to the car. He sounded like half of an old married couple. He could yell all he wanted, but there was no way of getting rid of Marilyn now.

When Andrey finally flew into the office after what seemed like hours in traffic, he made a point of not noticing the expression on his intern's face, which hinted loudly at something secret and weighty. Instead he rushed to the computer and pulled up *MK* online. Marketing experts might have said that the newspaper's website pushed the limits of bad taste. But Andrey wasn't there for the style. He needed an item that was probably two years old. He started searching, keying in two or three terms at a time—*organs suicide soldier, army stolen organs*, and so on—until he found it. There it was, the suicide of Private D., body returned home, something something something . . . Here. *General Ovcharov denies rumors of stolen organs, calling the allegations a deplorable provocation . . .* All right, nothing interesting after that. But now he had a last name. Andrey wrote the general's name in his notebook, along with the name of the reporter.

The phone rang and Andrey and Masha both jumped. Anyutin was summoning him to report on the investigation. Andrey was so pleased with himself this morning that he graciously invited the intern to come with him. This was her chance to get a glimpse of how real professionals operated, guys who weren't afraid to get their hands dirty. Nothing like the girl-talk she was probably used to at her fancy college.

"I really need to speak with you," the girl told him in the elevator.

"Later," said Andrey, committed to his role as the stern hero.

The intern shut her mouth. But when they knocked at the colonel's door and walked inside, it was Andrey's turn to shut up.

Anyutin wasn't alone. Katyshev was sitting there, too. Andrey just had time to wonder what the hell was going on before Anyutin, demonstrating all the hospitality of a polished host, seated the intern at the all-powerful prosecutor's right hand, and showed Andrey to a seat a little farther off to the left.

"So, how are we all getting along?" Anyutin began, while Katyshev practically winked at his little golden girl.

Andrey felt a wave of anger welling up inside him again. The feeling got even stronger when the little idiot grinned and said, "Fantastic!"

"Well, Captain? How would you evaluate Intern Karavay's contribution so far?"

"I give her an A plus," Andrey said, in a voice so full of scorn a deaf man could have heard it. "I'm glad to see Mr. Katyshev here with us. Just the man I was hoping to talk with today."

"At your service," the prosecutor said with a nod of his gray head.

"I'm investigating a hitman named Yelnik. Maybe you remember—he was charged with murder but acquitted in the Nungatov case. You were the prosecutor."

"Yes, I do remember," Katyshev said, nodding again. "Not a very pleasant story. The detectives were able to scrounge up only a few paltry leads, and the defense attorney—Tishin, I think—twisted the facts all around so that, by the end, it wasn't even clear who had killed whom. Yelnik only served a couple of years for failure to cooperate. So what's he done this time?"

Andrey sat at the ready, his chest puffed out proudly.

"Actually, Yelnik has been murdered, and I'm investigating. After he got out of jail, Yelnik got out of the game. He moved out to the village of Tochinovka and raised chickens and potatoes. But his place, which looks like a dilapidated shack from the outside, is a luxury resort on the inside."

"Did you have a search warrant, Yakovlev?" Anyutin interrupted.

"The door was open. Kind of," said Andrey. "But here's the strange thing. The last time he was in prison, Yelnik's cellmate was a guy named Zitman, also called the Doctor. The Doctor was famous for traveling around poor regions and getting people to sell their organs—and for pennies, compared to the going price abroad. When Zitman got out of prison, he moved to Israel. But I have a source who says that Yelnik received several visits from some unidentified military officers. And his call list includes multiple short calls, just a few seconds long, to a number at the Ministry of Defense." Andrey looked in turn at every member of his rapt audience. "Meanwhile, a couple years ago, the bodies of soldiers started getting shipped home—without their internal organs.

"What I think is this: Yelnik was inspired by Zitman, but decided to take a streamlined approach. Instead of a single kidney, he'd take both, plus the heart and liver. Basically, everything he might be able to sell. One healthy young soldier could make him big bucks, even if he split it with the medics and commanding officers. You might remember, Yelnik was known for making his hits look like suicide. Probably his military contacts would notice some dumb recruit, an orphan or someone from a poor family, somebody whose suicide wouldn't cause a scandal, and pass the information on to Yelnik. But he must have cheated somebody, sometime, and they came back to collect their share. That's why Yelnik's guts are missing. They decided to make up the difference at their supplier's expense!"

"Somebody? Sometime?" Anyutin said. "Rather a foggy theory, isn't it, Captain?"

But the chief's radiant face belied his doubt. He was especially pleased that Katyshev himself was there to see the top-rate work his people were doing.

"Colonel Anyutin, sir," Andrey said with a smile. "I already have the name of one general, and a journalist who wrote an article about the soldiers a couple of years ago. It won't be too hard to get to the bottom of this."

"So if I understand correctly," said Katyshev, swinging one leg, "this murder is not at all connected with my old case against Yelnik? I had been worried about that. A completely separate crime, eh?"

"Sorry, but I don't think it is separate," a young, clear voice rang out.

What the fuck! Andrey turned to glare at his intern. She was staring at the floor, a nervous but stubborn expression on her face.

"Tell us more, Intern Karavay," said Katyshev with an exaggeratedly official tone to his voice, and looking at the girl's pale face, Andrey felt like he might explode with fury any second.

Oh, she doesn't think so, huh? This fucking brat, all wrapped up in her books and her serial killers, doesn't think so!

"I only have a very raw theory right now," Karavay began. "But it seems to me that this is part of a pattern. A series of murders that started almost two years ago at the old electric station."

"Is that so? Let's hear an explanation," said Anyutin.

"I'm sorry," Masha said, raising her eyes, "but I'm not yet ready to provide a full analysis."

No fucking way, thought Andrey. Now what was he supposed to say? Anyutin also looked dumbstruck. If this were any other member of his staff, anyone other than this girl here as a favor to you-know-who . . . What the hell *was* this?

Andrey stood up with a grunt and said a curt military-style farewell to Katyshev. As he was leaving, he saw how Katyshev was looking at the intern. It was an attentive, appraising gaze. But there was something else in it, too: Katyshev was looking at her with admiration.

MASHA

Masha caught up with him in the hallway.

"Andrey!" Masha shouted, startling herself. She had never called him by just his first name before. He spun around, looking like a hurt child. "I'm sorry, I tried to tell you, but you—"

"'I'm not yet ready to provide a full analysis?'" the captain roared, and Masha thought for a second he was going to hit her. "Where do you think you are, some rich girls' finishing school? This is Petrovka! We have discipline here! If you have something to say, you sure as hell better back it up with facts!"

"I can," said Masha, quietly.

"I'm listening!"

"I'd like to bring in an outside expert for this discussion. Could we have lunch together?"

Her mannered tone made Andrey grimace like he had tasted something sour.

"With pleasure," he said with a fake smile, and with obvious scorn he clicked his heels like a nineteenth-century Prussian soldier. With uncharacteristic elegance, he bowed to her, then turned and took off down the hall.

Masha waited until he was safely around the corner, then took out her phone and dialed Innokenty.

"Kenty! Come rescue me, please!" she whispered. "I need your moral support, or this denim-clad crocodile of mine is going to eat me up."

"What sort of support do you require, my unfortunate Medea?" But Kenty's irony quickly turned to sympathy, and he added, "Is he really getting to you?"

"Yeah," said Masha, "but it's my own fault. I started to share my theory with the bosses before I told him about it. Now I need you to come in, show some authority, be the guy five minutes away from getting his doctorate in history, and back up everything Gluzman said yesterday."

"Not a problem, seeing as I really am that guy," Innokenty bragged. "And I know a great little place near your office."

"Just nothing too expensive," Masha warned. "My denim detective is obviously not swimming in money."

"Good! Given where he works, that's probably a sign of moral rectitude," Innokenty reasoned.

They hung up, and ten minutes later Kenty texted her an address. When Masha told Andrey, he just nodded, not looking up from his papers. Masha felt terrible. She looked at the back of his crew-cut head and cursed herself for not showing more restraint. But there was just no way she could keep this insane theory inside. It was tickling her lips, begging to be set free. How could Yelnik's bizarre murder be a one-off? Could Yakovlev really not see it?

Masha made herself sit patiently till lunchtime, thinking over every point all over again.

When the time came, Maria Karavay and Andrey Yakovlev took an awkward walk down the stairs together and stepped out of the building without exchanging a word. As she tried to match his stride, Masha noticed with surprise that the girls they passed were looking appreciatively at Mr. Denim. *They say there's a demographic crisis,* she thought, *but I didn't realize men were* that *hard to come by.*

✣

As usual, Kenty had selected the ideal place. Nice and quiet, with tables placed a discreet distance apart, and judging by the decor and the customers, not too posh.

When Innokenty stood up from the table to greet them, Masha saw Andrey's face go dark. Tall, broad-shouldered Kenty in his expensive jacket made the poor captain look like a nobody. Masha realized how much they both must irritate him, as a short, obviously provincial man without much money. *But to hell with him!* thought Masha. Did she have to please everybody she met? It wasn't her fault her father was a lawyer rather than a truck driver, or that her mother was a doctor who ran a private clinic. Why was she always apologizing to this guy? The revolution was supposed to have made everyone equal, and look how that had turned out! Why shouldn't Andrey look at her and Kenty, and see that they were different?

As she sat down at the table, Masha very deliberately, with a slow, genteel gesture, tucked a lock of hair behind her ear. Then she clearly dictated her order to the waiter, and turned to the captain in a rather majestic posture.

"What will you have, Andrey?"

Glowering, he ordered the first thing he saw on the menu. Then they settled in to wait for Innokenty, who after pondering for a while finally ordered the same thing as Masha. As he extended his arm to hand his menu to the waiter, the light reflected off his cuff links.

Masha smiled wryly, and took the file on the murders out of her bag.

ANDREY

"I think it's time to get down to the facts," said Andrey, thoroughly irritated by being talked at about medieval architecture.

"You're just like our Masha," said Innokenty, shaking his head. "I'm simply trying to explain that there is an actual system behind all of this."

"You want the facts?" asked Masha. "Look." She tapped with one trimly manicured fingernail at the cross on Red Square. "Doesn't it seem strange to you, this concentration of murders around one of the best-guarded architectural landmarks in the country? Actually, not murders, but bodies. Somebody worked hard to leave the mutilated corpses of his victims right there, on or near the square. This cross here at Lobnoye Mesto, in front of St. Basil's? That's the arm they found last winter. And this one is Kutafya Tower, where they found the drunk called Kolyan. Here, right at the Kremlin wall, is where they fished out Yelnik's body the other day."

"So what?" Andrey interrupted. "We don't know anything about that arm. Nobody's even found a body."

"So you think the arm's owner might be alive?" Innokenty quipped. "Listen, Yakovlev, the very center of the plan for a New Jerusalem was the Kremlin. More specifically, Red Square and St. Basil's Cathedral. In Ivan the Terrible's time, they even called the cathedral 'Jerusalem.' In the Book of Revelation, John the Prophet says that there is no temple in Heavenly Jerusalem, only a holy altar. So St. Basil's Cathedral was meant as the altar for the enormous open-air temple of Red Square."

"Andrey," said Masha, looking at him almost pleadingly. "It's all supposed to map onto Jerusalem. Lobnoye Mesto, the old public execution site, is supposed to stand for Golgotha, where Christ was crucified. Kutafya Tower is the Church of the Holy Sepulchre. The Moskva, where they found Yelnik, stands in for the Jordan River."

Andrey scowled and pointed to the other bank of the river, where there were three crosses marked on the map.

"Those are the three people killed along the Bersenevskaya waterfront," Masha explained.

"In Zamoskvorechye," Innokenty added. "Literally, that's 'the other side of the river.' In the seventeenth century, they built a hundred and forty-four fountains there, to represent the one hundred forty-four thousand believers in John's Revelation. Here, on either side of the river, there's a symbol for the Tree of Life, in the form of the terraced gardens of the Kremlin and the Tsar's Gardens, or the Tsaritsyn Meadow," he continued, practically singing as he warmed to his subject. "The famous icon painter Nikita Pavlovets depicted the scene—"

Innokenty suddenly broke off when his foot received a kick under the table. He gave it a surreptitious rub. Masha smiled and picked up the topic as if nothing had happened.

"Do you remember when the wife of the governor of Tyumen Province was killed and chopped into four pieces?"

"Sure," said Andrey. "They found her out at the Kolomenskoye estate."

"Right." Masha nodded. "In the actual Jerusalem, directly east of Gethsemane and the Golden Gate, there's an octagonal tower built at the spot of the Ascension of Christ, the Chapel of the Ascension."

Innokenty nodded, too, and went on. "But in Moscow, the line from Spasskaya Tower, our Golden Gate, to Tsaritsyn Meadow, our Gethsemane, runs north to south rather than east to west. If you continue along that axis, it runs straight to the Church of the Ascension at Kolomenskoye."

"Which is also an octagonal chapel with a steeple. And even though the distances aren't the same in Moscow as in Jerusalem, centuries ago the church at Kolomenskoye was perfectly visible from the Kremlin."

Their food came. Andrey had ordered some sort of pasta, and he immediately dove in. Innokenty tried a few times to make conversation, but neither Masha nor the busily chewing captain helped him out. When the waiter brought coffee, Andrey turned to Masha with a question.

"So is that all?"

"No," Masha hurried to answer. "There's also the architect. He died in a strange way, plus he was left in an apartment on Lenivka Street—"

"What about Lenivka Street? Make it quick, okay?"

"It's right by the Pushkin Museum. When you line up the maps of the two cities, that corresponds with the Jaffa Gate."

"Anything else?"

"That's it for now. But I'm sure I haven't found everything yet. There are other strange murders, we just need to match them up with—"

"Intern Karavay." Andrey scowled. "You're a real serial-killer fanatic, aren't you? Do you get a little excited over these guys? You're seeing them everywhere you look. Real detectives don't arrange real life to fit a theory. It's the other way around."

"Let me ask you something very elementary. Why these people, exactly? If this is a serial killer, how is he choosing his victims? A governor's wife, an old drunk, an architect, and a hitman? There's something about serial killers you ought to know, seeing as you're such an expert. They all have some signature, a modus operandi. Where's yours?"

Nobody spoke.

"Executions," said Innokenty, finally. "Each one was killed in a way people used to be executed in the Middle Ages. The governor's wife was quartered, Yelnik was drowned under the ice, the drunk was subjected to a kind of water torture, and those others had their tongues cut out."

"Pretty flimsy," said Andrey, not deigning to look at him.

Then he stood up, grabbed his denim jacket from the back of the chair, took out a couple of banknotes, and tossed them carelessly onto the table.

"One more thing, Intern Karavay. If this is the work of a serial killer, those numbers must mean something. So I'm sure you have an explanation?" He waited for a few seconds, then gave each of them a wry look and nodded. "See you around." And he walked out of the restaurant.

Andrey felt great. He had finally given the perfect speech, even if it wasn't in Anyutin's office. There were just three flaws to his perfect exit. First, there was something compelling about that crazy theory. Second, his dramatic gesture with the money would cost him and Marilyn Monroe a week's worth of provisions.

And third, Masha Karavay was a surprisingly good match for that pretty-faced jackass in the suit. For some reason, that really bothered him.

MASHA

"I'm positive we're right!" Masha said adamantly, while Innokenty slid his empty coffee cup from side to side on the table. "Before we talked it out today, I still had some doubt. But not anymore. There's a pattern here. Coincidences like these don't happen, you know?"

"Masha, it may be that the theory is too intricate, and the coincidences . . . they're just coincidences as long as we have no concrete facts. Your denim detective is right. We've built an intriguing theory, but as long as we have no motive, it's just fantasy. Like he said, why those people, exactly?"

"And the numbers." Masha sighed. "We haven't figured out those damn numbers yet. But still, it's obvious that we have a particular type of killer here: the maniacal missionary. I do think motive is clear, in general terms, at least. He kills in places symbolically connected to Heavenly Jerusalem in order to show us that we're all sinners, don't you think?"

"Tell me more about this maniacal-missionary type," Innokenty said.

"Why?"

"It's not for me, Masha. I'm interested, sure, but laying it out will help you. Try to be precise. You don't need to give examples. Try to build a system, and then compare your victims to every point in that framework, okay?"

Masha grinned. "Usually things work in the opposite direction: you lecture me, like you do about your precious Old Believers. But okay. Let's just order some more coffee first."

Innokenty waved the waiter over. While he took their order, Masha seemed to be studying the tablecloth, but as soon as he walked away, she raised her eyes and launched right into it.

"A maniacal missionary doesn't hear voices, either of gods or demons, and he doesn't see visions that urge him to violence. A missionary is on the hunt to destroy a particular group of people, to clean the planet of filth. There's any number of groups he could see as filthy: prostitutes, gays, blacks, whatever. He's a collector of sins."

"I'm more used to antique collectors than sin collectors. But there is what experts call a consistent motive, isn't there?" asked Innokenty.

Masha nodded. "Right. Consistency of motive is one of the main things all serial killers have in common. But only the missionary considers his work to be a sacred obligation. If you look at the four main reasons pushing someone to commit multiple murders—manipulation, domination, control, and sexual aggression—the missionary has none of the sexual compulsion, but the other three might be variously involved depending on the killer's personality. From what we know so far, judging from the current theories about missionaries, and from the fact that the bodies were moved to different places, I think that control is the strongest motive here. It also seems to me that, despite his fastidious methods of execution, our killer, like most missionaries, does what profilers call 'lightning murders.'"

"Explain," said Innokenty.

The waiter appeared with two strong cups of coffee. Masha slowly added two cubes of sugar to hers, and stirred.

"Well, lightning murders are committed by serial killers who don't get pleasure out of the act itself. Quartering a body isn't literally quick, of course, but for him, that was probably just a way to kill a sinner, not a way to enjoy himself. On the other hand, there are also 'leisurely murders,' where the whole thing happens slowly, because the killer enjoys his victims' suffering. The hedonists fit into that category, for example. Some of them thrive, somehow, on killing, and others get sexually aroused by it. Do we really have to talk about this?"

"No." Innokenty hadn't touched his coffee. "But it sounds like, out of all the types of serial killers, ours isn't the most terrible, right? He doesn't taunt or rape his victims; he almost seems to kill against his own will, simply because he thinks it needs to be done. Something like a conscientious soldier."

Masha winced sadly. "Lots of maniacal missionaries actually are soldiers. It has something to do with the habit of flawlessly carrying out orders, or being trained for a strict life in the barracks and then rejecting the mess of the ordinary world. Plus, I think that, for many soldiers, the value of human life is sort of negotiable. After all, they're basically told to sacrifice some people to clean the world up for the rest."

"Granted. Here's what is bothering me, though: you, and all the rest of the detectives who have investigated his crimes, have nothing solid on this monster. If he hasn't left a single clue, he must be more than just smart. He must have some special insight into the kind of work you do. What do you think? What about a—What did your supervisor call it, a signature, a modus operandi?"

Masha smiled, not too happily. "You must be spending too much time with me, Kenty! You're really taking to this stuff." She spread her fingers on the table as she talked. "We really don't know enough yet. How does the killer catch his victims, for instance? Does he ambush them? Does he lure them in somehow? Then, does he move things around at the scene, or take some sort of memento when he's done? And another thing. A modus operandi can be verbal, like some special text he makes the victim repeat. That wouldn't leave any trace for detectives to find. Right now, all we know is that he uses medieval methods to kill, all different ones. We need to figure out how he chooses his victims, what they have in common."

Innokenty was listening attentively.

Masha continued, "For example, if we look just at Russian serial killers, there's Slivko. He killed seven boys under sixteen years old. He was a Hero of Communist Labor and the director of a youth club. His victims were all members of the club—that's what they had in common. Chikatilo found his victims at bus stops and train stations. Pichushkin hunted in the park. They all chose children, the elderly, or women, often prostitutes, because they're easy targets. But imagine targeting the wife of a governor, one of the richest women in the world! Or a famous architect! Or sneaking up on a professional hitman! Kenty, our missionary is very smart, and—you're right—he knows how criminal investigations work. But he also must plan out every step of every crime in minute detail. It's terrifying, actually, and I feel like I don't understand anything at all."

Innokenty squeezed Masha's hand. "You do. I believe in you. Let's take things one at a time. From what I can tell, the only signature we have, so far, is the medieval-style executions. Maybe if we could break those down somehow, we would understand more?"

"How much do you know about executions?" Masha finally took a sip of her coffee, and scowled. It had gone completely cold.

Innokenty shrugged. "It's not a topic that ever really interested me. But if our missionary is so obsessed with Orthodox Christianity, maybe his murders have analogies in Russian history? And that's a subject I know something about."

I'm so lucky to have Kenty, Masha thought suddenly. She squeezed his hand encouragingly. Innokenty smiled.

"There was a document in the Middle Ages that regulated the Russian state's dealings with criminals. It was called the Council Law Code of 1649. Have you heard of it?"

"Maybe. Doesn't matter. Go on."

"This document appeared during the era Gluzman told us about. The Code described in great detail who was supposed to be punished, for what crimes, and in what fashion. The punishments were meant to be analogies for the torments of hell—and that, I think, may be important for understanding this killer of ours. It's why executions were often performed in public. It wasn't just to entertain or terrorize the people. The more important goal was to make sure everyone understood what might be waiting for them in hell. The symbolism was vital. By disfiguring a person—ripping out his nostrils or eyes, or slicing off his lips—the state also made sure he could never blend in with the masses. So a thief, for instance, could never pass for an honest citizen again.

"In the Middle Ages, different people who committed the same crimes were supposed to be punished differently. For example, for delaying a transaction, a clerk might be beaten with batogs, which were like sticks. But the clerk's boss would be beaten with a scourge, which could kill him. Basically, if I'm remembering correctly, sixty different crimes were punishable by death, including smoking tobacco."

"Wow," said Masha, sighing. "At least now it's only five."

"Which ones?"

"Well," said Masha, ticking them off on her fingers. "Murder. Threatening the life of a government figure. Threatening the life of someone working on a court case or a preliminary investigation. Threatening the life of a law-enforcement agent. And genocide."

"Well, that's good to know. I can't list all sixty crimes for you, but I do know that the execution methods were classified as either 'simple'— just chopping off someone's head or hanging him—or 'technical'— things like drawing and quartering, burning, dripping molten metal into someone's throat . . ."

A young couple sat down at the next table.

"Maybe we should talk about this stuff somewhere else," Innokenty suggested.

"It would take forever to go somewhere else. Traffic is terrible out there," Masha whispered. "Just finish up what you were saying. The short version." And she leaned closer.

"Hanging," Innokenty whispered in her ear almost intimately, "was the cheapest and most insulting method. They never executed respectable people that way, not here, and not in Europe. It was bad manners. If you wanted to take the life of a high-class individual, they seemed to think, it was worth at least spending the money to sharpen the axe and pay a real professional to do the job."

ANDREY

Andrey caught Masha on her way into the building, at the bottom of the staircase.

"Masha!" he called, and saw her shoulders tighten. Did she still expect him to call her Intern Karavay? Or was Masha afraid of him?

Earlier, that discovery would have given him a certain amount of satisfaction, like all was right in the world. Interns, even the kind who got in on connections rather than merit, were supposed to be scared of their bosses. But after lunch today, her fear suddenly seemed like an insult. *What the hell did I do to you to make you so frightened?*

Masha turned her head and smiled uncomfortably. "Yes, Captain?"

Suddenly, all his annoyance evaporated.

"I wanted to tell you," he began, "that despite my, you know, objective critique, your theory is a good one. Good, but incomplete, understand? This isn't about figuring out all the creepy medieval junk. If we're really talking about a serial killer, we'll need to go big, put a task force together. And for that to happen, first we need to make sure our reasoning is ironclad. Otherwise they'll never give us extra people or resources."

Masha grinned gratefully and tucked her hair behind her ear again, but this time with none of the haughtiness she had displayed at the restaurant.

Andrey's eyes followed her hand mechanically. Her ear was small, and it wasn't pierced, but there was a tiny freckle on her earlobe.

"Yes," she said, "I completely understand. I wanted to ask you—it would be nice to talk with the witnesses in those cases again. It seems to me that would be the simplest way to figure out how the killer caught his victims, what kind of pattern he was following."

"That would be a lot of work." Andrey forced his gaze away from her ear. The intern was looking directly at him. Masha Karavay's eyes were light green and glowed with calm expectation.

"I could get through a lot of it myself if you'd allow Innokenty to work with me," she said uncertainly.

Andrey didn't like that idea. He looked down at his worn-out sneakers, and remembered her friend's designer shoes.

"Doesn't he have anything better to do?" he asked.

"He's a historian, an antiques dealer. He specializes in seventeenth-century religious icons," Masha said quickly. "What I mean is, his schedule is flexible. He doesn't need to go into work every day."

"Fine. Work with him," Andrey said drily, and he turned and walked off without saying good-bye.

Andrey knew he was acting like a jerk, but he had no idea why. Could it be because he knew he could never compete with some fancy-pants antiques dealer? So if the game was lost from the start, why get so worked up about it? *What game, you moron?* he asked himself as he opened the door to his banged-up old Ford. *Are you tormenting her, like a school kid who bullies the girl he likes?*

MASHA

Masha watched her supervisor walk away, bewildered. What a strange person. Every time she started to think he might be a decent guy, he'd storm off without so much as saying good-bye. A total jerk! But still . . . Masha started climbing the stairs, her mood improving with every step. Andrey had just given her some actual encouragement. He called her theory "good." *Maybe I deserve to be here after all, Captain Yakovlev!* And agreeing to let her work with Kenty—that was a miracle.

Now all she had to do was call and deliver the good news. For the next few days, instead of appraising icons, cruising around antiques markets, and hobnobbing with collectors, he would be interviewing a dozen witnesses in murder cases.

"Kenty!" she pleaded as soon as he picked up. "Come save me! I have to interview a whole pile of people, and I can't do it alone." There was a heavy silence on the other end of the line. "I know I've been abusing you mercilessly, but there's no one else I can abuse quite like you. It's only for three or four days."

"All right, I'll do it," Kenty said, laughing. "I was just looking to see if I could cancel my appointments for the rest of the week."

"Oh, great!" said Masha. "We need to find out exactly what kind of sinners our victims were. I'll buy us some voice recorders."

"I have one already, Masha. Just get one for yourself. I'll come pick you up tomorrow. Right now I can't talk, I have visitors."

"Okay, sorry. See you tomorrow." And Masha hung up with a happy smile. Her real work was about to begin, and she was going do it with Kenty at her side, at a safe distance from her angry boss. What could be better?

The next day Kenty drove up at the appointed time. He found Masha waiting for him on the bench outside, calling all the numbers on her list.

"Hi," he said. Masha waved and turned her attention back to the phone. Innokenty sat down next to her. She said good-bye to the person she was talking with, then turned to him.

"Okay, check it out. I managed to set up a bunch of meetings for us. I decided it would make sense to start with the first set of mysterious numbers. I'll take number one. I'm about to go talk with the girlfriend of the guy who was the least mutilated in that basement on Bersenevskaya. He had the T-shirt with the number one written on it. Slava Ovechkin. Meanwhile, you'll meet with an athlete, a swimmer, at the Olympic Village. He'll tell you about his teammate: victim number three, Alexander Solyanko. Then I've got Tanya Shurupova, best friend of Julia Tomilina, victim number two. After that we need to find Kolyan's drinking buddies. I wasn't able to get through to them by phone, obviously. Can you try to find them after you talk to the swimmer?"

Innokenty nodded.

Masha handed him a list of addresses and jumped up. "Let's go!"

MASHA

Lyuda looked over the girl from Petrovka with a curious eye. So people like that were working for the police now? The young woman was wearing a plain sweater and black pants, but when she walked into Lyuda's kitchen and sat down next to the window, Lyuda knew that this plainness was deceptive. The girl's whole package was deceptive: her unstyled hair, her open face devoid of makeup, her supershort fingernails. She might have been a musician, a cellist maybe. An extremely successful one, judging from the brand of her purse. But here she was working for the government.

She was asking if there was anything unusual about Ovechkin, about his family. Well, it was true, his parents hadn't known much about their son—they were both too wrapped up in religion, God forgive her, but it was true! Lyuda had only met them once, by accident, in a grocery store. You should have seen Ovechkin's dad, with his mess of a beard and the kind of old-fashioned jacket and boots nobody ever wore anymore. His mom was even worse. She was wearing a kerchief, and a skirt so long it swept the dirty floor. Terrible. Slava had squirmed visibly, and he introduced them reluctantly. Like, *Oh, by the way, I guess these are my parents.* And Lyuda knew right away why Slava had never brought her to his house. What would that have been like? Lyuda's own mother wasn't much to look at, but at least it wasn't immediately obvious that she was a nutjob. With these two, it was right on the surface. What a face Slava's old man had made, like he wanted to put a curse on her right there in the store. Lyuda knew that in her miniskirt and war-paint makeup, she didn't have much chance of ingratiating herself to that priestly couple. His nun of a mother had even said to her, as she was leaving, *God save you, my child!* Lyuda had to admit she hadn't reacted too well, just giggled nervously and shot out of the store like a bullet.

Now Slava was gone, and, honestly, she wasn't drowning in grief or anything, but she still remembered how she had laughed like an idiot at that *my child*, and she even thought, sometimes, about going to visit the church where Slava's father worked. But his dad was so painfully depressing, and she didn't have any idea where to find his mom. And if she did find her, what would she say? She must be grieving her son, but Lyuda—of course she felt bad for poor Slava, but not as much as if she had been madly in love with him. They'd had a good time together. That was it, really.

That was what she was trying to explain to this elegant Detective Karavay when she asked her what kind of person Dobroslav Ovechkin had been. Lyuda had forgotten that Slava was short for Dobroslav. What a weird old name! His parents really must have been looney tunes. Lyuda furrowed her brow, looked at the girl from Petrovka, and said the first thing that popped into her head.

"He never stopped talking!" said Lyuda.

"What do you mean?" she asked, interested.

"Well, not like spilling state secrets or anything. I just got tired of it sometimes, you know? Usually, you go on and on, and the guy listens. But with Slava it was the opposite. You couldn't say a word because his blah, blah, blah filled up the whole room. He couldn't ever shut up. Not even in bed! I could say, like, oh, I just bought some new shoes near the metro. And right away, he's like, What were you thinking, they only sell garbage there, the heels will fall off the first time you wear them! As if he knew anything about stilettos! Or, like, I might say I wish I could get bigger boobs. What an idiot, you're not thinking about the consequences! Strange foreign substances, doctors say it's dangerous—"

"Maybe he just couldn't afford to give you presents?" the detective asked, her eyes laughing.

Lyuda laughed, too, out loud. "Want some tea?" she asked. And without waiting for an answer, she put an old teapot, which looked like it had boiled dry once or twice, on the burner.

"No," Lyuda finally answered, sitting down across from her guest again. "He wasn't stingy. Even if he'd only had enough money for one tit, he would have given it to me."

"That kind of relationship, huh?" the detective asked.

"Oh man. We were so good together. Before him I was going out with this real ass—" Lyuda pulled up short. For some reason, she really wanted this Karavay woman to like her. "An absolute, um, good-for-nothing. But I don't think Slava ever had a real girlfriend before me. He wasn't all that attractive, really. He was a joker. Skinny, kind of a wimp. I don't have, like, a maternal instinct when it comes to men. I need a guy who can take care of me. But he needs a girl with balls. Well, needed, I mean."

All of a sudden Lyuda felt like she might cry, but she managed to hold it in. In that pause, choking back tears, she got the tea ready. She put some cookies on the table, too. The detective remained tactfully quiet, then took a sophisticated sip from her cup while looking at Lyuda, who had sat down across from her again, legs crossed, swinging one foot nervously.

"I'm very sorry," she said quietly.

It was clear that she really was. Sorry for Slava, and maybe for Lyuda, too.

"Well," said Lyuda, snuffling noisily, "it's already been two years. And don't bother looking for any dirt on Slava. He could be a pain, but he wasn't a bad guy. The only thing I didn't like about him was the way he talked about his parents. He made fun of their 'churchly life,' as he called it, and laughed at how cut off they were from society. But how else could they be, given what they did for a living?"

"What do Dobroslav's parents do?"

"You know, preachers in that church."

The detective's hand froze in the air over the plate of cookies. She had gone pale.

"Kinda weird, right?" Lyuda said. "You know what happened one time? Once at church, while his father was up there droning on, Slava walked in and started singing loud in front of the whole congregation. And he had this terrible voice, really high, you know?"

"Falsetto," the detective said slowly.

"Yeah, that. So, in this falsetto voice, he sang a song, some old number about love, totally unbelievable, you know the kind."

The girl from Petrovka nodded uncertainly.

"He said his mom just about died on the spot, and his dad went totally red in the face. And Slava just ran out. So. I don't know what else to tell you. Have you talked to his friends yet?"

The detective shook her head no. Lyuda frowned. Before, this Petrovka lady had been listening close, all involved in the conversation. But now she seemed lost in thought, like she had forgotten about Lyuda completely.

"Thank you, Lyuda," she finally said, turning off her recorder and putting it back into her big black purse. "You've been a big help."

"Really?" Lyuda smiled. "Well, great! I don't know what I said that helped. Anyway, go and catch that monster."

The detective nodded, said good-bye, and left. But the aroma of her perfume lingered in the apartment for hours. Lyuda wished she had asked her what it was called.

INNOKENTY

"Listen, I already told the detectives everything I know," the swimmer told Innokenty as he tossed his wet towel on a bench. "If the investigation's at a dead end or whatever, that doesn't mean you've gotta come around asking questions for the twentieth time, does it?"

Innokenty didn't respond. He had just spent an hour waiting for this guy to finish his training session, watching through a window in the locker room as the swimmer cut through the pool's unnaturally blue water, back and forth, tirelessly. His head looked small against the smooth surface of the water and perfectly streamlined, disappearing and reappearing at even intervals. Innokenty, who preferred mental labor, was spellbound by this astounding concentration, this subordination of the self to the body.

But a whole hour of waiting around, breathing the stale smell of chlorine and sweat, was enough to sour his mood. Now they stood facing one another, one in a gray tweed jacket and a nice pair of trousers, the other almost naked, showing off the generous span of his muscular shoulders and his surprisingly sharp face, all pointy nose and jutting chin.

"I won't take up too much of your time," said Innokenty, quietly but with authority.

They were the same height. The swimmer tried to size him up, then shook his head like a wet dog. A few drops splattered onto Innokenty's shirt, and he looked down, annoyed, as they soaked into the fabric.

"Sorry," said the swimmer, and finally extended his hand. "Nikolay Snegurov."

They sat down right there on the wooden benches. There was nobody else around.

"You were Solyanko's friend and colleague. Could you try to tell me what kind of guy he was?"

Snegurov looked at Innokenty, and the blue sheen of the pool seemed frozen in his eyes.

"There's one thing you need to get straight," he said. "Solyanko wasn't my friend. Maybe writers or scientists can be friends, but in sports, it doesn't happen. You have to be a winner, third place at worst. And you don't have much time. We're like ballet dancers. One step closer to retirement every year. You work your ass off maybe twenty years tops, the injuries pile up, and you're off to the showers. When I hear people talk about 'healthy competition,' it makes me want to vomit. We're not some pansy fucking naval officers riding desks at the Admiralty. Here, if you don't make it at the Olympics, then you train for another four years, and in four years anything could happen.

"Know why I'm telling you all this? Because Solyanko was a piece of shit. I don't give a fuck that you're not supposed to speak ill of the dead. I was just a kid when I started swimming, I wasn't even ten, and I was always busy, away at sports camps. No reading books, no chasing girls. We give up our whole lives. All for a higher good, right?"

"I'm not sure I know what you mean," Innokenty said carefully.

"You don't? Maybe they didn't write it down before, didn't think it was important. Or they checked out my alibi. It's airtight, thank God. Solyanko and I were the leaders of the Russian team. Everyone thought either Solyanko or Snegurov would take home a medal, defend the country's honor. They even called us the SS Squad, for our initials. So naturally we trained like we were possessed. We were young, right? At our peak. It was our big chance. Solyanko and I hardly ever spoke in those days. Not just because I never liked him, but because we were too busy training. So, you know, rumors started to spread. That Solyanko was taking EPO."

"What was he taking?"

"EPO. Erythropoietin. It's a drug, improves your endurance. Increases the oxygen in your blood, or something like that. It can improve your performance by fifteen percent, basically."

"So, doping."

"*Oooo*, bad, right? The big bad wolf! Doping in sports!" Snegurov made a menacing face.

Innokenty was glad, suddenly, that Masha wasn't with them. The guy really looked monstrous.

"I'm so fucking tired of that. Know why? Because it's so—what's the word?—yeah, hypocritical. All these fucking bureaucrats, looking so serious, going, *Oh, we would never permit doping in our young champions!* But everyone does it, you know? Everyone! Every competition these days is all doped-up athletes. Furosemide, EPO, growth hormones for muscle mass . . . We get word about 'surprise' testing a couple days ahead, or the test results go missing, or you use blood you drew a couple days before. So the tests never find anything. And you know why I'm telling you this? Everyone out here has at least tried it once. And everyone thinks the International Swimming Federation is way too strict. But the government officials . . . On the one hand, they desperately want us to win. On the other hand, Russia needs to act like it's fighting doping as much as any country, maybe more. And then on the *other* other hand, at the Olympics in Sochi, we all heard what the president said about doping. And that's when they found a packet in my locker. Someone leaked it to one of the sports papers that same day and, since the Federation couldn't cover it up, they decided to make an example of me. Suddenly it was 1937 around here, a big fucking purge. You're presumed guilty, right? I was banned from competition for two years and I missed my Olympics. While my lawyer was trying to prove that the packet wasn't mine, I missed out on my gold."

"And the drugs really weren't yours?" Innokenty asked.

Snegurov huffed sadly. "I don't have any reason to lie about it now. But I know someone who could have benefited from making me look bad, who could have tipped off the press, who could have planted the packet, no problem. Except, as you know, Solyanko never made it to the Olympics. That freaky murder didn't have anything to do with doping, obviously, but you asked what kind of guy he was. A piece of shit."

Snegurov stood up, and Innokenty rose, too. They shook hands.

"We're not Olympians," said the failed champion, shaking his head. "We're gladiators, paying with our sweat and blood for the right to survive."

Kenty thought that Snegurov must have found the time to read a couple of books, after all.

"Who won your event?" he asked, when the swimmer's wide back had already passed through a doorway.

"Some guy from China." Snegurov turned back and grinned like a wolf. "And a couple of years later, they caught his coach with a suitcase full of growth hormones."

MASHA

Masha waited for Julia Tomilina's best friend next to the entrance to her apartment building. The woman was running late. Finally, the door opened a crack, and from the dark depths, a bright-pink stroller emerged. Masha jumped up and held the door open while Tanya Shurupova, squinting with the effort, shoved a double-wide baby limousine through the narrow doorway. Drops of sweat were rolling down her pretty face.

"Thanks," Tanya panted. "Phew." She wiped her forehead and smiled at Masha with embarrassment. "You don't mind if we talk in the park, do you? The twins just fell asleep, and I need to keep moving or they'll wake up and start yelling."

Masha smiled. "Girls?"

"No, they're boys. The pink stroller, huh? It's a hand-me-down from friends. Beggars, choosers, you know."

She and Masha crossed the street with the stroller and walked into Yekaterininsky Park. Masha stole a look at Tanya. Her ponytail was pulled back with an ordinary rubber band, and there were dark circles under her eyes.

"Not sleeping through the night yet?"

"Sleeping! Ha! First one sleeps, then the other. I don't even have time to eat. We don't have grandparents around to help us, they're all gone, both sides. And the government thinks those grants will make us have kids and solve the population problem!"

"What does make us have kids?" Masha broke in, having never considered the question before.

Tanya laughed. "Decent men. Men with their heads on straight."

"So raising decent men is an important job, I guess." Masha smiled, nodding at the two little bundles in the stroller.

"I'm doing my best," lamented Tanya. "But will it work? Do you watch TV? They're talking about polygamy! Those politicians think that if every man has three wives, we'll start breeding like rabbits. Are you kidding? We'd be nervous wrecks is all. If you want people to have more kids, you need society to tell men not to have affairs, that you're a shitty man and a shitty father if you cheat on your wife."

"Would they stop?"

"Probably not," Tanya said, tiredly. "But they might do it less. Nationwide, a good policy like that would make thousands of women decide to get pregnant. You can't tell right now, but I spent five years making ads at a consulting company. Believe me, if we had every television, every movie screen, every online think piece talking about protecting families, about respecting them no matter what, we'd see results within a year or two. Not to mention five years, or ten! Russian men are lazy. Half of them have mistresses just for the prestige of it, or because they're used to getting everything they want. And the female body is within their reach. Society says it's cheap. Nobody's going to judge you if you satisfy your physical needs. Our society is rotten. Right now, everyone's writing about that oligarch who dumped his wife for some young girl. But what are they talking about? About what restaurants he takes her to! What kind of yachts and airplanes he gives her! Not one of those bastards ever bothers to write that he ditched his wife and their five children. Five! Sure, he'll leave them some money. But kids need more than money."

Tanya stopped suddenly. "I'm sorry to dump all that on you. You're young, you probably don't have kids yet. But the thing is, the most defenseless people are the old folks, children, and the mothers stuck at home with them all day. I really don't care anymore what my husband is getting up to at eleven o'clock at night. I just want him to take over with these guys once a week, you know? It's been three months since I've had time to go to the beauty salon across the street. It takes forty minutes to get my hair cut. I don't have forty minutes!"

Tanya smiled at Masha morosely. "Sorry," she continued. "You don't want to hear all this. You came to hear about Julia, right? Actually, it's connected with what I was just telling you. You said on the phone you wanted to understand what kind of person she was. She was perfectly ordinary. We worked together. I got married early, and then I could focus on my career. But Julia was trying to find herself a husband, so she was on the secretarial track. Looking for Mr. Right is a lot of work, and it goes badly most of the time! I mention that because Julia slept at my place pretty often. She'd show up crying with a bottle of martini mix, and I couldn't let her go home alone drunk, so I let her sleep on the couch. My husband hated it.

"She went through some bouts of depression. No energy, something always ached, and she was always running into my office to whine, like a little kid. I actually talked her into taking meds for a while, an antidepressant called Smilify. Isn't that silly? She made up other names for it. Spoilify. Shittify. So there wasn't anything wrong with her sense of humor. I don't know whether the drugs made much difference, though.

"The problem, basically, is that Julia really wanted to fall in love. Her life was boring. There was nothing keeping her mind busy. So, eventually, she did fall in love. With a married man. It didn't bother her that he was married with kids. All these jerks have mistresses, so why shouldn't Julia be one of them? He worked for our company, too, but he was the head of the northwest regional office. He traveled down here from St. Petersburg pretty regularly for business. A friendly guy, a little over forty. He took Julia on vacations, always brought her presents.

"Julia was insanely happy. Once I even heard her singing a love song in the ladies' room. You know how it is those first months, when you get totally carried away. She kept coming to me for advice. Wore me out. She showed me all the lingerie she bought to wear for him, the new perfume, new stilettos with heels so high they're only good for the bedroom. I couldn't help being happy for her. The situation wasn't so great, but Julia wasn't depressed anymore, and I was grateful, just for that, to this Good Samaritan from St. Pete. So."

Tanya fell quiet for a few moments. One of the twins squawked faintly and went back to sleep.

"Then one day, the worst happened. She came to see me with this twinkle in her eye and made this big production of showing me a pregnancy test. Positive. 'What are you going to do?' I asked her. 'What do you mean?' she said. 'I'm going to tell him! Sometimes they just need a little push to, you know—' 'Julia,' I told her, 'he has his own kids back home.' I did my best, but it was too late. She insisted everything was fine. He could transfer to Moscow, they could sell her apartment and buy a bigger one, near the park . . . Basically, she had these huge plans, and I figured I should mind my own business. Maybe they talked about him moving to Moscow all the time, and I just didn't know about it. So I nodded, and she told me her boyfriend was coming in a week, and she would have time to put together some sexy romantic evening and share the happy news.

"I won't bore you with the details: the beauty spa, the manicures, more new underwear. Vanilla candles. Bubble bath. Roses. Some special recipe for ham. Sometimes I blame myself, you know? I think that if I had been able to bring her back down to earth, even just a little, everything would have turned out differently. But they say that when you tell the truth, you lose a friend. And since I wasn't even sure that I *knew* the truth, I kept quiet, I kept nodding, I gave her my approval, I even gave her the ham recipe.

"Finally it was D-Day. I ran into Julia's boyfriend in the hall a few times that afternoon, and at meetings, and I kept trying to read, from the look on his face, how he would take the news he was about to receive that night. He seemed like a serious kind of guy to me, and I thought, well, you never know, and we've needed a new director for a while . . ."

Without changing her rhythm, Tanya rocked the pink barge back and forth, and straightened the little bonnets (those, at least, were blue) on the boys' heads. She sighed, then turned to look at Masha.

"I'm an idiot," she said, shrugging. "I had a feeling it wouldn't end as well as Julia imagined. But I never thought it would be quite *that* bad. Apparently, after she delivered her news, Julia's knight in shining armor froze for a couple of seconds, then started racing to get dressed. He must have felt too vulnerable to stay naked just then. He told her something like: (a) he never loved her, (b) he had only been using her for sex, (c) he loved his wife and children very much, and he didn't need or want anyone else. Then he grabbed his coat, and that was it.

"Can you imagine how Julia must have looked? All her fancy makeup, not totally smeared away yet, her lacy lingerie. Her perfume all over the sheets. She lunged out of bed and starting breaking things. She said she went on a total rampage. Then she got dressed, tore her stockings, and went to the police station. She filed a rape complaint! I was terrified when she told me. I told her everyone knew they'd been sleeping together for months, and what about the baby? But she just turned away from me and said that the baby was gone.

"I tried to talk her into dropping the charges and forgetting all about that asshole. But honestly, I was pretty sure she was just trying to scare him. It's one thing to freak out and make threats, but who would actually accuse someone of rape? That only happens in bad movies. And, honestly, I had my own stuff to deal with. I was house-hunting, trying to get a mortgage. But I saw Julia sliding back into depression. A couple of times I tried to recommend a good psychiatrist, but she said if she got revenge on that piece of shit, her depression would take care of itself.

"So she went for it, all in. She even testified in court. But the trial didn't go well. It was as if she was the one on trial. They found people to testify about the affair. The guy testified about Julia telling him she was pregnant, and his lawyer demanded a pregnancy test. But Julia was the one who really ruined it. She described the whole sordid affair in such gory detail that she ended up going into hysterics right there on the stand. It was too over the top to be believable. And right in the middle, the guy's wife jumped up from her seat and started shouting, damning her to hell and so on, like she was actually putting a curse on her!

"After Julia died, I found out the guy had left our firm, but some people from the St. Pete office told me he was just fine. His kids were growing up, his wife pampered him—she was probably afraid he'd cheat again. But I think he's probably been scared straight. As for Julia . . . Julia quit, too, and went to work as a secretary at some little warehouse. I called her a few times, tried to get together, but it was like talking to a wall."

Tanya laughed mirthlessly. "We're all so alike, when it comes down to it. We all want love. Julia just ended up in a dark place. Somewhere you're not supposed to go, even if you've really been hurt, even if you really want revenge." Tanya mechanically brushed an unruly lock of hair away. "God, I really need that haircut."

"If you want," Masha said quietly, "I can walk the twins around while you go and get one right now."

"Would you really?" asked Tanya, looking at her with a new spark in her eyes. But it quickly went out. "No, you can't be serious. You're a busy woman, you're working. I'll figure it out somehow."

"I'm off for the day," Masha said, smiling. "If you'd feel comfortable leaving them with me . . ."

Tanya shook her head. "No, thank you so much, but I'd worry about you. They'll wake up any minute now. But thank you so much for offering, really! I'm very grateful."

And they headed slowly down the path out of the park. Both women were thinking about Julia. Tanya was pondering women's lack of power, how it could mutate into rage and villainy. Masha was thinking about what Tanya had said about the dark place. Julia had crossed over, blinded by the hatred that had grown out of love. And the door had shut silently after her.

She hadn't even noticed the murderer standing there behind her.

INNOKENTY

Innokenty sat on the stool and thought, gloomily, that he was going to have to get his suit dry-cleaned after this. Kolyan's friend's place was incredibly dirty. It wasn't just dirt; it was filth elevated to a philosophical principle. And for the past half hour, Kenty had been talking with a philosopher, and suffering terribly because of it. Kolyan's friend was not the simple kind of drunk, the conceptual kind. Instead, he was a drunk with principles.

The ordinary conceptual drunks limited their belief system to the dictate that a bottle should be split between three people, with some food to chase it down, if possible. But for the principled ones, drinking had a higher purpose, and it was a thinking man's most worthy endeavor.

Leonid, a young man with a weak chin and thin hands, was pontificating. "We don't bother anyone," he said. "We don't get involved in these managerial games of yours, sitting in an office, all these cheap attempts to justify our existence. We make no justification! *In vino veritas!*" he declared, jabbing one finger toward the peeling paint on the ceiling.

"I think you may be misunderstanding the meaning of that expression," Innokenty noted, trying to find a position that minimized the contact between the fine flannel on his rump and the sticky stool.

"The truth is in the wine!" the other man translated for him, offended.

"No, that's not quite it," said Innokenty, flashing a quick grin. "Or rather, when they said that, the Romans didn't mean that getting drunk put you in touch with the secrets of creation. They were only pointing out that someone who is drunk tells the truth, just like what we Russians mean when we say, 'Drunkenness reveals what sobriety conceals.'"

"Oh yeah?" Leonid looked puzzled. Apparently, Kenty's analysis had rocked the foundations of his philosophy.

"If you have no objection, let's move on to Nikolai Sorygin," suggested Innokenty.

"Kolyan? He was a good man. But he was a flower, you know?"

"A flower?"

"Yeah. I have this theory, see." Leonid wiped his bony nose, which was covered in tiny black spots.

Innokenty raised one eyebrow in a polite expression of surprise.

"Some drinkers are the tragics. They drink because life is hard. Their wife left them, you know, or they got fired, or they got fired and then the wife left. Then there's the Stakhanovites, the good Soviet workhorses. That kind has a wife, a girlfriend, all sorts of jobs and needy relatives, and nobody ever leaves him alone. Those guys do it just to relieve the stress, poor things. Next we have the black marketeers," continued Leonid, speaking more majestically now. "They drink for the company. And the spleenists. That comes from the English word *spleen*."

Innokenty nodded seriously to indicate he had heard of such a word.

"The spleenists have too much free time. Bored housewives, for instance. Or coddled little mama's boys. Then there are the machos. They drink for the same reason some people get laid, to prove their worth as men."

"Sorry—which group do you belong to?" By now Innokenty was desperate to get away from this disgusting place and its self-important drunkard. But the antiques business had helped him hone his conversational skills, and he knew that the only place to hook the golden fish that no investigators had caught would be in the stream of this speech. So he directed an attentive gaze into the man's watery eyes.

"Oh," said Leonid, languidly waving one hand. "I'm a philosopher. An observer of souls. For me, alcohol is a tool for learning about the world. But like I said, Kolyan was a flower. That's when you drink the same way that you breathe. For him, vodka was sort of like the sun, or water, or the soil where he put down his roots. No family, no work, no extra ideas. Life carried him along in its current, free and floating."

"Where did it carry him?" Innokenty asked, eager not to lose this gleaming fish in the murky water.

"Where do you think?" asked the increasingly unsober philosopher, surprised. "Same place it carries everyone. To death! He could never do anything to hurt anyone, see? Kolyan only wanted to drink and enjoy himself." Leonid looked at Kenty over the vodka bottle and concluded his story almost biblically. "Like a bird, he came by his nourishment easily."

He made a gesture, offering to split the rest of the bottle of Stolichnaya that Kenty had brought as an offering. Kenty shook his head, and the liquid flowed with a gentle gurgle into Leonid's glass.

"Kolyan was a flower," he said, drifting off now, "and they crushed him. Or they fed him the wrong kind of fertilizer." His head fell to the table. Almost immediately Kenty heard a plaintive, whistling snore.

Innokenty took a deep breath and stood up. He tried to wipe off the seat of his pants, and sighed sadly. All that time down the drain, and dry-cleaning costs, too, with zero results. Could a fish even survive in such poisonous waters?

A flower, he repeated to himself, jogging down the dingy stairs. Before his eyes, an incongruous image flashed: blooming chrysanthemums, inked in fine lines like a Japanese print. Words of poetry raced around his head. *Chrysanthemum buds, released by the rain again, rise from the soil.* A haiku by Matsuo Basho, composed around the same time that Moscow was being built in the image of Heavenly Jerusalem.

Not that poor Kolyan will rise ever again, thought Kenty as he finally surfaced outside. What a relief to expel the apartment's nauseating air from his lungs.

But Kenty was not pleased with himself. He hadn't found out anything for Masha, hadn't helped her at all. He got in his car and switched on the radio. Someone was singing a syrupy song about chrysanthemums blooming in the garden.

"Oh God," moaned Kenty, feeling even guiltier.

It was time to go and admit to Masha how worthless he was.

ANDREY

Andrey had put the fear of God into that reporter. He got everything he needed, including Alma Kutiyeva's address. Now he was pushing his way through another Moscow traffic jam. The drive wasn't just torturous because it was slow. He knew that his meeting with Alma Kutiyeva, the mother of a soldier whose body had been sent home hollowed out, would not be an easy one. Andrey was one of the many people in the world who didn't know how to express his sympathy. He stuttered, he blushed, and he felt terrible, he had tears in his eyes and a lump in his throat, but he could never find the right words. What could you say to a mother who's lost her son? That he was killed by a professional, so it probably didn't hurt? Would it help to tell her that her boy had been avenged, that the hitman appeared to have been executed by a homicidal maniac, drowned under the ice on the Moskva in accordance with some medieval Russian custom?

Andrey returned over and over again to his conversation with Karavay and her dapper boyfriend, and he tried to find some discrepancy that would prove all of this had nothing to do with creepy stories out of medieval mysticism. Maybe it was just dirty money, dirty politics, dirty passion, the three pillars that normally supported the logic of murder. But those banalities didn't line up with the ice, the freezer, the cut-out tongues at the electric station, the cut-off arm at St. Basil's, the quartered governor's wife at Kolomenskoye. On the other hand,

John the Prophet with his Revelations? Ivan the Terrible? They fit just right. He wanted nothing to do with this mess. But Masha had already plunged him through a hole in the ice, into a place where there were neither fish nor plants, just the thick, sluggish water, filled with insanity. He would have to face it head-on if he wanted to stop these crimes.

A murderer's logic is really killer, thought Andrey, punning badly in his head, and finally he turned his car off the crowded ring road.

Alma Kutiyeva's place was on the outskirts of the city. The apartment looked like a Gypsy camp, full of people all bustling around at top speed in the small space, talking at top volume. Alma locked herself and Andrey in the bathroom so they could talk. The room was full of damp laundry, and there were red rags floating in a tub of pink foam. Andrey was repulsed, at first, until he realized it was just cheap dye.

Alma offered him a low stool, and perched herself on the edge of the tub.

"Sorry about this," she said, nodding at the door. The many-voiced clamor of the big family rumbled on outside their refuge. "What did you want to ask me about?"

"Well, you see," said Andrey, pulling some paperwork out of his briefcase, "I'm investigating a case that might be connected to your son's death."

"Did they cut up another soldier?" Kutiyeva asked with a bitter laugh. "Or is this about the money?"

"What money?" asked Andrey, frowning.

"They already offered me money," said Alma, lifting her head. "Must have felt bad, I guess."

Andrey, worried, said nothing.

"You didn't know?" Alma shoved a hand into the pocket of her old green robe. "A detective came to see me, someone from the Military

Prosecutor's Office. He had a suitcase. He asked me very nicely to forget about it, but my brother and I kicked him out. We don't sell out our dead."

Andrey could see her clenching her hand into a fist under the ragged flannel.

"They brought my boy home without his insides! Gutted like a chicken! And they claimed he killed himself! What do they think, that we live out in the provinces, we'd never come here to Moscow to fight back? Did they think his mother wouldn't figure it out? That nobody would speak up for him?" Alma was shouting now.

Outside the bathroom, on the other hand, things had gone suspiciously quiet. Andrey pictured them all standing out there and listening. He frowned again, hard.

"I found other mothers! Their sons served in the same places mine did. All boys without fathers, too! Who's going to protect them? Well, I am. I've been in Moscow six months already, and I got them to put a good detective on the case. One from Khabarovsk, like us."

Andrey pulled out Yelnik's photo and handed it to Alma.

"Could this be your detective, the one from the Military Prosecutor's Office?"

Alma quieted down for a moment and slowly drew her hand out of her pocket. She took the picture, then gave it right back to Andrey, as if just looking at it made her sick.

"That's him," she said, her voice suddenly tired.

"All right," said Andrey. "Was anyone else at home when he came by?"

"Just me." Alma thought a bit. "Then my brother came home. Like I said, we kicked him out."

"All right," said Andrey again. Then abruptly, he took her hand. "I'm really sorry."

Alma jumped and pulled sharply away from his touch, and Andrey berated himself. Here she was a Muslim woman, and he was a strange man, sitting with her in these intimate quarters. A bathroom full of laundry! Andrey stood up and tucked Yelnik's photo away.

"I'm very sorry. Thank you. I think I'll be going."

She led him silently out of the bathroom, guided him past her relatives into the hallway, and saw him off with a "good-bye" as emotionless as the sound of the door locking behind her.

Andrey sat awhile on the bench outside the building and smoked. So, then, one more piece of the puzzle had fallen into place. Yelnik had come here himself. Why? Andrey looked thoughtfully at the lilac trees waving in the breeze. Someone had planted them around the neighborhood garbage heap, and they had bloomed early this year. After seeing in the paper that one of the mothers had figured it out, that she was coming to Moscow and making a stink, Yelnik had come here to buy her off—then kill her if she refused the money. But Alma's brother had shown up and Yelnik had put off finishing his plan. Then someone had finished him off instead. Alma had escaped death thanks to a medieval riddler. Andrey tossed the butt of his cigarette in the trash bin and rubbed his eyes.

It was time to go home to Marilyn Monroe.

MASHA

Masha and Innokenty stood waiting at the apartment door, both of them uncomfortable. Masha felt awkward because she knew they were about to ask one of Innokenty's acquaintances from his secret world of collectors about the vilest thing they knew: theft. Innokenty probably felt awkward because he didn't know how today's visit would affect his future business dealings.

The door finally swung open to reveal a gaunt elderly man in a faded old shirt and pants that had been ironed to a shine.

"Pyotr Arkadyevich Kokushkin," the collector introduced himself. His breath smelled of cheap sausage.

Masha forced herself not to shoot an astonished look in Innokenty's direction. He, meanwhile, seemed to have lost the keen sense of smell he was so proud of. He grasped the hand shot through with dark veins and contorted with arthritis, shook it heartily, and introduced Masha. Kokushkin muttered something welcoming and ushered them inside. It was completely dark in the apartment, and the only sound they could hear was the old man closing the door and setting at least ten locks in place. Then Masha felt a gentle prod at her back. Feeling her way along, she moved down the dark corridor.

The apartment stank of the frailty of old age: medicine, dust, mothballs. Finally, Kokushkin turned on a light, a single bulb hanging in the middle of the hall, and Masha gasped. Every wall was hung with pictures, crowded so tightly together it was impossible to see the wallpaper underneath. Lithographs, watercolors, pencil sketches, and scenes from the theater done in gouache paint. She saw famous signatures: Dobuzhinsky, Somov, Bakst. Masha froze in front of a sketch for the Ballets Russes, until she received another slight but palpable nudge. She turned around.

"This is for Nijinsky's *Afternoon of a Faun*, isn't it?"

"Yes, yes," Kokushkin grumbled in agreement, and Innokenty winked at her. Masha hoped that meant she was making a good impression.

The room they entered was no less claustrophobic. The window looked out onto the wall of another building, and it was covered with a metal grate. There was no sign of any attempt to make the place cozy. No curtains, no flowers on the windowsill. A bookshelf stood in the corner, stuffed with volumes about art. There was one armchair, and a small dining set from the seventies. The place was like a remote, provincial hotel before perestroika. But the walls! Just like in the hall, they were covered in artwork. Masha walked along one wall, fascinated. She saw photo collages by Rodchenko, classical still lifes by Robert Falk, Nathan Altman, and Aleksandr Deyneka, and original book illustrations by Vladimir Lebedev and El Lissitzky. Masha was no expert on avant-garde Russian art or surrealism, but even she could tell that a fortune hung on these walls. Innokenty watched her, obviously pleased. The old man trudged into the kitchen, where a kettle was already whistling.

He returned soon, his felt house slippers flapping, and poured the tea into old cups with chipped rims. Masha took a sip of the almost-transparent brew. It tasted like old straw. Innokenty had somehow smuggled in a box of candy, and now he took it out with a flourish.

"Drunken cherries?" Kokushkin grinned in delight, rushing to rip the gleaming wrapper off the box.

Innokenty smiled. "Your favorite."

"Ah, you remembered! You know what an old man likes!" Kokushkin's wrinkled face filled with a look of sweet rapture, which did not fit his physiognomy in the slightest. He grabbed a piece and tucked it away inside one cheek. "I never buy myself chocolate. My whole life, there's just two things I've loved: art and candy. I had to sacrifice one for the other. Actually, I sacrificed everything, not just candy!"

His Adam's apple jumped as he gulped some sweet saliva. Then he turned to look at Masha, a little more favorably this time.

"Young as you are, you must be thinking, here I am, an old man sitting on a fortune, and I won't even buy myself candy. A real miser, right? You wouldn't believe all the people who have come to see me. Vultures from the bank, idiots who think it might be fun to invest in art. Ha! Nobody in Russia has any brains left! No honor, either, and no taste! We had art, once. We had one moment of greatness, and then it was gone, thank you very much to the Father of Nations, that champion of realism, all those Repins and Surikovs and their ilk! Get out of here, I told those dirtbags, go invest in your Aivazovskys and Makovskys, for God's sake! But keep your dirty hands off my babies! Here's what I've got for you!"

Kokushkin's bony old hand flipped into an obscene gesture, and he thrust it proudly into the air. Masha gaped, alarmed and embarrassed by the man's fury and by the chocolate-tinted spray from his lips.

Exhausted by this outburst, Kokushkin started coughing. Kenty had to pound on his skinny, bent back, and lift the man's teacup to his lips. Their host slurped at the hot water, then sank, panting, into his armchair, which was covered with dainty flowers and less-than-dainty rips and tears.

"One of those little morons showed up here to fuss over me. Psychologists, they call themselves. This one said he's writing his dissertation on how collectors think differently from other people. He even thought up a system to classify us, the idiot!"

"Really?" asked Innokenty with a smile.

"He thinks we collect because of childhood trauma. That we just have to collect something, anything. As if I didn't even care what I collected! Stamps, candy wrappers, tchotchkes, whatever. Tchotchkes! 'Sure, or I could collect jackasses,' I told him, but he didn't get the hint. 'For you, Mr. Kokushkin,' this jackass told me, 'collecting is a psychological need dictated by your fear of death.' Must have gotten that idea from that old quack Freud. 'Collecting things protects you from the future and preserves your past.' For God's sake, what kind of past do I have that I should want to preserve it? My parents, shot? My two years in the gulag? And the future! In the future, this headshrinker said, we'll have more and more of the investment types of collectors. You already know what I think about them."

Masha sat and listened to the diatribe, uncomfortable. Even as he held forth, Kokushkin was racing through the box of candy. When it seemed completely empty, Innokenty winked at Masha again and lifted the padded sheet of paper, uncovering another whole level of treats. The old man grinned, and he picked up a new piece, turning it around lovingly in his fingers.

"That fool also told me about a type of collector who's mostly interested in the social aspect of collecting. Like dumb kids, you know? He said when a couple collects the same things, they're less likely to get divorced. Poppycock! I only had one love affair in my life, in the late forties, and she wasn't some silly little biddy. Never scolded me for not giving her silk stockings, nothing like that. But when I told her I wanted to buy a fascinating miniature by Somov, the woman went reactionary on me! She told me I was fetishizing bourgeois art, the fool!"

Kokushkin turned to Masha. "What about you, young lady? Do you like Somov?"

"Yes, very much," Masha said honestly. But even if she didn't, even if she agreed with the long-lost lover that Somov was sort of petit bourgeois, Masha wouldn't have had the courage to admit it.

"There you have it," said Kokushkin, smacking his lips. "There's a new generation now. Maybe they'll have better taste. And there was one last part to his classification scheme." Another in a long line of chocolates left its cushy, gold-plated nest. "This moron from the university told me that people collect art when they already have everything else. A house, a garden, suits from Savile Row. You know what really kills me, young lady? The idea that art is just a way to decorate their tawdry palaces in Rublyovka or some other ritzy suburb. Know how I bought my first paintings? There I was, still a grad student, a lab assistant. My salary was a joke. I couldn't buy myself shoes, much less an estate. I bought my Lebedev then—for pennies, but even at that I didn't eat for two weeks. I drank cheap kefir, I bummed bread from friends, I went around with holes in my socks. I let my beard grow so I wouldn't have to buy razors. All I ever did for fun was wander around antique shops and run errands for old women, who later sold me these priceless canvases at a friendly price. Pretty soon everyone knew who I was, and you know what they called me? Crazy Pierrot, like the clown! Now I'm always getting calls from the Tretyakov Gallery, inviting me to their parties. They think if they get me drunk on cheap champagne, I might leave my collection to them. But these paintings are like my children. It won't be too long till I die. Who can I trust to take care of them?"

Suddenly, the acrimony vanished, and the old man was all sentimentality, his eyes misting over. The transition was startling. *This man could bring an audience to tears,* thought Masha. His performance was worthy of Stanislavsky.

Out loud, she said, "Don't worry, Mr. Kokushkin, you have some time to think about it. You're still in very good shape! As it happens, Innokenty and I came to talk to you about the Chagall you lost a while back."

"Come with me." Kokushkin stood up with a wheeze and stalked out of the room.

Kenty and Masha exchanged looks, then followed him farther down the hall.

Kokushkin opened the door to a narrow room, and Masha and Kenty found themselves staring dumbly at a toilet, its plastic seat yellowed with age.

"You're looking in the wrong place," the old man croaked. He pointed around to the other side of the door. There, hanging perfectly at eye level for anyone sitting on the toilet, was a landscape of a Belarusian village by Marc Chagall. There were no lovers flying off into the dense aquamarine sky, but Masha—much as she did admire Somov—was always swept off her feet by Chagall. She gasped quietly in appreciation. Kokushkin was clearly pleased.

"That's right. Those oligarchs might piss in golden toilets, but I've got a Chagall in front of my pisser! The older I get—and you know I'm not modest about these things anymore—I have the honor and the pleasure of staring at this little Chagall of mine many times every day, for a good long while, too." Kokushkin pulled the door shut. "Is that the painting you're wondering about?"

Masha nodded. "Yes."

Kokushkin headed back to the living room and sat down stiffly in his armchair.

"They stole it from me. I get robbed all the time. It's the cross a lot of collectors have to bear. Six months ago, they ripped off that Chagall, then a month later the police brought it back. I remember thinking they must have finally learned to do their job. I didn't ask any questions—they just turned it over, thank God. A few years back I testified against a sonovabitch who robbed me and a couple of my friends. He got off, believe it or not! There he was, his face like a brick, the asshole! I'll teach you to take my Zinochka, I thought—I had this wonderful study by Zinaida Serebriakova missing—you're gonna rot in jail, you pig! Later Ardov told me—and he lost even more than me, ten paintings gone—that the thief had been hired by one of those gazillionaires to beef up his collection. So the guy was very selective. He knew what his boss wanted. He knew how to work the court, too."

Kokushkin nodded to himself for a bit, and Masha took advantage of the lull to take a file full of photographs out of her bag.

"Mr. Kokushkin, I have a strange favor to ask of you. But I think, maybe, with a professional's visual memory—" Masha laid out several enlarged photos of the arm found on Red Square the past winter.

"Well now." The old man put on some ancient glasses held together with tape. He looked the picture over for a while, frowning in revulsion. "I recognize it. Sure. That's him. The one who took my Zinaida."

Masha froze. "Are you sure?" she asked, not quite believing her own luck.

Kokushkin pushed the photo away impatiently. "Listen up, young lady. I've got arthritis, osteoarthrosis, bad veins, and high blood pressure. But I'm not senile yet! No problem there! The lout's name was Samuilov. He had two tattoos on his fingers. The whole time I was testifying, he was digging around in his ears with those fingers. Looks like he can't do that anymore!"

"No, he can't," Masha said quietly, picturing a one-armed body rotting in a ravine somewhere. She gathered up the photographs and put them back in her bag. "Thank you very much, Mr. Kokushkin. You can't imagine how much you've helped us."

"Oh, I can imagine." Kokushkin was still grumbling, but he was obviously flattered.

After a certain amount of ceremony at the door, she and Innokenty finally made their exit.

"There's nobody like that old guy!" said Kenty enthusiastically as they walked down the stairs. "I've met a few collectors in my time, but there are legends about Kokushkin. He could be rich as Croesus, certainly have enough for electricity, groceries, even his precious candy. He only parts with a painting when he can exchange it for one he wants more. You didn't even see his bedroom or his pantry. He's got canvases lined up there in rows, facing the walls, and he knows where everything is. He'll pull out whatever picture he likes, give it some light, dust it off, and hang it up—maybe in the bathroom!"

"He really did help us out, Kenty," Masha responded. "Now we know that the arm they found with the stolen Chagall belonged to a professional thief."

"Well, we could have guessed that, seeing as the painting was stolen."

"Sure, but now we can do some more digging about that guy, and—"

"Maybe, my dear," said Kenty, shrugging. "But it seems to me that the arm could be more like a symbol for thievery. We've been trying to figure out why these people, specifically, were murdered, right? With this Samuilov, it seems more straightforward than the others, doesn't it?"

Masha nodded, still thinking.

Back at home, Masha hung up the phone, dumbstruck. Katya's mother had just told her, in a strangled whisper, that Katya was dead. She had driven full speed into a concrete barricade on Nikolskaya Street. Death was instantaneous. The funeral would be Friday.

Masha's mother walked in and asked, annoyed, where Masha had left their car this time. When her daughter turned around to face her, Natasha saw with a start that something was terribly wrong.

"What happened?" she asked, taking her daughter's clammy hand.

Masha said nothing, just stared at her mother the way she used to stare at her father, pleadingly. *Please make my pet beetle come back to life! Please don't let the wolf eat Little Red Riding Hood! Please tell me that you, of all people, will never, ever die . . . Please!*

"Mashenka. What happened? What is it, sweetheart?"

"Katya's dead," Masha whispered, her throat clenching tight to keep back the tears.

"Oh my God. How can that be?" Masha's elegant mother was wringing her hands like a country babushka. She sank down heavily onto the sofa. "When?"

"Yesterday," said Masha softly. "It's my fault."

"What do you mean, sweetheart? Your fault?"

"Mama!" said Masha, staring at her with pain in her eyes. "Katya asked to borrow the car for the day. She came by and took the keys—then she crashed into a wall. Sorry, Mama, your car—"

Natasha waved that piece of news away and turned toward the window.

Katya. She seemed to be standing right there with them. Little Katya, enchanted by Masha's toys and picture books. Teenage Katya, awkwardly trying to fit in with Masha's bookish friends. Katya the struggling college student, wearing too much makeup and doing funny impressions of her neighbors.

Natasha sat down on the floor and wept silently, wiping away her tears. Masha went over and laid her head in her mother's lap. Katya had been her oldest friend, and not even a friend so much as family, a sister. Funny, uncomplicated, and unlike anyone else. Plus, Katya had known her father. Katya had known the Masha from before Papa had been murdered. That was a completely different Masha, a girl who read *Jane Eyre* under the covers at night. Masha laughed more with Katya than she ever had with anyone else, because it was only with Katya—and sometimes Kenty—that she could forget about her constant hunt for the mysterious entity that had stolen away her father, her childhood, that whole other life.

"The funeral's on Friday," she croaked.

"Poor Rita," Natasha said sadly. "Poor Rita."

❖

It rained the day of the funeral. Masha felt a strange lightness through-out her body. It wasn't the pleasant effervescence a glass of champagne might bring, but a kind of half-conscious numbness. She couldn't take the risk of driving. Her stepfather drove her, and Masha did not utter a single word the whole way there.

Why? Why had Katya lost control of such a manageable little car? Suicide, maybe? No. Masha shook her head sternly in the backseat, not noticing her stepfather's concerned glance in the rearview mirror. She just couldn't accept that Katya was the type of person who could bring herself to voluntarily depart this life in somebody else's Mercedes. Unless . . . Could it be about Innokenty? Hadn't she been madly in love with him? But Masha shook her head again. That was all in the past! Suddenly she desperately wanted to see Kenty herself, bury her face in his shoulder, and cry. She texted him.

Katya died. On the way to the funeral. Can I see you tonight?

The response was instantaneous. *Sure. Send me the address, I'll come pick you up.*

Masha tapped out the address for the wake she'd be going to after the service, at Katya's apartment, in what she had called her "blue-collar suburb," a place that Masha had never been. *Why?* she wondered. Katya had always been eager to come to her place.

The crematorium was not especially gloomy. There was a business-like air to the proceedings, like getting married at city hall. There were flowers and a small crowd of relatives. One ceremony finished up, and the next group filed in. A funeral march by Beethoven was playing, and Katya's neighbor girls in their short black dresses stood around sniffling. Masha and her mother kept to themselves. They didn't know any of these friends and relatives except Rita. Masha laid her bouquet of daisies on the gleaming, lacquered coffin and said a few words to Katya's mother. But there was a line of other people anxious to express their condolences, so she left quickly.

Natasha departed for another ordinary, hectic day of work at her clinic, and Masha took a taxi to Katya's apartment. She had promised Rita she'd help with the wake. Masha wasn't the world's best cook, so she'd picked up takeout from a restaurant nearby. Now she stepped inside, set down the heavy bags, and took a look around. She even sniffed the air, wondering if it would smell like Katya. The place was unattractive, both from a lack of money and a lack of taste. Masha could never have guessed that she was doing exactly what Katya had sometimes done in her home, tiptoeing around. The curtains were drawn shut, and the mirror was covered out of respect for the dead. Distraught, Masha touched a finger to a photograph of her and Katya, laughing, when they were little. There were more pictures. She recognized some—they'd been taken by her papa. Masha's copies were hidden away in albums, but here they had stood proudly, all these years, in plain sight. So in a way, Masha had been in this apartment after all. Still, the place was so foreign she couldn't even imagine Katya living here. She looked so much more natural, in Masha's memory, framed in the doorway of Masha's own apartment.

Masha found an apron and got to work. The table was already set, and she loaded it with the food she had brought, the cold salads and hardboiled eggs Rita had requested. She pulled a huge, sweating stockpot of soup out of the refrigerator and put it on the stove to warm up. She stood on a stool to reach the tray of freshly baked pirozhki Rita had put on top of the cabinets, up in the warm air near the ceiling, and she put them in the oven, preheated just as Rita had told her. Masha noticed she was breathing more easily now. That nauseating lightness was gone, her throat did not feel as tight, and the pinching feeling in her chest had disappeared, too. But still there was a name pounding away in her head, like a terrible metronome: *Katya, Katya, oh Katya* . . .

Soon the guests began arriving, and for a while, Masha was busy serving food to people she didn't know. She could tell they were looking at her, confused: Who was this girl taking care of everyone like some junior lady of the house? But to both Masha and Rita, it seemed perfectly natural. Their ghost of a relationship, through Katya, was completely clear to both of them. But they also both understood that this connection, like a thread made of the finest crystal, would splinter quietly and break the minute Masha left today.

For now, though, Masha was carrying away dirty dishes, half-listening to people toasting Katya's memory, soaping up dirty glasses and wiping them dry. She even tried washing the baking pan Rita had used for the pirozhki, though it obviously could stand to soak until the next day. She scrubbed away mercilessly, distracting herself from her own terrible thoughts, until Rita came into the kitchen and took the sponge from her hand.

"Leave something for me, all right?"

And Masha understood. Katya's mother needed a way to forget, too, and Masha, selfishly, was taking that away from her.

They sat down on a couple of stools, hiding in the kitchen like a pair of conspirators. Neither Rita nor Masha wanted to go back into the room full of people.

"I didn't do enough to protect Katya," Rita said abruptly. Masha felt sick at what might be coming next. "I didn't protect her. I knew she had it in her, that jealousy, that desire for what she didn't have. Desire to be *you*, to have your perfect apartment, the clothes you and your mother had, that car . . . And beyond all that, desire for what you knew, your mind, your focus on your career. Your friends, the boys you hung around with. I saw that, and I felt sorry for her. But I shouldn't have! I should have slapped it out of her when she was little!" Rita covered her face with her hands and sat silent for a second. "But I felt so guilty, bringing this child into the world with no father. I wanted so much for my little girl to be happy!"

Masha went to Rita and embraced her. She could feel her body jerking as she wept.

"I'm so sorry, Masha!"

"No, no, it's my fault!" The tears were welling up in Masha's throat now. "I'm the one who let her borrow the car!"

"The car!" moaned Rita. "And your clothing! She wasn't wearing a single thing that belonged to her. It was all yours, Masha, right down to her underwear! What was wrong with her? Why would she do that?"

Masha, worried, said nothing.

"Here." Rita fumbled in the pocket of her big, shapeless black dress and pulled out a set of thin bracelets. "These are the only things of her own that Katya was wearing. They sent them back from the police station. She used her very first student stipend to buy them, and she never let them out of her sight. I wanted to give them to you. To remember her by." Rita handed the jumbled pile of silver jewelry to Masha.

"Thank you," said Masha quietly.

"One more thing, too." Rita's cheeks flushed. "I'm ashamed to have to tell you this. But Katya didn't just take your clothes. I found this in her room. They're your mother's, aren't they?" Rita handed her a small packet. Masha peeped inside and found a flashy gold bracelet and ring. Natasha had loved them once, but for the past ten years she had preferred jewelry that she thought of as more distinguished—which turned out to mean less flashy but much more expensive, set with diamonds. Masha thought her mother must not have realized these neglected pieces had disappeared, and she figured she could sneak them back where they belonged. She raised her eyes to look at Rita.

"No," she said calmly. "You're wrong about that. Katya asked me if she could borrow these."

Rita's tense posture relaxed a little, and she sighed in relief. Nodding, she stood up and reached out to touch Masha's cheek with one hand. Then she wiped her red eyes and plodded sadly out of the kitchen. Masha sat back down on the stool and took out her cell phone.

Come get me, she typed.

It seemed to Masha that the moment they had admitted their mutual guilt and sin—for her, that she had let Katya borrow the

143

car, and for Rita, that she hadn't cured her daughter of that horrible jealousy—as soon as they had spoken those words, Masha and Rita had severed the thread between them. There was no more point to her being here, and suddenly she was desperate to leave. She found her coat and, without saying good-bye to anyone, slipped out. As she rode the elevator down, she mechanically counted Katya's bracelets. There were ten of them.

"Idiot!" she said to herself, out loud. Those damn numbers had infected her subconscious. She was automatically counting everything around her, looking for a clue. "Enough! Stop it! Katya is gone, and it has nothing to do with the numbers on those dead bodies."

She sat on a bench outside to wait, staring straight ahead, until Innokenty's car pulled up. He opened the door for her without saying a word, and Masha climbed in. Nina Simone was drawling gently inside.

"Let's go," said Masha softly.

Kenty had been waiting for a chance to ask Masha what was going on.

"So she died on Nikolskaya Street?" he asked. "Via Dolorosa."

"What's Via Dolorosa?" asked Masha. Then she understood, and recoiled in her seat.

"I'm sorry, Masha." He did, in fact, look ashamed. "It's becoming some kind of perverse game for me. Every time I hear the name of a place, on TV, on the radio, I can't help it—I do the calculations, I think about whether those places match up with Heavenly Jerusalem, or the earthly one."

"So? Do they?" Masha asked, uncertain.

"Not usually." Kenty rubbed pensively at the bridge of his nose. "But this one does. If you put the maps of the two city centers on top of each other, Nikolskaya Street takes exactly the same path as the famous Via Dolorosa—the route Jesus took on his way to the cross. It starts at the Lions' Gate and goes west through the old city to the Church of the Holy Sepulchre. Nikolskaya Street, as you know, runs from Red

Square to Lubyanka Square. But before they built Red Square, the street led directly to the Nikolsky Gate of the Kremlin." Kenty interrupted himself. "What a bunch of nonsense, though, right? Why am I telling you all this?"

Neither spoke for a while, and Masha thought their theory might simply be a way for them to avoid facing reality. Maybe it was easier to wall themselves off behind a preposterous barricade of smoke and mirrors, of historical, religious, and mystical allusions. Only now, hearing the sadness in Kenty's voice, did Masha understand that he felt guilty, too. And that guilt was a way to compensate for the absence of another sentiment. Maybe if he had returned some of Katya's feelings, she could have found a way to put her childhood jealousy behind her. And then she wouldn't have taken Masha's car and wouldn't have died on Via Dolorosa.

Maybe everyone had their own Via Dolorosa.

ANDREY

Andrey sat hunched over his computer, trying to figure out what sort of association the name Katya Ferzina was triggering in his subconscious. Danovich, the officer at the next desk, was talking about how this Katya Ferzina had died a couple of days ago in someone else's car, in a crash right in the center of Moscow, and a weird crash, too. Instead of running into a mammoth SUV being driven just as badly by some other woman driver like you'd expect, Katya had driven headlong into the concrete barrier surrounding a construction project at the Rusich Centre Bank. Plus, the officers at the scene had found evidence that suggested this was no accident, but rather an elaborate assassination. But who would have gone to such lengths to assassinate young Ms. Ferzina? And where the hell had he heard that name before?

He tried typing her name. Looking at it on the screen didn't trigger anything, so he must not have seen the name in print. He must have heard someone mention it. But who? Andrey couldn't concentrate. All he could do was sit there and whisper, trying out different intonations. "Katya? Katya Ferzina? Katya! FER-zina! Goddammit."

"Where's your intern?" Danovich asked, looking over at the neat, empty half of the desk, which presented a sharp contrast to Andrey's chaotic domain. Masha Karavay maintained impeccable order.

Andrey jumped. There, the memory had finally surfaced, and shot through him like the pain from a sore tooth. Masha had said the name on the phone, two days ago. Her friend Katya had died and she needed some time off to help with the funeral. Andrey remembered how uncomfortable her voice had made him, sounding strange and somehow dead.

"Hey," he said, jumping up from his chair. "Who owned that car your Katya Ferzina crashed in?"

Danovich glanced at him in surprise, but he flipped through his file.

"N.S. Karavay," he read. Then it hit him. "Karavay. The intern?"

Andrey nodded. His face had gone stiff and cold. Those weren't Masha's initials, but the car must belong to her family. And Masha's friend had been murdered. And the only case Masha Karavay was involved in was Heavenly Jerusalem. *No reason to worry,* he told himself. *No reason to worry!*

"Let me have that file," he barked, and with one more look at Andrey's distraught face, Danovich handed it over. Andrey scoured every page until he found the statement by Rita Ferzina, mother of the deceased. Ferzina said that her daughter had been wearing somebody else's clothes. And, she said, those clothes came from the same place as the car. They all belonged to the victim's oldest friend, Maria Karavay. Masha!

"Andrey! Andrey!" Danovich had been tugging on his sleeve for a while now, but Andrey hadn't noticed. "Maybe you should warn her, just in case?"

"Obviously I'm going to warn her," Andrey growled, and shivered in the sudden cold draft blowing up from inside his mind. Could it possibly be a coincidence? Andrey believed in accidents of fate, but he hated them. Especially this kind. Especially when it came to Masha. He ripped his jacket off the back of his chair. "Right now."

MASHA

Masha and Innokenty sat together in his car outside her building. He wasn't talking anymore, just holding her lifeless hand in his, and she felt like crying. Why shouldn't she cry here, with Innokenty? She had forbidden herself to indulge in things like that in front of her mother ever since her father's funeral. She didn't want to add to her grief. She wanted to protect her. But now she found she could not cry. Masha gently withdrew her hand from Kenty's and reached to grab her purse from the backseat.

"I'm gonna go," she said.

"Are you okay? Can I walk you to the door?"

"You sound like an American movie," she huffed. "I'm not okay, but I'm much better off than Katya. I think I can find the door myself." She got out, walked into the building, and headed for the elevator. The doors opened, and out walked Andrey Yakovlev.

Masha was surprised, but in a passive kind of way. *So you're here,* she thought. *Why is that?* Masha saw the pity in his eyes, and she looked away. She knew her eyes were puffy, and her face was pale. Damn it. She had wanted her boss to be impressed with her talents as a detective, but instead here he was looking at her with that mix of judgment and sympathy you direct at an old lady you're about to give your seat to on the subway.

"Hello," she said, surprised at the dull, heavy sound of her own voice.

"Masha, I was just talking to your stepfather. He said you were at the wake. I tried to call—"

"I turned off my phone. Did you need something?"

"Yeah," said Yakovlev, finally catching her eye. "Can we talk?"

"Sure. Come upstairs."

"Umm . . . I'd rather do this on neutral territory, if that's okay."

Masha nodded indifferently. She walked back outside and sat on a bench. Yakovlev settled down awkwardly next to her, unsure how to start. Masha didn't speak, either, remembering the bench she had sat on in front of Katya's building. A place she had gone today for the first and probably the last time.

"Too late," she said quietly.

"What?" asked Yakovlev.

"I'm a bad friend," said Masha, turning to look at him with a sad, almost childlike gaze, her lips twisted strangely in a contradictory grin.

He looked away. "We all feel like bad people when the people we love die," he said, looking down at Masha's delicate fingers, clasped tight between her knees. On one of her wrists a collection of thin silver bracelets sparkled in the deepening twilight. "Who ever says, when their mother dies, that they were a good child? Right? I'm sure you were a really good friend." Yakovlev looked right at her. His eyes seemed completely black.

"Why do you think so?"

He sighed, and spoke up. "Because if that wasn't true, you wouldn't be so upset right now, would you?"

Neither of them said a word.

"Masha. Listen, forgive me, but I need to talk to you about your friend's death."

Masha frowned. "What do you mean?"

Andrey heaved another sigh. "Katya's death wasn't an accident, Karavay. The autopsy didn't reveal anything conclusive, but it raised a lot of questions. Then we examined the vehicle and found things that confirmed our suspicions."

Masha said nothing.

"Your friend was murdered."

In a flash, Masha thought she must have been plunged underwater like that unlucky bastard Yelnik. She couldn't breathe. All she could feel was her own dark blood pumping in melodramatic slow motion through her veins, and coming to pound like mad in her ears.

"Masha!"

Yakovlev's voice seemed to come from far away.

"Via Dolorosa," Masha whispered. Then the darkness engulfed her.

She woke up on the ground by the bench, a painful cramp in her neck. She pushed herself up and tried, with a moan, to turn her head. Her eyes fell on a pair of blue jeans which smelled faintly of tobacco.

"Feeling better?" She heard her boss's voice above her. "I gave you a couple of slaps on the cheek. Sorry."

Masha put one hand to her face and felt the burning. Yakovlev propped her up slowly, one arm around her waist.

"I'm sorry," he repeated hoarsely. "This isn't how a professional is supposed to treat his intern, but when you passed out, I thought I'd better—"

"No. It's okay," Masha said automatically.

"Masha," he said, "listen to me, please. Katya's death was not your fault. But at the same time, we can't rule out the possibility that her accident was connected, somehow, with the killer we're investigating, the one I wasn't convinced actually existed." He cleared his throat nervously. "I think you were right—your theory. Though I guess that won't make you very happy, given the circumstances. You said something before you fainted, by the way."

"I've never fainted before," Masha said pensively.

"There's a first time for everything," Yakovlev replied. "But what did you say? Do you remember?"

"Via Dolorosa. Do you remember, Captain—"

"Look, just call me Andrey, all right? I mean, I slapped you, so we're friends now," Andrey tried to joke.

"Andrey, remember how we talked about Jerusalem and how it maps onto Moscow? Nikolskaya Street, according to Innokenty, corresponds with the Via Dolorosa."

"Oh," said Andrey, blinking.

"There's something else, too. But this is really nuts." Masha looked up at him. "The thing is, Katya was wearing my clothes."

"I know," said Andrey, nodding. He took her hand in his. The gesture seemed so natural that Masha didn't pull back. Instead, she squeezed his hand tight.

"Katya used to borrow clothes from me all the time. But this time, everything she had on was mine—even her underwear! You have to agree that's weird. And—" Masha faltered.

"You can tell me."

"The only things she was wearing that belonged to her were these ten bracelets." Masha held out her arm, and the bracelets jingled quietly. Andrey tossed a distracted glance at them. "And another strange thing: she took a couple of pieces of jewelry from my mother. These." Masha fished around in her purse. "It's another bracelet, and a ring. Nothing too special. My mom never even noticed they were gone—but that's not the point. They don't match."

"What?"

"They don't match, Andrey, and Katya paid very close attention to things like that. White gold doesn't go with yellow gold, your earrings should match your ring, and so on. I even made fun of her sometimes for it, but she always told me that since I never wore jewelry, I wouldn't understand. But, on a basic level, anyway, I get it."

Andrey raised his eyebrows quizzically.

"White metal. Silver. Does not match gold. Which is yellow."

"Huh," said Andrey.

"And then," Masha fiddled with the bracelets, thinking, "Katya's mom confirmed what I remembered: Katya bought these her first year in college." Masha raised her eyes to look at Andrey. "Now there are ten of them. But . . . there used to be more."

ANDREY

Andrey sat on his porch, in an old chair he had liberated from the dump, reading. It was a book Innokenty had recommended, by the historian Mikhail Petrovich Kudriavtsev, about the architecture of old Moscow. He trudged painfully through the text, motivated more by professional obligation than aesthetic interest. The practically unintelligible prose was painful enough, but Andrey's chronic exhaustion and the weak porch light also tested both his worn-out brain and his tired eyes.

Of course, Marilyn Monroe could also have been to blame. The mutt was lying in the corner tossing him dramatic, pleading glances. He must have caught a whiff of the cheap sausages Andrey had brought home with him. It was time for dinner, but despite the growling in Andrey's stomach and Marilyn's silent reproach, he didn't have the strength to get up out of his chair. When he finally tore himself away from the pictures—which, thank God, there were plenty of in that damn book—he stared absentmindedly through the dusty latticework of his porch out into the yard.

It was August now, and getting dark earlier. The night was milky with stars. Leaves rustled in the summer breeze, and an owl hooted. Andrey sighed and fought his way to his feet. Marilyn Monroe instantly leaped up, too, and hurried after him to the refrigerator. The fridge was so old it shook, and the door opened with a sound like a noisy kiss.

Andrey spent a few seconds examining its inner chamber. His examination yielded the following: one sausage—the soft pink Soviet kind called *Doktorskaya*, a pair of hot dogs, puckered with age, a piece of hard-as-rock cheese, and a few expired yogurts from that time he had tried to start eating healthier. He should probably throw them out, but Andrey hated wasting food, so usually he waited till the food in question was in a very advanced stage of decay. That way nobody, not even his own conscience, could think any less of him.

Andrey pushed the obnoxious beast out of the way with one foot, took out the hot dogs and the sausage, and set a pot on the stove. While the water boiled, he sliced some bread and greased each piece with a thick slab of butter. Andrey tossed the wizened old hot dogs into the boiling water and allowed himself a first bite of bread. Marilyn Monroe had transformed into a slobber machine, and if looks from pushy strays could kill, Andrey would have been long gone. That look said, *What do you think you're doing, scumbag?* so clear it might as well have been written in all caps in Kudriavtsev's book. Andrey knew that nobody else was going to teach Marilyn Monroe to behave, and a dog ought to obey and respect its master, who, by the way, had every right to sink his teeth into a nice slice of buttered bread after a hard day's work. He clung to his pedagogical principles for nearly a minute before tossing the beggar a heavenly smelling pink disc of cooked sausage. The hot dogs were nearly ready, and Andrey was nice enough to share those, too.

At first Marilyn Monroe eyed the hot dog suspiciously, but when Andrey downed his own serving with one fluent gesture, Marilyn decided to have faith, and he chewed up the ancient specimen happily enough. After that, they went on sharing sausage chunks until it was gone. Once there were no new meaty issues to worry about, the dog went to lie down in the corner again, and Andrey made himself some tea.

He drank it straight up, and with a pleasantly heavy feeling in his stomach, Andrey settled onto the broken couch and thought about what Masha must be doing right now. Probably dining on a salad made from—what was that stuff called? Arugula? Maybe with that fancy boyfriend of hers. Drinking a little wine, he thought, as his eyes started to close. A sauvignon, or something. Listening to live music. String quartet, or something. Andrey drifted off to sleep without even noticing.

He dreamed of a ballroom, like the ones he remembered seeing on school trips to old palaces. Couples spun by in an endlessly repeating waltz, and Andrey realized that Masha and Innokenty were among them. Masha was wearing a low-cut light-blue silk dress that reflected the light, and her hair was arranged artfully in a bun at her neck. Swept up in the dance, she was laughing and laughing, never taking her eyes off her partner. Andrey looked at the other couples, getting more and more nervous, because although he was sure that he was there at the ball, too, no matter how hard he looked, he couldn't find himself. Now every woman there had Masha's face, and she twirled around, her head flung back in rapture, now dressed in scarlet, now in navy blue, now in deep-black satin.

Finally Andrey spotted himself standing by the door, and a footman lurking on the other side of the room winked at him. That's when Andrey realized he was not there to dance. He was a servant. He raised his hand, alarmed, and felt the rough hair of a cheap powdered wig.

Andrey's eyes shot open in horror. The rough hair under his fingers belonged to Marilyn Monroe, who had crept over for a snuggle.

"What the hell!" Andrey said out loud, wincing. He turned his head to stretch his stiff neck, and shooed away some annoying little thought about Freud and the subconscious. Then he got up, intent on finding a nicer, more horizontal environment for sleeping.

And you, Karavay, he thought, as he kicked off his boots and climbed into bed, *you may know people in high places, but you're no fool. We could even say the opposite is the case.*

With that vague pronouncement, Andrey fell asleep. This time without dreams.

MASHA

Masha was sitting in the kitchen surrounded by books. She had only a very vague idea of where to look, but she wasn't the type to be deterred. First, the Bible. Then some of the old Russian philosophers, Berdyaev and Losev, and Daniil Andreyev's mystical tome *The Rose of the World*, and maybe even Gogol's *Dead Souls*. It felt cozier, somehow, to work in the kitchen at night than in her room. Next to the thick volume of Gogol was a bowl of crackers. Without looking, Masha fished another cracker out of the dish and crunched into it.

Heavenly Russia, she read, concentrating on the Andreyev, *is an emblematic image: a pink-and-white, onion-domed city on the high banks of the blue bend in the river . . . Heavenly Russia, or Holy Russia, is geographically situated within an area that approximately coincides with the borders of our country today. Several cities are major centers; between them are regions where nature flourishes in all its wonder. The largest of these centers is the Heavenly Kremlin, standing tall over Moscow. Its holy sanctuary gleams an unearthly gold and white . . .*

Close, thought Masha, *but not quite.*

Her stepfather walked into the kitchen, where he took in the sight of the books piled on the table. He spent a few seconds examining the titles on the spines, grunted softly in admiration, and put on the tea kettle. Masha's attention wavered, and at that instant she felt as if some important clue had slipped from her fingers. She went back to the same passage, annoyed. *The largest of these centers is the Heavenly Kremlin, standing tall over Moscow.* Her stepfather took a cup out of the cabinet and shut the door with a small thump. Masha jumped, then picked up the books and left the kitchen.

"Am I bothering you?" he called after her, too late.

"No," she answered flatly from her room. "I'm just getting tired."

Masha was in bed, still reading, when the doorbell sounded. She looked at the clock: it was eleven. Who could be visiting them at this hour? Indistinct voices came from the front hall—Natasha's, and somebody with a deep baritone. When they passed her room, Masha recognized the voice: the visitor was Nick-Nick.

"Sorry to come by so late. I've been slammed with work, as always."

"Oh, no, it's not too late. I'm sorry to bother you, I'm just so worried about—" The kitchen door closed, and Masha couldn't make out what came next. But she was certain it was her name.

So that's what's going on, she thought. *Mama's calling in the heavy artillery.*

In the kitchen, Natasha made some fresh tea and pulled out a box of candy given to her by a grateful patient, then sat down across from Nick-Nick. He looked at her, his eyes smiling under his expansive eyebrows, which were just beginning to go gray.

"You're more beautiful all the time," he said softly, and Natasha, just like in the old days, laughed quickly and slapped him on the arm.

"You're such a joker."

"No." Nick-Nick laughed with her. "I'm not joking. What's going on with Masha?"

"Well . . . Her friend died. She's had to cope with that along with working at this internship you set up for her at Petrovka. Nick, could you find her something else? Please."

Katyshev looked at her in surprise. "Would you really want me to? She's been working so long to get where she is—"

"Exactly!" Natasha interrupted him. "So long! Ever since Fyodor died! And I want it to stop. I was waiting and waiting for her to turn into a normal, happy college kid! Now she's almost ready to graduate, and all she's thinking about is serial killers! And your internship is encouraging it! I'm scared, Nick! Do you get that?"

"Natashenka," Katyshev said, pronouncing her pet name exactly the way Fyodor used to. "You have to understand, she's suffering. Her past is festering inside her. To pop the blister, Masha needs to find a killer. She needs to save somebody's life, even if it's not her father's. The sooner that happens, the better. Then she can move on, focus on other things. And this obsession of hers gives her a leg up, even compared to seasoned professionals. So give her the chance to finish the internship. Then, later, you can push her toward something more suitable."

Masha's mother said nothing, and there was no indication that she noticed how Nick-Nick was carefully, gently, touching her hand, one finger at a time.

"I don't know," she said, shaking her head and smiling tiredly. "Thank you, though." She patiently pulled her hand away. "You've always been such a good friend to us." The tea kettle had gone cold, and she went to turn the burner on again.

"Don't bother." Katyshev, tall and gaunt, was already on his feet. His face was impenetrable. "It's long past time for me to get home. And you should get some rest, too."

She nodded morosely, and brushed Katyshev's shoulder in a quick, fluttering caress, as if flicking away some invisible speck of dirt.

Katyshev gave her a wry smile and walked quickly back down the hall to the door, pausing, just for a second, in front of Masha's room.

INNOKENTY

Innokenty sat obediently and listened as the pale young woman told her story all over again. Two months ago, her husband had been found whipped to death, and she apparently considered that only fair. His photos portrayed him clearly as the stern Siberian type, with a nose like a duck's bill and deep-set blue eyes. For a good long while, he had doted on his wife, Larisa.

"He was very kind and considerate at first," she whimpered. "Then he started misbehaving . . . Well, you know how men are."

But Innokenty belonged to that small percentage of the Russian population who would define "misbehaving" as creative sexual practices, or, perhaps, having a little something on the side. How could that warrant such a brutal death? Apparently, his confusion showed on his face, because Larisa bowed her head and explained in a strident whisper.

"He started to beat me! I had my daughter from my first marriage, she was twelve years old at the time, and we're not from here, so where could we go? I kept begging him, 'At least don't hit me in front of my girl!' It was terrible. Any time he was in a bad mood, his fists came out. I was a chief accountant. I brought home more money than he did! And every day I had to cover up my black eyes to go in to work—I even thought up a new hairstyle, like a shaggy little dog, so that nobody could see my forehead or my neck. He beat me like he was a boxer and I was his punching bag. And I'd ask him, 'Sergey, why are you doing this?' And when he was sober, he used to say, very logically, 'Larisa, I'm not a bad man—you know that! I just have a bad temper! I can't fight back my anger, it possesses me, like a demon!'"

She looked briefly at Innokenty, but when she saw his eyes full of horror and sympathy, she lowered her gaze again.

"Happens a lot," she said with a forced shrug. "They say you should be patient at first, that maybe he'll stop. And I loved him, too. So I put up with it. Then one time it was so bad, I called the police. They took one look at my bloody face and said, 'You two work it out, lady. We're not getting involved.'

"After that he got smarter about how he hit me. In the stomach, on the chest, places where nobody could see it. So I thought maybe if I had a baby, that would calm him down. I got pregnant. And it worked. He was much gentler, and our son was born. But he was a fussy baby, cried all night, never let me sleep, and we had a very small apartment, so there was nowhere to hide. He got tired of it, and he started hitting me again, and I couldn't even scream, because I didn't want to wake up the baby." Larisa was speaking quickly now, as if trying to get through the story as fast as she could.

"One time he beat me up and I bled a lot. It's terrible, but I think it must have been a miscarriage. Now I realize maybe that was for the best, better to lose a baby early. How could another little one have survived in that nightmare? But then—one day I left him alone with our son in the bath. I left all the toys, so my husband didn't have to do anything but sit there. I went into the kitchen to make dinner, and—"

Larisa hesitated, and dropped her head even lower. "Just a minute." She pulled out a handkerchief and held it to her mouth.

"Are you all right?" Innokenty rose and bent over her.

Larisa just nodded. He opened a kitchen cupboard and found a glass, filled it with water from a plastic bottle on the table, and handed it to her. She took a drink, struggling to swallow through her tightly clenched throat.

"That was for the flowers," she finally said.

"Sorry?"

"You gave me the water I was keeping for my plants."

"Oh. I apologize."

"No, it's all right, I'll be fine. He killed my baby. That's what he did."

Innokenty shuddered, but Larisa just looked up at him, gloomy and resigned.

"I still don't know how it happened. Either the baby slipped, and his head went under the water, or my husband held him down. But one thing's for sure: he didn't help him. He was tired of the screaming, and hitting an eight-month-old isn't as easy as hitting a woman. Anyway, I really lost it then. I ran to the police station. There was a trial."

Larisa paused. Then she looked Innokenty right in the eye, her face utterly empty.

"They found him innocent. They said there was no proof any crime had taken place. They let him go right then and there. I tried to keep him out of the house. I had the locks changed. But he broke in, and beat me harder than he ever had before. That time I screamed. There was no baby to wake up anymore. The neighbors called the police, and they took him away. They were going to let him go again the next day. I packed our things—mine and my daughter's. I thought if he came near us I'd run, go back to my mother in the village. But he never came back. A week later, they found him in a ditch near that old church on Prechistenka Street." For the first time, Larisa smiled at Innokenty. It was a wide, genuine grin. "A dog deserves a dog's death."

MASHA

This was Masha's first time in the office of a real impresario. His name was Koninov, and he wore a brightly colored silk shirt and sharp-toed dress shoes. The sight of them made Masha's mouth pucker like she was tasting something sour.

"I don't understand. So they're still investigating Lavrenty's murder, then?" His voice was high and whiny, and Masha marveled at the idea of him talking to singers in that hysterical falsetto. Wouldn't they, of all people, value timbre and intonation?

"Yes. We're looking for his killer," she said, unconsciously moderating her voice into a low contralto and pronouncing every word crisply. "Please forgive the imposition. I'd like to learn everything I can about Lavrenty, not as a singer, but as a person, if possible."

"Oh my God! This old song again!" Koninov sighed as if exhausted, and propped his feet up on a chair. "What can I tell you about Lavrenty? We weren't lovers, and even our friendship was pure business. I helped him—a lot—but both of us knew that as soon as his star faded our friendship would, too. Still, as far as money went, he was a big deal." Koninov waved a hand at one of the many glossy posters decorating the walls of his office. In one, Lavrenty was dressed in a shining silver jacket. He had a thin face and a weak chin. "The ladies swooned over him, like Frank Sinatra," Koninov confided, and Masha nodded understandingly. "Here, I'll show you." Koninov pressed a button and the wall across from him transformed into an enormous screen. "Check out the kind of shi—uh, shenanigans he landed in with this one."

Masha wanted to ask whether those shenanigans had anything to do with the pop singer's death in the liquid muck that oozed out of the burst pipe on Lubyansky Drive, but she kept quiet.

On the screen, Lavrenty was wearing a black shirt embroidered with rhinestones, unbuttoned to expose his hairless chest. "I called you all day, and I followed you all day, like a shadow!" warbled Lavrenty in an unsteady little tenor, and Masha was offended at the Sinatra comparison. It was true, though, that his fans were enthusiastic. They shrieked, they sang along, they danced. The camera paused on a girl weeping, her mascara running down her cheeks.

"I could have made another Justin Bieber out of him. Just look at that smile!"

Lavrenty's smile was truly handsome. Even white teeth, dimples, eyes flashing naughtily from under a subtle line of dark makeup. But Masha found the singer oddly repulsive on some physical level.

"Do you have any interviews with Lavrenty?" she asked, and Koninov came out of his reverie.

"Well, of course, of course!" he crowed, clearly delighted to be rid of her. "I'll ask someone to escort you to our screening room. You can watch them all there."

Masha shook the man's slightly damp, soft hand, and then followed a long-legged secretary to the theater, graciously declining a cup of coffee. Then she sat through a shifting compilation of music videos and quick questions from interviewers, tossed at the star as he left a concert.

"What do you think of our fans here in Nizhny Novgorod?"

"Oh, they're the most gifted listeners in all of Russia!"

Questions asked in the makeup room before he went on stage.

"How does your new show differ from the previous one?"

"We're doing only the best songs, new and old!"

Questions in the studio on Valentine's Day.

"Tell us, Lavrenty, are you in love?"

"No, I'm still waiting for my one and only."

Masha was starting to lose patience. She hoped that in one interview or another, if only out of the boundless desire that public figures seemed to have to bare their souls, Lavrenty would offer up a little information about himself. Then Masha would latch onto it and dive into that dark wormhole where she'd extract the reason why a maniac had chosen this particular pop star to kill and then dispose of in the place where, in Jerusalem, the Mount of Olives stood.

But all she heard were inane questions with equally inane answers. Listening to them was like watching a ping-pong ball bouncing back and forth from one narrow-minded hack to the other—journalist to singer and back again. She had been sitting in the dark theater for almost two hours now, and was about to step out for some fresh air. Lavrenty and his gold and silver suits were driving her crazy.

Then, all of a sudden, a talk show host asked Lavrenty about his parents. Reclining in an armchair, the star spoke lazily about where he came from. His ancestors were aristocrats, naturally. His parents had passed away, he said, when he was just a baby, leaving him only a monogrammed silver cigar case, with which he would never, ever part (here he took the case out of his pocket and exhibited it to the studio audience). There was also a watercolor by Polenov depicting the family estate outside Moscow, which the Bolsheviks had "expo-expro-expropriated" (it took Lavrenty a few tries). In a tone of voice just bordering on irony, the journalist asked a couple more questions about the star's aristocratic forebears. Then, with an obvious air of satisfaction, the host told the television audience and his celebrity guest that he had "just a very, very short" video to show them.

The video cut to a generic five-story apartment building from the Khrushchev era. A completely ordinary, unglamorous residence for ordinary, unglamorous people. Cherry trees were in bloom, and those trees, plus the extraordinary blue of the sky, contributed to the impression that this building was located much farther south than Moscow. An elderly couple was sitting together on a bench in front of the building. They exchanged embarrassed glances as the camera rudely panned across their bodies, catching details like the woman's faded blue dress, her legs laced with varicose veins, her feet shoved into brown sandals from the eighties, and the old man's own ragged sandals, baggy jacket, and the white dress shirt which barricaded his wrinkled old neck and prominent Adam's apple behind a stiff collar. The camera zoomed mercilessly until their faces filled the frame. The old couple resembled each other, like a brother and sister. They had the same round noses, thin lips, and tiny network of veins visible on their kind-looking faces. The camera moved a little to one side, and the journalist from Moscow appeared, looking ridiculously out of place in his fashionable skinny jeans.

"These fine folks are Kapitolina and Viktor," he began smoothly. "They've worked together their whole lives in the painting and plastering business. Kapitolina," he said, turning to the old woman, "tell us about your son."

The old woman smiled abashedly, and in her soft southern accent laid out for the whole country how much she loved her darling Lavrenty, how proud she was. After all, he was a big man now, living in Moscow, singing on the television. Kapitolina took out a family photo album with worn, bent corners, and under the camera's watchful eye, began paging through the pictures of Lavrenty as a baby, as a curly-haired little boy, and as a pimply teenager, providing loving commentary for each snapshot. Then she took out a different album, one dedicated to Lavrenty the pop star. There were newspaper clippings from tabloids and magazines. A list of the "Sexiest Singers on the Russian Stage." Pictures from the Mr. Smile contest and awards ceremonies for she wasn't sure what.

"Only we never see him anymore, our Lavrenty," Kapitolina complained to the journalist. "He's off in Moscow, you know, and we don't have his phone number. We only see him on the television. He seems very happy and healthy. We read he had a girlfriend, very pretty, a singer, too. But then they split up for some reason. We would like to have some grandchildren to take care of, someday."

This moving speech was interrupted by a wider shot of the father, a tear creeping out the corner of one old eye.

The video ended with a thunder of exasperating applause from the studio, where the camera swept over the excited crowd of fans and stopped on Lavrenty.

"It's all a lie!" the star shouted, even his golden suit jacket trembling in rage. "Wait till my lawyers hear about this!" The lovely tenor voice had turned into a screech, and under his stage makeup his face was turning bright red.

Looking at that preening peacock, it was honestly difficult to believe that he was his parents' son. Scowling in disgust, Masha turned off the projector and walked out of the auditorium. She told the assistant she would find her own way out.

She didn't see Kenty until that evening, when he picked her up after his last interview and handed over the recording. Masha sat in the car and stared straight ahead at the darkening city, the old couple's faces looming before her eyes.

"I'm never having children," she said suddenly, and she sensed Kenty gathering his thoughts next to her.

"Funny, I came to the same conclusion today."

Masha turned her head and took in Kenty's pale, even profile. "Bad story?"

Innokenty only pressed his lips together without responding, and Masha understood that the story she was about to hear must be very bad indeed. Innokenty was unusually taciturn, and his eyes—his eyes looked not just tired, but tortured. He had been a bookworm his whole life, studying outdated moral systems, rules whose oppressive stench had long been dispersed by fresher air. Now, only beautiful things remained from that era: the onion-domed churches, their cupolas shining in the sun, and icons with their exquisitely drawn faces.

Poor Kenty, Masha thought ruefully, *stuck with me for a best friend. He has the refined company of antique collectors on the one hand and someone who collects human depravity on the other.*

Feeling guilty, she touched his hand on the steering wheel. That was the good part about having known each other since they were kids; they didn't need to say anything to understand each other. Masha sighed deeply and opened the window a crack. They were driving past the Sparrow Hills neighborhood, and the evening air was surprisingly fresh. Masha closed her eyes and fell asleep.

She didn't notice when Innokenty stopped at an empty intersection and turned to look at her, his face like a joker's mask: lit by a pale-blue streetlamp on one side and glowing in the red of the stoplight on the other. Kenty's eyes were very dark. What was in those eyes? Tenderness? A feeling grown tired of itself after all these years? The red light on his cheek changed to green, then back to red.

But Innokenty still sat watching Masha, as if he couldn't get enough of the view.

ANDREY

Andrey stood waiting outside a swanky-looking apartment door. He hadn't been surprised when instead of an ordinary buzz, the doorbell had produced a trill like a nightingale. *Screw this guy and all his rich-guy shit, seriously. And his girlfriend Masha, too, who just so happens to be my intern on the side.*

Innokenty answered almost immediately and stood framed in the doorway like some kind of Napoleon or something, posing for a full-length portrait. The celestial blue of his shirt matched the jeans he was wearing obviously just to kiss up to his guest. *Bite me,* thought Andrey. But he winced a little on the inside, because just that weekend he had bought himself some new pants, a classic cut in dark-blue velvety corduroy. They cost way too much, and he'd cursed himself as he took out his wallet. But he bought them, anyway, because he knew there was no way he could show up at this snob's place in his same old jeans again. Standing here now, he realized this was a game he could never win. Because first of all, his host really was going out of his way to be nice, even abandoning his usual elegance to make his guest feel more comfortable in his home; and secondly, Innokenty's jeans were so chic and expensive that Andrey's corduroys paled in comparison. All that put Andrey right back in his usual state of seething irritation, and when he caught sight of Masha down the hall, also wearing jeans—what had they done, planned their outfits ahead of time?—he merely nodded.

"Come on in! I'm just throwing something together in the kitchen." Innokenty pointed the way down the hall, and Andrey followed Masha inside, trying not to look around. The walls here in hallway, painted perfectly white, provided the ideal backdrop for the old icons. In the living room the furniture was an explosive mix of stylish modern design and antiquity: a bright-red sofa shaped like a teardrop, a lamp with steel flourishes, and next to them a very simple Empire-style writing desk with a leather top. Behind the desk there was a graciously curved antique chair upholstered in the same red fabric as the ultramodern sofa. This room had no icons on the wall. Instead, there was an enormous black-and-white photograph of a wide-open eye. The picture seemed strangely familiar to Andrey, and the decor reminded him of the cover of a fashionable design magazine.

There were more photos arranged on the desk, and Andrey paused before them, not wanting to be the first one to speak. But as he looked over the pictures—these were black-and-white, too—he was alarmed to discover that the master of the house was not alone in any of them. He was always with Karavay: ten-year-old Masha dressed in gym clothes and holding a rapier, for some reason, with a young Innokenty across from her; a teenage Masha gazing into the distance; Masha and Innokenty at some sort of black-tie banquet, smiling awkwardly at the camera. Andrey coughed, confused, and turned to Masha, who was sitting next to a low table which held a variety of bottles and three wine glasses. *Childhood friends, then?* he wondered. Masha caught him looking at her quizzically and blushed a little.

"Innokenty thought we should drink a toast, to the success of this case."

"We should eat something, too!" Innokenty walked in with a tray of warm petit fours. "But I should warn you that I'm not the baker. I only popped them in the oven. So don't overdo yourselves with compliments."

Masha laughed and took the first exquisite small pastry off the tray. "Thank you, Kenty. I'm starving!"

Andrey followed Masha's example. The dainty little treats proved delicious, and he felt like Marilyn Monroe galloping up to the gates of some gastronomical paradise. Just like the dog would, he stuffed a few of the treats into his mouth at once, keeping his fingers crossed that at least he wouldn't make the same gulping noises his dog made. Meanwhile, Innokenty opened a bottle of wine with a tasteful pop, poured some first for Masha, then looked at Andrey inquisitively. Andrey didn't dare open his mouth with all those stupid petit fours inside, so he just nodded at the bottle of whiskey, and Innokenty filled a massive tumbler for him and tossed in a couple of ice cubes. Andrey picked up his drink carefully, afraid of committing yet another uncivilized act, but then threw caution to the wind, clinked glasses with Innokenty (who was gallantly tackling the whiskey along with him) and with Masha, and gulped down the Johnnie Walker, which he didn't get too often but dearly loved.

"Well!" Andrey said, and smiled warmly at them for the first time ever as he felt the golden beverage find its way to his heart. "What's new?"

Innokenty and Masha exchanged meaningful looks, which for once didn't make Andrey angry. These two had known each other forever! They were friends. Just friends! Maybe it wasn't just the whiskey that had put him in such a good mood.

Surprised, Masha returned the smile, then dug through her bag until she found a stack of paper covered in small, tight handwriting.

"I started a separate dossier on each of the victims. I thought we should try to put all this in order, find some way to classify their possible sins, and collect them all together."

Andrey nodded and lifted his glass.

"So." Masha had been acting shy again, but gradually her voice became steady, and she began laying out her arguments calmly, never suspecting that her intonation was an exact replica of the lawyerly manners of the senior Karavay, her father. "What do we have? We have the numbers one, two, and three. Three murder victims on the Bersenevskaya waterfront. Two men, one woman."

"Number one," said Innokenty, "was a really inoffensive type of guy. Other than talking too much, nobody had anything bad to say about him. There is one interesting detail, however: his father was a priest, and they didn't get along. He used to monkey around in church during the service. Blaspheming, basically. Nothing major."

"The second," continued Masha, looking closely at Andrey, "accused her married boyfriend of rape."

"Whoa, really?" asked Andrey.

"She got pregnant, he wouldn't leave his wife—"

"Got it. Was he convicted?"

"No. But the wife was there in the courtroom, and they say she put a curse on the victim, right there in front of everyone."

"Well now. That's not hard to understand. I hope she's not a suspect?"

"I didn't check it out," admitted Masha, biting her lip. "But I don't think that fits our theory."

Andrey laughed. "That's what I've been saying! The facts fitting the theory, instead of the theory fitting the facts! Anyway. Go ahead."

Masha colored slightly, and Innokenty swiftly came to her aid.

"Finally, number three. Solyanko. He was a professional athlete, an Olympic contender. He's suspected of planting drugs on his main competitor, Snegurov."

"Suspected?"

"Snegurov suspected him, anyway. He's thinking along the lines of *cui prodest*. Find the one who benefits—"

"Is that how the jock put it?" Andrey asked with a smirk.

Innokenty smirked in response. "More or less."

"All right, so what do we have?"

"What we have," said Masha quietly, "is three bodies where the tsars had their gardens in medieval Moscow, a place that is a stand-in for the Garden of Gethsemane. One victim offended the church, the second gave false testimony, and the third slandered a colleague. All three had their tongues cut out."

Nobody spoke.

"Pretty harsh," Andrey said finally, but he had to agree. "Go on, Intern Karavay."

"Number four was the drunk they found at Kutafya Tower—in Jerusalem, that'd be the Church of the Holy Sepulchre. His number, four, showed up in the form of a new tattoo on his biceps. A cop from his neighborhood confirmed he'd never seen it before."

"I'm afraid I didn't make any headway on that one," confessed Innokenty, wringing his hands. "Just wasted some time and wrecked a good suit." He stopped when he met Andrey's wry gaze. "I had a long but fruitless conversation with a local alcoholic guru. All I learned was that Nikolai Sorygin was a flower drunk."

"What the hell is that?"

"Apparently that means he lived like a plant, drank vodka like breathing air. Never did anything bad, but never did anything good, either. An archetypal drunk. And vodka was used to kill him, too, in a medieval way perfectly suited to our dismal hero."

"The next, I think, was the architect, Gebelai," Masha went on.

"Is that the one who killed all those people when his metro station collapsed?"

"That's him." Masha looked Andrey straight in the eye. "Andrey, I'm pretty convinced that our killer did this one, too. We don't need to look too far for Gebelai's sin—there were hundreds of victims. There was even proof that he was at fault, but the charges were dropped. They found him in an apartment on Lenivka."

"In Jerusalem, that's the Jaffa Gate," Innokenty piped up. "He died of exhaustion. He was an award-winning architect, rich and pampered, with all kinds of medals. One of them was pinned to his body. Right into his skin." Kenty passed Andrey a photograph of the medal he had found online. "This is a third-degree Akhdzapsh medal, awarded in Abkhazia for exemplary service. It has eight rays. Three of Gebelai's were broken off."

"So five were left," said Andrey, doing the depressing calculations. He rubbed at the bridge of his nose. "All right. Let's go on."

"Then we were able to identify the arm."

"What arm?"

"Remember how, about half a year ago, a detached arm was found in a bag with a Chagall? We went to see the collector that painting was stolen from. He recognized the arm."

"He recognized it?" Andrey looked at them skeptically.

"This man has a fantastic visual memory," Innokenty insisted. "He recognized tattoos that he had seen on a thief named Samuilov one time in court. This wasn't the first time Samuilov had robbed the same group of art collectors."

"I think the arm is a symbol," Masha said. "The murderer didn't care what thief he killed, as long as it was a thief."

"I agree," said Innokenty, nodding. "The arm—or the hand, anyway—represents theft. And they used to chop off thieves' hands in the Middle Ages."

Andrey sighed. "Where?"

Innokenty knew what he meant. "The arm was found between Lobnoye Mesto, which maps onto Golgotha, and St. Basil's, which represents Mount Zion. Remember how in Ivan the Terrible's time St. Basil's was called 'Jerusalem'?"

Andrey did not remember, naturally. But he did suddenly feel as if an unnaturally cold breeze was blowing over him. And he was grateful that Innokenty was splashing some more whiskey into his glass.

MASHA

Masha didn't completely understand why Andrey's face, initially screwed up into a scowl, had smoothed out so nicely, but she figured the good whiskey must be responsible. *I should start bringing a flask to work at Petrovka,* she thought to herself, almost giggling.

But she couldn't help admitting that this new easygoing Andrey was much better looking than the old one. He was finally wearing something other than jeans, and his thin sweater emphasized his lack of paunch. *Probably works out like crazy,* thought Masha, ashamed of her own neglected gym membership. She liked his hands, too. The fingers that gripped his whiskey glass were startling—contrary to expectations, there was nothing crude about them. They were perfectly proportioned, and looked flexible and sensitive. And his eyes! When he looked at her without his usual fury, his eyes were piercing, even though she usually found that light-blue color sort of dull. All in all, Masha had to admit that Captain Yakovlev, even though he might as well have been an alien, a man of some other species and tribe, possessed a certain sullen *attractiveness.* Is that what it was?

Masha looked at him with her usual caution, but also with curiosity. *He's probably been with tons of women,* she thought, blushing. Thank God nobody was looking at her. Innokenty, ever the gracious host, was pouring his guest some more whiskey. Masha decided she'd better not have any more wine, if one glass was leading her mind down this titil-lating path.

"Way to go!" Andrey was praising them now. "That's great work, identifying the victim. It will be easier to hunt down the body now. Although we don't get that many bodies missing an arm, honestly."

"You heard it here, Masha!" Kenty said, winking at her. "Your first compliment from your new boss."

"I'm flattered." Masha smiled at Andrey, and he grinned in response. *I need to stop drinking right now,* she thought. She set down her glass and changed the subject.

"Let's move on to the governor's wife, Liudmila Turina. We don't know which number she is, but she was quartered, so clearly this is another medieval execution. Then she was wrapped up in newspaper articles about her excessive bribe-taking, and found at Kolomenskoye, exactly where a tower marks the Ascension of Christ in Jerusalem."

"I see." Andrey nodded, no longer grinning.

"And the singer Lavrenty." Masha frowned. "He was a weasel, but I'm not sure which of his sins got him killed. A pipe burst near the Polytechnic Museum, and he drowned lying facedown in the muck. His watch stopped at eleven o'clock, even though the time of death, according to the coroner, was around six in the morning."

"And what do we have there?"

"Lubyansky Drive travels over the hill between the Polytechnic Museum and the Kitay-gorod metro stop, and that hill is a stand-in for the Mount of Olives in Jerusalem."

"Got it."

The further they went down their list, the more serious Andrey looked. *He believes us,* thought Masha. *He finally believes us! And he's afraid.* But who wouldn't be? The killer could freeze over the deepest circles of hell. *Not only does he collect our sins,* thought Masha, *he numbers them according to some mysterious scheme, and picks the perfect places to leave the bodies, too.* As if he were a spider weaving a web or a careful accountant making a table in Excel.

"I'm cold," she told Innokenty, and her loyal friend left to get her a sweater.

"That eye on the wall looks so familiar," Andrey said. "But I can't figure out why. I'm not real up on contemporary photography."

"That's my eye," said Masha, embarrassed.

"What?"

"It's mine. Kenty took that picture maybe ten years ago. He was into macrophotography then. It was terrible. What if he'd made some huge version of my nose? I told him I'd never come to his place again if he hung a photo of my nose up on the wall. But an eye—that's not too bad, right?"

"No, it's fine," Andrey said, and furrowed his brow as he turned to look at Innokenty, who'd returned with an enormous fuzzy sweater.

"I keep this here just for Masha. She's always freezing," he said as he draped the sweater over her shoulders.

"Uh-huh," said Andrey. "Right, so, where were we?"

"Next was Katya," said Masha, pulling the sweater tight around her. "But that's just conjecture."

"It's not conjecture, Masha," Innokenty said gently. "Someone made that accident happen. She died on Nikolskaya Street, Via Dolorosa. And you said yourself that she had those ten bracelets. Number ten. She was wearing your clothes, driving your car, so—the sin of envy?"

"I guess," Masha conceded. "Why did it have to be *my* friend, though? Are there really no other envious people in Moscow?" Masha looked down. She hadn't meant to whine.

Andrey studied Innokenty's face which was suddenly transformed by pity. His host caught his gaze and smiled sadly.

"There's also the man who was whipped to death. He used to beat his wife, and may have been responsible for the death of his infant son."

"The place?" Andrey asked.

"Prechistenka, near the Church of the Assumption."

"And the number?"

Innokenty shrugged. "I only spoke with his widow. She thought her husband got what he deserved for what she called his 'excessive wrath.' I didn't think to ask about a number. But maybe we could find one in the file?"

"There's one more," Andrey added, by way of summing up. "Yelnik, the hitman who was drowned under the ice, kept in a freezer for months, then fished out of the Moskva, which matches up with the Jordan River. And Yelnik, like the thief you found, is probably just a stand-in for any old murderer. The number fourteen was shaved onto the back of his neck."

"So there are at least fourteen of them, then," said Masha, "which means we haven't found them all yet."

"About those numbers," Andrey asked, "have you dug anything up?"

Masha looked like a guilty schoolgirl. "Not really," she admitted. "The more I read on the topic, the less I understand. I mean, we need to find the system all these murders fit into, hopefully through the numbers. Something like a ranking of sins. In the Bible, for example, you can find the tax collectors, the prostitutes, and the Pharisees listed as sinners. But our victims don't fit into those categories. Then there's Dante's *Divine Comedy*. The first circle of hell is for unbaptized but virtuous non-Christians. The second is for people who committed crimes of passion, the third is for gluttons—"

"But Dante was a Catholic," Innokenty interrupted. "He was writing in the context of the seven deadly sins. In Orthodoxy, there's no such concept."

"So no sins are deadly?" Andrey asked.

"It's more like the opposite: every sin is deadly. Our killer is obsessed with the purely Orthodox, medieval idea of the New Jerusalem. In those days, the conflict between Catholicism and Orthodoxy was much more strident than it is now."

Innokenty couldn't help himself. He was off and running on one of his favorite topics. "Orthodox believers called Catholics 'Latins' and Catholicism 'heresy.' In the eleventh century, the venerable Feodosy Pechersky said there was no eternal life for those in the Latin faith. Later, in the sixteenth century, Maximus the Greek said something similar, denouncing Latin heresy in the same breath with all Jewish and pagan blasphemy. The Orthodox hated Latins almost as passionately as they hated the splinter Russian Orthodox groups like the Old Believers. Actually, no. You always hate your own kind more."

Andrey looked annoyed at first, but then decided this historical diversion was kind of a relief from their eerie dance around the unknown killer. He let Innokenty chatter on.

"Want to know the focus of one of the central debates between the Orthodox Church and the Catholic Church in the Middle Ages?" Innokenty asked.

Masha and Andrey both raised their eyebrows.

"Baked goods!" Innokenty declared with a grin.

"How's that?" Andrey asked.

"You see, the holy fathers of the Orthodox Church believed that communion bread should be leavened—that it should contain yeast. The Catholics wanted unleavened bread. Our side, being more poetically inclined, insisted that the living yeast symbolized a living God. Our bread was alive, we said, and the Catholic bread was dead. Plus, the poor Catholics only received their dead Christ during the sacrament of the Eucharist."

"Who do you think was right?" asked Andrey, in spite of himself.

"The Catholics, I think, as annoying as that is. The Last Supper is believed to have been a seder—part of the Jewish celebration of Passover. And during Passover, Jews refrain from eating anything with yeast in it, including leavened bread. Passover is a commemoration of the Exodus, after which they wandered the desert with only a dry bread called matzo. There are other differences, too. The Orthodox—and here

I think they're absolutely correct—reject the idea of God having a 'lieutenant on earth,' like the Catholic Pope. And one more thing," said Innokenty, looking serious again. "This, I think, is vital for our serial killer. In Orthodoxy, there is no purgatory. Everything is either black or white: heaven or hell. No shades of gray."

"Harsh," Andrey joked, but he felt himself shiver.

"That's our Russian maximalism at work—everything is a dichotomy, all or nothing," Innokenty responded sadly.

Andrey put down his glass, which had been empty for a while now, and stood up.

"Thanks for the hospitality. It's time for me to go."

Innokenty and Masha saw him to the door, where they hovered awkwardly as Andrey fumbled with his shoes. Finally, his face red with the effort, he got them tied. He shook Innokenty's hand and gave Masha a nod.

"You've both done good work."

"Wait!" Innokenty said. "Here. I jotted down some more places in Moscow connected to Jerusalem. Just in case."

"Just in case, huh?" Andrey chuckled gloomily, glancing over the list before tucking it in his pocket. "We're really going to need this, I'm afraid."

ANDREY

Andrey was not in the habit of lying to himself. If he had fed Marilyn all the food he wanted that morning, if he had put on his new pants and a clean shirt, if he'd driven to work like a madman while listening to some cheesy classical station, it must be because he was excited about seeing Masha Karavay.

But, Andrey told himself, that excitement was purely because the work was moving along nicely now, and if it weren't for Masha, they never would have linked all those cold cases. Intern Karavay had turned out to have a good head on her shoulders, and Andrey Yakovlev wasn't the only one who'd noticed. Terrifying as it was, he was beginning to suspect their unnamed killer knew it, too. Otherwise, why would he have picked Masha's best friend as a victim? *He's playing with her,* Andrey thought. Challenging her to a duel. And suddenly he was overcome with fear for Masha, deep in his gut. *That crazy fuck. Try coming at me, asshole! I'll—*

Unfinished thoughts whipped around in his brain. *You threaten a girl, but you don't have the balls to come after me?* Then he realized it wasn't a question of balls at all. Andrey simply didn't interest the killer. But Masha did.

He got out of his car and slammed the door, annoyed and maybe even jealous. There was something between those two. An intelligent young woman and a merciless killer. A mental connection could be more powerful than a physical one. But how could Andrey protect her from . . . coupling, in some horrible way, with a maniac? Andrey opened the door to his office, nodded to his colleagues, and strode right to Masha's desk.

"Masha!" he said gruffly.

Masha looked up with a smile, which quickly disappeared. Andrey was panting like he'd just run the hundred-meter dash. In fact, he had— up the stairs and down the hallways of Petrovka.

"Masha," he repeated sternly, sitting down across from her and trying to even out his breath. "I'm taking you off this case."

Her face went pale, enough to make her eyes glow behind the long eyelashes.

"Why?" she asked, her voice calm. "What am I doing wrong? Why do you hate me so much?"

"No, Masha," he whispered in response. "Seriously, for such a smart girl, you're an idiot! Do you think we're playing games here? He killed your best friend. Do you realize what that means? He walked into your apartment, dressed her in your clothes, put her in your car, and ran her right into a concrete wall! He knows who you are. And I'm not going to continue putting you in danger. You don't have enough experience. You haven't had time to develop the professional instinct that we have here, the sense that lets you sniff out danger—"

"But I sniffed out the pattern!" Masha interrupted in a furious whisper. "I had enough knowledge and intuition for that, when nobody else here had a clue! If he killed Katya, that means he was trying to tell me something. It's a message. Subconsciously, serial killers often want to be caught, right? If I don't figure out his riddle, that means Katya will have died for nothing."

"That's what I'm trying to tell you!" Andrey answered, roaring this time. "This isn't a riddle or a game! He's going to kill you for your sins, and only he knows what they are! And he's going to kill you in some twisted, medieval way, and it's going to be my fault!"

"Don't worry," said Masha, her voice devoid of emotion. She was already stowing documents in her bag. "Nobody's going to accuse you of anything. Definitely not gratitude, anyway." And she walked quickly out of the office.

"Karavay!" Andrey barked, but she didn't even slow down. *Woman's stubborn as a mule,* he thought. She was going to keep digging around, anyway, no matter what he said.

Andrey grabbed his jacket and took off after her, oblivious to his colleagues' silence and the astonishment in their eyes. Masha was already outside by the time he caught up with her, grabbed her by the arm, and pulled her silently to his car. She didn't resist, just walked along next to him, looking off in the other direction. Andrey opened the passenger door, put her inside, got in himself, and steered the car quickly, angrily, out of his parking spot.

"We're going to the morgue," he said after a while, though she hadn't asked. "Another woman got killed this weekend."

From the passenger seat, he heard a barely audible gasp.

"She might not be one of ours, but she lived at an address on Innokenty's list."

"Where?"

"Pushkin Square."

"Bely Gorod." Masha sighed. "The third fortified wall, after the Kremlin and Kitay-gorod. Built at the end of the sixteenth century, and, just like in Jerusalem, it had sixteen gates. The Tver Gate was where Pushkin Square is now."

"For God's sake," said Andrey, making a sharp left. "I'm starting to think you can't spit in Moscow without hitting something from Jerusalem."

"There are a lot of places that fit. Basically, the whole historical city center," Masha said. "He used to make more of an effort, try to leave the bodies in important places like St. Basil's. But now, I think he knows we're onto him, so he's rushing, looking for convenient spots closer to where the victims are."

"What?" Andrey slammed on the brakes to park the car. "How can you possibly know that he knows that we know? I mean—you know what I mean!"

Masha shrugged. "I just have this feeling."

"A feeling?" Andrey snapped. "You ought to do what my grandmother does, and cross yourself when you get a feeling like that!"

Andrey and Masha were standing on opposite sides of the car now, staring furiously at each other. When he realized what he'd just said, Andrey heaved another sigh. What had the world come to when a godless atheist like him was talking about sins and the sign of the cross!

"This is great, just great!" he grumbled under his breath. He turned and stalked into the morgue, not bothering to check that Masha was following him.

MASHA

Masha trailed Andrey, still fuming and off balance. The denim tyrant had practically kicked her off the case and out of Petrovka that morning! But Masha had to admit that she knew very well that Katya couldn't have just randomly caught the killer's attention as she drove down the road on her way to Masha's apartment. And Andrey was right; that meant he knew about her, knew who she was. The thought terrified her, but at the same time it sent off a wave of excitement, and Masha's whole body tensed like a greyhound ready to race.

I'm going to catch you, she vowed for the thousandth time. *You'd like that, wouldn't you? You're tired of proving how right you are about this soulless world. Come on, lay that burden down! Show yourself, phantom!*

Masha looked around, just in case a killer really did appear. But all she saw was the morgue, and Andrey holding the door open for her. Behind her was the hustle and bustle of the Moscow street.

While they walked down the hallway, its floor tiled with a cheerful yellow linoleum, Masha tried not to think about what she was about to see. Pasha's formidable figure appeared in the hall. He was just getting ready to go out for a smoke. Andrey introduced him quickly to Masha, and the coroner bowed chivalrously.

"Yakovlev, are you always this lucky with your interns?" he asked.

"Not always," Andrey muttered. "Thank God."

"He's such a boor!" said Pasha, leaning close to Masha's ear. "But there's a kind and noble heart beating somewhere under that hideous surface."

"Isn't that always how it is?" Masha smiled, joining in the game. "No good heart without a hideous surface. Is there any justice in this world?"

"Only in fairy tales," answered Pasha in all seriousness. "I'm reading a whole book of them to my youngest. The monsters with the good hearts always change into handsome princes at the end. But first, they need to be kissed. Even though they're ugly." Pasha winked. "What about giving Yakovlev a kiss, huh, Masha? What could he turn into? It would be nice to have something pretty to look at around here once in a while, since all I ever see is corpses, and nasty types, like, you know—"

Masha laughed, and Andrey narrowed his eyes at Pasha.

"Knock it off, Rudakov. Where's our corpse?"

"Your corpse has become a real celebrity. Quite the unusual cause of death. Let's go to my clubhouse."

Pasha gestured grandly, and they followed him into an autopsy room, where the corpse was waiting for them under a white sheet. Pasha must have noticed that Masha's face had gone green, because he paused.

"You know," he said, hesitantly, "I don't think I'm going to show you the whole thing. Pretty unappetizing, this one, even for the experienced connoisseur. For a young lady like you—here, let me just show you her hand."

Pasha carefully lifted up one edge of the sheet, and what a hand it was. There was no skin left at all, and in some places bone was visible. Masha yelped in alarm, and clutched at Andrey, who was pretty pale himself.

"What happened there?" he asked.

"I can't tell you for sure. I'm not an entomologist."

"A what?"

"A bug expert. Seems like it was ants. Ordinary ones, so far as I can tell. I kept some of them in a jar here. Turns out ants are not exactly vegetarians."

"Are you saying she died of ant bites?"

"No." Pasha removed his gloves, and tiredly wiped one hand across his forehead. "I did an autopsy. Her heart gave out. The guys at the scene said the place was swarming. They ate her alive, and nobody heard her screaming. Extra-soundproof walls, apparently. The woman worked out of her apartment as a psychic or a witch or something. She soundproofed the walls so the neighbors couldn't hear her speaking with clients. Turns out they were a little too soundproof. I can't really tell you anything else. I think I'm going to go have a smoke, all right?"

Masha and Andrey both nodded, and they trailed him to the exit. Without explanation, Masha flew out the door and dashed around the corner of the building. She vomited.

Andrey found her a minute later, gulping greedily at the polluted city air. He offered her his handkerchief. It was enormous, with an old checked Soviet design. Masha nodded in thanks.

"Let's go," Andrey said. "That's another reason I didn't want you involved in this anymore. Looking at dead bodies is no fun. And this killer is putting on a show that's too much even for an experienced coroner."

"I didn't say good-bye to Pasha."

"He'll understand. Come on, get in the car."

Without talking, they drove off. When traffic stopped, as it always did, Andrey looked over at Masha. Her face still looked pale, and dark shadows had appeared under her eyes. He was seized by an acute feeling of guilt.

"I'm sorry I got you into this," he finally said. "I'm afraid for you. This isn't the kind of case that should be your first, you know? Most detectives never see this kind of thing in their whole careers. And here you are, just an intern." He wanted to add that on top of all that, she was a law student, the daughter of a family of intelligentsia, a pampered girl who had only ever thought about ants as they related to picnics or fables.

"My childhood wasn't as easy as you think," Masha said, as if reading his mind.

"Sure, sure," Andrey said. He assumed his definition of an easy childhood was different from hers.

He drove her to her place, and even walked her to her apartment door, which Masha appreciated. Her legs had gone wobbly somehow, and her head was spinning.

"Okay," he said, almost propping her up outside the door. "Get some rest. We'll have a lot of work to do tomorrow. Oh, and ask your folks to change the locks, okay?"

He turned quickly and walked down the stairs. Masha wanted to say something, to tell him—what? *Thanks for taking care of me, even though you don't have to, even though you probably don't actually care at all. Thanks for turning out to be better than I thought you were.* Or something even crazier, like, *You know, I feel so calm and safe with you. Better than I've felt for a long time. Better than anyone since my papa.*

But Masha only turned her key in the lock and opened the door, almost falling into the quiet, familiar darkness of the apartment.

Masha caught herself smirking, but then felt bad. A crime scene was no place to be snotty. Still, it was hard, because this apartment—home to Alla Kovalchuk, or Adelaide, as she called herself—was stuffed to the gills with kitsch. Everything was gilded and twisted into the florid contortions of that baroque style particular to people with lots of new money. Andrey was examining the room where the murder had actually taken place and where Adelaide had received her clients. He hadn't let Masha in, even closing the door behind him. But the smell of decay, terrifying and sickly sweet, got through to her anyway, so she hadn't protested. In fact, Masha had decided to stop arguing with Andrey altogether—when possible. She also decided she would yell at him only when absolutely necessary, like when she had to prove she was (obviously) right, for instance.

Masha ran a hand over a velvety throw pillow and tried the divan, which gave way softly beneath her. The lady of the place had evidently pampered herself in every way, as if she could not bear the discipline of furniture with a straight back or a firm seat. Only things pleasant to the touch were allowed here, only objects that were soft and warm. The coffee table held romance novels with luxurious scenes on the covers, the stories as pink and fluffy for the brain as this couch was for the body. Though of course she hadn't known her, Masha suddenly decided that Alla Kovalchuk must have had a hard time as a child and teen. That was probably why she gathered so much sugary sweetness around her as an adult.

Masha pressed her forehead against a window and looked down on Pushkin Square. Not a single sound penetrated the three layers of glass, which made the people and cars rushing down Tverskoy Boulevard look unreal, like ghosts in some senseless masquerade. She heard footsteps behind her, but Masha didn't bother to turn around. Andrey stood next to her, looking down out the window with her.

"They look like ants," he said and grunted. They both shuddered, remembering the hand chewed through to the bone.

"Pushkin Square used to be called Strastnaya Square," said Masha quietly.

"I didn't know that."

"*Strast* means passion, but the square was named after the Passion of Christ. In Old Church Slavonic, *strast* meant suffering or torment." Masha shook her head, trying to escape the endless chain of associations stretching out in her mind. "I've been reading too much about this stuff."

"Come into the kitchen. I have something to show you."

There was a chair turned upside down, one that looked nothing like the others with their luxurious dark wood. This chair was shabby, probably cobbled together in a Belarusian furniture factory for some government office. Andrey spun it around so that Masha could see a metal plate, bearing the number fifteen, on its back. Masha drew in a sharp breath. So it was him again.

Andrey smiled gloomily. "Let's get out of here," he said, and they both hurried from the apartment and pulled the heavy door shut behind them.

Masha jogged down the stairs after Andrey. Her eyes kept catching on his neat, close-cropped hair. "You know," she said, "I checked the numbers against the *Arma Christi*."

Andrey slowed down to listen.

"Those were the instruments of the Passion, the things they used to torment Jesus Christ: the column, the whip, the crown of thorns. The quantities match, but—"

Andrey snorted. "But Christ never sinned."

One floor down, a door opened, and a young woman in a pink raincoat stepped out onto the landing.

"Right," Masha was saying. "But the place where the Passion took place was Jerusalem, so I thought maybe—"

She ran straight into Andrey, who'd stopped dead in his tracks.

"Sorry." Masha grabbed a handrail to steady herself, and felt her cheeks flush at the momentary contact with Andrey's back. But he didn't answer, or even turn around.

Then Masha saw that the girl in pink had stopped short, too, and was staring up at him. The dumbstruck expression on the girl's thin, almost doll-like face transformed into a flirtatious grin.

"Andreeeeeyyy! Hello! How long has it been?" she sang in a tone that exaggerated her already-high voice.

Andrey still hadn't spoken, and when Masha tiptoed two steps farther down and caught a glimpse of his face, she was shocked at its pallor.

"Hey," he managed finally, his voice flat.

Masha had been waiting for an introduction, but she realized Andrey had no attention to spare for good manners.

"I didn't think you'd escape old Garbage-grad and turn up in Moscow, too," the stranger went on as her eyes traveled over him, head to foot, with no hint of modesty. "Maybe I shouldn't have dumped you after high school, huh?" She winked artfully.

But Andrey just stood there, eyes wide, as if he'd swallowed his tongue.

Masha acted on impulse. She tucked her hand into his, which Andrey seemed not to even notice. But the girl sure did, and now she looked at Masha for the first time. That look was domineering, despite the fact that she stood half a flight below them. For a split second, Masha regretted that she wasn't wearing the expensive clothes her mother liked to buy her, ever hopeful that her daughter might finally answer the call of fashion. But almost immediately Masha got her bearings, led Andrey down the steps to the landing, and offered her hand.

"Hello, I'm Masha. Masha Karavay."

The girl apparently wasn't prepared for a handshake. Where she lived and worked, they were probably used to greeting each other with brisk nods.

"Raya," she said, and squeezed Masha's fingers halfheartedly.

"Nice to meet you!" Masha told her, putting on the smile her mother used when she didn't think something was nice at all, but still intended to behave. "I wanted to thank you. I mean, if you hadn't broken up with Andrey back then"—Masha pulled her shell-shocked supervisor closer with a proprietary flourish—"the two of us never would have gotten together. So, thank you *so* much! But now, you'll have to excuse us, we're on our way to go order our new kitchen. You know how you have to watch them every minute, or they'll send you last year's models from Italy instead of the new collection!" With that, Masha delivered another blinding smile. "Take care, now!"

"Um, bye," said the girl, her voice wavering. She hadn't moved, and she was no longer grinning.

"See ya!" said Andrey, his voice almost normal. He and Masha took off down the stairs again, but without talking this time. Now Masha was in the lead, pulling Andrey by the hand, and she didn't let go until they got to the car.

"Last year's models? From Italy?" Andrey gave her a crooked smile.

"Who knows!" Masha shrugged. "I needed a quick way to show her your happy family life."

"What for?" Andrey avoided her gaze.

Masha gave him an angry look. "I thought you needed it."

"A fake family?"

"No," said Masha, her voice hard. "Happiness."

"Well, yeah . . ." Andrey trailed off, then let out a low whistle. "Thanks, I guess."

"You're welcome, I guess." Masha smiled. "Lunch?"

"Absolutely, Intern Karavay." Andrey grinned in response. "And the boss is paying."

ANDREY

Andrey barely knew what to do with himself. On the one hand, the fact that Masha had caught him in a moment of weakness was humiliating. On the other, her response had been touching, the way she had immediately come to his aid, playing the role of his *wife*, no less. Touching, and flattering, too. He looked at her from across the table of the inexpensive café she'd thoughtfully picked. Andrey had to admit that if a girl like that actually were his wife, he never would have acted like such a helpless moron on those stairs. Of course, girls like Masha only married guys like . . . The intimidating figure of Innokenty rose up before his eyes. Guys who didn't freeze up like assholes when they ran into ghosts from their past.

Masha told the waiter what she wanted, and Andrey pointed to the first thing he saw with meat in it. As the waiter walked away, he called after him, "And vodka! For two."

"She was my first love," he told Masha apologetically, then winked to show her how silly the whole thing was.

"I thought so," Masha said, her voice serious, and she smiled uncertainly.

"We were supposed to take the capital by storm together, and my plan was to support her so she could focus on her writing. She wanted to get into the Institute of Literature."

Why am I telling her all this? Andrey wondered, but it was too late to stop now. He looked down at the polyester tablecloth. Out of the corner of his eye, he could see Masha's folded hands with their short, unpolished fingernails.

"I thought I'd come get a job. But she wrote poetry. Bad poetry, probably, but I didn't have a clue about that stuff." He laughed again. "I still don't." Andrey looked up at her. "Do you like Asadov's poems?"

"No," Masha answered honestly, frowning a little.

"Well, Raya loved them."

The waiter brought them a sweating carafe of vodka and some bread. He offered her some, but Masha declined. She took some bread, though, and started squeezing it in her fingers, molding it like clay. Andrey took a shot, then a long sniff from a crust of bread. Let her see how real Russians did it. And by real Russians, he meant provincials like him. He didn't need a chaser. Andrey knew Masha was waiting for the rest of the story, and he didn't mind giving it to her.

"She left me. Raya. Just like it always happens, for my best friend. For a little while, he really liked Asadov, too." Andrey smiled again, and poured himself another shot. The vodka went down warm and smooth, and splashed into his empty stomach. His mood still wasn't improving, but he was determined to finish the tale. "The problem was that she decided to leave me around the same time my father died of a stroke. There I was at his funeral, at the wake, and all I could think about was seeing her again, so she could console me or something, distract me from the nightmare at my parents' house. Well, she did. She totally distracted me, no doubt about that. I could recite some Asadov for you, if you want. Romantic bullshit." He tossed down another shot.

Masha smiled uncomfortably.

"A blow like that is nothing to laugh at, Karavay. Not when you're seventeen. And especially when your head is full of corny poetry. But it turns out I'm a unique specimen! Indestructible! I flew off the fifth floor, and walked away with only scratches. I took too many sleeping pills, and they pumped my stomach. I even lay down on the train tracks, but the bastard hit the brakes in time, and they locked me up overnight for being an asshole. I would have tried some other things, but I started feeling bad for my mom, and I didn't have enough imagination, anyway."

Masha looked distraught.

"Did you think I'd give up sooner? I had to show some genuine dedication to get a job serving my motherland like this one!"

Masha moved to say something, but couldn't make a sound. Instead, her eyes flashed suddenly, not with joy, but with a degrading, feminine pity, and something in her gaze made him tremble, made him desire the same thing he had hoped to find, so long ago, with Raya. Comfort. A reassuring hand on his shoulder.

But it's way too late for that now, he thought, suddenly angry. *And what right does she have to pity me? I've done enough of that for both of us!*

"I understand," Masha said suddenly, hiding her hands under the table as if trying to prevent them from reaching out to touch him. "That kind of thing can throw you off course. All you see in life is pain. It's unbearable."

"You understand, huh?" he said, smirking. Now Andrey was ashamed of his own cheap exhibitionism, and the mocking irony he had used to pose as the leading man in some sad romance turned abruptly into annoyance. The change was so powerful he could feel his eyes start to water.

"Is that right? You understand? What could you possibly understand, other than your serial killers? You play with them like Barbie dolls! You're sick, Karavay! Who have you ever lost? You ever lose a love and a best friend and a father, all at once? You're gonna tell me you know what it's like to jump from a fifth-floor balcony? What has ever been wrong with your life? Not enough, what, truffles? Oh, I know!" Andrey laughed, loud enough that people at the other tables turned around to look. "They sent you last year's collection from Italy!"

Masha stood up without saying a word. She put some cash down on the table and walked out of the café.

"You idiot!" Andrey shouted after her, even though he knew she probably couldn't hear him. "You're an idiot!" he called again, for the benefit of all those people at the other tables, who hurried to turn back around to their own plates.

The waiter brought Masha's salad and his stew. But Andrey had lost his appetite. He finished his vodka, tossed some money on the table just like she had, and left.

Generally speaking, it is a bad idea to ever reveal any regrets in front of one's pet. The animal might start to think its master capable of making mistakes, and that is impermissible, from the point of view both of the master's reputation and the pet's education. But Andrey had nobody to complain to but Marilyn Monroe.

"I'm such a jackass!" That had been Andrey's refrain all morning, and he repeated it to the very understanding mutt again as he fried himself some eggs. "I'm a total jerk. First I play up what a poor victim I am, and then, when I get the effect I'm looking for, I turn on her and cuss her out! I'm a cretin, right?"

Marilyn Monroe's furry face managed to express two things at once: *You're absolutely right!* and *You're not a cretin at all! You're the most wonderful person in the world!* That reminded Andrey that he hadn't fed his flunky yet. He sighed, and sliced the dog some sausage. Marilyn immediately switched his adoring gaze to the morsel in his bowl.

"You know what the worst part is? Yesterday she was acting like—" Andrey stopped to think and chew his eggs. *Like a real friend,* he thought. But he didn't say that out loud, not even to Marilyn Monroe. It seemed fitting to call Masha Karavay a real friend, but also, somehow, disappointing. Andrey sighed, and pushed aside the cup with the rest of his instant coffee. He gave Marilyn a pat and walked out of the house, intending to make it in record time to Petrovka. And to Masha, damn it!

Half an hour later, when Andrey walked into the office and saw Masha's part of the desk was empty, another sickening wave of guilt crashed over him. He picked up the phone, determined to call Masha all day, if he had to, until she answered. But then he remembered he didn't have her number. Masha had always been the one to call him. He stood still for a second, then began rummaging through the pockets of the lighter denim jacket he reserved for warm weather. Somewhere in there should be a sturdy white business card, inscribed *Innokenty Arzhenikov, Antiquarian* in fancy calligraphy.

Innokenty Arzhenikov, antiquarian, would definitely have Masha's phone number. And something told Andrey that Kenty knew it by heart.

Finally he found the elusive card. Innokenty answered.

"Hello," said Andrey. "This is Andrey Yakovlev, Masha's, um, boss."

"Of course." Andrey might have been imagining things, but he thought he caught a hint of irony in the antiquarian's voice. "What can I do for you?"

"Masha isn't at work," Andrey said flatly. He was mad. "Given what's been happening lately—" He paused.

"Right." Innokenty sounded worried now, too. "That's strange. Do you have her phone number? I'll give it to you."

Andrey wrote it down, said good-bye to Innokenty, and was just about to punch in Masha's number when the telephone rang with an internal call. Anyutin was summoning him for a reckoning. Immediately.

Katyshev was waiting in the colonel's office, too, trying to look as unobtrusive as possible, but Andrey knew the rules of this game. Without letting his eyes drift over to the prosecutor, he reported what he knew about the situation at Pushkin Square. The lack of clues and horrific crime scene matched the murderer's signature. There was no doubt, Andrey told them, a serial killer was loose in Moscow. Anyutin and Katyshev exchanged a look.

"Any theories?" Anyutin asked Andrey.

The captain made his decision. "My intern, Maria Karavay, has a theory that is somewhat unusual, but fits the overall scenario very well."

"Let's have it," said Katyshev, tilting his gray head to one side.

"Heavenly Jerusalem." Andrey had never actually pronounced that magical combination of words out loud before, and they resonated strangely in the colonel's office.

"How's that?" asked Anyutin, sounding lost.

Katyshev just stared at Andrey without a word.

"Heavenly Jerusalem. It's some sort of legend, from the Bible. A holy city in the sky," Andrey said, beginning to feel ridiculous. "There are points all around Moscow that are symbolically connected with it or with the real Jerusalem. That's where the bodies are turning up. At first, we weren't sure why the killer was moving the bodies, or parts of them. We thought he was trying to cover his tracks, maybe confuse us about timing. But he wanted to point us to places connected with Jerusalem and with the Middle Ages. He even uses medieval execution methods. We actually brought a historian in on the case," Andrey added coolly, looking Anyutin right in the eye. "Now he's predicted where we might find the next body."

"Ridiculous!" Anyutin blurted out, but Katyshev hushed him.

"Go on," he said.

By the time Andrey returned to his desk an hour later, he knew that his bosses believed him. Or, at least, they wanted to believe him. Andrey couldn't blame them for being skeptical. He couldn't completely believe it himself, even now. He needed to do some more digging. He would try to talk Anyutin into assigning a team to the case. They needed more help than a lone antiquarian could provide. He hadn't forgotten about apologizing to Masha, but his guilt had dissipated a little. How many times had he stressed to Anyutin that this bold theory was all the intern's work? It was kind of humiliating, sure, but it was only fair to give her the credit.

He really should try to reach her. But he also had a crapload of work to do.

MASHA

Masha was sitting on her bedroom floor in the empty apartment, listening over and over to her and Kenty's interviews. Books were heaped around her bed, stacked up on the chair, covering every inch of her desk. She was too tired to read, so now she was listening, thinking there must be something in their intonation, in the pauses between their words, in the subtle modulations of their voices, that could reveal a secret. A clue that would give her insight into those damn numbers written in blood, carved into skin, shaved into scalps. A broken medal. Bracelets on a dead wrist. Masha could almost hear the killer who collected sins whispering just over her shoulder: *Seven, eight, nine, ten . . . Ready or not, here I come!*

She shook her heavy head like a horse trying to scare off a fly and rewound the tape to the first recording.

"But I don't think Slava ever had a real girlfriend before me. He wasn't all that attractive, really. He was a joker. Skinny, kind of a wimp. I don't have, like, a maternal instinct when it comes to men—"

Masha looked up at the photograph on the wall. Her father looked down at her with his usual calm warmth.

"It's been another year, Papa," Masha whispered. "And I still haven't figured it out. What use am I? I've been trying so hard."

⁜

At twelve, Masha had put her dolls away, and started playing with maniacs and monsters instead. The young Masha had a ninety-six-page lined notebook, but it wasn't for song lyrics, or photos of pop stars, or dried flowers. It did not contain friendship oaths or names of cute boys from school. No, not quite.

Instead, it had a sketch of Gilles de Rais. He was the world's first convicted serial killer, a comrade-in-arms of Joan of Arc, and the inspiration for Bluebeard. He tortured and killed over one hundred forty children in his medieval castle. Then there was a reproduction of a lovely watercolor of Darya Saltykova wearing a lace bonnet. She was a pious widow with a fondness for using hot curling irons to batter her serfs. She also had a picture of Ted Bundy, the American serial killer who raped, tortured, and killed women from 1974 to 1978—and who practically made serial killers fashionable—and the darling young David Berkowitz, who operated from 1976 to 1977.

The Soviets were all there, too—Chikatilo, Slivko, and Golovkin—notable for just how ordinary they looked. She had newspaper clippings, printouts from web pages, carefully noted tables classifying mental pathologies, analyses of criminal profiles, and excerpts from the memoirs of FBI agents who specialized in catching serial killers. The excerpts Masha had copied out herself, point by point, when she was fourteen. *(1) Think of yourself as a hunter. (2) Become a psychologist to discover how your victim thinks. (3) Craft the perfect plan to lure the victim onto safe ground. (4) The hunter cannot afford to make mistakes.*

And there were pages and pages of quotes. Quotes from Chikatilo's interrogation. Quotes from Robert Ressler, the real-life detective who people say inspired *The Silence of the Lambs*. Quotes by Richard von Krafft-Ebing, whose groundbreaking *Psychopathia Sexualis* was published in 1886. There were even quotes from Sherlock Holmes, which were comparatively lighthearted in this company. Her favorite line was "Singularity is almost invariably a clue. The more featureless and commonplace a crime is, the more difficult it is to bring it home."

Two theories. There had been two theories about her father's death. The first, and most likely, was that it was a contract killing. Fyodor Karavay had a brilliance and sense of humor that allowed him to emerge triumphant from even the most complicated trials. There are always a few star lawyers in any legal sky, but the elder Karavay was undoubtedly the brightest of them all. He was known to quote Shakespeare fluently when defending a jealous husband. He hauled antique statues into court to demonstrate the angles at which a victim might or might not have been stabbed. He educated the judges, he confounded them, he made them laugh. But most of all, Karavay taught them to question their assumption that they'd always support the prosecution. He taught them judicial ethics. And they learned from him.

Once university students started to sit in on Karavay's trials, Masha's father had felt emboldened to take on a different category of cases. Karavay began representing journalists accused of slander, families whose children had been attacked by skinheads, and ministry officials accused of espionage.

Karavay had his enemies, certainly, and there were any number of people who might have had him killed out of simple spite. That kind of murder, halfheartedly disguised as a robbery gone wrong, was a very popular way out of sticky situations for a certain class of powerful people at the time. Masha had eavesdropped outside the kitchen door while Nick-Nick tried to explain to her mother that, even if they could catch the person who'd stabbed her husband three times, they'd probably never ID the man who'd ordered the hit. It was typical for hitmen not to know who they were working for—that way, they couldn't rat anyone out, which the cops didn't mind one bit. Why would they want to dig too deep into the schemes brewed up by local bigshots? It was a dead end.

"Is there a second theory, then?" Mama had asked, her voice flat and dull, and little Masha had pressed her ear to the door so hard it hurt.

"Well . . ." Nick-Nick had probably waved his hand in dismissal. "It's a silly one. Not really worth considering. Over the past five years, there have been a handful of murders around Moscow with similar types of wounds inflicted. Petrovka is exploring the idea of a serial killer."

Masha remembered the silence that had fallen on the other side of that door. Then she'd heard the sound of a stool being hastily pushed back and a drinking glass falling over. The syrupy smell of the Valocordin Mama was taking for her nerves had seeped out from under the door.

Months later, Masha had asked Nick-Nick a question. He was still stopping by regularly at that point, trying and failing to get Natasha to talk to him. He and Masha always ended up playing chess instead.

"How do you catch a serial killer?"

Nick-Nick had peered at Masha from under his eyebrows. "It's not easy. Serial killers are not so much a criminal-justice problem as an anthropological one." When he'd seen the perplexed expression on Masha's face, he'd smiled. "That means we don't really understand how a person can take pleasure in killing. In most cases, serial killers are mentally competent, and they lead seemingly normal lives. They go to work, love their wives, raise their children . . . Why, then? One fine day—or night, or morning—why does a model family man put down his crossword puzzle and go out to murder someone? And if we can't figure out why, then how are we going to find him? What clues would we have? Detectives also have another important challenge: How can they anticipate the killer's next victim, pick them out of millions of ordinary people?"

That was the first step down a long road. That was the day Masha found purpose. From the two possible explanations of her father's murder, she'd picked the second, less likely option. Contract killings, back in the late 1990s, were too ordinary. If it were a serial killer, though, that was strange, exceptional, and—according to Sir Conan Doyle—there was hope of finding the killer after all! She just needed to understand him. That understanding would help Masha finally banish the terror and grief that kept waking her up at night in a cold sweat. Every time it happened, she was relieved to realize she'd only been dreaming, until she remembered that her nightmare was all too real.

Masha finally tore her gaze away from her father's portrait. She stood up, gathered all the library books in an enormous shopping bag, grabbed the key to her stepfather's car, and headed for the front door. Suddenly, she turned and ran back to her bedroom to check an address on the computer. She heard her phone ringing, but she ignored it. There *was* someone who could help her! Why hadn't she thought of it before?

⁛

A thunderstorm was rolling in. The birds had fallen silent in anticipation, the old trees stretched upward as if preparing for battle, and the light-yellow hospital building in the depths of the park almost glowed in contrast with the darkness moving in from the south. Masha dashed through the humid air into the lobby, where an air conditioner hummed quietly.

"I'd like to see Professor Gluzman," she told the receptionist.

"Do you have an appointment?" the girl asked sternly.

"No."

The girl dialed a number, listened for a second, and then hung up.

"I'm afraid Professor Gluzman cannot see anyone right now."

"I must see him," Masha told her firmly. She pulled her Petrovka credentials out of her bag and gave the receptionist a strict look. The woman frowned, and Masha cringed a little at throwing her weight around like this.

"I'll call someone to escort you," the girl said drily.

A nurse silently led Masha to Gluzman's room. Masha never would have been able to find the right door herself in that endless corridor, as white and featureless as a hallway in some sci-fi thriller. The nurse knocked. When a voice inside told them to come in, she stepped aside and let Masha enter. Inside, the room was dimly lit. Gluzman's lap was draped with a blanket, and he was wearing pajamas. He sat facing the window, continuously smoothing the blanket over his knees, apparently bewitched by the scene outside. The rain had not yet started falling, but the wind had picked up, sending the summertime dust spinning.

"Good afternoon," Masha said, closing the door quietly behind her. Gluzman turned to face her, and she jumped in fright. The professor's eyes looked completely empty, and terrifying.

"Hi!" he said, and smiled ghoulishly, showing his snow-white dentures.

Masha had to force herself to smile back. Did this transfigured Gluzman even recognize her?

"Dr. Gluzman," she began cautiously. "I'm Masha, Innokenty's friend." He nodded. "Last time we were here, we talked about Heavenly Jerusalem. Do you remember? You were right. He truly is killing people he thinks are sinners in places connected with the City of Heaven. But I can't figure out what pattern he's following. Until I understand his numbering system, we won't be able to catch him." She stopped, waiting for the professor's response.

Gluzman suddenly leered at her, and he beckoned her closer with one finger. Masha cautiously stepped forward and bent over him. She heard a quiet giggle.

"I wonder . . ." The professor's whisper tickled her ear. "What sort of sexual fantasies do you think Inno-centi has about you?"

Masha jumped back. "Dr. Gluzman, Innokenty and I have been friends since we were little!"

Gluzman cackled again, leaning back in his wheelchair. "Oh, of course, a childhood friendship! That blameless little flower, which often conceals a monstrosity!" Gluzman's eyes were no longer empty. Instead there was madness boiling up behind them, gathering force. Masha tried to retreat to the door, but he rolled himself forward, slowly but steadily, still holding her gaze and cackling frightfully.

"And what sort of fantasies do you have, my lady?" His voice sounded smooth, almost gentle. "Or has your generation suffered a castration of the imagination? No elementary logic, no intellect!" Gluzman's voice was rising. "I've never seen anyone so stupid!" he shouted.

But Masha was shoving the door open, and there were nurses and aides rushing in—they must have been standing outside at the ready. *They probably have security cameras everywhere,* Masha thought, feeling at a strange distance from events, as though this were all a bad dream.

She watched the medical staff restrain Gluzman. A nurse tried to guide a needle into his vein while the professor worked his way up to a howl, never taking his terrible gaze off of her.

"The Torments!" Gluzman was shouting.

And Masha, as if awakening from her dream, finally bolted out of the room and ran down the hall.

"The Torments!" he wailed after her. "Wallow not in fornication, but rather pay the tolls for your sins!"

Though her hands were shaking badly, Masha managed to unlock the car. She slammed the door and sat there awhile, trying to catch her breath as the first rumblings of thunder heralded rain that soon drummed on her roof and windows. Masha closed her eyes. Gluzman was the second man in twenty-four hours to call her an idiot. *That must be some kind of record,* she thought. They were probably right. And her boss had called her sick—he was probably right about that, too. But maybe it took a sick person to understand a serial killer. Masha could imagine things that Andrey's mentally healthy, experienced detective brain simply could not. She could take an excursion down the dark paths of another person's madness, and search him out there, even if she ended up in the room next to Gluzman's as a result. She had to do this. She had no choice. Otherwise, all her suffering over Papa's death would have been in vain.

Calmer now, Masha pulled her hair into a ponytail and sped off through the driving summer rain. If she had turned around, she would have seen Gluzman silhouetted in the window, swaddled like a baby, sadly watching her go.

❖

Masha's turn came, and she handed the reference librarian her request slips.

"I'd like to see everything you have on medieval Russian literature, especially the source texts themselves."

The librarian looked up at her. "The originals have to stay in the reading room."

"That's fine."

The librarian nodded. "What about schismatic texts? Do those interest you?"

"Probably," said Masha, uncertainly. "Of course, they're out of date now."

"Well, all medieval texts are 'out of date,' aren't they?" noted the librarian. "But before the revolution, those Old Believers made up thirty percent of the population. They're still around today."

Masha lifted her tired eyes. "Really? I always thought they were history."

The librarian snorted.

"I'll take those, too, please," Masha said.

She found a place to sit alongside some scholarly looking women with old-fashioned hairdos, and settled in for a long wait. Someone tapped her on the shoulder and Masha's head jerked—she'd nodded off. The librarian was stacking a pile of books on the table. Zachariasz Kopysteński's *Book on Faith*. A Book of Hours. And there were more . . .

Masha signed for them mechanically, and the librarian walked away, shooting her one last pitying look. She must have taken Masha for a beleaguered graduate student. Masha wiped her eyes determinedly and read the title of the first book in the pile.

Was she still sleeping? The reading room seemed to spin under her feet.

ANDREY

Andrey didn't notice twilight falling over the city after the thunderstorm. Petrovka had gradually emptied out, the telephones were no longer ringing—it was the best time of day for workaholics. There, in the silence, it was easier to think, easier to analyze the lab reports and interview transcripts that had arrived over the course of the day. Andrey sighed, stretched, and opened a window, letting in a gust of rain-cooled air. He put the kettle on. It was already beginning to boil when the preparation of Andrey's signature brew—a shot of yesterday's tea in yesterday's cup, with one cube of sugar—was interrupted by a telephone call.

"Yakovlev," he answered, adding fresh water to his not-so-fresh cup.

"Hello, good evening, Captain," came Innokenty's voice, nauseatingly polite. "I'm very sorry to disturb you, but I'm worried about Masha."

Andrey slowly put his cup down on a pile of paperwork. "Oh yeah?"

"Were you able to reach her?"

"No," he said.

"I called all day, too, but she hasn't picked up. It's probably nothing—she's always leaving her phone somewhere or forgetting to charge it. But as you noted this morning, given what's been going on . . . And since the anniversary is this week, and I—" Innokenty stopped and cleared his throat. "I mean, we, her family and friends, try not to let her out of our sight for long this time of year."

"What anniversary?" Andrey asked, a nasty feeling of dread creeping across the back of his neck.

Innokenty paused. "Masha probably wouldn't want me to tell you, but I think you should know. Masha's father was Karavay, the famous defense attorney. He was murdered when Masha was twelve. She's the one who found the body."

Andrey sat down. "Fuck me," he said.

"Excuse me?"

"Sorry. I've gotta go." Andrey dropped the phone and stood up quickly, almost knocking over his teacup. He just managed to grab his jacket on his way out the door.

He could tolerate the feeling of guilt while he was running down the stairs and pulling out of his parking spot. But it became unbearable as soon as he hit the eternal Moscow traffic jam. Once his car was firmly lodged up against the back end of some sort of SUV, Andrey noticed that he was clenching his jaw to keep from roaring in anger as the rage and self-loathing overtook him. His inner masochist was forcing him to relive the details of his drunken outburst and Masha's silent departure, over and over again. He punched the steering wheel, which responded with a loud honk. The Jeep ahead of him stood stock still, like some sort of monument to the American auto industry. Andrey turned the wheel sharply and pulled out onto the shoulder. There must be a metro station somewhere around here.

He would take the train to Masha's place, just to be going somewhere, just to be moving toward his own possible absolution.

MASHA

The Torments, or St. Theodora's Journey Through the Tollhouses read the cover. This one was a reprint. The foreword maintained that, thanks to the intervention of a lay monk named Grigory, a ninth-century nun named Theodora had conveyed the story of her own death—a tale of the agonies of hell and the blessings of heaven. But most important of all was this: in her revelation to Grigory, Theodora described how she passed through twenty stations of torment, which she called aerial tollhouses, and was tried for her sins at each one. In Greek and Russian Orthodox literature, *The Torments* was the most complete and lively description of the transition from temporal life to eternal destiny. *And so,* Masha read, as everything inside her trembled (she was so close now, she could reach out and touch the killer), *after death the human soul, guided by angels, ascends a divine ladder past a series of tollhouses. At each stop, the soul is beset by evil demons called the Torments.*

She remembered Gluzman shouting at her, *The Torments! Wallow not in fornication, but rather pay the tolls for your sins!*

She continued to read. *At each tollhouse, the Torments put the soul on trial for its sins. The souls of the righteous are saved, but the demons spear the sinners on their flaming lances and carry them into the everlasting darkness.* The foreword noted that the poet Batyushkov had called this journey an "epic of death," designed to terrify the medieval reader. Well, Batyushkov could go to hell, she didn't have time for him. Masha flipped impatiently through the introduction and started in hungrily on the main text.

And then came Death, roaring like a lion; its appearance was a terrible sight . . . Masha scanned the pages quickly, feeling like she might be sick. *As we rose from the earth to the heights of heaven, we were soon met by the spirits of the first Torment, where souls are tried for the sins of Idle Speech; that is, for speaking without thought or without need, or uttering what is vile and shameless.*

He couldn't ever shut up, she heard Slava's girlfriend complain. *Not even in bed!*

Masha pulled out her notebook and began sketching a new table. *Torment 1: Idle Speech. Who: Slava Ovechkin. Where: Bersenevskaya Waterfront. Connection to Heavenly Jerusalem: Tsar's Gardens (Garden of Gethsemane).*

She turned back to the book. *Thence we ascended and drew near the second tollhouse, where I underwent the Torment of Falsehood. Here I was tried for every false word: failure to keep oaths, the use of God's name in vain, and false testimony.*

She went for it, all in, said the exhausted mother, the pink stroller swimming before Masha's eyes. *She even testified in court—*

Masha swallowed. *We reached then the third tollhouse, the Torment of Denunciation and Slander.* She remembered Snegurov's recorded voice: *The packet wasn't mine* . . . *But I know someone who could have benefited from making me look bad, who could have tipped off the press, who could have planted the packet, no problem.*

She kept reading. *We reached the fourth tollhouse, for Gluttony, and evil spirits immediately rushed forth to meet us. Their faces resembled those of sensuous gluttons and despicable drunkards.*

Kolyan, wrote Masha. *Kutafya Tower. Church of the Holy Sepulchre.*

As we conversed, we reached the tollhouse of Sloth, where sinners are tried for all those days and hours they have spent in idleness. Here, too, are detained the parasites who did no work themselves, but rather lived off the labor of others, and men hired to work who took their wages with no regard to the performance of the tasks which they had undertaken.

Masha had to think about that one. Then she remembered the address: Lenivka Street, which even *sounded* like "Lazy Street." The Jaffa Gate, the western gates of Jerusalem. Gebelai! A hired architect who took his wages with no regard to the performance of the tasks which he had undertaken.

As her chart filled up, it began to take on a horrifying clarity. There was the seventh tollhouse, for Avarice, and the eighth, featuring the Torment for Usury, where *there stand accused those who gain riches by the ill use of their neighbors, the bribe collectors, and those who take what belongs to others.* The all-powerful governor's wife could fit either of those. It went on and on. Theft. Murder. Pride. Disrespect for one's elders. Envy. Masha's hand shook as she wrote Katya's name. The Moskva River . . . the Jordan. Lubyansky Drive . . . the Mount of Olives. Masha's cheeks were burning, and her pen flew over the paper. She was on his trail, and running fast.

The dark shadow was just up ahead, leading her to a meeting place known only to the Sin Collector himself.

ANDREY

Andrey sat outside Masha's building, looking uneasily between the dark sky and the street where, he hoped, Masha would appear. Her mother, whose dinner he had interrupted an hour ago, had looked him over appraisingly from head to toe and then told him her daughter was out. Judging by the reduced collection of books in her room, she was probably at the library, she'd said. No, she didn't know which library. Yes, Masha had left her cell phone at home again. Andrey had already called Innokenty to reassure him. He kept his tone very official as he reported that Masha had left her phone at home and was probably just slaving away over some books. But he'd also called to make sure she wasn't at his place. Innokenty had thanked him for calling. Masha wasn't there. That news was slightly reassuring.

Finally, a car drove up, and Intern Karavay climbed out. Andrey hopped off his bench and ran up to her, without any real idea what he was going to say. Masha didn't seem surprised to see him. She only nodded. Andrey suddenly noticed the dark circles under her eyes, and sympathy won out over the shame that had been eating him up inside the whole day. He wanted to grab her, hold her close, tell her everything would be okay, that they would catch the bad guy. He stuffed his hands deeper into his pockets to stop himself.

"It's good that you're here," said Masha coldly. "I have something new on our investigation. And I think—"

"Hang on a second," Andrey said, feeling the sweat drip down the back of his neck. "I came to tell you I'm sorry. I was rude yesterday, and I didn't have any reason to be. I mean"—he ran a hand over his buzzed head and laughed sadly—"there is a reason. You really piss me off."

Masha's face went hard, and her eyes dropped. Andrey hurried to explain.

"I really like you. But probably the pissing-off part is . . . bigger. Because I also *like* you. You're out of my league, I know—don't think I don't get that. Innokenty would say we're from different worlds or something—"

"Stop," said Masha, her voice quiet.

"No. Let me finish. I like you. I want—well, everything about you. But there's nothing between us and there can't be, can there? That's why I'm going crazy!"

Masha broke into a grin. Andrey barely had time to be offended before her arms were around his neck, and she was kissing him, his forehead, his eyes, his cheeks, and saying, "God, you're such a dummy! I'm serious, has there ever been anyone dumber?" He stood there for a moment in shock, then finally took her face in his hands and kissed her.

The last thing that flashed through Andrey's mind, before he stopped thinking altogether, was how nice it was, after all, that they were the same height.

MASHA

The two of them were perched on a low windowsill in the stairwell of Masha's building. Her notebook was open on her lap, and she was completely happy.

Just the day previous, Masha had thought she would never be able to go back to Petrovka, not after that bucket of scorn Andrey had dumped on her in the café. The pain she felt had finally made her understand that she was head over heels in love with this denim-clad detective with the everyday blue eyes.

But that meant nothing, she had told herself. Her own stupid feelings weren't important. The only thing that mattered was the killer roaming Moscow, seeing Heavenly Jerusalem everywhere he looked. She had almost managed to convince herself. But then when she'd seen Andrey outside her building, her heart had seemed to beat everywhere in her body at once. And then, when they'd kissed, first standing there outside, then sitting on the bench, long enough for their eyes to go cloudy and their lips to be rubbed raw . . . And then when he'd pulled her head gently down onto his shoulder, and they'd sat there side by side . . .

The downstairs neighbor had finally broken things up when he came out to walk his enormous Newfoundland. The dog adored Masha and had no idea he should be discreet. The abashed neighbor had tried to pull the beast away, purposefully averting his eyes, but Masha had laughed and petted the dog's shaggy head. Neither of them had felt like talking about the murderer, but they knew they had to, so they'd decided to hold an impromptu work meeting there at the third-floor window.

"So you like dogs?" Andrey had asked as they'd climbed the stairs.

"I love them," Masha said. "Why?"

"I have one for you to meet. Name of Marilyn Monroe."

"A girl?"

"No, a boy. And cocky, too. You'll have to take a tough line with him when you, um, come see my place." And he'd smiled such a bashful, happy smile that Masha had felt like kissing him again, but she'd decided to control herself.

"So. I figured out the numbers," she now told him, flipping to the new chart. "And surprise, surprise, it's totally medieval. It turns out there's an Orthodox text called *The Torments, or St. Theodora's Journey Through the Tollhouses*. Remember how Kenty mentioned that the concept of purgatory was only accepted by Catholics?"

Andrey rolled his eyes, and Masha poked him in the ribs.

"Stop it! This is important for understanding the criminal's mind. It turns out that these tollhouses are the only way for Orthodox Christians to atone for their sins."

"How's that?" asked Andrey.

"At each tollhouse, the soul is tried for everything it ever did, said, and thought. Finally, it gets sentenced either to heaven or to hell. Here, look." She handed Andrey the notebook. "It all fits! These Torments are our Sin Collector's manual, and Moscow is his New Jerusalem, where no sinful souls should be allowed to live! He's already up to the fifteenth tollhouse. Read this."

"'We passed the fifteenth Torment: Magic, Sorcery, Poisoning, and the Summoning of Demons.'"

"That's Adelaide, the psychic eaten by ants!"

"Super," Andrey said glumly. "How many are left?"

"Five," Masha answered quietly.

ANDREY

They didn't have to wait long. Artyom Minayev had been torn in half between two trees near the Florus and Laurus Church, close to the former site of the Myasnitsky Gate. While they were getting the corpse down out of the trees, Andrey pondered the logistical difficulties. The killer had to choose trees with two important qualities: not old enough to break, and not young enough to stay bent under the weight of the body. Minayev wasn't a big guy, maybe one hundred thirty pounds, and it occurred to Andrey that the sinner's size might have been decisive in attracting the Sin Collector's attention.

There was no doubt that the victim had, in fact, sinned. Only the most serious tollhouses were left now, where the demons interrogated their captives for bigger transgressions than verbal diarrhea. But as terrible as Minayev's sins might have been, Andrey couldn't think of a single crime bad enough to justify getting torn apart alive.

As he climbed the stairs to Minayev's apartment, he noticed the frightened but curious faces of two little boys peeking out from a doorway one floor below. An unsteady female voice called from inside, and the small faces disappeared behind the upholstered door. Andrey made a mental note to have a talk with them afterward. Kids that age notice everything.

Minayev's place was a typical bachelor pad. Maybe a little tidier than most, Andrey had to admit, thinking of his own mess and vowing to clean soon. After all, he might be getting a visit from one Masha Karavay—something he still couldn't quite believe. Minayev's refrigerator held just enough to feed one person a basic lunch and dinner for two days, so he probably hadn't been expecting company. A plate with the remnants of some smoked fish from the night before was sitting in the living room, stinking up the whole place. But Andrey agreed with the forensics guys: he'd smelled worse. He took a slow stroll through the room.

Nothing much, just an imposingly big computer with a separate hard drive. Cartoon fish swam lazily across the big screen. Andrey gave the forensics expert nearby a questioning look and got a nod in response. He touched the mouse, and the screen came to life. A video window was open on the desktop. Andrey clicked "Play."

Music started up, a rhythmic, thumping beat, and the action on the screen was rhythmic, too. Andrey was soon surrounded by curious colleagues. It was obvious from the first frame that it was porn, but the man standing with his back—and thrusting buttocks—to the camera seemed strangely large compared to his partner. When the camera moved, someone next to Andrey gasped.

"But that's just a kid!"

Andrey rushed to click "Pause." The boy's face looked strangely familiar, and Andrey tried to will away his nausea. It was one of the kids downstairs. He minimized the window and spotted two more behind it with the same sort of content.

As he saved them onto a flash drive, he noticed that each video lasted eighteen minutes. What had Masha said yesterday? They were past the fifteenth tollhouse. He didn't want to tell her about this. But he knew that he'd have to eventually, so it might as well be now. Besides, he needed to consult her and the neat table in her notebook.

"Hey!" breathed Masha into the phone, in such a sleepy, gentle voice Andrey couldn't help smiling. His whole heart felt warmer. Maybe he hadn't been dreaming? Maybe everything that happened yesterday was real.

"Hi!" he answered, already regretting his next words. "We have another body. At Myasnitsky Gate."

Masha took a sharp breath.

"Could you tell me again what the sixteenth tollhouse is supposed to be?"

There was a rustling of paper. "The Torment of Fornication. Inappropriate dreams or thoughts, lustful touches. Does that fit?"

"Yeah," said Andrey, "but not completely. What's the seventeenth?"

"Adultery, rape," read Masha in her honor-student voice.

"Go on," said Andrey.

"How many bodies do you have there?" she marveled, but obediently kept reading. "Eighteen is the tollhouse of Sodomitic Sins: miscegenation, masturbation, bestiality, and sins horrible and unnatural."

"There!" declared Andrey. "That's the one."

"But that means—"

"That means he skipped two victims, or we missed them," Andrey confirmed.

"I'll be right there," Masha said. "What's the address?"

"You can't tell Mama," said Petya, the younger of the two boys. The older one had scowled with worry when Andrey told him Minayev was dead, and run off into the apartment.

"I won't," Andrey promised, and he meant it.

"Mama drinks. She's not an alcoholic. It's just because of the divorce is all. Papa left her the apartment," the little boy told him, in a very dignified tone of voice. "And the car. But she sold the car," he said, wrinkling his nose. "It was such a cool car! A Hyundai, with a really big engine!"

The apartment had been nice at one point, but a dozen small details—darker patches on the faded wallpaper where pictures must have hung, an awkward empty space on the TV shelf—made it clear that this household was not as well-off as it once had been.

"Tell me about Minayev," he asked Petya.

"He's Kolya's best friend. Mine, too!" the little boy told him proudly. He wrinkled his nose again when he corrected himself. "*Was* our best friend. Kolya used to go watch movies at his place and he gave him books about ninjas. They're these Japanese guys."

Andrey smiled. "Yeah, I know."

"He gave us food, too! Mama forgets to buy groceries sometimes," he said with a disarming grin. "We hid it. It was fun. And we went to the planetarium one day, too. Kolya and him were friends. He went over there every day."

"What about yesterday?" Andrey asked, trying not to react to the idea of "friendship" between Minayev and Kolya.

"Then, too. He left us some food, and Kolya said he had to go say thank-you. He didn't take me with him. But I ate all the candy, see?" Petya pulled a handful of brightly colored wrappers out of his pocket.

"I need to talk with your brother," Andrey said, standing up.

"But he doesn't want to!" objected Petya.

"It's okay, I need to try, anyway," Andrey told him.

"Kolya!" called Petya, running off toward the kitchen, and Andrey heard a muffled conversation coming from behind the door.

Andrey walked into the kitchen himself, and found a woman with red eyes and matted hair spreading butter on slices of bread, which she followed, for some reason, with a layer of mayonnaise.

"You stay away from my kids," she told Andrey, assaulting him with the stale booze on her breath. "He says he doesn't know anything!"

Andrey paid her no attention. "Kolya?" he coaxed. "I just want to ask you one question: What did you see yesterday evening? You need to tell me so we can find out who killed your neighbor."

Kolya turned silently to the window.

"I said go!" The mother pushed him toward the door. "Get out! Go figure it out yourself!"

Andrey turned and left. He could have insisted on interviewing the kid, but the idea made his heart ache, and besides, he was ashamed. Ashamed that nobody had identified the pedophile earlier, but even more ashamed that this was the kind of shitty world where a predator could be a lonely child's only friend. Andrey walked outside and smoked a cigarette, thinking Masha should be there any minute.

The door banged behind him, and Kolya ran out, probably hurrying off to school. Andrey watched him carefully as he passed by, went maybe twenty steps, then turned around and ran back.

"I didn't see anyone," Kolya said. "But I heard something. The voice was, like, thin. He was saying something weird. Kind of in Russian, but I couldn't understand it really."

"Can you try to remember?" asked Andrey.

Kolya frowned. "Something about demons in dirt and stench. Do you know what *stench* means?"

Andrey nodded. "Yeah. It's a bad smell."

"Ah." Kolya nodded. "Like it stinks?"

"Something like that. Do you think you could recognize that voice if you heard it again?"

Kolya, serious, nodded again. "Oh yeah. It was really squealy, like somebody was hurting him. Okay, bye, I'm gonna be late to school!"

Andrey watched the little figure run off. He probably needed a therapist more than he needed school. Andrey made a note to put a social worker on the case.

When Masha drove up, Andrey opened her car door to help her out, then pulled her close. They stood that way, pressed up against each other's bodies in an attempt to share the last bit of heat they could muster. But somehow they both felt colder every minute. The problem wasn't the execution methods, or how merciless the killer was proving to be. The problem was that the further they pursued the Sin Collector, the more horrible the whole world seemed.

MASHA

Masha took a visual survey of the men Anyutin had assigned to help them. They had a team now, the Sin Collector Investigative Group, but Masha still hadn't shaken her fear that these skeptical detectives would laugh her out of the office. So she'd asked Andrey to brief them on Heavenly Jerusalem. As he laid it out, all the crazy details somehow fell into place, and nobody so much as raised a doubting eyebrow. Some of the men even took notes, which made Masha a little embarrassed. It scared her, too. It was as if, before the name was official, before they had this team dedicated to hunting him down, the Sin Collector had existed solely in Masha's imagination, regardless of his all-too-real crimes. *Like a vampire, or the Abominable Snowman,* Masha thought. If one person sees Bigfoot, they're nuts. But when a big group of serious men at Petrovka take out their legal pads, it's the real deal.

"I believe," Andrey was saying, "that we need to go back to the first victims. If even one of them knew the suspect personally, they might have inspired the whole series of killings. Let's look more closely at Dobroslav Ovechkin. His father was a preacher at the Old Believer church at Basmanny. And the story of the tollhouses, as I'm sure you know"—Andrey smirked, because he was pretty sure nobody in the room had ever heard of it—"is an Old Believer text. They're zealots. You've heard the stories." Andrey paused, catching Masha's wry look.

"And now," Andrey continued, gesturing grandly like a ringmaster announcing the next act, "Intern Maria Karavay will brief us about her profiling of the suspect."

Masha clutched her notes nervously. Her voice shook a bit as she spoke.

"I'm passing around copies of a table with geographical locations corresponding to these murders. We have an outside consultant working on this for us, a historian. He's listed locations we've already identified with certainty and other sites with potential, too, because we may have missed a few victims, and we also have to assume our suspect plans to keep killing. The second page contains some information that might help us understand the suspect. He is a serial killer, apparently highly organized. As you know, this type is characterized by their self-control. They have a clear plan for stalking and seducing their victims."

Masha paused and swallowed. The detectives were still listening attentively.

"If a plan breaks down, this killer is capable of putting off his crime for another day. He acts in socially appropriate ways. He's likely to live with a partner, but in his domestic life, he may be unstable or violent. Geographically, he's mobile. He follows the news. He returns to the scene of the crime to check on the progress the police are making. He probably drives a big car that he uses to move bodies."

She stopped to catch her breath and steal a look at Andrey. He was standing against a wall, looking at her with undisguised tenderness and a pride that was almost paternal. Masha barely restrained herself from grinning back at him. Instead, she looked over the rest of the men sitting before her.

"I'd like to talk over every point of this profile with you. You might see something we missed."

"Is this really supposed to help?" A young man stood up. "Gerasimov," he introduced himself. "Who cares about the homicidal triad or whatever it's called? What difference does it make whether the guy wet the bed as a child? Seriously, that's just intellectual masturbation. It's a bunch of foreign baloney."

Andrey had already straightened up to come to Masha's defense, but she beat him to the punch.

"If the psychological model is a match, it will help us identify the perpetrator, and even if it doesn't, it can at least help us strike some suspects off the list. Think of how many people the police arrested on false leads before they caught Chikatilo."

"Our own researchers don't think profiling is a bad idea, and you wouldn't talk to them like that," a gray-haired detective added, frowning at the young man. "Go on, miss."

"The Sin Collector is a maniacal missionary." Masha looked around the room again. "He chooses his victims carefully, because for him, it's not the murder itself that's important, but the message it sends to humankind. So. Let's start with general personality characteristics. What can you add, based on how these incidents occurred?"

"He's pedantic," Andrey said, starting them off.

Masha thanked him with her eyes.

"Elaborate executions like these require all sorts of preparation, so he must he highly organized, as you said," the gray-haired detective chimed in.

"He takes charge at the scene of his crimes, because he's frustrated with his life?" added Fomin, a freckled red-haired guy to his left.

"No," Masha objected. "This isn't frustration. It's more like control. Control over sin and retribution for sins."

"Like he's playing God?"

"No," said Masha, shaking her head. "He doesn't see himself as God. He's playing a demon, a toll collector. So he doesn't think he's free of sin himself." Masha suddenly fell silent. She met Andrey's gaze and could tell he was having the same thought.

"Maybe he's done time?" Andrey suggested. "Is that where he gets his insider knowledge of law enforcement? Plus, he knows Yelnik, and he's cruel."

Masha nodded. She would need to think that over some more, play with it in her head. She went on.

"Now, what about habits? Skills? Any ideas?"

"He probably keeps his house and his car superclean. Sterile. Because he's so hung up on cleanliness and purity, in every sense," suggested Gerasimov.

Masha nodded, surprised that the young man had come around so quickly. "I agree."

Now other members of the group were offering ideas.

"He knows police work inside and out, seeing as he never leaves tracks."

"He's strong. Otherwise how could he have quartered that woman?"

"He's probably middle aged, say between forty and fifty-five. Confident, knowledgeable. People trust him."

"Where does he live?" asked Masha, then answered her own question. "He's got a very clear kill radius, the old Bely Gorod fortress walls, which is the Boulevard Ring Road today. He only leaves bodies there, in the middle of downtown. But as you all know, his choice of victims and crime scenes is based on the religious pattern we've identified, not convenience. Still, seeing how well he knows the area, it seems to me that our suspect lives and probably works downtown."

"What about education?" Andrey reminded her.

"Definitely a higher degree. Above-average intelligence. As for profession"—Masha cast a glance at her notes—"his job probably involves decision-making, something where he can be confident that he never makes mistakes. There are several occupations that would give him a feeling of absolute power . . ."

"A teacher!" called Gerasimov, like the troublemaker in the back of the classroom.

"Physicist or mathematician."

"No, a historian!"

"Maybe a doctor?" suggested Fomin. "A surgeon! He knows how to dismember people."

"A crusty old general who doesn't know the meaning of love and is used to making everyone else follow orders."

Andrey raised a hand to settle them down. "I think there's a good probability that he works in criminal justice or defense."

The men looked doubtful. And frightened. "One of us? For real?" they murmured.

"He got to the governor's wife too easily, and other powerful people, too," said Andrey, almost as if he were talking to himself. "We don't have enough clues. Actually, we don't have any. Everything is circumstantial. Maybe he has a blue car. Maybe he has a high voice."

"About that, I don't think he does," said Masha, frowning. "I think he's reciting things from the tollhouse story to his victims before they die. But that's part of his signature. When he's in the middle of the ritual, he might feel like another person. Or," she corrected herself, "a demon. And if he thinks that demons whine and howl, that means he'd naturally make his own voice higher, too."

ANDREY

Andrey left Gerasimov waiting at the bulletin board outside and walked into the church on Basmanny. Masha had told him this temple was new. But as far as Andrey could tell, there was no difference. It had the same golden onion dome, the same bell tower, the same whitewashed walls.

But he only made it two steps onto church grounds before his way was blocked by a bearded man in a dull-gray suit and a shirt out of Russian folklore. The man asked him, in a formal but perfectly courteous voice, who he was. *Understandable,* thought Andrey. Compared to the Old Believers, after all, he probably looked suspicious, clean shaven and strange. Andrey showed him his badge, and the bearded man, nodding curtly, suggested they go have a chat next door.

Andrey was surprised to learn that there was an Old Believer-style café right there next to the church, and he looked around curiously when they got inside. The decor included brick walls, simple tables with dark-wooden benches, and an icon of the Virgin Mary on the wall.

The bearded man closed and locked the door, then sat down across from his uninvited guest at a corner table.

"I am Yakov."

Yakov's eyes looked like nails pounded deep under his bony brow. "Ovechkin is not at the church right now. But I am in charge of the café and the souvenir stand. Perhaps I might be of assistance?"

Andrey glanced again around the dim room, which smelled maybe just a little like incense. He had been hungry all morning, and couldn't help asking his host, "What kind of food do you serve here?"

Yakov smiled behind his beard and apologized that the café was closed for the beginning of the week and there was nothing he could offer. But other days, people could eat here for a reasonable price, and find food that didn't violate any religious strictures. No meat or dairy during Lent, of course, but the rest of the year they served traditional food. Meat pies, cabbage soup, *lapshennik* . . .

Andrey nodded, and although he had never heard of *lapshennik*, he felt even hungrier than before.

"Let me tell you what I came for," he said, afraid his stomach might growl. Yakov tilted his head to one side, ready to listen. "We have a particular suspect we're working on. We think he might be connected to the Old Believers."

Yakov winced. "You believe your suspect is a member of our community? Could I ask on what basis you ground this belief?"

"No." The refusal sounded harsh, but Andrey didn't want to get into the whole Jerusalem mess. "We're thinking a middle-aged man, physically strong, well educated. A doctor, teacher, soldier, or"—Andrey smiled wryly—"a police officer. Most likely drives a dark-blue automobile. I'd appreciate it if you could let me know if any of your parishioners meet that description. Especially ones with a tendency for fanaticism."

Yakov sighed and frowned. "You have come here because you are under the impression that Old Believers are religious fanatics. Is that so?"

Andrey didn't answer.

Yakov held the awkward silence, drumming his neatly clipped fingernails against the dark-wooden tabletop.

"You know," he began, "in the nineteen seventies, Soviet geologists stumbled upon a plot of potatoes growing deep in the taiga. The Old Believers who cultivated that field had lived there for fifty years completely cut off from the rest of the secular world. They missed everything about this modern world, but they never felt as if they were missing a thing. For me, being in the family—and that is what we call ourselves, a family—is akin to that plot of potatoes. A glimmer of civilization in the dark wild, where the dangerous beasts go creeping. If this suspect of yours has committed a terrible sin . . ." He stopped and peered at Andrey with his small, sharp eyes. "That means he has not come to terms with the beast. He is reacting against it. That beast, that human beast, frightens him. We have been taught to be frightened. Do you understand? All around us the world has been changing, ever since 1666, that diabolical year of our schism with the tyrants and religious innovators. All of these present-day reality shows of yours, these vulgar faces, the naked bodies splashed sinfully across millions of screens in every home, are no more dangerous to us than the medieval, tsarist, or Communist commissars with their heretical new ideas. Our community has seen this all before. They burned our homes down around us, but *we* never responded in kind, you see. All we have done is held to our own."

"So you don't ever get new converts?" Andrey asked skeptically.

"Some do search us out," Yakov admitted. "But they are people looking for their roots. As much as Russia has suffered, as much as people's souls have been made to twist and turn in the wind, our minds sent spinning in different directions, turning now to communism, now to the blossoming of capitalism . . ." Yakov shook his head sadly. "Yet still, there are young people who wish to retreat into the depths of tradition. There is nobody deeper in tradition than the Old Believers. You know yourself that the Russian people are beset with rot. Everything here is as rotten as the rod they use to beat us. Just think! In all of history, only once have the Russian people said no to the state, no to the tyrants. Our people kept hold of their dignity through all the persecution, the executions, the torture. We have survived for four centuries now. And look what sort of blindness the Lord has sent down to curse us! Ours is a history full of hardship and miraculous courage, but nobody sees anything other than religious obsession!"

Yakov thumped the table with his fist, then suddenly calmed down again and stroked his beard. "Go with God, and do not look for your fanatic among the Old Believers. None of us have picked up the sword, not for a long time. We ensconce ourselves in our cells or we leave this life. That is our way."

"So nobody is crusading for purity? You never get anyone who wants to, you know, clean up this rotten country?" Andrey pressed.

"You, young man," Yakov told him quietly, "have forgotten the meaning of the word *dignity*. But I do not blame you. Forgetfulness has become a national trait." He turned to face the icon on the wall.

Andrey stood up and said good-bye to his bearded informant. Yakov hadn't convinced him of anything, and obviously, if Andrey wanted some insight into the church, he'd have to find a different source. He stopped outside for a cigarette. The night before last, sitting on that windowsill in the warm circle of his arm, Masha had told him that these schismatics did not smoke, didn't even drink coffee or tea, much less anything alcoholic. She knew that thanks to Kenty, who had imprinted her since childhood with his tales of the Old Believers. "They used to keep a full bottle of vodka at home," Masha had relayed. "Just to show that the man of the house didn't drink."

That would have been a good choice in Andrey's own home growing up, he thought. Maybe his father would have lasted a little longer. There were other families that could have benefited, too. The pale little faces of Petya and Kolya flashed before his eyes.

Suddenly his cigarette tasted bitter. He tossed it into a trash can nearby.

INNOKENTY

Innokenty couldn't resist. He unwrapped the soft linen cloth and carefully lifted up the little board. Time had darkened its color, and hundreds of hands over the centuries had polished it to a shine. He ran his fingers over one uneven edge, covered in darker scorch marks. Maybe the icon had been rescued from a burning cabin, the most valuable thing in the home. It needed some serious restoration, but he could see the thin face peering out, as if from the depths of a forest lake. St. Nicholas, the Wonderworker. The saint's left hand pressed a Bible to his chest, but where his right hand should be, the whole surface layer of the piece was missing. Kenty could only guess which sign of the cross the thin hand would have been making: one with two fingers, Old Believer style? Or with three?

"Vandals!" whispered Innokenty. Were the marauders from the twentieth century or the eighteenth?

He decided he wouldn't restore that part. Let it stay the way it was, as a memorial to intolerance. But he would ask Danechka to work on the face. For an icon painter, he was young, but he'd already earned an excellent reputation among antiquarians. Even aside from his devotion to his work, it was fair to say that Danechka did not truly belong to this world. His skin was clear of adolescent blemishes, and long blond lashes framed the light-blue eyes that only came alive when they encountered icons like this one.

Innokenty looked again at the Wonderworker's face and sat still, mesmerized, for a few minutes. These figures had enchanted him ever since he was little. Every element was intentional. The high forehead, the perfectly spaced brows, the fish-shaped eyes (the fish, of course, a symbol of Christ). The narrow, elegant nose, the surprisingly full lips hidden in the woolly beard, the thinnest possible spiraling line drawn to represent every individual curl. And those eyes looking at the viewer sternly, dispassionately.

Kenty's thoughts were interrupted by the doorbell. He shuddered, then put the icon aside. At the door stood his father, a broad-shouldered man of fifty, seemingly enormous in his long dark coat. His beard was black with a sprinkling of gray, and though it was short, it came up almost to his eyes. A healthy, youthful blush lent color to his cheeks, and his sharp eyes regarded Innokenty with something like a squint. This massive individual ushered in his companion, a man much shorter and more slightly built, with a long beard gone almost completely gray, then shut the door behind them both. Only then did he offer his hand to Innokenty to shake. It was enormous, practically a shovel.

"Hello, son!" He glanced respectfully at the older man. "You've met the head of the diocese."

Innokenty gave a slight bow to the old priest, standing calmly at his father's side. "Could I offer you some tea?" he asked, but then corrected himself. "Herbal, of course?"

The older man nodded. He looked around dispassionately, his heavy eyelids half-lowered, letting his gaze wander silently down the hallway and over the dark icons on the white walls, then contemplating the designer lamp, a waterfall of crystal droplets. Innokenty's luxurious surroundings embarrassed him now, and he noticed how his father's lips tightened, although the old priest's face remained impassive.

Kenty sat his guests at the kitchen table and bustled about. He ran boiling water into a white ceramic teakettle to warm it, then

wiped it dry and filled it with a fruity brew that was not techni-
cally tea. All the while, the question plagued him: Why had they
come? His parents hardly ever visited him, and a prestigious visitor
such as this priest was unprecedented. Why had his father brought
the man? Innokenty answered his own question: it was the other
way around. His father was here at the whim of the single-most-
important figure in the Old Believer community, which meant the
reason for their visit must also be of singular importance. But what
was it? Kenty poured the bright-red, aromatic brew into their cups,
smiling mechanically.

"Your young lady," his father began, and a shiver ran down
Innokenty's spine, nearly making him splash tea on the tablecloth. "The
one you've been shadowing all these years—"

"Masha?"

It was not really a question. Had he ever been anyone else's shadow?

Innokenty put the tea kettle neatly back in its place as two pairs of
eyes watched him closely.

"Maria Karavay," the head of the diocese affirmed, his voice soft.
He paused and pursed his lips like a peasant to blow on his hot tea.
"She seems to be leading a group of detectives from Petrovka looking for some sort of serial killer. Today they came to the church on
Basmanny to ask questions. Yakov spoke with one of them. But we
know full well that these people are going to keep sniffing around,
and that will not do us any good. On the contrary." The old man
looked up from his teacup. His swollen eyelids had suddenly lost their
sleepy look, and his eyes were bigger now, drawing Kenty in with a
gaze that was young and sharp. "On the contrary, this will only bring
us misfortune."

"It is your duty to protect your own, Innokenty," his father added.
"These people are reckless. It will only take the slightest nudge to send them
on a new witch hunt. Just one article in the tabloids about a psychopathic
Old Believer, and that will be the end of everything we've worked to build

these past years. It will all collapse, as it has happened before, all too often. They will cast out all the Old Believers who have only just returned from South America, they will halt the plans to restore our churches to us—"

"We have no desire to reveal to the world how many members of our community are living a secular life," the priest cut in, never letting his pointed gaze drop from Kenty's face. "Not because this is a transgression, but because when we shout the faith of our fathers from every street corner, we betray them. More fitting, for us, is silence, which was created before the Word."

"I'm not sure I can talk Masha out of it." Kenty shook his head. "She's very stubborn. And she almost always achieves what she sets out to do."

"Let her achieve it, then." The older man stroked his beard. "Catching a killer is a sacred endeavor. But she is not looking where she should. By the time she recognizes her mistake, the evil will have already been done. One must not use evil means to strive for good. One must not."

No one spoke. The Old Believers might have said an angel was flying by.

"I'll try," Innokenty finally said. "But I can't promise you anything."

"Very well." The head of the diocese nodded gravely.

"Please try," added Kenty's father.

With that, both men stood and proceeded to the door. There, the priest made the sign of the cross over Innokenty before he walked out, and Kenty's father quietly laid a heavy hand on his shoulder, then followed. As he closed the door behind them, Kenty wondered what they would have said if they had known that he personally was part of the investigation now threatening to discredit the whole community. He walked back to the kitchen. The three teacups still sat on the table, looking for all the world like chalices of blood.

The priest's words spun in his head. *One must not use evil means to strive for good. One must not.*

ANDREY

Andrey worked up the nerve to invite Masha over only after he had pulled up to her front door.

"So, if you want," he said, exhaling smoke out the open window of his old Ford, "we could go to my place?"

He could have said, *Let's go to my place and I'll introduce you to Marilyn Monroe. Or I'll show you what kind of place a cop who doesn't take bribes can afford. I'll show you the vinyl cloth on the table outside, worn down to its thready white skeleton. Or the creaking, mismatched chairs, the stained towel hanging near the rusty washbasin, the wallpaper that's warped and uneven from the last freeze. Yeah, I have so much to show you, like nothing you've ever seen. No exquisite antiques here!*

Why was it, he had asked himself many times, that in order to get a girl to come home with you, you had to offer to show her something completely beside the point? Like your old blues records or whatever. He looked at Masha and blushed.

"But only if you promise not to let my mess frighten you away," he added out loud.

Masha turned her pale elfin face to him and let him see her eyes, which looked almost transparent in the darkness.

"Let's go," she said, and squeezed his hand hard.

And with a squealing of the brakes (now this was what his super-charged engine was good for!), he tore away from the curb before she changed her mind, heading for a place where the darkness would make the differences between them disappear. Faster. He had to go faster. The prospect of what remained of the night before them sent blood to Andrey's head, and he felt himself growing warm, despite the breeze buffeting him from both open windows.

He handled the car expertly, as if he were playing a computer game or taking drugs. He *was* on something, actually, but this high was natural. This euphoria made his vision sharper, his reflexes quicker. Masha was curled up in her seat watching the road as if she, too, were willing the car to go faster.

Now they were past the outer ring road that circled the city, now they turned onto the highway that led out into the countryside, and now they were on a local road, where silent, dark houses lined both sides and the air smelled of fresh grass and wet sand. Finally, he stopped the car, turned off the engine, and sighed. He said it again, like casting a spell.

"Just don't let my mess scare you away."

But Masha had already gotten out of the car. She stretched like a cat, took a deep breath, and smiled at him, then took his hand. Andrey pushed open the gate and they walked up to the porch. From inside, Marilyn Monroe was begging for his freedom, barking and whining happily. When Andrey finally opened the door, the dog jumped on him, almost knocking him off his feet, and did the dance of a happy dog who knew he was finally about to have some dinner and play outside.

"Hey, look, buddy! This is Masha! It's Masha!" he told him.

Marilyn took one look and unceremoniously stuck his snout under her skirt, then butted his woolly head into her hand and pawed at her bare knees.

Andrey fed the beggar and let him out to race around the garden. Then, for the first time since reaching his house, he turned to Masha, his euphoria giving way to trepidation. Where the hell were all the things he was supposed to have on hand for romance? Candles? A bottle of good wine? Silk fucking sheets, for God's sake? He knew for sure, suddenly, that Kenty had all that at the ready.

"Want some tea?" he asked. "I don't have any food, but—"

Masha shook her head without speaking and took a step forward. Andrey roughly pulled her closer to him, and with one hand behind her head, he moved his lips over her neck near her ear, hungrily breathing in her scent, and that smell—so right and so much hers—suddenly turned off his brain. Instead of thinking about his sheets (not only were they not silk, they weren't even very clean), he was now operating on instinct. Who needed wine or candles?

Damn it, Masha Karavay, he thought, *how can you be so smooth all over, everywhere my fingers and lips can reach?* Every curve of her body felt like it was made for his hand. Her bare knee, her satiny shoulder, her small, soft breasts, the gentle hollow of her stomach. How could she have ever seemed foreign to him, when they were made for each other? Did it hurt her when he held her so tightly? His fingers were starving—what were they going to touch next? *Masha, Masha, what are you doing to me? Look at me, Masha! Look me in the eye!* But her eyes were shut tight, and she was writhing under him, moaning in the ultimate spasm of pleasure, and pressing her hot body against his. Andrey couldn't hold back any longer, and he closed his eyes, too, letting a rush of release overtake him.

Andrey would have given almost anything for a smoke, but Masha's head was resting on his shoulder and he was afraid to move. The sound of a gentle nighttime rain shower came in through the half-open window. The sheets were damp, but Andrey could feel the sweat slowly drying on his chest—the room had started to cool down. He pulled the blanket up over her. He listened to the rain and Marilyn Monroe trotting around outside, enjoying his long-overdue romp. Andrey was full of happiness, full as that old metal pail he'd left outside yesterday morning, hoping to catch some rainwater.

It wasn't the floorboards creaking under the dog's tread that awakened them, nor the rays of sunlight that stubbornly shot through the uncurtained window, nor even the morning clamor of his neighbors. It was the soft ringing of a cell phone. Andrey sighed with relief, because that wasn't his ringtone, which meant the call wasn't about work. But Masha got up, giving Andrey a look at her long, graceful back, and began digging through the heaps of clothing on the floor.

"Yes, Mama," she said, her voice husky from sleep, when she finally found her phone. "Did you get my text? Yeah, everything's fine." The murmur on the other end broke into a sobbing sound, and Masha sat down, pulling a blanket up over her chest. "What is it, Mama? What happened? Why are you crying?" She sat there listening, her eyebrows raised high, nodding. "Anything could have happened, right? He lost his phone, he decided to stay at a friend's place, who knows! Or maybe one of his patients had a crisis. There's a first time for everything. It's the weekend, maybe he had a couple of drinks, and—" More sobbing came through the phone. "Mama! Can you just hang on a little? I'll be right there, okay?"

She hung up and turned to Andrey, looking distraught. "My stepfather is missing. I have to get back to Moscow."

Andrey took Masha's cheeks in his hands. Framed by his fingers, she looked like a scared, worried little girl. He kissed her on her forehead, her nose, on her warm lips, and on her cheek, which still retained traces of a crease in the pillowcase.

"Good morning!" he said. "You get dressed, and I'll go put on some coffee."

He grabbed yesterday's shirt off the floor, gave it a quick sniff, and promised himself he'd switch it out for a clean one as soon as he got coffee started. Though that plan might fall through, Andrey admitted to himself as he walked into the kitchen, if he couldn't find a clean shirt. And did he even have any real coffee? For two little cupfuls, at least? Or just one?

He nudged the pesky dog out of the way with one foot while he emptied his cupboard onto the table, learning a few new things about himself in the process. For instance, it turned out that he owned cinnamon. At least, that's what the faded label said. As he turned the packet over in his hands, Andrey wondered whether you could put cinnamon in coffee. Or drink it instead of coffee? Then he discovered a box of spaghetti and a rusty bottle opener, a metal can of uncertain contents (good until October of last year), and a few stale crackers. But not a single goddamn trace of coffee, other than the instant garbage. He angrily threw the mystery can into the trash, even though he'd ordinarily have risked opening it and generously splitting whatever was inside with Marilyn.

The dog looked at him reproachfully, while the small pan Andrey had put on the rickety old gas burner in anticipation of the nonexistent coffee started to boil over and listed to one side. Without thinking, Andrey grabbed the aluminum handle, yipped in pain, and swore, just as Masha Karavay appeared before him. She was completely ready to go, and gave him a skeptical look.

"Uhhh," said Andrey. "Sorry, no coffee in bed today. No coffee at all, actually. Unless you want instant?" Like an idiot, he picked up the container of Nescafé and dangled it before her.

"Maybe some tea?" Masha asked innocently, cheering him up beyond all measure—because he definitely had some Lipton.

She embraced him, hiding her smile in Andrey's strong young chest.

"I'm stinky and gross," he whispered, embarrassed, in her ear.

"That's okay." She looked at him and grinned. "If it gets me some tea, I'll put up with it."

She started kissing him, and pretty soon they both got carried away. Marilyn Monroe watched appraisingly, not yet ready to give up hope of breakfast.

But then Andrey's own ringtone cut through the room.

"What?" he snapped into the phone.

He froze, and Masha did, too.

Again? her eyes asked him, all the dreaminess gone in an instant.

I don't know, Andrey answered with a glance, squeezing her shoulder as if holding tight to the only solid mooring he could find in this nightmare.

They did not talk as they drove. Masha stared out the window, and Andrey squinted hard, concentrating on the road flashing by. He had just ordered Intern Karavay to go home to her mother and take care of family business—reassure her mom, track down her truant stepdad, make sure the two patched things up—and told her she didn't need to mess around in murders on the weekend.

Masha was offended, which he certainly understood, but Andrey just couldn't take her with him. Fomin, who had been first on the scene, had said it was fucking horrible and he had never seen anything like it, so that was one good reason. The other was some funny feeling, deep in his gut, which had given up whispering and was now shouting in his ear: *Do not let Masha anywhere near this one!*

They reached her building, Masha already opening the door so she could leap out without a word, but he pulled her inside and kissed her, even though she resisted like a proud little bird. Andrey hoped the kiss would sustain him through a day that was sure to be long and terrible. *Poor girl,* he thought as he watched her walk away. *Nice boyfriend you found. No candles, no coffee in bed, not even tea on the veranda. He loved you and left you—for an unidentified corpse.*

✤

The crime scene was a rented apartment inside the boundaries of the old Bely Gorod walls, a line on the map Andrey thought of, these days, as a barrier of blood and flame. By the time he arrived, it was difficult to push his way up the crowded stairs. Even though it wasn't a work day, every member of the investigative team had shown up, and they were standing around smoking and talking quietly, waiting for the forensics experts to wrap things up. Andrey bummed a cigarette off Fomin while the detective piled information on him in an excited whisper. The body had been found in some kind of coffin thing shaped like an enormous doll, with sharp nails poking into the hollow inner chamber. The murderer had closed the victim inside, so the nails pierced his arms, legs, stomach, eyes . . .

"You can't even get a good look at him!" Fomin told Andrey, his eyes wide and serious. "Blood everywhere! Poor bastard tried to wriggle out of the way, and the fucking nails only dug deeper." Fomin took a deep breath. He apparently did not relish the memory.

"Who called the police?" Andrey asked.

"Only about three different neighbors, all on their own. Apparently, the killer hit him over the head to knock him out, then stuffed him into that doll-thing. But the guy woke up and started yelling." Fomin went pale again, imagining the screams.

Andrey told him and Gerasimov to go interview the neighbors, and he headed up to visit the apartment in question. He stood next to the forensic examiner and leaned over the body. It really was hard to look at it, smeared all over with blood, and the face . . . Looking for long at that face, frozen and distorted in a spasm of terror, was completely out of the question.

"Anything in his pockets?" Andrey asked hoarsely, tearing his eyes away from the dead man's hideous, white-toothed grin.

"Here."

Someone handed him a transparent plastic sleeve holding a photograph of a man smiling happily, holding a woman close to him. The man was obviously the same one lying before them now, being covered modestly with a sheet. Andrey gestured that they could take the body away. But the woman—the woman in the picture looked strangely familiar. When it occurred to Andrey that her lips were just like Masha's, his stomach turned. How fucking lovestruck must he be, to see her face everywhere he looked? Then he remembered the face at the door to Masha's place. *Masha's not home. Her books are gone, so she's probably at the library.* That was Masha's mom in the picture, and the guy had to be her missing stepfather. Which meant he must be the poor soul who'd spent the night in the iron maiden. *Masha!* Andrey's legs went out from under him, and he sat down hard on a chair. It was all leading back to her again. Could it possibly be a coincidence? Even the question seemed ridiculous. The Sin Collector had chosen this victim purely because he was close to Masha. And, of course, because Masha's stepfather somehow fit into that fucking table that Masha herself had copied out for the team.

Andrey pulled the sheet of paper out of the back pocket of his jeans. Her stepfather hadn't been missing for long, so assuming the killer was working in order, his sin must be even worse than that pedophile Minayev's. There were only two tollhouses on the list after the one for sodomy: nineteen and twenty, heresy and cruelheartedness. Masha's stepfather, as far as Andrey could guess from Masha's conversation with her mother that morning, was a doctor. Maybe he had been too stern with one of his patients? Or, cruelheartedly, hadn't realized how sick one actually was? A mental patient would be easier to finger for the crime than an Old Believer. Not a bad theory, but it would need work. Masha's stepdad could just as easily have been, say, a Baptist, which was definitely heresy to the Orthodox faithful. Then he'd fit the bill for the second-to-last tollhouse.

He would have to tell Masha. He would have to call her, and interrupt the painful and humiliating routine she and her mother must be going through right now, calling around to all the hospitals asking if he had been admitted, calling all their friends and relatives to see if he had spent the night. What was that humiliation, though, compared to the truth: that he was a cold dead body, poked full of holes, with a picture of Masha's mother in his pocket? No. Andrey wanted to give himself just a few more minutes before he dialed the number he already knew by heart. A few more minutes to think.

He read the table again, frowning. It seemed like the suspect had been making mistakes in his order, jumping around. It was as if, once he realized the police were onto him, he stopped taking the trouble. The pattern skipped forward and backward like kids playing a game. And another thing: Why had the killer put a family photograph in his victim's pocket? Was it because Masha's mother was somehow tied up in his plot? Andrey sighed out loud, and with a heavy heart, he took out his phone. He needed Masha's help. Awful as it was, she wasn't just a detective in this case anymore. She was a witness, too. It was as if the killer wanted to involve her in every part of the process, from theory to practice, from investigation to evidence, from evidence—Andrey couldn't help but finish the thought—to complicity.

Fomin was sitting across from the downstairs neighbor, a middle-aged woman with an unhealthy pallor. The color of her skin was explained by the stale odor of cigarette smoke, which permeated the miserly little apartment, and by the woman's profession. She was a technical translator. In her kitchen, which also served as her office, there was an old laptop and a stack of instruction manuals for all sorts of high-tech kitchen gadgets: microwaves and pressure cookers, bread makers, blenders, and deep fryers. The only machine that graced her own tiny kitchen was an ancient refrigerator trembling in a senile state of exaltation. Wrapped up as she was in the written word, the woman had little opportunity to speak with live human beings, so she was eager for a nice talk, even if it had to be with a police officer.

Fomin had already given up asking questions. Why bother if the woman was going to tell him everything with no prodding? She was doing a good job, too, speaking precisely without getting distracted by the details. This might be a lucky day for the redhead. Fomin classified every circumstance in his life one of two ways: either the redhead was lucky, or he was not. Conveniently enough, those two categories had been all he needed for the past twenty-six years. New girlfriend? The redhead was lucky. No place to start a family? Unlucky. The girl leaves him for some other guy? Probably the redhead was lucky, because what was he going to do with her with no place to live? And so on and so forth.

The apartment above hers, the neighbor said, had been largely empty, used exclusively for lovers' frolics. That's how she put it: *frolics.*

"Are you certain?" Fomin asked.

"There's no mistaking it," said the translator. "You can hear everything. The couple would come over, sometimes at lunchtime, sometimes in the evening. And they'd have *sex.*" She spat the word. "Basically," the woman went on, nodding, "around a year ago, a very sophisticated couple rented the place. He looked like a professor." Fomin felt goose bumps tickling his skin, remembering the man in the wooden doll. "And she looked like a professor's pet student. Much younger than him, very pretty. It was the usual story. An older man drawn to some fresh meat." The translator snorted and sneered dismissively, hoping for some sort of reaction, but Fomin did not play along, just nodded calmly to encourage her to go ahead.

These sophisticated-looking people had made love in a very unsophisticated manner, moaning and screaming, bothering the downstairs neighbor (and the neighbors next door, she pointed out) as she tried to cook dinner, take a shower, or watch the evening news. The passionate struggles up above made the translator's old Czech chandelier swing from the ceiling, and made her smoke nervously and ponder her fate as a single woman. But the funniest part was that she would sometimes run into them on the dimly lit stairs or in the elevator, and somehow she never could say a cross word to them. That's the benefit of looking so sophisticated. It intimidates people. It wasn't worth scolding them, anyway. Those two didn't rendezvous so often, not more than once a week, and the moans from above were honestly easier to tolerate than, say, the young couple with the new baby who were always fighting and had already let their tub overflow into her place three times now. At least there was the excitement and suspense of secret passion with the people upstairs.

"But yesterday—" The neighbor frowned. "Everything started like usual. He arrived first, probably around four o'clock. I can tell it's him by the heavy shoes. She wears these little heels. I heard his key turn in the lock and then the door open and shut. But *she* never turned up. No heels tapping on the stairs, no elevator stopping on the floor above me."

Fomin laughed to himself. The secret romance had drawn the neighbor woman in a lot deeper than she wanted to admit.

"Maybe half an hour passed, I was already getting dinner ready, when the door opened and shut again. I thought the man had gotten tired of waiting and left, but no. It was somebody else going into that apartment."

"You're sure it wasn't the woman?" Fomin asked.

"No!" the translator answered him excitedly. "I didn't hear any noise on the stairs. And the elevator makes a terrible racket, you can't miss it. No. It was somebody who came down from the floor above that one."

"So that person had been waiting?" Fomin asked thoughtfully.

"Maybe." She nodded and reached for her packet of cigarettes. "I heard the doorbell ring up there, a long ring, and then I think I heard a male voice."

Fomin was giving the neighbor all his attention now.

She blew cigarette smoke out the small, open window, with its peeling paint and crooked hinges. She paused. "It sounded like he said—"

"Yes?" Fomin pressed.

The translator looked at Fomin again, and for the first time, she looked frightened.

"'Open up! It's me!'"

MASHA

Masha held her mother in her arms, but her arms were clearly not enough. Maybe they were too short, or maybe Masha was simply the wrong person for the job. But there was nobody else. No Papa, no UnPapa. Natasha was slipping away, falling like Alice down the deep, dark rabbit hole. And Masha knew what she would find at the bottom: Papa's death, and pain and terror, and her own aloneness. It had only been five minutes since Andrey's call, but all that morning, as she'd telephoned every place she could think of, Masha had known. She'd felt it in her bones, the same way you can feel someone else breathing in a dark room: it was hopeless. He wasn't with friends, he wasn't with colleagues, he wasn't in any hospital. It was too late. He was somewhere his wife's gentle pleading could never reach him.

At long last, Masha realized what Belov, and his unobtrusive presence in her life, had meant to her. The perfectly brewed coffee in the mornings, the gentle gaze that restrained her mother's urge to badger Masha with too many personal questions. Even his kindly therapist act, as she thought of it, had helped to keep her afloat. She had been genuinely and tightly attached to this big, gentle man. Her customary annoyance about him was gone.

Meanwhile Natasha's whole body was trembling, despite the emergency double dose of Valocordin, and her fingers, digging painfully into Masha's forearm, were cold as ice. Masha made a decision. She dialed the number of an old medical-school friend of her mother's who worked a few blocks away, and tried to give her the short version of everything that had happened: her stepfather was dead, her mother was apparently suffering from nervous shock, and Masha didn't know what to do.

"Masha!" the friend exclaimed, her voice trembling with worry. "Hold on, dear, I'll be right there. You stay with her, all right? Get her into bed if you can."

Masha hung up and turned to her mother.

"Let's go, Mama. You're going to go lie down. Nadya is coming soon." Her mother looked right through her, and Masha felt a flash of terror. She grabbed Natasha by the hand and tried to stand up, pulling her mother after her. "Come on," she repeated, gently. "I'm going to put you in bed."

Natasha stood up, and with tiny steps, like a truck pulling a trailer, they inched out into the hallway. It occurred to Masha that it would be a mistake to take her mother into the room she had shared with her second husband, so she pushed open the door to her own room.

Natasha stopped short in the doorway, and her eyes came alive when they focused on something right in her line of vision. Masha craned her neck to get a glimpse of what her mother was staring at so intently, and swore to herself. Her room wasn't a safe option, either. The black-and-white photo of her father regarded his wife and daughter from the opposite wall. He seemed more alive than both of them put together. The standoff lasted maybe ten seconds, until Natasha turned to her daughter and said, very quietly, "This is all your fault." Then she clutched at her heart and, as if she were in a movie, slowly crumpled to the floor.

"Mama, what's wrong? Is it your heart?" Masha shouted.

That same instant the doorbell rang, and Masha ran to answer it. She slipped on the rug and pulled the door open almost in midflight.

"Nadya!" She was no longer trying to act as if she were in control. Masha felt like she had shot back in time eleven years, and she was standing there, small and lost, over her father's dead body. "There's something wrong with Mama. I think it's her heart!"

"All right, all right," Nadya told her reassuringly and hurried inside. "Natasha!" Nadya squatted down on the floor next to her friend, and in one quick gesture took some sort of tablet out of her purse and slid it under Natasha's tongue. She wrapped her long fingers around the patient's wrist and felt her pulse. "Natasha, you need to be strong now. You need to pull yourself together, Natasha," she was saying in a quiet, almost sing-song voice, while Masha stood by silently behind her and tried not to cry. "I'm going to give you a shot and bring you in to my clinic. My car's outside. You'll have a few days of rest. Masha can pack your things."

She nodded back at Masha, who obediently turned around and walked to the bathroom, where she forced her trembling hands to gather up her mother's makeup and the bathrobe hanging on the door. What else? A change of underwear? Masha hurried down the hallway toward the master bedroom, catching a glimpse of Nadya expertly inserting a needle into her mother's arm, still talking soothingly.

"Wonderful! I've always been jealous of your veins, nice and big!" Natasha was staring straight up at the ceiling.

Masha grabbed the first pair of underwear she found, and was turning to leave when she caught the scent of her mother's perfume. Her throat tightened. She must not cry! She also saw, out of the corner of one eye, an empty silver picture frame. But she didn't stop to look closer. Masha ran back into the hallway. Her mother was on her feet now with her coat on, standing at the door. Nadya took the bag Masha had packed and patted her on the cheek.

"I'm going to take care of her for a few days. Will you be all right?" Masha nodded.

"Wonderful. You can come visit when she's feeling better."

Masha nodded again. She couldn't take her eyes off her mother's pale, frozen face. Nadya was opening the front door now, taking

Natasha by the arm and steering her toward the elevator. Masha waved good-bye, the elevator door clanged shut, and she slowly retreated back into the apartment. She gave the lock four full turns, and turned away to look at her own reflection in the mirror.

The play of artificial and natural light made Masha look like a ghost, belonging to neither this world nor any other. Only now did she realize what her mother had said before collapsing on the parquet floor. It was all her fault. For some reason, Masha was not at all surprised. As always, Natasha was right.

Everything that had happened to their family was her fault. Hers and nobody else's.

ANDREY

For the first time in his life, Andrey walked into a psychologist's office, and despite his sour mood, he couldn't help smiling. *Lordy lordy lordy,* his old grandma would have said. Quiet music was playing, slow enough to be hypnotic. Some extremely calming fish swam reassuringly in an aquarium. Soft rugs covered the floor, further muffling the unhurried footsteps of the staff walking to and fro. The sun was shining through the high windows, and Andrey squinted, wishing for a second that he could trade places with any of the poor saps sitting in this waiting room.

His own psychological dilemma was straight out of a classic novel. Andrey was caught between duty and emotion. It was his duty to go straight to Masha's and grill her and her mother. His feelings, though, were whining as desperately as Marilyn Monroe. *Give them time,* his heart pleaded. *Let them get their bearings.* Lurking behind that generous notion was a quieter one: *She's going to hate you, and her mother's going to hate you, too, and even if it helps you find the killer, you will lose Masha for good, Andrey, you provincial schmuck.*

To distract himself, Andrey picked up a brochure off a table in the waiting room and started to read. *A psychologist helps a patient look at a problem differently. With expert help, you will learn something new about yourself.* Andrey smirked. It was true that he was hoping to learn something new, but not about himself. *You will come to new conclusions about what you have experienced, arrive at a comprehensive understanding of your problems, and, finally, discover a path to a solution.*

Not bad, thought Andrey. *Maybe I should make an appointment.*

He flipped over the brochure and found the price list. A personal consultation with Dr. Yury Arkadyevich Belov, whose photograph graced the cover (apparently, Dr. Belov was the head of the whole operation), cost two hundred euros. VIP consultations were available for two hundred fifty euros. So this place was too fancy to list their prices in rubles? Andrey made a face. He wondered what was included in a VIP session. A deep-tissue massage to ensure the patient was totally relaxed? Suddenly he lost all desire to finish reading the brochure. The whole idea of VIP therapy sessions had made him lose faith. What's more, even if he spent all that money and arrived at a comprehensive understanding of his own problems in return, surely new problems would arise: financial ones.

A tall, imposing woman had walked into the room. Her hair was dyed the color of old gold and arranged in a low bun. She looked over the small crowd of patients, their faces tense despite the Mozart and the fish, and easily picked out Andrey.

"Tatyana Krotova," she said, offering him a warm hand manicured with light-pink polish. "I'm second-in-command here." She coughed and dropped her eyes. "Or I was, before Dr. Belov . . . Let's go talk in my office."

Andrey rose obediently and followed her until they reached a door bearing the sign "T. A. Krotova, D.Psych." She opened the door to reveal a spacious office with the expected couch for patients bowled over by life, and Dr. Krotova gestured fluidly to Andrey to sit on it.

"Well now." Krotova smiled sadly, and sat down behind her massive desk. "From what I understand, you'd like to ask me some questions about Dr. Belov. But I'm, ah, not sure that I can help you. Everyone here loved him. His colleagues and his patients. He was an expert in his field, and we are, well, mourning."

Andrey fidgeted on the couch that was the tool of this woman's trade. How could people pour out their deepest, darkest secrets here? Wasn't it too awkward? He took a deep breath. It was clear that Doctor of Psychology Krotova was not about to share with him the things that were most paining her. She wasn't the one on the couch, after all.

Andrey expected himself to start with the standard questions, but instead he blurted out, "Did your boss have an affair here at work?"

Dr. Krotova's lips tightened, almost unnoticeably.

"No. Yury loved his family very much."

Andrey kicked himself. Why on earth had he asked this lady about adultery? Maybe because of the family portrait the man had in his pocket? Or the tollhouses on Masha's list? In any case, Andrey had to get his questioning back on track.

"How long have you been acquainted with the victim? Was he in any sort of conflict with colleagues at work? Or with patients? Have you noticed any recent changes in his behavior?" And on and on down the list. But Krotova didn't give Andrey even a tiny toehold, nothing to work with.

He hadn't actually expected much. After all, the Sin Collector never left a trail. Why would there be one this time? Andrey suddenly felt incredibly tired. These past few days had been shot through with helplessness, terror, and blood, and he was worried sick over Masha. He desperately wanted to hear her voice, so he could better remember what had happened between them the night before. But all he could recollect was their sad kiss outside her building that morning. He wrapped things up with Krotova quickly, shook her hand one more time, and almost ran past the enormous aquarium and away from the place where his childhood fears were supposed to evaporate to the sound of cloying music.

The air felt fresher outside. Twilight had fallen, and the city smelled of rain and gasoline. Andrey was reaching into his pocket for a smoke when a whole pack of cigarettes suddenly materialized before his eyes. A thin, bony hand was holding the pack up for him. He turned and saw a man next to him, probably thirty years old, tall but slouching. He wore a long jacket he had thrown on right over his white lab coat.

"Thanks," Andrey said, taking the cigarette. Then he leaned over to take advantage of the elegant gold lighter, which seemed strangely out of character for this odd-looking stranger.

"Timofeyev. I'm a psychiatrist and sexologist here."

Andrey shook his hand gingerly and tried to imagine, awkwardly, what kind of work a sexologist must do.

"Sexology," Timofeyev explained, as if catching the glint of alarm in his eyes, "is not the same thing as gynecology. Or urology." He smiled. "We work on things above the belt, not below." He leaned toward Andrey again and added, "The brain, I mean."

"Huh," answered Andrey, grateful that the cigarette was providing him an excuse not to fan the flames of this conversation.

"You're a detective, right?" Andrey nodded, and the sexologist went on. "I saw you walk into the Serpent's nest."

"The Serpent?"

"Yeah, that's our loving nickname for our unloved Tatyana." He made a grand gesture in the air with his glowing cigarette and quoted Pushkin. "'And she was called Tatyana!' She calls herself a doctor, too, which isn't actually very funny."

"She doesn't have a doctorate?" asked Andrey. Now he was curious. Krotova had seemed perfectly suited to the title after her name.

"Oh, she does," Timofeyev said dismissively. "Maybe she bought it somewhere, or maybe she just plonked her ass down in the library until she learned everything by heart. Psychology isn't an exact science, if you know what I mean. But, honestly"—he moved his long face even closer to Andrey's—"she's just tickled pink that Belov is gone. He was the only person in this whole nuthouse who actually knew anything, hadn't just memorized some Carl Jung. The only one who actually cared about his patients. Too much, sometimes." The sexologist snickered.

"What do you mean?" Andrey hurried to ask.

"What else could I mean? It was clear as day. He's a doctor, a king, and a god, and she's a patient tortured by her own psyche. And a pretty one, too. It's risky business, sure, and medical ethics forbids it. But more important, she had a husband. A cop. The kind who, if you gave him a leather jacket and shaved his head, he'd be the perfect thug. That sometimes happens with your kind, sorry to say. And his eyes—well, they weren't kind, to put it gently. That kind of guy, he's as likely to stab you as a Young Pioneer is to help an old lady across the street."

Andrey couldn't believe his luck. "You happen to know this lady patient's name?" he asked quietly, afraid of jinxing himself by showing too much eagerness.

"Nope," said Timofeyev, tossing away his cigarette butt. "But I can look in the files. It was probably two years ago. I saw her getting into his car after a session, and they drove off. Then she canceled the rest of her appointments."

"Is that why you figure they were having an affair?" asked Andrey, faking disbelief, as Timofeyev opened the door to the clinic.

"Oh man." The sexologist lifted one long crooked finger into the air. "If you had seen the way he looked at her? And her, too. Believe me, it was obvious."

The patient's last name turned out to be Kuznetsova, and Andrey got her address, too, and her phone number, which he called right from Timofeyev's office. A toneless female voice said hello.

"Anna Kuznetsova? Good afternoon. My name is Yakovlev, and I'm a police detective. I'd like to have a chat with you about Yury Belov. Could we meet? Right now?"

"Certainly," Anna answered quietly. "Please come. You have my address? The door code is 769."

"On my way," Andrey said, and hung up before she could change her mind. By the time he pulled out of the parking lot, he realized why the short conversation had felt so weird. Anna Kuznetsova had seemed neither surprised nor frightened. Very odd for a person receiving an urgent call from a detective.

INNOKENTY

Innokenty hung up the phone and sank down heavily onto the dark-green leather ottoman in the hallway. That had been Masha's denim detective, Yakovlev, again. He was driving, and apparently in a serious rush. Yakovlev had told Innokenty that Masha's stepfather was dead. He had given no details, but Innokenty knew enough to understand that Belov must have been murdered in some hideous medieval manner. And Innokenty knew just as well as Yakovlev did that the death of Masha's stepfather was no coincidence. The Sin Collector was breathing down Masha's neck now. The fact that she was still alive might be just an oversight, though that was hard to believe. More likely, it was a vital part of his devious game, part of his obsessive control over events. He was saying that he could take Masha's life, purely by his own will, any time he chose.

Yakovlev had asked Innokenty to pick up Masha and her mother and bring them to Kenty's place. "Just for a while," he specified. Innokenty could hear the fear and exhaustion in his voice. There was a new tone, too, a note of pleading.

"Of course. I'll go get them right now," Kenty had agreed. Then he added, "Don't worry. My apartment is like a bank vault. They'll be relatively safe here."

"Relatively, right," Yakovlev had answered, but he also thanked him sincerely.

"Not a problem," Innokenty had said automatically, but something nagged at him. Who the hell did the denim detective think he was, thanking Kenty for taking care of Masha Karavay? He had taken care of her for the past fifteen years, without anybody ever asking him to! But he quickly made himself see reason. Masha's gloomy-looking boss was turning out to be a good guy, and it was natural that he was worried about her. Innokenty ran downstairs to his car and headed for Masha's house, without even bothering to call first.

When Masha opened the door, Kenty gave a start. She looked thin and unhealthy, her collarbones standing out at the neck of her bathrobe, her elbows too sharp, and her face . . . Masha's face was drawn and pinched, with dark circles under her eyes and sunken cheeks. Her hair hung in long, disheveled strands, and even her eyes looked pale, as if all the light had gone out of them. She moved quietly to one side to let Kenty in and led him, her feet dragging, to the kitchen, where she sat down facing the light. She smiled, unhappily.

"Mama's in the hospital," she said. "Her heart was giving her trouble. I guess you already know what happened?"

Innokenty nodded and tried to take her hand in his, but she pulled away, then looked down to concentrate on picking at a hangnail. She succeeded, and tore a considerable swath of skin away with it. Masha didn't even wince. She licked the blood off her finger and grimaced at him again with that same empty smile.

"Masha," he began, "you shouldn't be here. It's too dangerous. Even if you were able to convince yourself that your friend's death was a coincidence—"

"Her name was Katya," Masha said.

"Yes," Innokenty conceded. "But we know that Katya's death was no accident, and your stepfather was targeted for a reason, too."

"Right," Masha agreed. "This is about me, and it's all my fault."

"That's ridiculous! Why would you—"

"No, Kenty! Stop. It's obvious!" Masha said, her words rushed now as she frantically pulled at another hangnail. "Even Mama said so!"

Innokenty grabbed her hand, but he felt her palm quiver and her fingers wriggle like insects as she tried to break free.

"Your mother said what?"

"Yes, Mama, too! If I hadn't gotten involved in this Jerusalem thing, nobody would ever have figured it out! Maybe he even would have stopped killing, maybe he would have gotten bored with it. But now he has an audience, he has somebody to play with, you know? I mean, who would go and hide in the woods like an idiot, all alone? But if there are reasonably intelligent people looking for you, it's different, and I'm closer than anyone else. It's fun for him to play with me. And there are so many sinners around me. That's what he's trying to tell me. He's saying I've been blind! I'm following his trail, but I can't see what's right in front of my face!"

"Masha!" Innokenty squeezed her hand harder. "We need to get you packed. Pick out what you need for a couple of days."

"What's the point, Kenty? Do you think he won't find me?"

"My place is safer," Innokenty insisted. He stood up, went to her bedroom, and opened the closet. Masha stood in the doorway and smiled at him strangely.

"You don't get it, Kenty," she said softly. "I'm not the one who needs to be protected. You are. You, my mom, everyone around me. You're all in danger."

Kenty did not turn his head. He found some jeans and sweaters and her favorite black T-shirts and put them in a bag. Masha sighed. With a hint of her old sense of humor, she added, "What, are you going to pack my underwear, too?"

"Well, where do you keep it?" asked Kenty, turning to her and smiling. And, thank God, she smiled back. For real, this time.

They walked out of Masha's apartment ten minutes later, carrying the packed bag, and Innokenty closed and locked the door.

ANDREY

Andrey had never seen such a beautiful woman. Not beautiful in the contemporary sense, when some disproportionate feature gives a face its charm or makes an actor famous. No. This woman carried a kind of nineteenth-century grace about her. The regularity of her features combined to make the perfect portrait: the gentle oval of her face, the big blue eyes, the even, light-colored eyebrows, the slight nose, the smooth forehead. The face was astonishing, but Andrey was surprised to find that it did not seem to affect him. Was it because he was in love with Masha? Or was it just that perfection like this inspired only chaste admiration? That was probably a load of bull. According to Fomin's interview with the downstairs neighbor, Masha's stepdad's feelings hadn't been chaste in the least.

"Ms. Kuznetsova," he began. "Why didn't you show up at your meeting with Dr. Belov yesterday?"

Anna raised her perfect eyebrows just a bit. Evidently, her repertoire of facial expressions was limited.

"He canceled it."

"Did he call you?"

"Yes. Well, no. Someone he works with called, and said that Yury—Dr. Belov—was stuck at the office. They said he wouldn't be able to come."

"Had he ever canceled a meeting with you before?"

Anna paused to think. "Yes, two or three times. But he always did it himself. I didn't think he trusted his colleagues enough to give them my phone number and let them in on that, uh, side of his life. It startled me a little."

"And how long have you two been—meeting?"

"About two years," she answered calmly, brushing a shining lock of hair out of her face. Andrey couldn't help watching. Beauty really was a force to be reckoned with. "I used to be his patient." She smiled simply, revealing her perfect teeth. "He felt sorry for me."

Andrey didn't have time to be surprised before she looked him straight in the eye and asked, "Did something happen to him?"

"He"—Andrey cleared his throat—"he died. He was murdered yesterday evening. I'm very sorry." Andrey thought he was ready for any sort of reaction, from crystalline tears to muffled sobbing. But the beauty surprised him. Her face, up to then so exquisitely immobile, suddenly began to shake as if she were having a fit. Her lips gaped open, contorting her mouth; her temples throbbed; her chin jutted forward, then back again; and her eyebrows shot up high, buckling her perfectly smooth forehead into accordion-like folds. The whole effect was so ghastly that Andrey jumped up, nearly knocking over his chair.

"My medicine!" Kuznetsova moaned, in a strange, low voice, through a clenched jaw, and she pointed to a cupboard.

Andrey yanked open the door and saw it right away, a vial in the very center of the lowest shelf. There was a stern warning on the label: "BY PRESCRIPTION ONLY."

"Thirty drops," she wheezed, and Andrey began counting out drops into a glass that was waiting conveniently nearby. Time seemed to stand still. Andrey switched off his peripheral vision. He could see nothing but the drops of medicine splashing one by one into the glass. Fifteen. Sixteen. He couldn't make a mistake, and he couldn't look at the terrifying sight sharing the room with him.

When the medicine was finally ready, he held the glass as she drank it down, her lips trembling, and fell back in her chair. Andrey turned to the window. Kuznetsova's apartment was on the third floor of an old building, and it looked out over a quiet courtyard. How many of these were left in Moscow? *Must be expensive,* he thought suddenly. *I wonder what she does for a living. Or is she just the fortunate spouse of some crooked cop?*

"Excuse me," a calm voice finally pronounced behind him. "I didn't expect that. I should be used to it by now."

Andrey turned around, and saw the flawless beauty restored.

"It was all so strange. The phone call, the fact that Yury didn't cancel himself. He knew how important it was for us to meet at least once a week. You probably think he was just my lover," she said, bowing her head a little, and laughing sadly. "But he was my therapist, too. Do you have any cigarettes?"

Andrey nodded and got the pack out of his pocket.

Kuznetsova took an awkward drag. "I really don't smoke much. But Yury said it was all right after an attack. It calms me down. Anyway, yes. My husband was the one who first brought me to the clinic. He didn't even know the difference between psychologists and psychiatrists. They were all just head doctors to him. That's what I thought, too. It seemed all right, fancy, nice and clean. Not some haunted old asylum. But Yury—he realized quickly that I needed a different kind of doctor, not a psychologist. He was scared for me. My husband was, too." Kuznetsova laughed again. "But I was only scared of my husband. Anyway, Yury prescribed some medicine and some intensive therapy. My husband got jealous. He thought I wanted to go to the clinic just to see Yury. And that was true, actually, but Yury didn't know it. To make a long story short, my husband forbade me to go back, saying he'd kill Yury if I did. By that time, I had stopped being afraid of dying myself. So Yury volunteered to go on treating me, but somewhere other than the clinic. I don't think he really knew, at the start, how things would end up."

"What about your husband? Did he ever guess? From what I understand, he's—"

"Yes, he's a police officer, too. But no, he never knew. I filed for divorce. He didn't want to let me go. He watched me like a guard dog. A nervous, vicious guard dog! I knew," she said, lowering her voice, "that he had killed people before. He swore he hadn't, but I could feel it! I couldn't go on living with him. Before Yury came into my life, I had thought about leaving him some other way. I tried suicide, but he always caught me in time. When I met Yury, though, it was like someone had switched on the light at the end of the tunnel. As long as I saw him at least once a week, I wasn't afraid anymore. So it's actually hard to say what he was for me. Did I need him as a man or as a doctor? He actually said I didn't need him anymore. He said I was almost all better and that I'd learned how to control myself."

Kuznetsova paused. "So now I get to test that theory out." She turned to look out the window. One shining tear rolled down her perfect face. She looked like a fairy-tale princess.

Andrey waited a few moments before asking her the next question, the decisive one.

"Ms. Kuznetsova, how can I get in touch with your husband? Your ex-husband, I mean."

"That would be difficult." A remarkable smirk crept across her face.

"I can go see him at work, or—"

"He's at Vostryakovsky."

At first, Andrey didn't understand.

"The cemetery. My husband is dead. He was killed in the line of duty a year and a half ago. He never did give me that divorce. And he never planned to. Yury and I didn't meet in this apartment, because it was too far for him to travel. Besides, I shared this place with my husband, and Yury was squeamish about things like that."

Andrey said nothing. A police officer, capable of murder. Someone indirectly acquainted with Masha's stepfather. Judging by his disappointment, Andrey could tell how much he'd been counting on this interview to confirm his new lead. He stood up slowly and said good-bye.

As she showed him out, the princess made one more comment, seemingly less to Andrey than to herself.

"They were both so scared for me. But here I am, alive and almost well. But not them. It's so surreal."

MASHA

Masha followed Innokenty into his apartment and felt as if she were exhaling, finally, for the first time this whole long day. There were suddenly so many things she wanted to do. Sleep. Call Andrey just so she could hear his voice. But the first thing, probably, would be to get some food.

"Kenty?" she asked beseechingly as she kicked off her shoes. "I don't suppose you have anything to eat?"

Innokenty put down Masha's bag and shot a wry glance in her direction.

"I'm so glad you associate my home with sustenance, my dear. Come on."

In the kitchen, Masha sat on a high bar stool and swiveled around quietly, this way and that, while Kenty studied the contents of his enormous French-door refrigerator. He adored it for its capacity, and referred to it lovingly as his root cellar. Now he pulled a stock pot, wet with condensation, out of cold storage and put it on the stove. The deep recesses of the machine also yielded up some fresh dill, and Kenty got out a huge heavy-looking cutting board and set to work chopping the herbs up. He turned on the oven and slid in a tray of pirozhki. When the pot started boiling, he removed it from the burner, ladled out some chicken meat, and cut it up into small pieces. He got out a serving bowl with a delicate floral pattern—Dutch, he explained, a Delftware piece—and neatly poured the broth into it. He selected a linen napkin from a drawer and set it on the table next to Masha, along with a solid-silver spoon.

Usually Masha teased him about the care he took, his desire to make sure everything in his life, especially everything pertaining to the stomach, was just right. Even when it was his one and only best friend at the table, someone he had known forever, and whose stomach was growling in a completely indelicate way. This time, though, Kenty's dance around the table had a calming effect on Masha. After all, in a world where a Delftware tureen could survive since the eighteenth century, how bad could things be?

"So where's the silver napkin ring?" Masha couldn't help ribbing him now. "No respect, I tell you!"

Innokenty looked up from the last step in his ritual (he was pouring vodka from a bottle into a crystal pitcher already chilled to readiness), smiled, and reached out a finger to tap her nose. He poured some vodka into a small, thick-walled shot glass, ladled the broth into a deep bowl, and moved a plate full of pirozhki closer to her. Masha breathed deeply, lifted her glass, and, without pausing for a toast, took her shot. She chased it down with a bite of the pirozhki and tossed some of the lovely bitter dill into her bowl to soak.

"Kenty—" she started, then stopped. He froze with the spoon in his hand. What could she say to him? *Thanks for being you? You're my best friend in the world, and I don't know how I would have survived all these years without you?* Could she tell him the things she might have said, but never did, to her other best friend, Katya? Or to her stepfather? But thinking like that scared her. It was as if she were getting ready to say good-bye to him, too. So instead of finishing her sentence, Masha took her first spoonful of the radiantly golden chicken broth. Only after that did she lift her eyes to meet his again.

"Who taught you to make such excellent broth?"

For a second, it seemed that Innokenty had been expecting some other sort of declaration. But he smiled and wiped his mouth with a napkin.

"My only teacher is Elena Molokhovets, the Russian master cook." He could even quote her: "'To be sure the soup comes out clear, let it simmer on the lowest possible flame while removing any scum. Then your soup will taste delicious and will be so transparent that you will not need to skim off the fat, but merely strain it through a napkin.' That's the 1911 edition."

"Oh God," moaned Masha in exaggerated horror. "And to think, all I can make is an omelet!"

"Sure, but what an omelet it is!"

"Sometimes I think you're just a mirror there to reflect my own faults," Masha told him, finishing up another bite. "Did you bake these yourself, too, Mrs. Tiggy-Winkle?"

"The pirozhki came straight from the bakery," Innokenty admitted gracefully. "But what do you mean about the mirror?"

"Oh, I dunno. It just occurred to me. You have so many good qualities that when I look at you, I see all my own faults. You understand, right? You're good-looking and elegant. You're a great housekeeper. You can cook! Any girl would be happy to share your well-equipped household."

Innokenty smiled, and turned back to the stove.

"Want anything else?" He cleared his throat. "Dessert?"

"No, Kenty, but thank you," said Masha sincerely. She walked over to him and for a second leaned up against his broad back. She could feel the muscles tighten, just slightly, under his thin, silky sweater. *Cashmere,* thought Masha. *Dear little fashion plate!* She stepped away again.

Kenty sighed, then turned to face her. "Masha, there's something I need to talk to you about."

His somber tone and the look on his face were so alarmingly out of character that Masha knew, suddenly, that all the effort he'd made to lure her out of the dark woods she had been wandering in—the hot soup, the cold vodka—would be in vain. She could feel her heart dropping, then freezing solid.

"Sit down, please," Innokenty said, and he sat down next to her, resting his large, handsome hands on the table before him. "There's something you don't know about me. I never thought it was important. I still don't think so."

"Kenty," said Masha softly. "Just tell me."

He sighed again, looked her in the eye, and tried to smile.

"It's about my family, Masha. You never asked, but my family . . . They're Old Believers. My great-grandfather donated the money to build the church on Basmanny. My great-grandmother came from an Old Believer community in the Urals. None of that ever mattered much to me, since I'm not a very religious person. But my father . . ." Now he was looking down at his hands. "That's why I almost never invited you over to my place when we were kids."

Masha stared at him. Hundreds, even thousands, of memories that had collected over the course of her childhood danced before her eyes like dolphins cresting at the surface of the water. Innokenty's father, with his full beard and archetypically Russian face. His mother, who always had a kerchief wrapped tightly around her head, no matter how warm the weather. The shadowy icon in the kitchen. The smell of old books in their home, their time-worn leather covers embossed in gold, lined up on the top shelf, out of the reach of children. The thesis Innokenty had defended two years ago about the Old Believers, the one the dean had told him ought to be turned into a dissertation. Why hadn't she guessed? After all, they had told her practically the same thing about her own thesis on murder. Innokenty had always been obsessed with the schismatics, and he told endless stories about them, some terrifying, some strange, some even funny. None of that could have come out of nowhere, any more than her own fascination with serial killers did.

Masha looked at Innokenty and felt like she no longer recognized him. He seemed to have grown. He was enormous now, and he took up every square inch of the kitchen. And there were things about him buried so deep that Masha had never even suspected.

"Don't look at me like that! It's just a branch of Russian Orthodoxy, you know, one with a difficult past. You wouldn't be staring at me like that if I had told you I was a Protestant! And I'm not even religious! You know that. I'm a historian, first and foremost!"

Masha gulped. "You said your great-grandfather had something to do with building the church on Basmanny?"

Innokenty ran a hand over his face. "Yes. That's actually what I wanted to talk to you about. Some people came to see me. The head of the church, in fact. He asked me to talk to you, to try to convince you that the killer you're looking for isn't one of us. He's worried that the detectives will ruin things for them, that there will be articles in the paper. The Old Believers have only just started growing again, building churches, and people have begun returning home from the US and South America. All of that progress could be stopped by stupid prejudices, gossip, and rumors with no basis in reality."

"And you agreed?" Masha asked. "You agreed to talk me into dropping it?"

Innokenty smiled morosely. "I told them I'd try, Masha. I didn't promise anything."

"Well, great." Masha's lips twisted into a frown. "At least you won't have to break your promise! I wouldn't want to be responsible for you violating any sacred vows."

"Masha, please!" said Innokenty, leaning closer to her, but Masha slid back away from him. He hunched back in his chair unhappily. "I have only one thing to say in my defense," he said. "It's a historical argument, and it might not seem convincing to you and the detectives, but for me, and for all the Old Believers, it puts the schismatics beyond all suspicion. This Heavenly Jerusalem our Sin Collector is so obsessed with? It's directly connected to the life and work of Patriarch Nikon, who promoted the idea of Moscow as a second Jerusalem. Nikon wanted to unite all branches of the Orthodox Church under the patriarchate in Moscow, especially the Greek and Ukrainian churches. To that end, among other things, he replaced the Russian two-fingered sign of the cross with the three-fingered sign the Greeks used. He revised the liturgical texts to follow the Greek versions. And you know what happened as a result. Some refused to follow the new rules, there was the schism, and the Old Believers split off from everyone else. For the Old Believers, Nikon and everything that he stood for is the lowest point in our history. Every ideal he worked for is diabolical to them, Masha. He wanted to be like the Catholic Pope, and he even built a new monastery, called New Jerusalem, outside Moscow. Nikon did it all in an attempt to imitate the Vatican. All of that is anathema to us. Believe me, no Old Believer would ever drink from that poisoned cup." Innokenty lifted his hands, seeming to give up. "I could tell you more, but—"

"I get it." Masha slipped off her stool. "I need to think about this. Sorry. I really need to get some rest."

"Sure, sure, of course," Innokenty said, fussing around her again. "Sorry. I just didn't want to keep that from you any longer. Forgive me, Masha, I'm not—I don't know what's wrong with me. I'll fix up a bed for you in the study."

He rushed off, but Masha sat still for a minute. Then she made herself put her dirty bowl in the dishwasher and lug the soup pot, still slightly warm, back to the refrigerator. Innokenty reappeared in the kitchen doorway. He looked harried, but Masha didn't feel sorry for him. She didn't feel sorry for herself, either.

All she wanted, desperately, was to sleep. When Kenty left her in the study and quietly pulled the door shut behind him, she wasted no time in tossing off her clothes and slipping into a cool forgetfulness there between the crisply ironed sheets. She was asleep in an instant.

ANDREY

Andrey regarded his boss's blood-red face. Usually when the tyrant was angry, Andrey worried. But today he definitely did not care. No boss man could possibly make him feel any worse than he already did. There was a monster after Masha—*his* Masha. And he did not know a single way to chase the killer back into the foul, dark pit from which he had emerged. Andrey's shame was propelling him forward, nagging him onward every time he stopped for half a minute to toss back a sandwich to fuel himself. But the whole race had been pointless. He was running on a treadmill. Every clue led to nothing, and all the suspects were dropping off the track. The police officer resting in his grave. The Old Believers. The military officers, interviewed just yesterday by the guys from his team about whether they had ever worked with Yelnik. There were too many murders, and he had to dig in dozens of different directions, like a mole, hoping to sniff out the slightest lead in this vast field of data. Any clue would be a miracle.

"Of all the fucking things!" Anyutin slammed his enormous fist on the desk. "Did you see this?" He tossed a newspaper down in front of Andrey with the headline "NEW CHIKATILO IN DOWNTOWN MOSCOW!"

Andrey dispassionately ran his eyes over the page, then went back to his own thoughts. If he couldn't catch the killer, then maybe he'd be able to hide Masha from him? No, he told himself. Hiding her wouldn't work. The only thing to do would be to keep her by his side, twenty-four hours a day, and maybe, just maybe, he'd be able to protect her. Not that she'd go for that.

The colonel was raging, "Can you imagine what kind of shitstorm is going to come down on me? How long can I feed them stories from the Old Testament?"

"It's the New Testament," Andrey corrected him without thinking.

"What the hell is going on?" Anyutin went on menacingly. "Everyone at Petrovka's a Bible scholar now? Do you think we're playing pick-up sticks here? Or are you just waiting for him to get through all of his, what are they, tollhouses, and disappear back to hell?" He slammed his fist down on the desk again, and paper flew in all directions. Somebody knocked at the door. "Yes!" Anyutin barked, while he and his subordinate collected the documents strewn across the floor.

"May I come in?" The voice at the door was a calm baritone.

In walked Katyshev. Anyutin's face went even redder, and he stood up and shook the prosecutor's hand. Katyshev nodded in Andrey's direction.

"I was just thinking about you. I was wondering how your investigation is getting along."

Andrey shook his head tiredly.

"It's not," Anyutin answered for him. "The guy's a ghost."

"Well," said Katyshev, settling into a chair with a cold chuckle, "that happens with serial killers, you know. Remember how many people the original Chikatilo got to." He nodded toward the open newspaper. "And how many of the wrong people were arrested for what he did."

"Don't try to make excuses for these so-called detectives," said Anyutin with a scowl, not even deigning to glance in Andrey's direction. "The clock is ticking, the bodies are rolling in, and these idiots haven't gotten one iota closer to solving the case."

Katyshev crossed his legs and calmly swung one foot back and forth. Andrey noticed how worn out his shoes looked.

"At least your men have figured out the rules of the game, which was no simple feat." He smiled sadly. "You know, I walk around Moscow myself, sometimes, without even recognizing it. I always wonder what happened to the city of my childhood. All these new nightclubs and strip shows, the abject poverty alongside the Bentleys and the champagne fountains . . . This suspect of yours doesn't have to operate under any of our rules or limitations. He slices up, or, I suppose, quarters, people we in law enforcement can't seem to get our hands on. Like that governor's wife."

Katyshev rose to his feet and sighed.

"Sometimes you have to wonder. Maybe we should give the guy the chance to finish what he started."

MASHA

Masha woke up when the front door slammed. She stayed in bed for a minute, listening. Not a sound. Kenty must have left for a meeting with a client, or maybe he'd gone to buy more groceries to cook for her, try to make amends. Masha wasn't mad at him anymore. And she realized now that she hadn't been convinced, not really, that the killer was as religious as all that. It was more likely, she thought as she got dressed, that he was just using religion as a cover. The idea of Heavenly Jerusalem, coupled with the list of Torments, gave him a precise pattern to work with. A path he could follow while doing just what his heart desired. And speaking of hearts . . .

Masha called her mother's cell phone, but landed in her voice mail. She was probably still sleeping.

Masha walked to the kitchen and poured herself some juice. She really was feeling better, here in Kenty's apartment. She decided she would not think about her stepfather. She would not think about the Sin Collector. She would think about those things tomorrow, and she was sure she'd have to keep thinking about them for a good long while. But today? Today she would try to read a book, maybe one from Kenty's collection. Nothing too serious, though, just something from when they were kids. Maybe a book from that Adventure Stories series. She had seen some of those in the study. Or Sir Walter Scott, or Thomas Mayne Reid. Masha leaned over the couch, one hand holding her glass of juice, the other hand running over the familiar book spines. Aha! Jules Verne, *The Mysterious Island*. Perfect! Masha hooked the little volume with one fingernail, and it slid off the shelf and into her waiting hand.

In the gap where *The Mysterious Island* had been, she could see the dark wood of the book case, and also something white. An envelope? Masha frowned. Was Kenty hiding money in his bookshelf? That didn't seem like the kind of thing he would do. So what was it? Masha wavered. She downed the rest of her juice and tossed the book onto the sofa. Still frowning, she reached for the envelope, and carefully slid it out from between the books. For a second, Masha stopped, ashamed of herself. The envelope was obviously supposed to be hidden away from prying eyes. But her curiosity won out. Kenty had already let her in on one huge secret, so, Masha reasoned, it made sense to check, just to make sure he wasn't hiding some other nasty surprise, right? She'd just take a quick look, she told herself, that was all. The envelope was not sealed.

Inside, there were photographs. But these weren't photos of both of them together, from the days Kenty and Masha made the rounds of youth festivals and parties. These pictures—black-and-white, glossy— were of Masha alone. Every single one of them.

After seeing the first one, she gasped and dumped out the rest. There was one shot of Masha leaving home in the morning, walking, laughing carelessly, with one of the boys from college who used to have a crush on her. There she was drinking champagne with her mother at a premiere at the Bolshoi. There was Katya, and other friends of hers, too. What *was* this? You could track her whole life through these pictures! School, her family, her friends, different events . . . Innokenty had been following her! For a long time, too. Masha remembered very clearly that outing to the Bolshoi five years ago, because her mother had forced her to wear a low-cut, floor-length dress. Innokenty had not been there with them. Or apparently he had been, but she hadn't seen him. Was he hiding behind a column or something, focusing on her through the lens of his camera? Masha looked with horror at all these snapshots from her life, spread all around her. Why had he done this? Why had he spied on her?

Masha swallowed nervously and stood up, brushing the pictures off her like poisonous insects crawling up her legs. She needed to get out of here, and now. She dashed into the hallway, where the cow-eyed faces of the old icons watched her from the white walls. Shaking all over, she struggled to put on her shoes. For God's sake, how could she have ever felt safe here? There was nowhere in this city where she could feel safe anymore! And she didn't think there was a single person she could trust, either. One thought nearly made her physically ill. She would have to go back to the empty apartment she had deserted, just a few hours before, where everything reminded her of her father and stepfather, and where—she knew for sure now—the killer had certainly set foot. Masha pushed open the heavy front door with clammy hands, and ran out into the echoing stairwell.

Suddenly Masha heard movement on the stairs below. The measured, confident step of a tall man, taking two stairs at a time. Innokenty. She scurried in the other direction and walked one flight up, and stood concealed behind the grating of the elevator shaft, watching him unlock the door.

"Masha?" he called, his voice worried.

The door closed behind him, and Masha flew like a bird down the stairs, rushing headlong to confront her own solitude.

ANDREY

From the moment he left Anyutin's office, where the colonel and Katyshev were still bemoaning the morals of the day, Andrey knew there was no way he would be capable of thinking, or engaging in any investigative activities whatsoever, until he saw Masha. He needed to embrace Masha Karavay, press her body to his and never let her go, until either they found the killer or he stopped killing. He would hold her that long, or maybe even forever. Eternity in Masha's embrace didn't seem like such a bad deal. Andrey didn't really trust Innokenty, but still, he felt better knowing she was with him rather than all alone. When he called and heard her expressionless voice on the line, pronouncing just two words—"I'm home"—Andrey did not stop to ask questions.

I just need to remember to stop at the store, he thought as he parked in front of Masha's building. His fridge was empty again. But that would be later, with her by his side.

As Andrey climbed the stairs, he heard voices. One male, speaking quietly, and the other female, slightly hysterical, which sounded as if it were coming from behind a closed door. He couldn't make out the words at first. But the higher he climbed, the more distinct the dialogue became. He recognized Innokenty's voice. And the first words he understood stopped Andrey in his tracks.

"Masha, please!" Innokenty was saying. "Please forgive me! I feel like all I'm doing is apologizing, admitting things I've done wrong.

What do you think? That I'm insane and I've been stalking you for years? Don't you think that might not be it at all? Isn't there—" Innokenty paused for a second. "Don't you see any other reasons, aside from me being some sort of bloodthirsty maniac, that I might have—Masha, why can't you see? I—"

"You lied to me!" Masha interrupted him, the panic sounding in a long, high note in her voice.

Andrey couldn't wait any longer, and he sprang forward.

"You hid so much from me!" Masha yelled. "I don't trust you now. I don't trust anyone!"

Andrey reached the landing and saw Innokenty standing with his forehead pressed to Masha's apartment door. He turned to Andrey, his eyes lost and unseeing.

"Masha!" Andrey called. "It's me. Open the door."

Andrey stepped forward, and Innokenty stepped aside, his shoulders shaking. "Please, Masha," said Andrey.

The door cracked open and there she stood, tears in her eyes.

"Where have you been?" She took a step toward Andrey. "Why did it take you so long to get here?"

Andrey hugged her then, the way he had dreamed of doing all day long, and he felt her hot, damp cheek pressed against his neck. He held her head to his shoulder, and moved his lips over the silky hair covering the back of her neck. He whispered, as soothingly as he could, "Hush, now. *Shhhhh.* Hush. Everything will be okay. Let's go to my place. We'll feed Marilyn. We'll eat, too. We'll go to bed and get a good rest, okay?"

And Masha only squeezed him harder and sobbed for a while before her breathing gradually returned to normal. Then he turned her to face him, and when Andrey looked into her sad, moist eyes, he thought he had never seen them look so piercingly green.

"Anything you want to bring with you?"

"That would be the third bag I've packed this weekend," she said. "No. I don't want anything. Just let me grab my purse."

Without letting go of his hand, Masha rummaged in the coat rack for her purse, turned off the light, and pulled the door shut behind them. This time she didn't bother to lock it.

Only then did either one of them remember Innokenty. They looked around, worried, but he was nowhere to be seen.

"Come on," said Masha, pulling Andrey by the hand. "Let's go. Marilyn Monroe must be starving."

THE SIN COLLECTOR

Moving with an easy, athletic stride, the man vaulted over the fence around the park and walked quickly toward the playground. The car was there, in place, black in the early-autumn twilight. He opened the door, sank down onto the worn seat, and sighed. He cranked the window down and lit a cigarette, then took a long, appreciative drag. The spicy smell of the leaves outside mixed with the cigarette smoke in his lungs. *Now the trees are covered with colorful leaves,* he thought, *but soon all that will remain of these trees is their black branches, like a cryptic script written on the pale sky. In the mornings, those benches will be covered with frost. And then the first snow will fall, and finally it will seem that everything has become lighter. But that is an illusion, a trick of the eye. Winter will come. Catharsis. Death, with no hope of clemency.* This year, too, would die. And he would die with it. No reason for regret.

The man carefully put out his cigarette in the ashtray, closed the window, and drove away. For some time, the road was completely empty. But suddenly, with a wailing of sirens, a fire truck flew into view from around a corner, and another one after it.

That was quick! The man laughed disdainfully. *Everyone's afraid of fire. They even say if you're being attacked, you should cry, 'Fire!' instead of shouting for help. Who would ever respond to a call for help?*

The man swallowed back a familiar bitterness in his mouth. He knew that bitterness would not pass, no matter how often he tried to gulp it down or how much alcohol he used to wash it away. He had driven as far as Kutuzovsky Avenue when the rotund silhouette of a traffic cop, waving his striped baton, emerged from the darkness on the side of the road to pull him over. The man frowned. He knew he had not broken any rules, simply because he never broke any. But he did not wish to be delayed here. Instead of his driver's license, he handed the traffic cop his badge, and he watched as the officer's gelatinous face quickly transformed into something like the formal grimace of a man in a military parade. "Have a good day, sir!"

The man could smell something burning. The wind must be blowing from that direction. His hands smelled like it, too. And a little bit like gasoline. He would have to remember to wash them with antiseptic. That would never fool the crime lab, but by the morning, at least, the smell would have to be gone, so that more inquisitive noses at work wouldn't sniff anything out. He had work yet to do. Masha Karavay would suspect there was one more left when she heard the news tomorrow. But she would be wrong. There would be two more. And he smiled again, the honest smile of a hard worker who had just a short way left to go before a well-deserved rest.

But back where he had come from, farther and higher up Poklonnaya Hill, deep in Victory Park, the enormous bonfire raged, leaping with joyful, bright flashes of flame against the blue-black night.

MASHA

Masha woke up because she was cold. They hadn't bothered to light the stove last night and settled instead for the space heater, which had been a mistake. She huddled against Andrey as best she could, warming one icy foot against his side, then a frozen hand under his arm. They had slept all night, interlaced like a strange kind of jigsaw puzzle. But at about two in the morning, Andrey had gotten up to turn off the heater, not wanting to risk a fire, and by morning, the small bubble of warmth generated by their combined bodies had drifted away. Masha finally gave up that blissful state of forgetfulness she had forged out of Andrey's sleepy breath on her cheek. It was time to get up and do some thinking.

Carefully, so she wouldn't wake him, Masha stretched out her legs and swung her feet onto the cold floor, then jerked them back again, shivering. But the thought of turning on the heater in the kitchen and of the old fleece Andrey had lent her last night gave her courage. Masha got out of bed, grabbed a small pile of clothing, and hustled into the kitchen, where Marilyn Monroe was already sitting at the ready. The mutt watched absentmindedly as his master's girlfriend slipped into a T-shirt and jeans in record time, then added a sweater, his master's fleece coat, and then, with a satisfied hum, his master's wool socks, which had been drying near the stove since last ski season.

Then Marilyn's new mistress disappeared again into the bedroom and returned with the heater. She put on the tea kettle . . . and she opened the *refrigerator!* Marilyn Monroe couldn't wait any longer. He stood up and went to press his flank against his mistress's legs, just in case she might have forgotten the poor hungry dog in the house. And the mistress, who was a kind soul, not yet spoiled by a strict master, offered Marilyn a pair of sausage links *right away*. She watched thoughtfully as Marilyn gulped them down as noisily as ever, and then gave him another one. Marilyn tried to handle that one with a little more sophistication, out of respect for the lady, and then he went to wait meekly at the front door. And the mistress understood him. She unhooked the latch and let him out to run around.

As Masha watched the dog forge a new path through the frosty yard, she wasn't thinking about anything. She simply let her eyes absorb the fog outside the window, the dark mass of the hedges that separated their little cottage from the next one, and the absolute silence. All she could hear was Marilyn's muffled tread over the freshly fallen, damp leaves, and the sound of his curious canine snout snuffling through the grass, crunchy with frost.

The boiling kettle brought her out of her reverie, tossing its poorly fitted lid. The lid landed with a crash on the wooden floor and rolled around the kitchen. A creaking sound from the bedroom told Masha she had woken Andrey after all. She frowned guiltily. He walked past her, looking adorable in just his jeans, his eyes still half-closed, and Masha couldn't help reaching out for him, pressing his sleep-warmed body against hers for a second. But Andrey, trying to stifle a yawn, muttered something about having to take a shower before he let anyone get near him. Soon the makeshift outdoor shower was gurgling aggressively on the porch, and she could hear him whooping and hollering like a child.

Laughing, Masha set the table, putting out almost everything they had brought from the twenty-four-hour supermarket the night before: yogurt, cheese, ham.

A couple of minutes later, Andrey returned, fully awake now. He kissed her on the cheek and poured some hot water over the grounds in the new Turkish coffee pot. Yesterday, in a weird housekeeping frenzy, they had even bought extra coffee for the future.

Once the coffee was ready, they sat down at the table. Masha warmed her hands around her mug. Andrey made himself a ham sandwich. They looked at each other awkwardly. Their first breakfast together. Andrey put his sandwich down and reached across the table, palm facing up. Masha smiled and put her hand in his.

"Everything's going to be okay," Andrey said, with the confidence of someone who has slept well and woken up in a good mood.

Masha nodded, and urged him back to his bread and ham with her eyes.

Andrey laughed. "Who do you take me for, Marilyn Monroe?" he asked and took a huge bite, then a swig from his mug.

"I was thinking," Masha began, then stopped.

"Yes?"

"I was thinking that I was wrong to treat Innokenty that way. I was just so scared. First my stepfather . . ." She gripped her coffee cup a little tighter. "And then they took my mom to the hospital, and Kenty told me about his family, and then all those pictures . . ." She looked up at him. "But none of that means anything, Andrey! I know Kenty inside out. I'd have to be insane to suspect him of murder! Cliché as it may sound, he truly would not harm a fly. Do you believe me?"

Andrey nodded.

"I've known forever that his family was unusual somehow. But that never mattered. I was too shy to ask about them back then, when we were kids, like, *Why are your mom and dad so weird?* I bet, if I had asked, he would have told me the truth. But I wasn't curious enough. I was too obsessed with my own little demons. Then he picked the worst possible day to reveal that secret to me. As for the photographs . . ." Masha lowered her eyes and used her fork to trace a flourish on the tablecloth.

"Well, it's pretty clear what *they* mean," Andrey said, sighing.

"Sure," said Masha, quietly. "I guess I must have known on some level, but I just never wanted to admit it to myself. I was so happy having him as my friend, but from a certain perspective, I was taking advantage of his feelings for me. I—well, to be honest, I've been a bad friend. A terrible friend!" Masha looked at Andrey sadly.

He wiped his mouth and made himself another sandwich. "There's no point punishing yourself, Masha. Yesterday it was your mom, and today it's Innokenty. Think about it. There's no way you could possibly have been a good friend to him. We can't be a good friend to someone who's in love with us. Because our friendship will never give them what they really want. So we hurt them, no matter what. But Kenty's a big boy and he made his own choices about your relationship. He had plenty of chances to tell you he loved you and see how you would have responded, try to win you over or whatever."

Masha suddenly giggled. "'Or whatever,'" she mimicked him. "What do you mean *or whatever*?"

"Well," said Andrey, pulling her by the hand over to his lap. "For example . . ."

Masha nodded thoughtfully. "Right. We all know how long and hard *you* courted me."

"I'm more interested in the result than in the process," Andrey whispered in her ear.

"Uh-huh. Kenty would be horrified if he knew how easy it was."

"No, you're not easy. You're just—very selective."

And with that momentous declaration, Andrey kissed her.

ANDREY

Unfortunately, Masha pulled away from him all too quickly. Andrey thought it must be the ham on his breath, but she was thinking of something else.

"I have to call Kenty and apologize." In a kittenlike move, she gave his cheek a pat, and then took her phone out onto the veranda.

Andrey wondered how he could ever have been jealous of Kenty. Now he just felt sorry for him. He even felt sort of superior, which was really funny when he thought about it. He was finishing his coffee when Masha returned. She looked worried.

"He's not answering. Not his cell and not his home phone, either. Where could he be?"

"Maybe his parents' place?" Andrey suggested, putting the rest of the food back in the fridge.

"No," Masha said, shaking her head thoughtfully. "He never spends the night there."

"Hey now," Andrey said, leading her toward the front door. "Don't worry too much over him. And don't get suspicious all over again. Maybe he's just singing in the shower and didn't hear the phone ring. Or maybe he got drunk last night to ease the pain, and he's sleeping, with the phone switched off."

"Innokenty, getting drunk?" Masha asked doubtfully.

"So you admit he sings in the shower, then?" Andrey teased as they climbed into his car. "A Verdi aria in the original Italian, I'll bet, none of this pop music nonsense!"

Masha laughed, but sadly. Andrey laid a hand on her knee—this time for reassurance rather than romance.

"I'm going to drop you at the clinic to visit your mom. Spend as much time with her as you need. Then take a taxi straight to Petrovka, okay? I don't want you out of arm's reach."

"All right," Masha answered obediently, and her knee shook a little under his hand. "But you don't need to worry, I told you—"

"You told me, and I heard you. The killer's going after the people you love, not you. I heard that yesterday when you said it in the supermarket, too. So let's frame it another way: you'll be protecting me with your presence, okay?"

"Okay, okay! I'll stay close by."

They stopped by the store again to pick up some juice, Natasha's favorite crackers, and some flowers. Half an hour later, he dropped her off in front of the clinic.

Andrey watched Masha walk in, and he spent a moment hoping that the events of the coming day wouldn't add to her worries. *Masha needs a break,* he thought as he pulled out of the clinic parking lot. She needed an intermission, or she'd need to be admitted herself. Her heart already ached too much to let her brain make any logical connections. Maybe that was exactly what the Sin Collector was counting on. Maybe he was clobbering her with pain to switch off her mind? Did that mean that regardless of how pointless all their poking around had seemed, they were actually getting close? He hoped Masha could concentrate fully on her daughterly duties for now. A new little idea was dawning in Andrey's head, and he wanted to check it out right away.

But the loud ringing of his phone disrupted that train of thought. It was Fomin. "Andrey. Looks like we have a new body."

"Hang on," Andrey told him, and swerved sharply to park on the shoulder, ignoring the furious honking that followed. "Are you sure it's one of ours?"

"Not positive, but seems like it. Last night, the fire department got called to Victory Park. The blaze was big enough to see from across the city. Then they found a burned corpse, and an ID with the name, uh, hold on . . ." Fomin rustled some papers. "Innokenty Arzhenikov. And since the place was the only one on our table outside the Boulevard Ring Road—Andrey? You still there?"

"Innokenty?" Andrey asked, his voice hoarse.

"Yeah, you know that name?"

"Yes, I do. He's the guy who wrote that table."

A short while later, he was back at the clinic. He spent some time sitting in the car, staring dumbly out the window, putting off the moment he would have to tell Masha the terrible news.

MASHA

She had just finished talking with Nadya. The doctor, as stern and calm as ever in her white lab coat, had told her that Natasha was in stable condition. She wasn't eating much and she was sleeping a lot, but that wasn't surprising, given the sedatives she was on. But there was no need to worry. Nadya smiled then, for the first time.

"Your mother is a very strong woman, Masha, dear. Believe me. The drugs she's getting will give her nervous system a break. But she'll be better soon, and then, terrible as it may sound, she'll be too busy making funeral arrangements to get bogged down by her own thoughts. So don't you even think about making those arrangements yourself, all right?"

"Got it," said Masha, remembering her fit of dish scrubbing in Katya's kitchen.

"Good girl!" Nadya smiled and gave her a pat on the head. "I've already looked in on her today. Don't just sit next to her while she's sleeping. Go outside and take a walk, find something to do with yourself."

"Okay," said Masha, and smiled back. But her smile was forced.

Nadya nodded good-bye and walked off down the corridor, and Masha stood there for a few seconds, watching her go. Then she dialed Kenty's number again. Again she got his voice mail.

When she left her mother's room, Masha caught sight of a familiar figure standing near the nurse's desk.

"Irina?" Masha walked over, and the woman turned around. Masha was surprised, as she always was, by her almost sickly thinness.

"Mashenka!" The woman broke into a smile and reached out to embrace her. "Such sad news, Masha! Your poor mother! Losing Fyodor, and now Yury, too! How is she?"

"She's sleeping," said Masha. "They're giving her sedatives, and—"

"Sure, sure," Irina said, tilting her head to look at her, and Masha saw that she had been crying. "And how are you doing? Holding on all right?"

"Yeah, I think so." Masha felt the tears welling up in her eyes.

"Now, now, don't cry," Irina said, stroking her shoulder. "Nick-Nick is very proud of you. Did you know that? He thinks you have a real knack for what you do. Just like Fyodor. A gift, if you want to put it that way."

That's when Masha finally broke down. She couldn't hold it back any longer. She took a breath, intending to say something, explain her sudden tears, but Irina was still stroking her back and whispering, "It's all right, it's all right."

There was something absurd about how it was only then that Masha was able to cry. Not on her mother's shoulder, and not to Innokenty or Andrey, but there with Nick-Nick's wife, someone she hadn't seen for probably ten years. She wiped her eyes and blew her nose into the lace handkerchief Irina offered her.

"I'm sorry. I'm so tired," Masha said.

"Of course, of course!" Irina said again, tucking the handkerchief away in her bag. As she did so, Masha caught sight of a bruise on the woman's arm. Irina hurried to adjust her dress. "Well, Mashenka, I've got to go and visit your mama. Come and see us soon, all right?"

And she stood up and walked off, with a heavy tread that didn't match her thin frame, down the hallway toward Masha's mother's room.

Masha decided to take Nadya's advice about going out for a walk while she waited for Natasha to wake up. She wanted to see her mother, tell her it would be okay, give her a kiss. Then, finally, she would go back to Petrovka. She felt irresistibly pulled to the place, like an addict needing her fix.

But as soon as she stepped outside she saw Andrey waiting, and then he was walking toward her quickly. Masha felt her heart freeze. The feeling of foreboding was so powerful that she stopped where she stood, not wanting to take a step to meet him. No matter what kind of news Andrey was bringing, she knew she would be much happier in the last few seconds before he opened his mouth.

"Poklonnaya Hill?" she asked after Andrey had told her about the most recent body.

"Yes. Moscow's own 'Hill of Worshipful Submission,' where pilgrims traditionally stop before entering a holy city to pray, bow, and—"

"I know what it is," Masha interrupted him. "Tollhouse?"

It was a refrain by now, a call-and-response routine.

"The nineteenth. Heresy. Deviation from the tenets of the Orthodox faith."

"Who?" Masha asked in a whisper.

"Masha," he began. "I'm so sorry."

But the deep, empty oblivion engulfed her before he could say the name.

ANDREY

Andrey barely managed to catch her as she fell. Masha lay in his arms, pale, her eyes rolled back in her head.

"Hey! Somebody, help!" Andrey shouted.

Clinic staff rushed toward them with a stretcher, and he stumbled over his words, trying to explain that Masha's mother was here already, shoving his badge under their noses. He said her mother was a friend of Nadya's, the name springing from his memory like a ping-pong ball even though Masha had only mentioned it in passing. Thank God, Nadya herself soon ran out, and she slapped Masha on the cheeks, trying to bring her around. Andrey stood there gaping like an idiot, shame pounding in his head like a migraine. He trotted along next to the men carrying her stretcher, which they were now loading into an enormous elevator.

Suddenly, Masha woke up and sobbed. "What's happening to me?"

"You fainted," Nadya said. "You're under a great deal of stress. Your mother has an empty bed in her room. We'll put you in there with her for the day, to rest."

Andrey swallowed hard and gave Masha's hand a squeeze. He felt a gentle pressure in response.

"I'll be back this afternoon," Andrey said, his voice hoarse. "What can I bring you?"

"Nothing." Masha closed her eyes. "I don't need anything."

"Masha's best friend died," he told Nadya when they left the room.

"Good Lord." She covered her mouth with her hand. "I don't suppose it's a coincidence?"

"No, it's not," Andrey answered, shaking his head. "This is the third murder of someone close to her, all in a row. I think—I think this is a terrible time for her. She's going to blame herself."

"But that's nonsense!" Nadya objected.

Andrey smiled morosely, nodded, and walked out of the clinic.

A very simple idea still had its hooks in him. It hadn't stopped nagging at him since the evening before. Andrey just needed one day to check it out, or half a day, if everyone would leave him alone. Andrey passed out assignments to each member of the Sin Collector team. He had one guy drive out to the military post where the soldiers had died, he sent one to interview witnesses at the Victory Park fire, and he asked another to do some research on the governor's wife's closest associates.

He could have come up with a hundred other urgent assignments, but they all had the same ultimate goal. He needed to get every member of the group out of the way, get all the secondary problems out of his head. He even ignored a call from Anyutin (blasphemy)! Relieved to find the office empty at last, Andrey locked the door from the inside, yanked the phone cord from the wall, and, in one decisive gesture, swept all the last few months' worth of papers, business cards, and file folders off the top of his desk. Then he exhaled, and dove into the dossiers on the Sin Collector case that had been delivered to him yesterday. He looked through all of them, right down to the photos of the lacerated hunk of flesh that had previously been Masha's stepfather.

Andrey scrutinized each file. He had to tease out the ties that bound the killer to the dead. How had the first victims caught the Sin Collector's eye? What if Innokenty was right and the Old Believers had nothing to do with it? Actually, the Old Believers were out of the question now, weren't they? Innokenty had been burned as a heretic, after all, so the one doing the punishing must be from some other camp. Could Kenty have been in the army? Or under criminal investigation? The killer was obviously no amateur, so somehow, Kenty must have caught the attention of the professionals: Andrey's own colleagues from defense or law enforcement.

Garrulous Dobroslav Ovechkin had once been charged with a misdemeanor and gotten off with a suspended sentence. The trial had been half a mile from here at the District Court. Then there was Julia Tomilina, who testified in court against her ex-lover; Alexander Solyanko, who was a party in the case against his competitor over planted drugs; not to mention Kolyan the drunk, who any police station might have hauled in once or twice. Andrey unfastened the top button on his shirt and opened a window. Then again, what if this was another dead end? What if he was wasting time while poor Masha lay in the clinic, sedated?

But Andrey forced himself to control his yearning to run off somewhere, anywhere, and do something, anything, quickly. He needed to be methodical. In control. He would not look at the clock, just at this dossier, page after page. The architect who got the amnesty. The thief, a repeat offender. Turina and all the countless bribes she took. But wait. Yelnik! The murderer they fished out of the Moskva. What had that hapless kid, that other Andrey, told him back in Yelnik's village? Andrey froze. He remembered Anyutin's office, their first conversation about the Sin Collector. And their most recent one.

All at once, Andrey understood everything. He jumped up and grabbed his coat. He needed to see Masha. But before that, he needed to prove his theory beyond a shadow of a doubt. He went down to the reception desk, handed in his key, and signed his name in the book. He asked to see the sign-out sheets for the day Masha's stepfather died. There was Anyutin's name, and next to it a brief signature executed with military precision and the time he'd turned in his keys. Andrey ran out of the building. He noticed he had started to breathe again. Now he could go see Masha.

Masha was lying with her face to the wall. She wasn't asleep, and neither was her mother. But they weren't talking, either. Natasha's eyes were swollen from crying, and when Andrey came in and said hello, she gave him a look that made his blood run cold. He put a hand on Masha's shoulder, and she turned over, slowly, and attempted a smile.

"Any news?" she asked.

Andrey glanced over at Natasha's bed. Without a word, the older woman stood up and quietly left the room.

"I know who it is, Masha," Andrey told her, even though he hadn't been sure, on the drive over, that he wanted to tell her the whole story.

"You know?" Masha sat up a little on her pillows.

"Take it easy. You don't want to get worked up," he said, then immediately regretted the cliché.

Masha's brow furrowed and her eyes narrowed. "I'm not sick, Andrey. I can handle it. If you found out who it is, and you're planning on doing anything without me, I'll never forgive you. Got it? I have to be there to help you catch him. Because of Katya, and my stepfather"— tears shone in her eyes—"and Kenty."

"All right," said Andrey. "Get dressed. We're getting out of town."

"Where to?" Masha asked, pulling on her fleece.

"Your friend Katyshev's dacha."

Masha frowned. "How did you know Nick-Nick has a—"

"I guessed," Andrey said, smiling sadly.

"But I don't know where it is! The last time we went was before Papa died. I remember there's a little brook, and a forest, but I don't remember the name of the train station or anything."

"The village of Narino, off the Kaluga Highway. House number twelve, I think. It *is* across from the woods, you're right about that."

Masha and Andrey turned around. Natasha stood in the doorway, pale as her white nightgown and terry-cloth robe.

"Mama." Masha sounded unsure.

But Natasha was looking Andrey straight in the eye. "Go. Go right now, before it gets dark."

They made good time on their way out of Moscow, but Masha said nothing, staring straight ahead.

"Why?" she finally asked, once Andrey had left the city limits.

"Ever since your stepfather died, and ever since Katya, I've been asking myself one question: Why you?" Andrey began. "Why was he weaving his web around you, specifically, and why did he seem to be performing for you? As if he were showing off for you or something. Didn't you ever wonder the same thing?"

"Well," said Masha, slowly. "I thought it was because I have a sense for how he operates."

"All that sensing is a load of crap, Masha. It's metaphysics, fortune-telling." Andrey sounded angry. "I can't believe we didn't see it right after your stepfather died! He knew it was you who had spotted him. Nobody but you had made the connection between those murders. You had teased out his motive, you had connected the crime scenes with Heavenly Jerusalem, you had unearthed *St. Theodora's Journey Through the Tollhouses*. You did all that, Masha!"

"Innokenty helped," she said quietly.

"Stop it!" He slammed one hand against the steering wheel, trying to control himself. He was really angry, but not at Masha.

"Fine," she said. "So what?"

"So you became extremely interesting to the murderer!"

Masha's face went pale, and she turned toward the window.

"I've known that for a while now. Just yesterday I told you that all this is my fault."

"You're such an idiot!" Andrey couldn't help it. "You're so smart, but you're such an idiot! Think! Who knew that you were the one who connected the murders with Heavenly Jerusalem?"

"Lots of people. Please don't yell."

Andrey took a couple of deep breaths, and gripped the wheel harder. "I'm sorry. Damn it! The solution was right there in front of us this whole time, and we were stumbling around like blind kittens, distracted by all our fancy theories. Lots of people? Not that many, Masha." He glanced over at her. Masha was still looking out her window at the parade of country cottages strung along the road. "Remember? Our investigative team didn't know who first discovered what. Only five people actually knew for sure. You, me—"

"Innokenty, Anyutin . . . and Nick-Nick."

"Right, Masha. Your friend Nick-Nick. Chief Prosecutor Katyshev, who took an interest in this case from the very beginning. Katyshev, who straight-out told Anyutin, last time we met, that maybe we should let the killer finish what he started!"

"That's crazy, Andrey," Masha objected, her voice hoarse. "He only meant that his own hands are tied, since the justice system—"

"Exactly! Remember our psychological profile. *Your* profile, again. The killer most likely works in law enforcement, probably served in the military. Katyshev was in the army, wasn't he?"

Masha nodded without speaking.

"And this sick desire to take justice into his own hands? You told me yourself that's the hallmark of a maniacal missionary! Who better to judge us all than Mr. Bigshot Prosecutor himself?"

Andrey stopped talking. He took out a cigarette and rolled down his window. He could see Masha out of the corner of his eye, and sensed that she was beginning to believe him.

"And there's something else. I've spent the afternoon going back through all the Sin Collector case files trying to find the link. How does the killer meet his sinners? I still wasn't sure if it was my boss, Anyutin, or Katyshev. Both of them fit pretty well. Then I realized: all the victims had a run-in with the courts, in one way or another."

They passed a sign: "Now Entering Narino."

"Turn right up ahead," said Masha softly.

Andrey nodded. He made the turn and slowed down.

"Know how I figured out I was on the right track?"

Masha went on looking silently at the country road.

"I remembered the day I went to visit Yelnik's place in the country. He had Andreyka, the village idiot, working for him. The kid hadn't seen the killer, just his car. But he said something I didn't pay attention to at first. On the day he disappeared, Yelnik sent Andreyka away, telling him a friend had come to see him, a very important man Yelnik owed his life to. Now, Masha, can you remember who the prosecutor was at Yelnik's last trial? The prosecutor who allegedly didn't have enough evidence to convict?"

They pulled up in front of the very last house on the main road, and Andrey switched off the engine. Masha turned to face him, her chin jutting out stubbornly like a child's.

"I still don't believe it. Nick-Nick was my father's best friend, and he loved my mother." Masha shoved her door open, then looked back at Andrey. "What if it's really Anyutin?"

Andrey shook his head. "I checked it out, and it couldn't have been him. An unidentified visitor rang the doorbell at four thirty, when your stepfather was in that rented apartment for his, um, usually scheduled appointment. But Anyutin was at the office until eight—the logs say so. That's not a guarantee, I know, so I haven't told him anything about Katyshev."

The two of them walked along the edge of the forest. The ground was slippery with fallen leaves and springy with moss underfoot. Andrey took Masha's hand to steady her. It was damp to the touch, but her face looked calm and focused now, and Andrey was relieved. He knew that giving Masha's brain some hard work to do would help distract her from other more dismal thoughts. Masha suddenly stopped walking. There in front of them was an old wooden fence, strips of ancient paint hanging off it.

"This is it," Masha whispered. "Nick-Nick's dacha. I think the gate is over there."

They circled the cottage warily. Everything was still. It had been cold enough the past few days that vacationers in the neighboring dachas had gone back to the city, and there weren't many locals around, either. Just smoke rising from a chimney or two at the other end of the village. Andrey tried to ram through the locked gate with his shoulder, but Masha slipped a thin hand between the boards and opened the latch from the inside. She turned to Andrey.

"Remember what he said? 'Open up. It's me!'"

"I remember," said Andrey. "Your stepdad didn't know Anyutin, but he did know Nick-Nick. The killer came down from one floor up and rang the doorbell. When your stepdad asked who was there, the killer didn't even need to say his name. He knew he'd be recognized."

Masha gulped. "They're not here. I saw Nick-Nick's wife today at the hospital. She came to check on my mom. She had a bruise on her arm." Masha shook her head desperately. "I know serial killers often abuse their families, too, but maybe she just hurt herself somehow? Are you sure it's him and not Anyutin? I mean," said Masha, looking at him pleadingly, "Nick-Nick has never been religious. I would have known!"

"Do you want to wait outside?"

"We can't go in without a warrant," Masha said, but Andrey had already walked up to the door, raised one hand, and magically summoned up a hidden key. In one ordinary twist of the wrist, he unlocked the door. It swung open with a creak, and Masha followed Andrey inside.

MASHA

The first thing she saw was an icon. It had its own honored place in one corner, as tradition dictated. Masha jumped and exchanged a glance with Andrey, who was nice enough to say nothing. As she looked around, memories crowded in. Memories from her childhood, from the days she hadn't yet been poisoned by her father's death.

There, at that table, they had sat together cleaning mushrooms they'd found in the woods. Irina had taught her to string the right kind of mushroom on a thick white thread, which they would hang over the round stove like a Christmas garland to dry. And there on that veranda, Mama had laughed while she and Nick-Nick washed the lunch dishes in a tub. In the old rocking chair, Papa had stretched out his legs and talked with Irina, who was always stitching away at something, mending or knitting, and listening uneasily to Natasha's laughter pouring in from the veranda, which Fyodor never seemed to notice. The memories were so vivid that Masha almost forgot why they had come. She looked at the row of folded-up cots on the veranda and ran a hand over the worn lacquer of the old buffet. It held ceramic knick-knacks, probably heirlooms from Irina's parents. A little boy in ice skates. A little girl with skis. She thought she could even remember Irina saying how much she loved those little pieces of bourgeois charm, kitschy as they were. Mama hadn't understood, of course.

A loud scraping noise shook her out of her reverie. It was Andrey, moving the heavy table aside and lifting the cheerful little striped rug. Underneath was the trap door leading down to the cellar. Masha nodded. She remembered the cellar, too. As a girl, she had helped Irina carry jars of pickled mushrooms and jam down there.

Down they went, into a room that stank of mold and neglect. Masha's foot knocked against an empty jar, which clattered away in the darkness. Andrey pulled a cord, and a dim, swinging light bulb illuminated the room. The walls were lined with racks of shelves, which in Masha's childhood had been full of provisions for the winter, sacks of potatoes, and apples. Now all that decorated those shelves were rows of large, empty jars. There were gaps in the rows, like missing teeth.

"I thought—I was sure, actually, that the cellar was bigger than this." Masha's voice echoed strangely in the neglected, dusty place.

"Everything looks big when we're kids," Andrey answered glumly.

"I wonder why Nick-Nick's wife quit gardening." She ran a finger thoughtfully over one of the dusty jars. "She used to get so excited about her jams and pickles! They don't have kids, you know, and—"

"*Shhhhh!*"

Andrey was rapping his knuckles on the back of one of the racks of shelves.

"You're right. This cellar really is a lot bigger than it looks. Come help me."

Together, the two of them began taking jars off the shelves. When the rack was completely empty, Andrey gave it a tug, first in one direction, then the other. All of a sudden it gave way with a groan and swung slowly away. The sickly light bulb only illuminated a few inches into the space hidden on the other side of that shelf, a room that did not look dusty at all.

Andrey told her to wait, and Masha obeyed. She didn't want to see what was in there. She yearned for knowledge, as her father used to say, like a sunflower reaching for the sun, but she also realized that she had reached a certain boundary, a limit. And that boundary was drawn right there, where this uncertain light met the deep blackness on the other side of the cellar. Andrey took out a flashlight and walked in, and Masha sat down on an old overturned bucket to wait, struggling to keep her eyes fixed on her dusty fingers.

For a while, the flashlight danced over a hastily whitewashed wall, but then Andrey found another switch, a far brighter light poured down, and a brilliant new world emerged from the darkness, ruled by a remorseless truth. Masha felt left behind in the dark. In that other world, she could see things on the walls. An enormous map of old Moscow hung next to a map of Jerusalem. Next to that was a modern-day map with red flags neatly pinned onto it. Masha gulped. She had one of those, too, and hers had pins in just the same places. She saw the eyepiece of a video camera. Did he observe his victims through that lens? There was a massive professional-grade refrigerator where, apparently, Yelnik had spent half a year. Some carpentry tools. Masha remembered, with a start, how her mother used to urge her father to be more like Nick-Nick, who was a real handyman. *But you, Fyodor! You couldn't hammer a nail into the kitchen wall!* Farther back, there was a simple, solid workbench. Masha didn't need to get any closer to see that it was covered with dark stains.

"Look at this." Andrey walked over to a bookshelf and pulled out one thin volume. *St. Theodora's Journey.* He opened the fridge. "It's switched off, but it's definitely the right size," he said, and pulled out something that looked like an aquarium.

"What is that?" Masha asked, her voice trembling, still not getting up off her bucket.

"Maybe some kind of incubator?" Andrey turned the glass box over carefully in his hands. "To hold—"

"Ants." Masha finished his sentence in a whisper. "Let's get out of here!"

Andrey picked up a metal-tipped whip, and put it down again.

"Yeah. Let's go," he said. "I've seen enough."

He had raised his hand to turn off the light when Masha stood up and called, "Wait!"

Trying not to look around, she marched across the room and, in one quick swipe, ripped the map with the red pins off the wall. It rolled up in her hands.

"Now let's go," she said. But halfway up the stairs, she couldn't resist looking back at the black hole where the secret hideout had been. *So that's where you were,* she told herself. Heavenly Jerusalem. Right here in this dark basement, for Nick-Nick—her Nick-Nick!—the light had shone down from on high and the angels had sung in chorus. *Oh my God . . .* She stumbled up the last few steps, ran out of the house, leaned over the railing of the porch, and threw up. Then Masha sat on the steps for a long while, gasping in the frosty air, while Andrey kept an arm wrapped around her shoulders, trying to fend off the trembling that wracked her body.

When they got in the car, Masha had almost stopped shaking. She looked silently at the map rolled up in her lap. Andrey called Petrovka and told them to send some forensics experts out to the dacha. He decided to leave the front door, and the entrance to the cellar, wide open. He also asked Fomin to stop by and see if Katyshev was in his office. He turned out not to be, and he wasn't answering his phone. Masha called his home number. Irina answered and said her husband wasn't at home. After a pause, she asked, "And how's your mom?"

So Masha got stuck updating Irina on her mother's progress and her own, trying hard not to ask any sort of question that might tip her off. She listened submissively to Irina's worried advice. ("You need to get more rest, Mashenka! At least eight hours of sleep a night, try some mint tea or chamomile.") It was enough to make Masha think that she, and the whole world, had finally lost their minds. Masha made herself glance in the rearview mirror at the forest disappearing behind them in the early dusk. There was only one person she knew who was crazy—though of course he must not think so.

When their conversation was wrapping up, Masha asked casually, "Do you two go to your dacha much anymore?"

For a second, she thought the call might have been disconnected. But then Irina answered, her voice sad.

"You know, we never go at all anymore. He doesn't have the time, and it's no fun when it's just me. And Nikolay says the house is falling apart, and he never gets around to fixing it up, because he spends all his energy bringing his bad guys to justice." She laughed, awkwardly, and Masha shuddered at what an apt description that was.

"Well, Mashenka! Tell your mother I said hello, and get well soon," Irina said, and they hung up.

"So," said Andrey, "that means Katyshev isn't anywhere. Do you think he knows we've fingered him?"

"I don't know," said Masha. "But I think so," she added, more confidently.

Andrey gave her a worried look. "If he knows we're on his trail, he might try to run."

Masha shook her head. "No. If he knows we're on his trail, he'll try to finish what he set out to do."

"Are you sure?" asked Andrey, glancing over at her.

Masha laughed sadly. "Positive. I know Nick-Nick. He's very conscientious."

THE SIN COLLECTOR

He still had time. He had done the calculations many times over. He didn't trust taking the car—there could always be a traffic jam—and he didn't feel like going underground to take the metro. Instead, he walked the Boulevard Ring Road, and when it came down to it, he had earned this walk.

He wore an old Mackintosh-type raincoat, frayed at the wrists. His wife had fixed up the lining more than once, but she couldn't do anything about the fraying. He loved this old jacket though, loved even the disrepair it was in. The raincoat lived his life with him from the start of fall until it got cold enough for a wool coat, then again from midspring to summer. And he always preferred these middle seasons to the winter cold or the intense summer heat. Between seasons, when the sun shone gently and the air was wet and carried a stronger smell of gasoline, it was easier for him to believe what his heart could see. What he saw now were not the cars flashing by, the tacky billboards, the sordid advertisements, or the current of people flowing past him, none of whom even noticed the man in the decrepit old raincoat and scuffed shoes, the man with the face that looked tired of life.

No, he had become invisible even to himself, like the changeable air in those times between the seasons, and he could see the urban landscape around him changing as well. The walls of Bely Gorod rose up, the walls Boris Godunov had called Tsargrad, the white rock emerging to conceal the river of filthy garbage below. Above the walls there was only the sky, the same as it had been in 1593, when Fyodor Kon finished the construction, and the Khan and his marauders rode right up to the fortress walls and left again empty-handed. He smiled cunningly, as if he himself were sitting under that pyramid of a roof and watching the Tatar horde retreat into the distance.

He had almost reached his second-to-last stop: an enormous C-shaped building with three wings just off the Boulevard Ring. One wing had an exit onto Znamenka Street, the "Street of the Sign." He thought he'd walk along that street, too, afterward. Then he'd get to see two small churches before him, through the advancing dusk, as if they had never been demolished: the Church of St. Nicholas the Wonderworker, with its three domes and bell tower, where they had built a garish new chapel, and the Church of the Sign of the Holy Mother, where now there was nothing but a playground. He'd need only half an hour to do his work, and then he'd take a leisurely walk to Borovitskaya Square, and from there, on to the waterfront.

He showed his ID at the desk and they handed him a pass. *MMMD*, the pass read. Main Military Medical Directorate of the Ministry of Defense of the Russian Federation. The corner of the little card featured a complicated emblem: the traditional serpent, wrapped around a chalice. And there was something inside the cup. A dagger? A mortar? Oak branches on each side, an eagle posed above it, a red cross below. *My, oh my!* He chuckled. Such ridiculous heraldry.

He knocked at the door. The secretary had already left, as he had anticipated, and he walked in, welcomed by a low, rumbling voice. Leontiev even stood up to greet him. There was a certain apprehension in his eyes. Clearly, he wondered what the prosecutor might want from him. But in the end, you don't turn down meetings with people like Herr Prosecutor, even after you've worked your way into a directorship, into a vast office with a view of the Kremlin. They shook hands, and then Leontiev sat down in his leather chair at the end of a long table, polished till it gleamed like ice. He gestured with one broad hand that his visitor should have a seat, too.

"I've heard of you, of course!" he boomed, taking a look at the man in the old raincoat. "To what do I owe the pleasure?"

The man smiled, baring some poorly made dentures.

"Oh, I'll be quick. I know your time is valuable. Just one small question," he said. "I've received some information about a series of suicides. Or, I should say, apparent suicides. All the men who killed themselves had been soldiers in Afghanistan. Now, here's what I figured out." Was the man in the raincoat's smile turning into a sneer, or had it always been that way? "I learned that they all had been denied wheelchairs. That same decree—dictated, officially speaking, by the need to conserve resources—also canceled the veterans' prescription-medicine discounts."

"I'm not sure I understand your interest in this ministry's affairs." Leontiev was trying to remain polite, but on the open face that had been such an asset in his career, a hint of annoyance was visible. "You know as well as I do how much the federal budget has shrunk."

The man nodded in time with the tapping of his old shoe on the floor, and he went on as if nothing had happened. "However, according to the information I have, at the same time, a new suite of furniture was purchased for your office." He ran a finger gently over the shining tabletop. "Cherry, is it?"

Leontiev nodded.

"For a little more than five million rubles," the man continued. "All of this carving work, the bronze and the good leather, it all costs good money, doesn't it?" He stood up and walked around the table, very close to Leontiev, his voice friendly. "Doesn't all this expensive garbage give you a rash on the ass?"

"What is the meaning of this?" Leontiev was rising slowly out of his chair, upholstered in that incriminating leather. Standing, he was the same height as this uncouth prosecutor. Suddenly he heard a click. His eyes darted to one side, and there, just an inch from his temple, another eye stared at him, unblinking—the barrel of a pistol. He also saw, for the first time, the eyes of the man in the ragged raincoat. Compared to them, the pistol looked almost kind.

"What are you—?" Leontiev began, but the man ordered him to shut his mouth, and with the easy gesture of a practiced magician, pulled a gag over Leontiev's head and fastened it tight around his mouth. From the other pocket of his raincoat, the man took a roll of packing tape, which he used to tie Leontiev to his extravagant chair. There was a moment when Leontiev could have broken free. But that pistol . . . And the prosecutor seemed so sure of himself, not even the slightest bit nervous. Now he laid an ordinary black briefcase on the table. In no more hurry than before, he began taking wooden pegs out of the case, one after another, and he arranged them neatly on the table.

Leontiev thought he must be going mad. The events taking place here in his office, with no particular ceremony, simply did not compute. What could the man need those pegs for? Before Leontiev found an answer, his eyes stopped darting around like a frightened bird's and he froze. Moving just a little, he rolled closer to the table. The new furniture did not creak, and the carpet concealed the sound. With the sole of one long soft-leather dress shoe, Leontiev felt for the alarm button under the table. There was the usual button that alerted building security, but there was a second one with a direct connection to the police. One more inch, just one more . . . He coughed a little, to distract the prosecutor from what he was doing, and finally—oh, thank God!—his foot hit the alarm button.

ANDREY

The call came in when they were almost back in the city. Fomin was shouting into the phone that headquarters had gotten an emergency call relaying audio from an important functionary's office.

"I heard him ranting and raving about something!" Fomin yelled, excited. "A thin voice, like a woman's, but it wasn't a woman, and it was—"

"Where?" Andrey asked, cutting him off.

"The army medical office, on Znamenka Street. There's an entrance on the Boulevard Ring."

"Why aren't you there?"

"We're driving over now, Captain. We'll be there in five minutes, ten tops. It's rush hour, you should see the fucking traffic."

"That was part of his plan," Andrey said quietly. "Fine, go ahead, do what you can."

"What was he ranting about?" Masha asked Fomin. She had not missed one shouted word of the phone conversation.

"They sent me the recording," Fomin said. "I'll play it, you can listen."

Andrey switched to speakerphone. At first, all they could hear was a muffled moaning.

"He gagged him," Masha whispered.

Then there was a terrible voice, high and thin, chanting, "Here we were met by the evil spirits of the last and twentieth Torment, the station of Heartlessness and Cruelty. Cruel are the tormentors of this place, and their prince is terrible, dry and depressed of countenance. Even if a man performs the most outstanding deeds, mortifies himself by fasting, prays ceaselessly, and guards and keeps the purity of his body, if he has been merciless, then from this station he is cast down into the abyss of hell and will receive no mercy in all eternity. I sentence you, sinner, to a hasty descent into hell, by impalement."

"Did you hear that?" It was Fomin's voice on the line again. "Creepy, right? Okay, we're here."

"Stay on the line," Andrey told him. He groped under his seat for his police lights, and without slowing down reached out the window and shoved them into place on the roof of the car. They could move faster now, but their progress was still slow, monstrously slow. Meanwhile, Fomin provided them with terse narration.

"We're here, boss. We're surrounding the entrance. We're inside. We're splitting up, one group on the stairs, the other on the elevator."

Masha sat next to Andrey, on the edge of her seat. They could hear the pounding footsteps, then a fire-escape door opening with a creak, then more footsteps, and a pause. There was the crash of a door getting blasted open, and then—silence.

"Fomin! Are you okay?" Andrey shouted. "What do you see?"

"Oh my God," Fomin breathed into the phone. "I'm here. We're all okay. But this guy—"

"Ask him to describe it," Masha whispered.

"Uhhh," Fomin began. "There's a man sitting in a chair. The chair's on the table, like a monument or something. There's, uhhh, stakes sticking out of his ribs. Like a fucking bloody porcupine, for God's sake."

There was a sudden burst of shouting, and Fomin's voice filled the whole car.

"He's alive! Get him down, he's alive!"

311

Masha and Andrey sat transfixed. At the other end, they could hear chaos, chairs crashing to the floor.

"No," someone else said. "His body was just spasming before death. Get the forensics guys over here."

Fomin spoke up. "That's it. He's dead."

"Fomin. Listen to me." Andrey was speaking slowly, knowing that poor Fomin must be in shock. "Go down to the reception desk. Look at the list of visitors the dead man had this afternoon. Look to see when they came and when they left. Hurry! I'll still be on the line."

He asked Masha to use her phone to call Anyutin.

"Colonel, sir," said Masha, her voice shaking. "We know who the Sin Collector is. It's Nikolay Nikolayevich Katyshev."

Anyutin coughed carefully. "Intern Karavay, forgive me, but are you feeling all right?"

But Andrey had already grabbed her phone.

"Colonel, we were at his dacha. We found everything. Maps, torture tools. There's no doubt it's him. I don't have time to explain more. We've just found a new body. I need you to spread the word, okay? Alert all the traffic checkpoints, send SWAT teams to his home address and to his dacha."

"What about you?" Anyutin asked. Judging from his lack of objections, Anyutin must believe him. There was something in Andrey's voice that could not be denied.

"I'll call you back, sir," Andrey answered, and he hung up.

MASHA

At almost exactly the same time, Fomin came back on the other line.

"Okay, I have the visitor log. Today the victim had three afternoon meetings. Here's the last one: N. N. Katyshev. In at 7:15, out at 7:45."

"Which door did he use? Did he leave through the reception area?"

"Well, yeah," said Fomin, not understanding. "It was all by the book. Here's the signature, they gave him a pass—"

Andrey swore, glancing at Masha. "Get back to Petrovka," he ordered Fomin. Furious, he slammed the phone down on the dashboard.

Masha knew why he was so livid. It wasn't even eight o'clock yet. They had come so close. The killer could have been any one of the ghostly silhouettes of pedestrians hurrying by.

"He'll never go home again," Masha said quietly. "And I doubt he'll go back to the dacha. Let me think."

They parked, and Masha spread the map from the cellar across her knees. She peered at the web of downtown streets and at the holes from the pins scattered here and there over the pale-green background. *So,* Masha thought. *Now we look at it the other way around.* She started very methodically, one by one, to count off the places the murders had been committed. Bersenevskaya waterfront. Lenivka. Pushkin Square. Kolomenskoye. As she counted, she smoothed over each pinhole in the paper with her finger. She felt as if she were releasing those old names of the streets and squares from their terrible history, setting them free again. Her finger faltered for a moment when she came to Poklonnaya Hill. Andrey opened the window and smoked a cigarette, never taking his eyes off of her. Lubyansky, Nikolskaya, Prechistenka. One remained. One mark, almost in the center of the map, where there were already more than enough pinholes.

Masha picked up the map and held it closer to her eyes. She read the name, then turned her pale face to Andrey.

"There it is," she said. "Do you see? He had everything ready for us."

"What do you mean?" Andrey tossed his cigarette out the window and took the map from her.

"A few of the tollhouses, a few of the murders, were missing. I thought that Nick-Nick—that the killer—must have committed them, but we didn't know where to look. But here on the map, there are exactly enough pinholes for every victim we've found, including the murder he committed today . . . and one more. There was an extra pin on the map, Andrey."

"And what does that mean?"

Masha spoke slowly. "I think he allowed for the possibility that we might find his lair. And if we did, and found his map, then he would have no way back. So he left just one extra pin on the map, a place he could return to, if necessary, after he made it through all the tollhouses. That pin marked a place we haven't connected with a killing yet. But . . ." Masha paused, then went on, her voice flat. "But it *was* on the list that Kenty made."

"Are you saying he's asking the two of us for a meeting?" asked Andrey, incredulous.

Masha nodded.

"At"—Andrey squinted and read the tiny lettering, barely legible in the dim light of the car—"Vasilevsky Slope?"

"At Vasilevsky Slope."

MASHA

"You stay in the car," Andrey told her.

He kissed her, his lips taut, then pulled a gun out of the glove compartment and left. There were fewer lights here, and it was completely dark. A few lingering tourists wandered around the square, on the hill leading from St. Basil's down to the Moskva, where it flowed past the Kremlin. Masha sat there terrified as the air inside the car gradually got colder.

Maybe I should call Anyutin? Why did Andrey go by himself? Or maybe he called everyone as soon as he got out of the car and the place is already surrounded? In that case, why haven't they gotten all these foreigners out of the area?

Masha thought time must have stopped. She looked around. This was the obvious place to meet, now that she thought about it. The perfect scene for the final act in this nightmare. The Kremlin wall seemed higher here than anywhere else. This road flowed like a wave, in a wide ribbon, down to the river, crowned on the high end of the slope by St. Basil's Cathedral. The building was brightly lit, and from here, it looked like an elaborate gingerbread house. It was a favorite spot for teens and tourists to come for pictures, the kind of place where you could reduce a complex, amazing city to one nice glossy picture.

As Masha looked at the wall of the ancient fortress, almost black in the night, she thought about how the history of any city, any point on the map where people have lived pressed close together for centuries, was a history of blood and cruelty. Human beings were pitiless creatures. If all the blood that had ever been spilled on the streets of those ancient cities were to rise up over the cobblestones, we'd all be wading around in it up to our ankles, maybe our knees. And we'd never agree to live in a city again, because of all the cities in creation, only one was free of sin—and nobody had ever seen it. The City of God, Heavenly Jerusalem.

A phone rang, and Masha realized in horror it was Andrey's. He had left it on the dashboard, which meant he couldn't call anyone for help. And *that* meant he was out there alone in the dark, hunting for a killer, who was lying in wait for him in some dim shadow of the fortress wall!

In one swift move, Masha grabbed the phone, tumbled out of the car, and, like a baby bird fallen from its nest, helplessly looked around in all directions. The phone had stopped ringing and she couldn't see Andrey anywhere. People hurried by, intent on their own business, and she suddenly wanted to take a deep breath of the cold, wet river air and shout at them all, *Get out of here! Save yourselves!* Instead she let out a short, spastic breath and started scrolling through the phone's contact list for Anyutin's number.

"Mashenka," a quiet voice said then, and for a split second she sighed with relief. Thank God, Nick-Nick was here! He'd know what to do! But then she remembered, and she froze.

He was standing right behind her. Masha thought she could even smell his old-man breath.

"Mashenka," he said again, in a voice that was at once dear to her and utterly repulsive. "Your papa would have been proud of you. You always were a very smart and very stubborn girl." He chuckled softly, sounding pleased with himself. "And I very much believed that you and I would meet one day, right here, at the end of my journey. I really had no desire to be here by myself. But I was sure you would seek me out! Fyodor also trusted me at the beginning, do you see? But that night he started asking questions. Before I had even answered, he knew. He knew me so well, Fyodor! We were best friends! Nobody else could see through my lies, but he always knew!"

Masha gritted her teeth and turned to face him. Nick-Nick was standing with his hands stuffed into the pockets of his ripped old raincoat. Masha remembered that jacket. It must have been fifteen years old. Nick-Nick smiled at her, a smile that was tired and sad.

"You—" Masha could not finish her sentence.

"Yes, Mashenka. I killed him. Not with my own hands, of course. The people who had bribed me killed him. You understand." He tried to step even closer to her, but she moved away. "It was a time when everything was so confused, Masha. There was such poverty, such chaos. Economic, political, moral. I was lost and confused."

"Papa wasn't confused!" Masha screamed, her eyes full of tears. And she jutted her chin forward determinedly. What was she doing talking to him, defending her father to a monster? But she couldn't help it. She had been waiting for this conversation since she was twelve years old.

"No, your father was not confused," Nick-Nick agreed, and his face twisted painfully. "Fyodor always had that moral compass. But I only discovered mine later, when I found God. I found peace, Masha. I became a different man."

"A different man?" Masha's voice was getting higher, and as she spoke, another voice rang out, just like in a bad movie.

"Freeze!"

Andrey was five steps away, his gun pointed at Katyshev's head.

Nick-Nick grabbed Masha by one shoulder and yanked her toward him. She felt the cold gun against her temple.

"Not so fast!" said Katyshev. "We haven't come to terms yet, young man. Put your gun down. Put it down!" he bellowed, and Masha saw Andrey slowly laying his pistol on the ground. "Hands behind your head!" Katyshev ordered. Masha heard his voice changing. She knew every intonation of his speech by heart, but these new tones, with the hysteria that ran through them, were completely unfamiliar. A wave of horror washed over her.

"Now then," said Katyshev, and Masha felt the steel trembling against her forehead. "Where were we? I became a judge. I could no longer tolerate the licentious or bear the sight of their lawlessness. I could not! They were all liars! Both the ones who pretended to be running away and the ones who chased after them. Yes, I have sinned! And no earthly court can ever serve justice!"

Now his voice was soaring even higher. It howled and vibrated in the crystal-cold air. Katyshev licked his lips.

"The only just court is the court of heavenly judgment. An angel and a demon exist inside each of us! In their names, I sentenced the guilty to be cast at once to perdition." He laughed good-naturedly, making Masha shudder all over. "But I would be a poor judge, indeed, if I could not judge myself. I will not pass through the ninth tollhouse, the Torment of Injustice. Here are punished the unjust judges who acquit the guilty and condemn the innocent for their own selfish ends. My place is in hell, and I shall die here, on Vasilevsky Slope, symbol of the fiery mouth of hell!"

In a burst of strength, the old man who had once been her father's closest friend shoved Masha forward. She stumbled and fell directly into Andrey's arms. Katyshev pulled a small vial out of his ragged pocket, and while Andrey rushed at him, slowly, oh so slowly, his teeth crunched through the fragile glass that held death. He fell to the pavement, his body spasming uncontrollably. He saw Masha bent over him, and he spent his last second staring, focused, at those light eyes, so like Fyodor's. In their depths, he saw only pity without measure.

Then silence fell. The shouting stopped, and so did the hum of passing cars, and the nearing sirens, and some distant music. The smell of the wet asphalt slipped away, and the scent of the fallen leaves and the gasoline. The new penthouses vanished from the opposite bank of the river, and the river itself disappeared, along with the tall brick towers of the Kremlin. But along with them all the trouble disappeared, too, all the blemishes, all the suffering. All human moaning and lamentation.

And it seemed to him that out of the crystalline nothingness around him, new, high walls were rising, slowly, triumphantly, gleaming with a cold fire.

ACKNOWLEDGMENTS

I would like to thank my family for their infinite support, my friends Anastasia Piatakhina and Anastasia Golotyk for their always-positive critiques, producer Yury Moroz for giving me the very idea of writing the novel, my agent and my friend Thomasin Chinnery for all her hard work, my editor Gabriella Page-Fort for believing in my book, and my translator Shelley Fairweather-Vega for allowing Masha and Andrey to express themselves in English.

ABOUT THE AUTHOR

Daria Desombre was born in St. Petersburg, Russia, where she studied at the Hermitage Art School and received a master's in English and Spanish from Saint Petersburg State University. In 2000, she moved to Paris, where she completed an MBA in fashion marketing and management and was head of advertising for the jeweler house Mauboussin before devoting herself full-time to scriptwriting. She writes for leading film companies in Russia and Ukraine. She also adapts American and European television programs for the Russian market. Desombre lives in Brussels with her husband and two children.

ABOUT THE TRANSLATOR

Photo © 2017

Shelley Fairweather-Vega lives with her supportive American family and skeptical Russian cat in Seattle, Washington. Her academic background is in international politics, and that, plus a passion for puzzles, led her naturally to a career in translation. Since 2006, she has worked as a freelance translator for attorneys, academics, authors, and activists around the world.